Also by Jayne Ann Krentz

A Coral Kiss
Crystal Flame
Gift of Fire
Gift of Gold
Midnight Jewels

Published by
WARNER BOOKS

JAYNE ANN KRENTZ

Sweet Starfire

WARNER BOOKS

A Time Warner Company

WARNER BOOKS EDITION

Cover design by Diane Luger

Cover illustration by Michael Racz

Warner Books, Inc.
1271 Avenue of the Americas
New York, N.Y. 10020

 A Time Warner Company

Printed in the United States of America

First Printing: March, 1986

Reissued: January, 1994

10 9 8 7 6

For Claire Zion, an editor with enthusiasm,
good timing and that rarest of assets,
the willingness to try something different.
My thanks.

Chapter One

The tavern was awash with blood. Cidra Rainforest saw splashes of crimson everywhere—seeping from a gash in a man's forehead, staining the front of another's shirt, trickling from still another's mouth. Glancing down, she saw that there was even a spatter of blood on the hem of her early-evening surplice robes. To Cidra the delicate yellow-gold fabric spun of the finest crystal moss was not just soiled but frighteningly scarred.

She was surrounded by a scene she had never before experienced, never even been able to imagine, and she found herself incapable of coping with it. It wasn't just the sight of so much blood that held Cidra immobilized with shock. All around her the viscious fighting continued unabated, even though Cidra knew that by now the combatants must be experiencing unutterable pain. Yet they raged on. The violence of it horrified her.

Grunts, obscene oaths, and desperate shouts filled the long, low tavern hall. One man had been knocked unconscious by a deftly swung tankard of Renaissance Ross ale, but no one paused to help him. Rather, everyone was participating in the free-for-all with an air of what Cidra could only describe as lusty enthusiasm. No one was lying in a fetal huddle, whimpering on the edge of insanity, as Cidra would have expected, as indeed she herself would be doing had she not been using every ounce of her disciplined training to control herself. The scene around her was incredible. It was, she thought, just as the novels had described it.

A large, scarred, brutally strong hand clamped around Cidra's arm, shocking her out of her stupor.

"Come on, lady, unless you want to explain your presence to the guards. Let's get out of here."

In a daze Cidra turned to the hard face of the man she had met only moments earlier, the man she had come to this rough tavern to find. Teague Severance hadn't been quite what she had expected, and Cidra had been trying to adjust to that fact.

"The guards?" she asked, clinging to the look of strength she saw in the man's gray eyes.

"Port Valentine's safeguards enjoy breaking up this kind of thing. Thrive on it, in fact. And they'll be here any minute. Let's get going. I think we can make it out through the back."

Cidra didn't argue. The stunning violence going on around her had not only disrupted her ability to think coherently but also seemed to be playing havoc with her normally excellent sense of balance. When her escort yanked Cidra toward the door and out of the way of a falling mountain dressed in a miner's kirtle, she stumbled and fell to her knees. Teague Severance's hold on her arm was broken, and he was whisked away by two men in a fist fight who suddenly saw him as a preferable target.

But Cidra barely noticed. The huge man who had just fallen

lay beside her feet, blinking groggily as he rubbed a bleeding jaw. Instinctively Cidra turned to comfort him, murmuring words of hypnotic comfort.

"Focus, my friend. Focus, focus. The pain is receding. See how it fades. Focus on it. The oblivo is being brought to you. Soon all will be serene. All will fade. All will fade. You must relax and let it flow away from you, let it flow—" Her soothing words ended abruptly as Cidra was hauled to her feet. Severance's scarred hand was once again clamped tightly around her arm; part of her had a moment to wonder how he had come by the odd lacing of scars.

"What in a renegade's hell do you think you're doing? Get up off the floor, woman. We've got to get out of here. The Wolves are howling tonight, in case you hadn't noticed."

Cidra's escort pulled her unceremoniously around a writhing mass of human beings and continued to forge a path toward the tavern's kitchen.

"But that man was in such pain. . . ." she murmured, feeling more lost than ever.

"Don't worry, he won't feel a thing until morning."

A hulking figure rose in front of Cidra, all bloody grin and glazed eyes. It wore a ship suit not unlike Severance's, but the diagonally slung utility loop was of a cheap, functional synthetic, not fine rantgan leather. Cidra noticed long before two hands that, to her startled gaze, resembled grappling hooks reached for her.

"Don't run off, little lady. You and I can go somewhere peaceful for some special handling. How does that sound?"

Before Cidra could sort through her list of appropriate responses to a question she had never before encountered, her impatient escort dealt with the grisly man before her.

"Don't touch her, you renegade idiot. Are you so drunk that

you can't tell she's from Clementia? What's more, she's a patron. My patron."

The glassy-eyed man blinked, frantically trying to focus his eyes. "I'm sorry, lady—I mean, Otanna. Didn't mean nothin', uh, rude. Had no idea what I was doing. No offense intended, I swear to Saints."

Cidra hurried to respond to the man's apology. She realized that he was under a misapprehension, thanks to her escort's comments. "Do not concern yourself. All is serene. And you have inflicted no real pain. I am—" But again she was not allowed to finish her sentence. With a dazed sense of surprise she realized that the hulk with the grappling-hook hands wasn't listening to her at all. He had turned to Teague Severance and was apologizing to *him*.

"Sorry about that, Severance. Never meant to interfere between you and a patron. Just a little misunderstanding. Better get her outa here, though. She'll probably go crazy any second."

"I'm working the problem. Unfortunately she's not exactly cooperating."

Cidra felt a rush of emotion that was decidedly akin to annoyance. She responded to the accusation in a tone of voice that was neither properly modulated nor serene. "I am trying to cooperate, Otan Severance. But circumstances are making it difficult."

"Just close your eyes and stop digging in your heels every time one of these Wolves gets in your way." And with that, the man called Severance once again hauled Cidra toward the tavern's back door.

Once inside the relative safety of the small kitchen, which was protected by a makeshift barricade of hastily arranged food heaters and ale dispensers, Cidra and her escort found the tavern's owner and his employees sitting around a table, playing a game of Free Market. The stacks of gleaming sardite chips in the center of the table indicated the seriousness of the stakes involved. Several bottles of ale resided at the players' elbows. The balding proprietor glanced up with a frown as Cidra and her companion burst into the room.

"Now, look here, kitchen's off-limits. You know that," the owner growled.

"We're not participating," Severance assured him, not bothering to slow down as he headed toward the rear door. "Just looking for a way out."

But by now the owner had noticed Cidra's appearance. Everything from the expensive comb of fire beryl in her carefully braided hair to the slippers embroidered with genuine emerald floss spoke of Harmonic wealth and refinement. "What do you think you're doing bringing her here? She looks like she's from Clementia."

"She is."

"Sweet Harmony, get her outa here."

"I'm trying," Severance said, his hand on the door latch. "Saints know I'm trying."

"There seems to be some misunderstanding," Cidra began hurriedly as she glanced back at the scowling tavern proprietor. "I'm from Clementia, but I'm not a . . . a Harmonic."

"Forget it. We'll straighten everything out later." Severance had her outside on the gently glowing fluoroquartz pavement. Maintaining his grip on her arm, he broke into an easy, loping stride and forced Cidra to match his pace.

In the distance the arrogant shriek of a safeguard runner sliced through the balmy night air. Cidra was suddenly very grateful that she wouldn't have to endure the indignity of being questioned. Kyrene, her mentor, would have been shocked, to say nothing of her parents' reaction.

The glowing bands of fluoroquartz supplied all the light

they needed to follow the path easily in the warm darkness. The pavement was still wet from a recent rain, and drops of water, illuminated by the natural light of the fluoroquartz, glittered like jewels. Cidra wanted to stop and examine the prismatic effect. Such naturally occurring phenomena, so close to artifice in their beauty, were meant to be appreciated. But her escort clearly had no intention of slowing down, and Cidra felt it was an inauspicious moment to debate the issue.

But as she raced along beside Teague Severance, she found herself instead savoring the rich assortment of fragrances that floated on the damp, balmy breeze. Clementia was a subtly perfumed delight, it's odors carefully generated by exotic, hybrid flowers to complement the delicate noses of its inhabitants. But here in Port Valentine, Cidra's olfactory senses were bombarded by new sensations, causing her to alternately wrinkle her nose or inhale sharply. Here, Cidra had discovered the faint scent of the sea at low tide, complete with a hint of rotting vegetation, and the sour odor that could only be from some tavern's garbage bin mingling with the rich smell of the recent rain. She thought she detected a waft of fernweed smoke as Severance urged her past a dark doorway. Cidra wanted to stop and find out why anyone would actually smoke the dangerous substance when everyone knew how bad it was for the body, but Severance gave her no chance.

Two blocks later Severance finally slowed to a brisk walk. "All right, I think we're clear. The guards will be concentrating their attention on the ones inside the tavern. They won't be looking for a few who had the sense to leave. You okay?"

Cidra, her breath coming quickly even though she'd had no real trouble maintaining the pace of the last two blocks, nodded. "Yes, of course. I'm fine. Thank you for inquiring." For Cidra, such polite inquiries had always been expressed in the formal, ceremonial form, but remembering where she was, she tried to use her companion's colloquial style. "And you? Are you, er, okay?"

"Sure. Let's get off the street. There's another tavern up ahead. One that's usually quieter. We can get something to eat. I haven't had dinner yet, have you?"

"Well, no," Cidra said. "It's only two hours past the evening change, and I eat at three past."

"Is that so? Me, I'm starved. Nothing like pulling patrons out of tavern brawls to work up a postman's appetite." He gave her a roguish smile that made her strangely uncomfortable. "You can sip nectar or whatever it is you folks normally drink."

Cidra contemplated the situation. "Actually I am rather hungry. Perhaps the unplanned exercise is responsible."

Severance grinned down at her, his strong, white teeth gleaming, although the glow of the pavement lighting cast his fog-gray eyes into pools of shadow. The rest of his hard features complimented the carnivorous impression. "Perhaps."

Cidra watched as the quick, feral grin disappeared, and wondered how an expression normally intended to convey laughter and humor could be so totally devoid of either. She shivered mentally. No wonder they called them Wolves, she thought fleetingly. "As a point of general information, I'd like to inform you that we don't sip nectar in Clementia."

"Another illusion shattered."

But Severance seemed philosophical about the matter as he led his patron into a different tavern. According to the illuminated sign over the entrance, this one was called The Valentine; presumably a name coined in honor of the surrounding sprawl of Lovelady's chief port town. A heart-shaped logo enclosed the words.

Once inside, Cidra glanced around with interest. The room was gently lit with a glowing pink light and was much quieter and far more refined than the first tavern had been. Here a mixed crowd of diners and drinkers occupied booths and a dispenser bar that lined the back of the room. The atmosphere was warm and comfortable and reasonably clean. Humans, both Wolves and Harmonics, still preferred to be served by humans, and the dining room was not automated.

"I take it this meets with your approval?" Severance was watching her expression as they stood in the doorway.

Cidra flushed, sensing his sarcasm. "This will be fine. All I need is a chance to discuss my business with you."

"Wait'll I order my food. I prefer to talk business over a good steak." Severance pinned a nearby member of The Valentine's staff with a steady gaze that eventually got the woman's attention. She glanced at him and then at Cidra. As soon as she took in the sight of Cidra's formal clothing and quietly regal bearing, she moved forward in an apologetic rush.

"Sorry to keep you waiting, Otanna. I have a very pleasant booth available across the room. It's out of the way. Quite peaceful."

Cidra inclined her head in polite acknowledgment. "You are very kind." A moment later she was seated. A waiter materialized out of nowhere, bowing a little awkwardly as he set out utensils.

"I have to admit that you've got your uses," Severance said as he slid into the booth across from Cidra. "I don't usually get such good service." He glanced at the holotape menu card only briefly before coming to a quick decision. "I'm going to order the torla steak. Maybe with you here they'll make sure it's cooked the way I order it. What suits you?"

Frantically Cidra scanned the menu, looking for an item that didn't contain meat. Finally she spotted the holotape images of a familiar Lovelady tuber and something that appeared to be a pile of greens. Politely she gave her order to the waiter, who was so interested in getting it right, she finally had to ask him to listen to Severance's demands.

"I want the steak. Large size. And I want it cooked on the grill, not in a heater, understand? And when it gets to the table, I want it rare. Bloody in the middle. *Rare.*"

Cidra hid her dismay behind a serene expression. Severance went on to order two mugs of expensive Renaissance Rose ale before she could explain that she never drank it. Cidra knew that the distinctly dark and potent brew was distilled from the thorn of a flower that was lethal, and too much of the ale was also considered dangerous. She managed to maintain a look of contentment as the waiter bustled away, but once he was gone, she sighed.

"Feeling like a fraud?" Severance leaned back in the booth and stretching his booted feet out under the table.

He had been sprawling with the same rangy casualness when she had first seen him. Conscious of her own gracefully correct posture, Cidra wondered if Severance ever really sat properly in a chair. The close-fitting gray ship suit pulled taut across his shoulders, emphasizing his broad, hard chest. The suit itself was a standard pilot's outfit, cut in a severe style with functional collar and cuffs that could be worn open for comfort or neatly clipped closed for a more formal look. Severance wore both open, the cuffs pushed up on his sinewy forearms. The trousers followed his long legs neatly and disappeared into the tops of his boots. Severance was built along lean, tight lines but had a sense of solid weight that strangely disturbed yet comforted Cidra. His black hair had recently received a short no-nonsense cut, and she guessed he'd had it trimmed as soon as he'd hit port after the long trip from Renaissance. In the soft light of the fluoroquartz lamp Cidra could see that the rantgan leather utility belt he wore had been handwrought with an eye for exquisite detail. She wondered whether Severance had carved the tough leather himself and then shook herself out of her reverie and considered his question.

"Yes, I am feeling a fraud. Everyone seems to be jumping to the conclusion that I'm a Harmonic."

"Let 'em jump. It gets action, doesn't it?"

"So it seems." Cidra studied him a moment. "You knew right away I wasn't a Harmonic, though, didn't you?"

He shrugged. "I wasn't drunk when you approached me, and I had a chance to get a good look at your eyes before that brawl broke out. I'll admit that I haven't met many, but there's something about a Saint's eyes . . . something different."

Cidra nodded. "I know." She paused. "Harmonics hate that nickname, you know."

Severance's quick, humorless grin flashed, then faded. "Saints? Impossible. Harmonics are constitutionally incapable of hating anything, least of all something as unimportant as a nickname."

"You're right, of course. I should have said that they prefer not to be called Saints."

"Then they shouldn't be so damned perfect," Severance told her blandly. He held up a hand as Cidra started to protest. "All right, all right, I withdraw the comment. I don't want to argue with you. Not if you're from Clementia and not if you're serious about doing business." He paused then for a minute, a strange look coming into his eyes. "You are from Clementia, aren't you? Not just an actress or something?"

"I was born there," Cidra stated, and immediately regretted the show of pride. A true Harmonic was above pride. "My parents are Harmonics," she finished more quietly.

Severance eyed her with what could have been casual interest if not for the flicker of cold assessment in his gaze. "An aptitude for the Way is supposed to be hereditary."

"There are exceptions to most things, Otan Severance. I'm afraid I'm one."

"Obviously. If you weren't, you would have fainted when some drunk miner got blood on your fancy dress." Cidra cringed at the truth of his words. She had wanted to believe that she had remained relatively coherent because of her training but had to admit now that even the most rigorous discipline wouldn't have protected a true Harmonic from the violence she had seen. "So," Severance continued, "you're an exception, but you *are* from Clementia. And you want to do business."

"That is correct."

"Suits me." His glance shifted to the expensive fireberyl comb in her hair. "You look like the kind who pays her postage, and I'm always looking for patrons—" He broke off as the rich, dark Renaissance Rose ale was placed in front of them. Taking a long, obviously satisfying swallow, he met Cidra's steady gaze over the rim of the mug. "What is it you want delivered?"

Cidra cleared her throat. "Myself."

Severance put down his mug. "You'll have to try it again. A little more slowly this time. I'm just a Wolf, remember? I'm not intuitive or telepathic. I'm not even wildly good at guessing games."

"It's simple enough, Otan Severance."

"Teague."

"I beg your pardon?"

He made an impatient movement with his hand. "My birth name is Teague. Severance is my chosen name. Use either one you like, but skip the formality. No one in my line of work uses Otan."

Cidra nodded with grave politeness. "You'll have to forgive me, Teague Severance. In my world formality is everything."

Severance's mouth twisted wryly. "I know. I'm sure it works

just great in Clementia. Out in the real universe it tends to be a waste of time. Why don't you finish explaining your business before we get sidetracked by a philosophical discussion on the role of the formalities."

A faint flicker of amusement touched Cidra's expression. "Are you capable of being sidetracked by such an esoteric discussion?"

"Sidetracked or bored. One of the two."

"I see." She drew a breath and went back to business. "As I said, I wish to mail myself."

He considered her intent face. "To where?"

"Wherever it is you happen to be going. I have no single destination in mind, although Renaissance is high on my list. Postmen are famous for their unorthodox schedules. According to what I have read about your profession, you'll go almost anywhere in the Stanza Nine system to pick up a package. Nor are you particular about where you deliver your cargo."

"As long as someone's willing to pay the postage," he reminded her. Severance leaned forward, planting his elbows on the table. Even the gentle light of the lamp could not soften the hard lines of his face. "But we rarely carry passengers, except in emergencies. And we never take tourists."

"I know it's not common practice."

"Do you know why?"

"I assume it has something to do with the fact that most postmen tend to be loners," Cidra ventured. "Psychologically speaking, people in your profession are often temperamentally unsuited to close social contact."

"It has to do with the fact that the ships are small and every spare centimeter has to be used as profitably as possible. Compared to packages and mail, passengers aren't a paying proposition. For one thing, passengers tend to eat. That means extra food has to be put on board. Passengers tend to sleep. That requires bunk space. Passengers also tend to want to be entertained. That's a damned nuisance. Pound for pound it's cheaper, more profitable, and infinitely less wearing to carry the mail. Go buy a ticket on one of the regular freighters if you want to tour the system."

Patiently Cidra shook her head. "The freighters only go to the main port towns on Renaissance and QED. From there I would have to find transportation to the various outposts. From what I understand that's an uncertain matter at best. It's also very expensive. And I don't have a great deal of credit to spend. I can't even afford extensive traveling here on Lovelady, let alone the other planets and their moons. Please don't be deceived by my appearance. Most of what I am wearing is a gift from my parents."

Severance stared at her. "Excuse me for being a little slow, but I seem to be missing something rather vital here. If you can't afford commercial travel, how in a renegade's hell did you expect to pay postage for the scenic route?"

Cidra smiled brilliantly as they reached the heart of her plan. "Actually, I intended to hire on as a member of the crew. I want to work my passage, Teague Severance."

Whatever he would have said in response to that was lost for the moment as the waiter appeared with the heated trays of food. A still-smoking slab of meat was thrust in front of Severance, who eyed the crosshatch grill marks with satisfaction. Cidra studiously avoided looking at the meat as she examined her own plate of vegetables. The waiter hovered anxiously until she glanced up and realized why he was hanging around.

"It's lovely. Just what I wanted. Please thank the kitchen staff."

The waiter beamed and disappeared without waiting to see how Teague Severance felt about the condition of his steak.

Severance didn't mind; he was too busy slicing into the bloody heart of the meat. He was unaware that Cidra was swallowing uncomfortably as she tried to avert her eyes and struggled to control her stomach.

"Just right," he declared, chewing a chunk with the thoughtful concentration Harmonics reserved for a glass of fine ether wine. "Like I said, lady, you do have your uses. Do you know how hard it is to get a place like this to use the grill instead of the heater?"

Cidra didn't pay any attention. She was lost in her silent recitation of the chant that by Harmonic custom preceded the evening meal, a ritual that was also helping to take her mind off the bleeding carcass across the table on Teague's plate. When she was finished, she hunted unobtrusively around the table for the proper vegetable-eating prongs. Failing to find them, she settled for the all-purpose bowled fork that was lying beside a sharp-edged blade near her plate. The sight of the knife gave her a start. The idea of a weapon at the table was unsettling. She was going to have to become familiar with the informal eating habits of Wolves.

"Are you going to finish your ale?" Severance asked.

Cidra glanced at the mug she had left untouched and shook her head. The famous brew didn't look terribly appealing.

"I'll finish it for you," Severance said, reaching across the table to help himself to her mug.

"About my passage on board your ship, Severance, I want to make it clear that I am fully prepared to work. I am not proposing that you take me along as excess baggage."

"Lady, mail ships are made to be operated by one person. They don't require any extra crew."

"But I've heard that mail pilots sometimes hire a crewmate," she protested. "Surely there must be plenty of small tasks required on board."

He stopped chewing long enough to give her a hard, steady look. "The kind of crew situations you're talking about are generally called convenience contracts. I tried it once and it was a disaster."

"Why was that?"

He stifled a muttered oath and went back to sawing on his meat. "Because the woman I contracted with nearly drove me crazy. She and I were at each other's throats by the time we reached Renaissance. I had to put her off ship at Port Try Again with enough credit to buy a commercial ticket back to Lovelady. I decided after that experience that a little loneliness was probably good for the soul and a hell of a lot cheaper than companionship."

Cidra smiled gently. "The one thing you would not have to fear is me going for your throat. I was raised in Clementia, remember?"

"Uh-huh. And what's going to keep me from going for yours?"

Cidra blinked, unsure if he was teasing her. He didn't look as if he was, but how could she really tell? Whatever sense of humor Severance had, it seemed to be on the savage side. "When I inquired into potential ships' masters, I was told you were considered a reasonably honest man. Somewhat rough around the edges and basically a loner, as are most mail pilots, but generally honest. Insofar as it is possible for Wolves to trust each other, your acquaintances appear to trust you, Severance. Among Wolves, I understand, that is not a common occurrence."

Severance drummed his fingers on the table. "Any Wolf dumb enough to completely trust another Wolf deserves what he or she gets. Just the opposite of how things work in Clementia, hmmm?"

Cidra's eyes softened. "For obvious reasons."

"Lady, you don't know what you're getting into with this plan of yours. Talk about being a Saint among Wolves!"

"Would you mind terribly calling me by my name? I would prefer it to 'lady.'" She kept her tone rigidly polite.

"Far be it from me to annoy a near-Saint. What was your name? Cidra Something? I didn't have time to catch it back in that tavern."

"Cidra Rainforest."

"Rainforest," he repeated, tasting the word. "That's your chosen name?"

"Yes."

"Have you ever seen a rain forest, Cidra?" Severance asked, his tone unexpectedly gentle. "A real rain forest?"

"No. This is my first time away from Clementia."

"How did you come to choose the word as a name?"

Cidra wanted to point out that they were not here for purposes of casual conversation, but she was too fundamentally polite to say the censuring words. "I read about rain forests on Renaissance when I was fifteen. There were holotapes and slips of them in the Archives. They seemed so beautiful, so rich and full of life. Endless blooms and endless green. I suppose the forests were very much in my mind that year, and fifteen is the age at which Harmonics traditionally choose their names. I understand that among Wolves the age of choice varies."

"You could say that. The truth is that we sometimes go through two or three names before settling on the right one. Occasionally a Wolf finds it very useful to select a new name quite frequently." When she just looked at him with a puzzled expression, Severance abandoned the subject. "Never mind. Tell me what made you decide to go planet-hopping."

"My reasons are personal, Severance."

His eyebrows climbed. "Is that so?"

She flushed a little at his tone. "In Clementia privacy is greatly respected," Cidra reminded him.

"Another good reason to abandon your idea of bunking down on a mail boat. There's very little privacy available on one of those ships."

"I am prepared to accommodate myself."

"Oh, yeah? How far?"

"I don't understand."

"Those convenience contracts we just talked about? Do you know just what that entails?"

"I assume it implies a sharing of responsibilities and tasks."

"Sweet Harmony, what an innocent. It means a sharing of bunks, Cidra. Convenience contracts are short-term sexual alliances. Contracted for purposes of sex and companionship. The six-week run to QED can be very long and lonely, Otanna Rainforest. Now do you understand?"

Her face grew very still as she contemplated his words. Then Cidra nodded thoughtfully. She should have realized that something like this was involved in the contractual situations she had heard about. Wolves were said to be prodigiously interested in sex. "Yes, now I understand. Well, I would not be interested in that sort of arrangement."

"Somehow I didn't think you would."

"Is that the only type of contract you would be willing to extend?"

"If you had been listening carefully, you would have heard me say that I'm not even interested in a convenience contract. I told you, I tried it once and it was a disaster. I'll stick to finding a little special handling in between mail hops. I'm grateful to you for getting this place to serve me a decent steak, Cidra, but I'm afraid we're not going to be able to do business together."

Cidra tried to hide her disappointment behind her mask of

17

serene acceptance. "So it would seem. You must allow me to pay for your meal, Otan Severance. It is the least I can do under the circumstances."

He looked vaguely irritated. "Skip it. You said you were running on short credit, and I just had a fairly decent run from Renaissance. I'll get the tab."

"Oh, no, I could not allow you to do that," she protested, genuinely shocked. "It was I who approached you and took up your valuable time."

"I was sitting in a tavern about to get drunk. You didn't waste any of my time. I can always get drunk. I can't always get my steaks cooked properly." He picked up his mug and downed another healthy swallow of the potent ale. "So. What are you going to do now? Go back to Clementia?"

Cidra's eyes widened in astonishment. "Of course not. You are only the first mail pilot I have approached. There are half a dozen more here in Port Valentine at the moment, or so the Port authorities told me. I will work my way through the list. Surely there must be someone interested in a working passenger. And if not, I will wait until other postmen or postwomen arrive. They come and go constantly from what I have been told."

Severance regarded her coolly. "I don't think that's such a good idea, Cidra."

Some of her anxiety bubbled to the surface and emerged in a flash of hostility that took Cidra by surprise more than it did her companion. "Still, it is *my* idea, is it not, Severance? You needn't concern yourself with it or with me."

"Isn't there someone in Clementia who might be concerned with your notions and where they're liable to take you?"

She put down the all-purpose fork she had been using and sat very straight in the booth. "I am not a child, Severance. I reached the age of maturity four years ago and am fully responsible for my own actions. Just as you are."

"Far be it from me to give advice to someone reared among Saints," Severance growled. "Good luck, lady. Just watch out what kind of contract you end up signing. Don't forget to read the fine print." He got to his feet. "If you've finished eating, I'll see you back to wherever you're staying."

"That won't be necessary."

"It is, unless you want a scene." He slipped a credit plate into the small slot embedded in the table. When the faint glow confirmed that the meal had been paid for, he removed the plate and reached for Cidra's arm.

She hadn't argued, Severance thought later, after having dropped Cidra off at her hotel. But, then, Harmonics rarely argued, except about philosophical or mathematical problems. He remembered how his brother Jeude had always backed away from a disagreement, putting on the same mask of serene contentment he had seen on Cidra's face that evening. Emotional confrontations with other people were very uncomfortable for Saints, Severance knew. Belatedly he reminded himself that Cidra wasn't technically a Harmonic.

It was easy to forget. He could understand why others such as the restaurant personnel reacted to her as if she were indeed a full-fledged Saint. There was something very serene and innately dignified about Cidra Rainforest. Perhaps it had to do with the way she wore her long, red-brown hair in that formal coronet of braids. Or it might have been the way the elegant yellow robes flowed around a body that was as slender, graceful, and proud as that of a dancer. The clothing worn by Harmonics was naturally as dignified and graceful as those who wore and designed it. The women's high-collared gowns, with their long, wide-banded sleeves, fit closely to the waist and

19

then flared in an elegant line from hips to ankles. The fabric was uniformly the fine, beautifully worked crystal moss. Cidra's gown was no exception. She was not a tall woman, but her robes provided an illusion of height. She was a young woman, probably about eight years younger than himself, but her eyes held more refined intelligence than a man usually saw in a woman that age. Of course, Teague reminded himself, if she'd been raised in Clementia, her education would have been thorough and sophisticated.

Severance grabbed a runner outside Cidra's hotel to take him to his ship, but his thoughts remained with the woman he had just left.

The essentially gentle quality that usually characterized Saints was a part of her, too, he mused, but in Cidra it came across differently. In true Harmonics Teague had always sensed a distant, controlled, broadly humanistic compassion. In Cidra he had seen something much more immediate, a more vivid and impulsive empathy. Severance remembered the way she had stopped to help the downed brawler in the first tavern and shook his head. It had been a long time since he'd enjoyed any special handling in the arms of a woman. Too long. Chances were that his imagination was interpreting Cidra's actions in the wrong way. He was probably just hungry for the kind of gentleness a man sometimes needed from a woman. And, for some reason, a part of him had gone ahead and decided that Cidra could give him what he needed.

A picture of her soft, slender body lying under him, her gilded nails clutching his shoulders snapped into Severance's head before he could stop it. For an instant he knew a sense of self-disgust. Surely he wasn't one of those perverts who were attracted to the cerebral and remote female Harmonics. Such men were only drawn by the sick need to despoil something they could never understand or accept.

No, Severance reassured himself, his brooding awareness of Cidra was reasonably normal. She was, after all, by her own admission a Wolf in Harmonic clothing. And while he hadn't been around many Harmonic women, he had met enough to know that they didn't project any real sense of sexuality. Cidra, on the other hand, had struck him as a very sensual creature, even though her air of serenity partially masked the raw vitality in her. He had the feeling she wasn't even aware of it herself.

A Saint among Wolves. To a certain extent Cidra would be safe because most people felt a certain instinctive protectiveness toward Harmonics. But there were all too many exceptions to that rule. Severance could think of several offhand, many of whom were fellow mail-run pilots.

At least she'd had the sense to choose a hotel in a reasonably safe section of town. Mankind's penchant for building cities around ports had changed little during the course of human development; nor had the basic characteristics of those cities changed. There were still good and bad sections, safe and unsafe areas. Cidra Rainforest had been wandering through some of the less desirable streets of Port Valentine when she had found him earlier that evening. Severance tried to ignore the fact that she'd be back on those same streets tomorrow evening, searching for a more helpful postman.

She would probably find one, he reflected as he sprawled in the back of the runner and listened to the faint shushing sound of the vehicle's twin blades on the pavement. Some renegade such as Neveril or Scates would lick his chops and produce a very neatly worded convenience contract before Cidra quite realized what was happening. She would be on her way to Renaissance, only to discover that her Harmonic trappings weren't much protection from certain kinds of Wolves.

Severance shifted restlessly as the lights of the port facilities came into view. It wasn't any of his business, he told himself angrily. By all accounts, Harmonics were quite intelligent; someone from Clementia had the ability to make her own decisions. She certainly didn't need Severance's help.

As the runner hissed to a halt Teague paid the fare with his credit plate and climbed out. He stood on the glowing sidewalk, staring at the tapering, floodlit outline of his ship out on the field. *Severance Pay* was poised for an immediate liftoff, her stubby, swept-back wings seeming to strain at the inconvenience of being planetbound. She was always ready to leave at a moment's notice. The competition for lucrative mail runs was stiff, and Severance had no intention of missing out on prime cargo simply because his ship wasn't ready to leave.

Automatically he removed one of two small remotes he carried on his utility loop and punched into *Severance Pay*'s primary on-board computer. He queried for messages and read the response on the small screen of the remote. A couple of friends had hit port and left word that they could be reached at one of the nearby bars if Severance happened to feel like a game of Free Market. There was a fuel tab that the computer had already been authorized to pay. And there was a terse message from one of the local postal agents saying that he'd had a special request from a client.

Severance knew what that meant. A patron had asked for him and his ship by name. With any luck that meant an important run. He started for the bank of comp-phones that were housed in a nearby terminal.

"Hey, Severance, you son of a renegade, where's the little Saint?"

Severance hesitated and then decided that he couldn't shake Scates by simply ignoring him. The other postman grinned and waved from the terminal doorway.

"I took her back to her hotel." Severance made to step

around the man who had obviously been doing the port-strip taverns.

"Heard she was looking for a contract."

"Not the kind you mean."

"I'm not particular," Scates assured him. His broken nose twisted at an odd angle when he leered. "I take it you're not going to give her a lift?"

"No."

"You're missing a great opportunity, Severance. Me, I could think of plenty of things to teach a little Saint between here and QED."

Severance didn't bother to respond as he started through the open terminal door. But as the clear diazite panels slid shut behind him, he glanced back and saw that Scates was grinning more widely than ever. In the up-from-under pavement lighting his features seemed almost ludicrously demonic. Severance cursed his imagination again and turned away.

Even as he found a vacant comp-phone and punched in the postal agent's code, Severance knew what Scates was going to do. And as he listened to the agent tell him that there was a rush shipment of small but vital robot sensors that would pay twice the usual rates, Teague Severance was visualizing Scates offering Cidra a contract of convenience. Scates's convenience.

Chapter
Two

He shouldn't have tried to touch her.

Cidra found herself shaking uncontrollably. Perhaps, she told herself, if the man who called himself Scates had only continued to wheedle or argue, nothing would have happened. But he had reached for her, and Cidra had seen the hot lust in his eyes. She had reacted instinctively because there had been no real time to think.

All her life her body had been kept supple and strong with the ancient exercise. The training had begun before she could walk. Cidra couldn't remember a time when she didn't know the essentials of Moonlight and Mirrors. Intellectually she had known, too, that the flowing, deceptively simple movements were based on an ancient form of self-defense, records of which had arrived with the First Families of Stanza Nine nearly two hundred years ago.

But no one she knew in Clementia had ever actually used

it in self-defense. She was shocked by how her body had reacted to the first genuine threat it had ever known. One moment Scates had lunged for her, and the next he was lying half conscious on the floor. The instant in between had been a shifting pattern that hadn't required any thought or preparation on Cidra's part. She had known the basics since she was a child. But she had never known herself capable of using them so effectively in this way.

The hem of Cidra's black-and-silver sleeping surplice was still swirling around her ankles and Scates had just hit the floor when the hotel room's communication panel announced another visitor. Cidra tore her stunned gaze from the man at her feet and stared at the softly lit door panel. Just then Scates stirred, groaning, and Cidra stepped quickly out of the way of his hand. The door panel hummed softly, demanding her attention. Because she could think of nothing else to do, Cidra went to the panel and switched on the screen. The fine tremors in her body seemed to grow worse when she saw who stood outside her door.

"Severance," she whispered.

On the small screen his hard, unforgiving features were etched in impatient, irritated lines, as if he didn't approve of either his surroundings or his business in the hotel. Indeed, he did look out of place in the elegant hall, his lean, dark figure a harsh contrast to the silvered carpet and the soft, waving patterns of soothing hues that decorated the walls. Behind him the subtly concealed security monitors turned politely toward his profile and then moved on, not yet alarmed.

"Cidra? Let me inside. I want to talk to you. If you don't open the door, the hall monitors are going to start recording my actions, and then we'll have to explain everything to the front desk." When she didn't respond immediately, he went on more harshly. "Come on, lady, I haven't got all night. I'm in one renegade hell of a hurry. I've got to get my ship off the ground within the hour."

"Severance, you'd better go away." Cidra's voice sounded strange to her own ears. "Something's happened. I don't think you'll want to get involved."

His eyes narrowed. "Cidra, let me in. *Now.*"

The soft crack of command in his words jolted her. She was unfamiliar with such an approach to the giving of instructions. Cidra found herself releasing the computerized locks on her door without even thinking. A moment later he was striding into the room, shutting the door behind him. His gaze slid quickly over her form, assessing the apparent lack of physical damage. Then he stared at Scates, who was still out of commission. Swearing softly, Severance knelt beside the other man, feeling for a throat pulse.

"I knew it," Severance said. The words were full of morose resignation. "I knew he'd come here, and I knew you'd probably let him into your room without a second thought. Naive little fool. What did you do to him?"

Cidra locked her hands in front of her. "When he came to the door, he said he would be willing to take me with him on his mail run. I let him in and we started to discuss the matter. Then he made it clear that he was only offering one of those convenience contracts you mentioned. When I declined and asked him to leave, he . . . he touched me. Tried to grab me. His eyes were strange, Severance. Almost wild. And his hand was damp. I think he wanted to have sex with me."

Severance shot her a sidelong glance. "Yeah, I'd say that was one way of putting it. He probably thought you'd be easy game. I guess you surprised him, though."

"There was no time to think." Cidra stopped as she heard the apology in her words. Then she went on with grave honesty.

"But even if there had been time to analyze the matter, I believe I would have done the same thing."

"What, exactly, did you do?"

"It's called Moonlight and Mirrors. It's a kind of dance. An exercise, really. But it's based on a very old self-defense technique. My instructors always said I had a unique style of interpretation," she added lamely.

"I can see what they meant."

Cidra watched with a frown as Severance pulled a small object from his loop and held it to Scates's temple. He pressed the small touch pad on the end of the device, and the other man's body jerked once. Then Scates went ominously still.

Deeply disturbed by her victim's new appearance, Cidra touched Severance on the shoulder. "What have you done?"

"Bought us a little time." He got to his feet, and then saw the horrified expression on her face. "Don't worry. He's not dead. I just finished what you started. He'll be out until morning, and by then we'll be long gone."

"I don't understand."

"I've changed my mind. I'm taking you with me." He began moving around the room, opening the door of the closet. "I know I'm going to regret it, but I can't seem to think of a way around having to take you along. Maybe I can dump you off in Clementia before I head out to Renaissance."

"I am not going back to Clementia, Otan Severance. I can't go back. Not yet."

He swung around, her travel pack in his hands. "We'll discuss it on the way to Lovelorn." He thrust the pack toward her. "Here, get your things together and let's get out of here. As long as Scates stays unconscious in your room, the privacy locks will protect us. Once he gets on his feet and wanders out into the hall, the security monitors will pick him up, and then the questions will start. I vote we leave him alone here to answer them. He's not likely to file any complaints against you. How could he explain that he got knocked unconscious by a lady from Clementia? His pride will be our best protection. Unfortunately it won't protect us from his friends, who will be looking for blood. So get packed, *now*."

Somehow it seemed easier to obey when he used that cold, hard tone. She was still trembling from the violence she had caused and had no desire to question Severance's decisiveness. Numbly she began to remove her formal robes from the closet and fold them in the proper manner.

"We haven't got time for you to practice the fine art of elegant garment folding. Here, I'll take care of the clothes. You get everything else together." Severance grabbed the liquid-soft garments from her hand and began stuffing them into the travel pack.

"My books," she said, trying not to watch as he treated her lovely gowns as if they were dirty ship suits. "I'll get my books."

"There's room in this pack for them," he told her.

She glanced at him in surprise as she began pulling the beautifully bound volumes from the autostorage unit beside the bed. "Oh, no, there couldn't possibly be enough room. I have a separate pack for them."

"I could get a couple hundred data slips in here," he assured her before glancing over and seeing what she was doing. "Saints in hell! Those aren't slips. They're books. Real books."

"Of course." She touched one of the handworked covers reverently. "No information storage system ever invented can compare aesthetically with a genuine book. They are such beautiful things."

It was Severance's turn to look shocked. "They must weigh as much as an exploroprobe. What do you think *Severance Pay* is, a cargo freighter? Leave 'em here. I just arranged for a crate of Rose ale to be put on board. There isn't room for your damn books."

Cidra clutched the volume she was holding to her breast. "If the books stay behind, then I stay too."

Severance lifted his eyes beseechingly. "I knew I was going to regret this. The Renaissance sinkswamps will freeze before I make a mistake like this again. All right, all right, bring the damn books. But move, will you? I've got a hot run, and it's COD."

"What's that mean?" Cidra asked, hastily placing the books in a travel pack.

"It means," Severance said as he locked the pack he had just finished stuffing with delicate clothing, "that I don't get paid unless the shipment gets delivered on time. Credit on Delivery. I don't intend to make the run to Renaissance for free, so let's get going. Here, you take the robes. They're a lot lighter. Let me have those damn books. Anything else?"

"No, that's everything." She edged around Scates's prone body. "You're sure he'll be all right?"

"Unfortunately yes. Now just act normal out in the hall, understand? Pretend you've changed your mind about staying here and have agreed to spend the night with me. You've paid for the room?"

Cidra nodded and then asked, "It's true, isn't it?"

"What's true?" Severance closed the door and set the locks. Then he shouldered the travel pack and started down the hall, Cidra following close behind.

"Wolves think constantly about sex. It's what that man Scates wanted from me, and it is the excuse you think the hotel security system will accept for our unexpected departure."

"By now you ought to have learned for yourself that Wolves aren't nearly as elevated in their thinking as your friends back home in Clementia."

"It's not a question of refined or elevated thinking," she responded seriously as he herded her out of the hotel lobby and onto the glowing sidewalk. "It's a matter of the relative importance of the subject to an individual. Sex is obviously a great deal more important to Wolves than to Harmonics."

Severance opened the panel of a waiting runner and stuffed Cidra and her packs inside. Then he slid in beside her and punched in their destination. When he was finished, he leaned back in his characteristic lounging fashion and folded his arms across his chest. "Maybe if sex were a little more important to Harmonics, they would be able to increase their birthrate. Everyone knows they don't produce enough children to keep up their population. If it weren't for the random occurrence of natural Harmonics among the Wolves, there probably wouldn't be enough Saints to keep Clementia running."

"The system works fine the way it is," Cidra told him firmly. "It's good to have the new blood constantly being introduced into the Harmonic society."

"If everything is so great in Clementia, what are you doing here?"

She looked out the runner's diazite window, staring at the passing town, which had been founded according to a careful plan but had since grown into an eclectic and sprawling mix of architectural styles on meandering streets. The glow from the sidewalks illuminated everything from old, squat buildings fashioned by the early colonists of enduring anthrastone to the newer, gleaming structures built of obsidianite. Both materials had proven plentiful and cheap once the colonists had discovered how to pull them from the heart of the eastern mountains. One adventurous designer had done an entire hotel in the ubiquitous fluoroquartz. It was quite garish and tacky to Cidra's eyes. But, then, much of the town was. The jumble of styles and materials was visually unsettling when Cidra mentally compared it to the beautiful proportions and harmonies that dominated Clementia's graceful, simple architecture.

All this passed before Cidra's eyes fleetingly, as she gathered her spirits to answer Severance's question, since he was helping her, she felt she owed him the truth.

"You don't understand, Severance," she finally said quietly. "I can't go back to Clementia. Not as I am. I don't belong."

Raising a skeptical eyebrow, he turned to her. "A person either is or is not a natural Harmonic," he pointed out gently. "If you aren't one, there's no use fighting it, is there?"

Her head snapped around, and all the years of grim determination blazed for a moment in her vivid green eyes. "I will find a way to be one of them, Teague Severance, if it takes me to the end of the Stanza Nine star system and beyond. I will find the answer. It's out there. I know it is. I have traced the legend since childhood, and now, at last, I'm actually going after it."

He looked at her blankly. "Going after what? What legend?"

Cidra bit her lip and sank back into her corner of the seat. "It's out there, Severance. The tool with which I can become a Harmonic. The instrument that can fit my mind into the natural patterns and rhythms of everything I see or touch. Maybe it won't quite duplicate the way a Harmonic's mind vibrates in tune with whatever it chooses to focus on, but I think it can imitate the telepathic element. I think it can help me bridge the gap that my lack of natural ability has always put between me and the world I was meant to join." Her hands tightened in her lap. "I have almost all of it, Severance. I have the training, the rituals, the education. I have studied the Klinian Laws and the Rules of Serenity as the most devout of students. All I lack is the ability to achieve communion with the others and that intuitive element that makes the Harmonic mind so unique. But I'll get it. Or something almost as good. I swear I will."

The silence in the runner seemed frozen as Severance regarded her taut features. Finally he said, "That's why you want to ship out with me? You're searching for a legend?"

She nodded once, sharply, wishing she had kept her mouth shut. "A Ghost legend."

"Ah, Cidra. There are a million Ghost legends. All of them created by humans after they reached Stanza Nine and found all that junk lying around on Lovelady and Renaissance."

"It's not junk! We're talking about the artifacts of a vanished civilization. And this legend is based on one of those artifacts. I found too many hints of it in the Archives. The tool is out there somewhere, and I'm going to find it." She shook her head wonderingly. "How can you call the artifacts junk?"

Severance's mouth curved wryly. "I'm sure that when they originally encountered the Ghost ruins, the First Families were suitably startled. But that was a couple hundred years ago, and when everyone realized how common the leftover Ghost garbage was, the novelty wore off. Even the Harmonics who are archaeologists are interested in only the most unusual finds. They don't want to be bothered anymore with every little shard or carving that turns up. If Stanza Nine ever attracts any tourists, we'll all make a fortune selling Ghost junk, but until then, it's practically worthless. The legends are even more worthless. We invented them. Every company explorer who ever had a bad dream while camped out on Renaissance has a new so-called legend. And the miners on QED are just as bad. Hell, for that matter there is still enough unexplored territory right here on Lovelady to breed tales. If you're chasing a legend, Cidra, you're chasing moonlight."

"Moonlight," she said, thinking of the dance patterns that

had recently subdued Scates, "is something I have been taught how to chase."

Severance groaned. "I should have had the ship off the ground the minute I had the mail on board. I knew this was going to be a mistake."

"Then why did you change your mind and come after me?"

"When I think of a sufficiently sound answer, you'll be the first to know." And with that, the runner that had been slowing as it neared the port terminal slid to a stop.

A few minutes later, her pack of clothing in hand, Cidra followed Severance toward the small, streamlined mail ship. She watched as he punched codes into both a computer remote and the gadget he'd used on Scates. Then he led her aboard.

The interior lights came on as they stepped over the threshold. Cidra stood looking around at the compact, painfully limited cabin space and wondered for the first time if she had really given due consideration to the problems of living in such confined quarters with another human being, and a Wolf at that. She was still worrying the question when the scruffy rug beneath her feet moved abruptly. Startled, Cidra glanced down in time to see the motley piece of rug silently display three rows of tiny needle teeth.

"Watch out for Fred," Severance said as she backed hastily. "He hates being mistaken for a rug."

"Fred?" She watched the creature move in an undulating motion toward the seat in front of the command console.

"Fredalius is his full name. But I just call him Fred."

"Who named him?" she asked.

"My brother," Severance answered, his back to Cidra as he stowed away his pack.

"Does your brother fly with you occasionally?"

"Not anymore," he answered in a clipped tone. "He's dead."

"Oh." It didn't take a Harmonic's empathic abilities to realize that she had blundered onto a painfully raw topic. Automatically Cidra sought to soothe the discomfort she had caused. "I'm sorry, Severance. I had no idea. It was thoughtless of me to ask after him. I seem to be causing a great deal of unpleasantness tonight."

"Forget it." He busied himself with sealing the ship. "Stow your packs under my bunk for now. That's where I had the ale put, so you'll have to fiddle a bit to find room. We'll decide what to do with those damn books later. Right now I just want to get off the ground."

"We're leaving for Renaissance?"

"First we're hopping over to Lovelorn. I got word of another good shipment. Then we'll off-planet for Renaissance. Once we're in space we'll have two solid weeks to drive each other crazy. If we reach Renaissance without having murdered each other, we'll talk about extending the contract."

Cidra decided that this wasn't the time to argue her intention to stay aboard. It also didn't appear to be a good time to discuss the exact nature of the contract she had apparently entered into. She finished shoving her travel packs under the safety net beneath Severance's bunk. It wasn't easy. The crate of Renaissance Rose ale took up a great deal of room. Cidra wondered if Severance intended to drink all of it before reaching Renaissance. The thought was unsettling.

Then she took the single passenger seat located behind and to the left of the pilot's seat. Fascinated, she watched Severance run fluidly through the pre-liftoff procedures. It seemed to her that the computer had barely signaled that permission had been received to take *Severance Pay* into the air before they were, indeed, off the ground.

The lights of Port Valentine hung beneath them for a moment and then receded into the distance as Severance set a course that would take the ship to the mountain town of Lovelorn.

Cidra knew that within the confines of the planet's atmospheric envelope *Severance Pay* was powered by standard jet engines. Only when the ship thrust into the freedom of space could they safely switch to the distance-crunching power of the STATR drive. Cidra studied Severance covertly. She admitted to herself now that he had been occupying her thoughts since the moment she had met him.

He was all business as he worked, his intent expression illuminated by the glow of the console lights. She was aware of being strangely fascinated by him in a way that was new to her, and the knowledge was disquieting. She should be viewing him simply as a man with whom she was doing business, but Cidra was honest enough and uneasy enough to admit that her reaction to him right from the start was far more jumbled and complex than such a simple arrangement warranted.

When he had first been pointed out in the tavern, she had experienced serious doubts about approaching him. It was obvious from the start that he was a hard man, a true Wolf. There was an aggressive harshness about him that made it clear he was a man who had not been softened or refined by too much contact with Harmonic values or ways. But she also sensed a quietly brooding element deep within Severance and wondered what had happened in his past to cause it. Something told Cidra it would be instinctive in Severance to avoid those ritualized behavior patterns and codes of conduct favored by people who tried to emulate Harmonics. He would have his own way of doing things, his own code of ethics and standards. And he would stick to it.

The people whom she had questioned at Port Valentine had been in agreement about one thing when it came to Teague Severance: He was a man of his word, and among Wolves that meant something. It had to mean something. It was all the general population had when it came to insuring trust. Wolves were forced to depend upon such things as reputation and experience to judge their acquaintances. They could never be completely certain of each other. They were forever denied the unique telepathic communion of minds that allowed Harmonics to establish such firm bonds between themselves. Trust was implicit in the way Harmonics lived and communicated; it was an unavoidable given, because they could know each other's minds. But when trust existed absolutely between a man and a woman, and was combined with the indefinable chemistry of shared pleasures and intellectual interests, it could lead to a lifelong commitment that was unique among mankind.

Cidra's parents shared that type of commitment. Talina Peacetree and Garn Oquist had a bond between them that Cidra had always longed to experience, herself, with the right man. Knowing that was impossible as long as she lacked true Harmonic telepathy had been the misery of her life. And her determination to overcome her own shortcomings was the driving force of her existence.

The covenant of marriage had taken on new meanings as Harmonic society had evolved. It stood now as so many Harmonic ways did, as an ideal. Wolves frequently used portions of the formal Harmonic wedding ceremony for their own nuptials.

Harmonics had always appeared at random in the human population. For countless generations many had died young. Others were driven insane by their instinctive efforts to reconcile reality with the inner harmony they saw in the world around them. A few had lived lives that appeared normal to others who never guessed at the effort it took to survive as a Harmonic among Wolves.

Special aptitudes and genius were common among Harmonics, and a few of the early ones had been strong enough to achieve a great deal before they died. Usually the achievements came in spite of a life racked with trauma and mental strife. Many others had simply perished without ever flowering.

The world of Wolves was a harsh one, and true Harmonics seldom coped well. A few hundred years ago, just prior to the unprecedented outpouring of mankind into the galaxy, it had been recognized that both Harmonics and Wolves fared better if they lived a separated, if symbiotic, existence. When the first of the beautiful, interstellar shimmer ships had left the home star system carrying colonists to new worlds, they had carried small contingents of Harmonics aboard.

No one had been egocentric enough to believe that the galaxy could be colonized into a tightly knit empire. Distances were too vast, and the demands of different worlds required too much physical and emotional adaptation, and the streak of independence in human nature was too strong. But the early planners had felt the need to insure that the best of what was human went with the colonists. Sending a small group of harmonics along with each colony ship had not only guaranteed philosophical continuity, it had also provided a resident brain trust for each new world.

But, beyond that, each world had proved unique. Cidra knew from her work in the Archives that the Stanza Nine social structure was different in sometimes subtle, sometimes elaborate, ways from that of the home worlds. And since the ability to maintain contact with the home planets had been lost, the distinctions between Stanza Nine and other human systems no longer seemed to matter. Adaptation meant survival. And both Harmonics and Wolves believed in survival.

The crash of the colony ship that first reached the Stanza Nine system had been a complete disaster. Not only did the home planets believe there had been no survivors, but the First Families, thus isolated, had been deprived of much of the technology that should have been their heritage. The need to dig in and establish a foothold on a new planet without the aid of the machines that would have made the task relatively simple had bred a rugged sense of independence in the colonists. That sense of independence had even permeated the Harmonic contingent of the culture, where it was quietly accepted that each individual had both the privilege and the responsibility of achieving success on his own.

Technology had developed erratically from the bits and pieces of information left in the heavily damaged data banks after the crash of the colony ship. Regaining spaceflight had been of paramount importance because the human population was intent on establishing itself throughout the Stanza Nine system. After finding the remains of the Ghosts it had become even more important to determine if humans were going to have to share Stanza Nine with anyone or anything else. It had taken a hundred and fifty Lovelady years to get back into space, and the secret of the faster-than-light speeds that had brought the colonists to Lovelady had still not been found.

The majority of the population, the Wolves, respected the levels to which the Harmonics raised human virtues because the seed of those virtues lay in all humans. When a Wolf viewed a Harmonic, he saw the best of himself; he saw the most valuable essence of his own nature developed and channeled. Intelligence, integrity, honesty, serenity, and an appreciation for every element of the universe were traits to be protected and respected. Every human knew this. Not every human reacted in a positive manner to the knowledge, but none could avoid it.

Cidra drew the first deep breath she'd allowed herself since the man called Scates had lied his way into her hotel room. She was tired, but the adrenaline was still flowing through her system. Through the cabin window she could see the white disc of Lovelady's single moon, Gigolo. That small, dead world was also shining on Lovelady's southern town of Clementia. Her home was a serene, protected landscape of beauty and order. There lay everything she understood and loved. For a moment her heart yearned for another glimpse of the delicate fountains and the formal gardens that lined the white stone paths. But she had never been truly a citizen of Clementia. The magic of it had been denied her, even though she had been raised in its midst and taught its ways. Her own shortcomings had been pointed out quite graphically this evening.

Severance finished one last procedure at the command console and then swung around in his seat to face her.

"You look exhausted. Maybe you'd better grab a nap before we reach Lovelorn."

"I couldn't possibly sleep."

"Still seeing Scates coming at you?" he asked gruffly. "Don't worry. You're safe now."

"It's not that." She glanced out into the darkness and then back at Severance. "Do you realize that tonight was the first time in my life I've done violence to another human being?"

"You've led a sheltered life."

"It's not funny, Severance."

He sighed. "I know. But it's not the end of the universe, either."

"Perhaps not, but it worries me."

"Listen, Cidra, you want to worry? Worry about what would have happened if you hadn't had all that fancy Moonlight and Mirrors training. Now that's something to fret about."

"You don't understand," she snapped. "I should be begging for a shot of oblivo. I should be flat out on the floor, half catatonic."

"And instead you're just sitting there shaking like a leaf?"

"Don't laugh at me, Teague Severance." She was near tears

now, and the knowledge infuriated her. Quickly she used her years of training to regain her self-control. "I want to be one of them. All my life I have been trained in the ways of the Serene path. Surely I have some Harmonic sensitivity in me. I was born to Harmonics. Yet tonight I used the ways of a beautiful dance to hurt someone else."

"Who was trying to hurt you. It's called self-defense, Cidra, and I know enough about Harmonics to know that they're not philosophically opposed to self-defense. They're just lousy at being able to act on that belief. Be damned grateful that your only problem right now is that you've got the jitters instead of a full-scale anxiety attack. I've seen what happens to a Harmonic who runs into real violence and it's not very pleasant."

She eyed him curiously. "When did you see a Harmonic deal with genuine violence?"

Severance ran a hand through his thick black hair, his face drawn, gray eyes suddenly bleak. "My brother was one of those random occurrences you mentioned earlier. A Harmonic born among Wolves."

"Why wasn't he sent to Clementia?" she asked, frowning.

"It's a long story, and I'm not in the mood to tell it right now. Take a nap, Cidra."

"I don't think I can sleep yet."

"Suit yourself. I'm going to sack out for a few minutes. It's been a long night."

Severance got to his feet and brushed past her, heading for the sleeping area at the rear of the cabin. He unlatched the upper sleeping berth so that she could climb into it if she changed her mind, and then he threw himself down onto the lower bunk. He was already half asleep when he felt Fred undulating up onto the bed to drape himself over his master's feet.

Severance awoke once during the flight and realized that

Cidra hadn't tried to nap. He peered through the gloom of the dimly lit cabin and saw her seated cross-legged on the metal deck. Her eyes were closed in silent meditation.

Probably still worrying about Scates and how she'd handled the situation, Severance reasoned in sleepy irritation. She looked very soft and gentle sitting there with her black-and-silver gown flowing around her. A little lost. But it would have taken a fair measure of strength and coordination to throw Scates. She couldn't be all sweetness and light, even if she wanted to believe she was.

Beneath the fine crystal-moss fabric of the robe she wore, he could see the rounded upsweep of her breasts. It seemed to him that the womanly curves would fit his hands perfectly. Then he recalled what she'd said about Wolves being very interested in sex. Severance turned over to face the wall and ordered himself to go back to sleep.

Chapter
Three

Cidra felt the shift in altitude and speed as *Severance Pay* automatically began its approach. The subtle changes jerked her out of the meditative trance she had been using to calm her mind and body. Opening her eyes, she saw new console lights wink on, while others changed color. For the first time she noticed there was a second computer on board. It didn't appear to be involved with the landing operation, either. A glance over her shoulder told her that the ship's master was still sound asleep.

She got to her feet, feeling delightfully rested, and went to the nearest viewing port. A few scattered lights in the distance heralded the presence of Lovelorn, a manufacturing town that had been located near the ore-rich deposits of the continent's western mountains. Beyond the mountains lay an ocean that extended most of the way around Lovelady. It was almost totally unexplored, although research indicated it would ultimately prove even richer in raw materials than the continents.

There was a lot of Lovelady waiting to be thoroughly explored and even more of Renaissance and QED. Beyond the three close-in planets lay one other, Liquid Assets, a frozen ocean of a world that lacked a breathable atmosphere. It hadn't experienced more than a few exploratory landings so far. The Stanza Nine system was still a frontier, its population centers small, even on Lovelady, which was its most heavily populated planet.

Cidra felt a glimmer of excitement rush through her. She was on her way, off in search of a legend. For the first time she acknowledged that the search, itself, was going to prove fascinating.

The ship altered course again, and this time Cidra turned around a little anxiously to see if Severance had awakened. When she saw him lying spread-eagle on his stomach, face to the cabin hull, she decided to act. She went over to the bunk and reached down to touch his shoulder, only to find she had made a terrible mistake.

There was no startled shout or sleepy, questioning groan. Severance simply exploded off the bunk at the touch of her hand. He was on the deck, feet spaced apart in a fighter's crouch, before Cidra quite realized what had happened. The small weapon he had used on Scates was in his right hand. Somehow he had gotten it out of the utility loop he'd hung beside the bunk.

Cidra froze, not daring to breathe as his eyes flickered in recognition. With a muttered oath Severance dropped the black metal object back into his loop. The poised tension went out of his body. On the bunk Fred exposed his teeth briefly, and then went back to posing as a rug.

"A few more surprises like that, Cidra, and one of us isn't going to make it as far as Renaissance."

She cleared her throat. "I just wanted to tell you that we're approaching Lovelorn. The ship seems to be altering course. I assumed that, as pilot in command, you might have some interest in the matter."

"Not much," Severance assured her. "This baby can land herself if necessary." Nevertheless he went forward to check the winking lights on the command console. "Saints know she's done it before." He yawned and massaged the back of his neck with one scarred hand as he stood staring down at the controls.

"Severance?"

"Hmmm?"

"What is that instrument you carry? The one you had in your hand a moment ago?"

"It's a remote for a Screamer." He leaned down and depressed a red-lit control, watching the screen in front of him as he did so. *Severance Pay* banked gently into a turn.

"I've never heard of a Screamer," Cidra said.

"I don't imagine you've got a lot of use for them in Clementia. They're not exactly legal."

"But what does it do?"

"It's very good at making uninvited visitors scream."

His obvious preoccupation bothered her. "That's not much of an explanation," she said reproachfully. Cidra was accustomed to an educational system that answered all questions as completely as possible. She was also trained to keep asking questions until she was satisfied with the answers.

Severance shrugged, still watching the landing setup on the screen. "It's a device that's designed to jam the frequency of human nerve impulses. That's about the only way I can explain it. I've got the main system installed here in the ship. I carry the remote with me."

"Scates didn't scream when you used it on him."

Severance glanced at her. "He was already half out. The remote just finished the job you'd started."

Cidra stiffened. She wasn't sure if she had been rebuked. But her curiosity persisted. "Does the device function automatically whenever someone comes aboard?"

"It can be set that way. I leave it on when I'm gone and switch it off with the remote when I'm ready to come back aboard. But it can also be triggered manually. See that switch there on the console?"

"Yes."

"That will trigger it. There's another one back near the head of my bunk."

"You would turn it on while you, yourself, were on board? What about your own nerves?" she asked.

"Curious little thing, aren't you?"

"I'm sorry," she apologized formally. "I don't mean to pry into your private business."

"Uh-huh." He sounded skeptical. "Well, the answer is that I can set the remote to protect me from the effects of the main system. Fred's safe because his nerves work on a different frequency than ours. Have a seat, Cidra, we're ready to hit dirt."

She realized that his patience had reached its limit, so obediently she strapped herself into the passenger seat and fixed her gaze on the lights of Lovelorn. A few moments later *Severance Pay* settled gently down into the landing field, and Severance cracked the hatch.

"I'll be gone for about an hour. No more than that. We haven't got time for you to wander outside and have a look around. You wouldn't find much of interest, anyway. This is a pretty dull town. You stay here and guard the castle. When I return, I'm going to put this ship into space as fast as possible.

If you're not here, you'll get left behind. Clear?" He sealed the collar of his gray shipsuit as he spoke.

Cidra nodded, and then asked impulsively, "Have you ever seen a real castle, Severance?"

He glared at her. "It was a figure of speech, not an invitation to more questions."

"I've heard that the Ghosts left behind a structure that might have been a fortress," she ventured thoughtfully. "On Renaissance."

"Why don't you take a nap, Cidra?"

Her eyes widened. "I couldn't do that. You're leaving me in charge."

Severance muttered something unintelligible and started through the hatch. "That was a figure of speech too. Forget I said it. Fred is in charge. Stay out of trouble, Cidra, if you want to see Renaissance." With that he vanished into the cool Lovelorn night. The hatch hissed shut behind him, sealing and locking itself.

Cidra felt movement near her sandaled feet and looked down. Fred was investigating the hem of her black-and-silver robe. Even as she watched, Cidra saw his three rows of teeth appear. She yanked the fabric out of reach just in the nick of time.

"Don't you dare chew on my clothes! Just because you're the one who is officially in charge, don't get the idea you can terrorize innocent passengers." Then she smiled at the creature. Fred continued to expose this teeth, and Cidra chose to believe he was smiling back. She reached down to scoop him up into her arms and discovered it was difficult to pick up a rug. There seemed to be no stable bone structure inside Fred.

He didn't appear to mind the awkwardness of her grip, however. He simply wrapped himself around her forearm and continued to grin. Cidra looked for something resembling eyes.

"You're a Lovelady rockrug, aren't you? I've seen holotapes

of your kind sunning themselves on mountain rocks. How do you like shipboard life?"

There was no answer, but the three sets of teeth disappeared into the tatty fur covering. As Fred settled down to sleep on her arm Cidra thought she saw a couple of small black eyes wink shut. It was hard to be certain because of the scraggly fur. Her arm felt pleasantly warm with the rockrug wrapped around it.

She wandered around the tiny cabin, investigating the functional, if spartan, lavatory facilities and the miniature galley with its preserver and heater. She checked the preserver to see if there were enough nonmeat food packs aboard to hold her until Renaissance. It was a limited selection, at best. Teague Severance was definitely carnivorous. Typical Wolf. Well, if he were willing to do without some of the vegetable packs, she might not starve to death. For someone who had been brought up to appreciate exquisitely prepared food, the prospect of two weeks of preserved vegetables was not a pleasant one.

But one had to make sacrifices when one set out on a quest, Cidra reminded herself as she shut the preserver. The heroes in the First Family novels always sacrificed comfort when they went adventuring. She ought to know. She was an expert on Frist Family novels. The only real expert in Clementia. She wandered over to the sleeping berths and fished around beneath Severance's bunk for her precious pack of books. Before she found it, she encountered a small metal chest wedged in behind the crate of ale.

She was far more intrigued by the unimposing storage container than she should have been, perhaps because she knew immediately that the box would contain something that was very personal to the enigmatic man who was taking her into space. For the first time in her life Cidra found herself wanting to explore the private side of another human being without waiting for an invitation. It took an amazing amount of fortitude to push the unopened chest back into the sticky storage net. But the ingrained rules of privacy were far too strong in her to allow Cidra to do otherwise. She pulled out the pack of books.

Her mind and body had settled down again. She would happily occupy the next hour reading. She deliberated between the elegantly worked volume of Nisco's *Serenity and Ritual* and the anonymous collection of essays and poetry known as *Passages to Appreciation*. She knew she ought to choose something from one of them, but somehow she wasn't in the mood. Cidra dug a little deeper into the pack and came up with a hidden bundle of data slips that contained her collection of novels. Novels didn't warrant much more than cursory interest on the part of Harmonics specializing in social history. She'd had no competition when she'd chosen to become an expert on them. But Cidra loved novels. She had acquired a sizable collection on slips, and when the time had come to leave Clementia, she had been unable to abandon them.

Cidra removed the reader and a slip that contained one of her favorite tales and curled up on the lower berth to read once more the adventurous story of a mythical First Family colonist. Without any hesitation at all she skipped along until she came to the love scenes. The love scenes in such stories held an interest for her that she had never stopped to analyze. But she was more exhausted than she realized. Cidra was in the middle of a torrid seduction when she fell asleep.

It was the distinct impression of wrongness that awoke her a few minutes later. For a moment she lay quietly, eyes closed, and tried to analyze the feeling. She immediately realized that Fred was no longer wrapped around her arm. She could feel the warmth of him lying on her stomach, but he didn't seem quite as boneless as he had earlier. There was a tension in him that had communicated itself to her and awakened her.

Cidra opened her eyes and looked up into the muzzle of a Garing Immobilizer. A part of her recognized the classic safeguard sidearm, even while her brain sought to adjust to the shock of seeing one pointed at her. A large, gloved hand was wrapped around the grip.

"Just keep calm, lady, and nothing's going to happen to you."

At the sound of the rough voice Cidra managed to jerk her eyes from the Immobilizer to the swarthy face of the safeguard holding it. When he saw her stricken look, he smiled bleakly and used his free hand to display his certificate of authorization.

"I don't understand," Cidra murmured, confusion replacing some of the initial fright. Harmonics never had trouble with the authorities for the simple reason that Harmonics never committed crimes. Both safeguards and Harmonics knew it. She had grown up with that serene knowledge. It was built into her. Then she remembered Scates lying on the floor of her hotel room. "What's wrong? He's all right, isn't he?"

The man holding the Immobilizer appeared amused. "Who? Severance? As far as we know. Don't worry about him, he'll be back in about forty minutes. He ran into a little delay collecting his mail, you see. We arranged it that way."

They didn't seem to know about Scates. Feeling simultaneously relieved and guilty, Cidra relaxed slightly. "But what are you doing here?" She realized that a second uniformed man was standing near the command console, and her searching gaze rested briefly on him. "How did you get on board? The hatch was sealed."

The man standing over her answered. "Didn't you look at my certificate? We're port security. We have bypass plates for all registered mail ships. Now sit up very slowly. You from Clementia?"

She nodded. Fred scuttled down into her lap as she sat up cross-legged on the bunk. Her hand brushed past the small switch that could activate the Screamer, but Cidra hardly noticed. She was watching Fred bare his teeth. He didn't appear to be smiling this time.

"Good. That should make things nice and simple. We won't have any trouble with you, will we?"

Obediently Cidra shook her head. "Of course not."

"Fine." He glanced at his companion. "We won't even need to put a tangler on her, Des. She's a Harmonic. She'll stay out of trouble."

"But what do you want? If you have business aboard, I would have been happy to open the hatch. I don't understand what this is all about." Cidra turned an unwavering gaze on the armed man. "Whatever it is you're after, you should consult with the master of the ship."

"We're not quite as formal here in Lovelorn as you folks are in Clementia. We don't always have time for good manners. What we're after is in the cargo bay, and on this kind of ship it can only be unsealed through the command console."

Cidra kept her hands carefully folded in front of her. "Then you should definitely speak to Teague Severance."

The safeguard grinned. "He's not likely to be very helpful under the circumstances. We're here to remove some cargo he picked up in Port Valentine."

"But the shipment from Port Valentine is scheduled to be taken to an outpost on Renaissance." Cidra kept her voice very clear and polite. She betrayed nothing of the uneasiness she felt, realizing that her best defense right now lay in maintaining the impression these men had of her. They couldn't have dealt with many Harmonics. In their line of work they simply weren't likely to encounter people from Clementia. Her appearance and dress had led them to mistake her for a Saint, so she would play the part.

"Don't worry yourself about it, Otanna. This isn't Harmonic business. This is a matter of port security." The man holding the weapon spoke to the silent figure by the console. "Find what we need, Des?"

"It's here. The bypass is working through possible code combinations now. We'll have the bay opened in a minute or so. What about her?"

"She's not going to give us any trouble."

The first man holstered the Immobilizer and smiled again. He smiled a lot, Cidra thought. Too much. She didn't like him, and neither, apparently, did Fred. There was a curious humming sound coming from the vicinity of the three rows of teeth. Automatically Cidra reached out to stroke the rockrug.

"We're all set," the man called Des announced with cool satisfaction. "The bay's open. Let's get the stuff and get out. I don't want to be hanging around here when Severance returns."

"I couldn't agree more." The first man started for the rear of the cabin where the inside cargo hatch was located.

The valuable shipment lay undefended. It was COD, Severance had said. He would get nothing for it if it wasn't delivered. With a kind of stark clarity Cidra realized that she had to act. In Severance's absence she was in charge of his ship. "Guard the castle," he had told her.

Yet these men were official representatives of Lovelorn law. The law was one of the few formalized institutions Wolves had. It was to be respected. Harmonics knew it often fell short of the ideal, but that was no excuse for failing to honor it. Still, she felt she had to do something.

"Wait," Cidra called urgently as the first man was about to

step into the cargo bay. "I must protest this action. I insist you wait until Teague Severance returns. This is his ship and his cargo. You must discuss this with him."

"Why don't I just go ahead and put her out?" Des unholstered his weapon and calmly pointed it at Cidra.

"Forget it. She's not going to get in our way. Give me a hand, Des. I knew we should have brought a servocart. This thing's heavy."

"Please," Cidra said, "I'm asking one last time that you wait and take this up with the ship's master."

"Shut up, lady. You're beginning to annoy me. Why don't you meditate or something?" Des started to follow his companion into the cargo bay.

Fred suddenly leapt from Cidra's lap, undulating with incredible speed across the cabin floor. Des whirled around, aiming his sidearm at the small creature.

"No!" Cidra stopped debating the philosophical quandary in which she found herself. Her hand swept out, yanking at the Screamer trigger imbedded in the wall behind her.

And then she found out why the shipboard defense system was called a Screamer. She was barely aware of the strangled cries of the two safeguards. Her own mind was suddenly bursting with the screams of every nerve in her body.

She had never experienced anything approaching such pain, and after the first few seconds, it held her totally immobilized. Lights flashed in front of her eyes, her ears seemed to hear every harsh, discordant sound in the universe, and her skin was on fire with a rash that made her want to claw at herself with her own nails. But she couldn't even move her hand far enough to switch off the screamer. Cidra could only sit on the bunk and struggle to maintain some hint of sanity, for a primitive part of her was still alert enough to fear being driven insane by the cacophony. And that was the most terrifying prospect of all.

Instinctively she mentally grabbed for and clung to the intense discipline that was a fundamental part of her Harmonic training, using it to search for and find a thin sliver of consciousness and sanity to guide her through the pain. A true Harmonic would not have been able to apply her training under such fearsome circumstances. It was an ironic indication of Cidra's lack of true talent that she could use the training now in a way for which it had never been intended. But Cidra was not contemplating the right or wrong of it all; she was simply holding on for her life.

Severance was worried even before he got out of the runner. He stood for a moment on the curb, the small courier pack locked to his wrist. Then he fished the computer remote out of his utility loop. The tiny notation on the screen informed him calmly that the Screamer had been activated. He stared at the object in his hand, unable to believe what he was seeing. He picked up the package of preserved vegetarian meals he'd wasted valuable time purchasing on the way back to the ship and broke into a run.

Severance Pay sat in heavy shadow on the landing field, giving no hint that all was pain and chaos aboard. The Screamer put out no audible sound. When Severance punched the remote to open the hatch, he found that it hadn't been locked. Had Cidra left the ship after all? The knowledge infuriated him, but he found himself praying that she had. If she was still on board when the Screamer had activated, she would be limp, quivering marshjelly by now. He knew what the Screamer could do to the most hardened of Wolves. He couldn't bring himself to imagine what it would do to someone who was almost a Harmonic in so many ways.

Damning everything and everyone around him, Severance used the Screamer's remote to cancel the defense system. But he knew that if Cidra was inside, the damage had been done. He leapt aboard, his eyes sweeping the ominously still cabin.

For an instant he couldn't see his passenger. She wasn't on her bunk and she wasn't lying on the floor. He saw the prone bodies of two men near the open cargo bay before he realized that Cidra was slumped on his bunk.

"Damn it to a renegade's hell. Cidra. *Cidra.*" He crouched beside the berth, searching for her throat pulse. It beat far too rapidly beneath his fingers. The stiffness in her body alarmed him more than anything else. She should be unconscious by now. Even a minute of the Screamer's effects was sufficient to knock most people out. Yet the tension in her body indicated that on some level she was still aware, still trying to fight the nerve-jamming impulses even though they had ceased. He began stroking her, petting her as if she were a wild creature he was trying to soothe and tame. There was no quick remedy for the Screamer's damage. It took time to recover. Victims knocked unconscious generally awoke a long time later with a headache that could only be described as violent.

"Cidra, can you hear me? It's over. Listen to me. It's over. Let go, lady. Let go."

Severance caught a brief movement out of the corner of his eye. He glanced toward the cargo bay and saw Fred release the leg on which he had been gnawing. The rockrug flowed toward his master. "What the hell happened in here?" Severance asked softly, wishing the rockrug could answer.

Fred hummed a little in response and undulated up into the bunk to settle on Cidra's stomach. Then he began shifting his pliable body in a rhythm that didn't take him anywhere but seemed to emulate the stroking movements Severance's hands were making.

"It's all right, Cidra. It's all over. Can you hear me? All over. You're safe now."

Very slowly some of the unnatural tension seemed to seep from her body. Beneath his hand Severance could feel the gradual unknotting of the muscles in her arms. Her head began to move restlessly. He kept talking to her, muttering meaningless words of comfort. Even though he knew there was no instant cure for the Screamer's results, Severance decided to get Cidra to the nearest med facility. If nothing else, they could tranquilize her into unconsciousness.

Her lashes lifted just as he started to get to his feet. Instantly he knelt again beside the bunk.

"Cidra?"

She seemed to have trouble focusing on him, but at last she realized who was beside her. Her lips moved, shaping soundless words. She touched her tongue to the dry surfaces and tried again.

"Is the castle . . . safe?"

"Everything's safe, Cidra. Don't try to talk. Just try to sleep. It's the only way out of this. Try to sleep."

"I know you left Fred in command," she whispered, "but they were going to shoot him. There wasn't anybody left . . . except me."

Relief poured through Severance as he realized that she was starting to breathe normally. It didn't look as though he would need the med facility after all. Gently he continued stroking her.

"We'll talk about it when you wake up. Go to sleep, Cidra. Close your eyes and go to sleep."

He watched her relax slowly into unconsciousness, and then he got to his feet once more. He studied the two men lying near the cargo bay while he unlatched the courier pack he had just picked up from a patron. It was being sent to Renaissance, and the shipper had been most anxious that it travel under computer lock. To humor him Severance had performed the little drama of latching the pack to his wrist. It was an ancient shipping custom that could still impress customers although Severance privately thought it wasn't very practical as a security technique. But it seemed to have reassured the patron. It had also taken up precious time.

Dumping the pack carelessly into a nearby storage bin, Severance went toward the cargo bay to investigate the intrusion that had apparently caused Cidra to pull the Screamer. With the toe of his boot he nudged one of the unconscious uniformed men onto his back. Then he went down on one knee and pulled out the man's certification card.

For a long time Severance studied the port security identification. It appeared almost genuine. It would easily have fooled Cidra, who wasn't accustomed to double-checking a stranger's ID.

The second man was sprawled halfway through the cargo bay opening. His arm still lay across the shipping container bearing the red COD seal.

Suddenly it all made sense to Teague Severance.

All except one small matter.

Twenty minutes later, as *Severance Pay* lifted off for the long trip to Renaissance, Severance was still pondering the fact that Cidra Rainforest must have gone against everything she had ever been taught when she'd used the Screamer to stop two safeguards from stealing the shipment.

A postman could do worse than go into space with a woman who was willing to risk her life for the mail.

Chapter
Four

Cidra's first thought when she awoke was that a giant torla had accidentally stepped on her head. Such a thing could only happen accidentally, as torlas were too stupid to do anything on purpose except eat. They were also too stupid to move once they had accidentally stepped on someone. So, of course, Cidra assumed, the beast was still crushing her.

Unless, of course, this was the first assault in a war of revenge against the human population of Lovelady. If it was, Cidra could hardly blame them. The big, dumb, placid torlas had become a prime source of meat shortly after the First Families arrived. Knowing torlas, it might have taken them two hundred years to wake up to the fact that they had an enemy.

"I'm a vegetarian." Cidra didn't even try to open her eyes as she squeaked her protest. The torla on her head didn't move.

"I know," came the response from somewhere to her right.

"Just one more problem. Here, I've got some 'gesics. They won't knock you out like that oblivo stuff does, but they'll help the headache. Open your mouth, Cidra. They have to dissolve under your tongue."

A strong, sinewy arm slid under her shoulders, lifting her. The pain in Cidra's head changed from a steady state of heavy pressure into sharp bolts of lightning. Tears burned beneath Cidra's eyes. The humiliation washed over her, momentarily more intense than even the agony in her head.

"I apologize," she gritted.

"For what?" Severance asked, calmly shoving two small objects under Cidra's tongue. "The tears? Forget it. Most people would be screaming about now."

Cidra sensed a faint fizzing sensation as the tablets dissolved. Experimentally she lifted her lashes and found herself looking up into Teague Severance's gray eyes. He didn't appear especially pleased with her as he knelt beside the lower bunk, cradling her in one arm. There was a grimness around the edges of his mouth.

"The act of screaming would only make it worse," Cidra explained with grave logic. She managed to blink back the incipient tears.

"It can't be as bad now as it was when you cranked on the Screamer. Saints in hell, lady, that thing must have ripped you apart."

"I thought that's exactly what it was doing." Automatically she looked down at herself. The black-and-silver surplice was a mess, stained in places from her damp, perspiring body. The finely spun crystal-moss fabric looked as crumpled as she felt. But she seemed to be all in one piece. Then she realized she didn't feel quite right even though nothing appeared to be missing. "Are we in space?"

"Two hours out of Lovelady. I've got the grav on."

Severance steadied her with one hand while his other went to her braided coronet.

The artificial gravity explained the faint strangeness she was feeling. "What are you doing?" Belatedly Cidra realized that Severance was freeing the fireberyl comb in her hair.

"I thought your head might feel a little better if you loosen those braids." He tossed the expensive comb down onto the bunk beside her and deftly began unpinning her hair.

The intimate touch of his hands was vaguely alarming. Cidra wasn't accustomed to much physical contact. Harmonics had a great respect for the privacy of another person's body. Instinctively she tried to draw away from Severance. His grip on her shoulders tightened in response.

"Hold still. I'll have these down in a minute."

"I'll do it." She lifted her hand to her hair, trying to take over the small task. Her fingers came in contact with his, tangling for an instant. He ignored her efforts, pushing her hand aside. She felt the roughness of his scars.

"I've almost got it. This must be harder to put together than a coalition of free miners on QED. How long does it take every morning?" Two long braids tumbled free, falling down over Cidra's breasts. As if intrigued by the intricate braiding, Severance's fingers followed the line of one braid all the way down to the tip. His hand hovered there, filling Cidra's body with a new tension.

Her concentration was abruptly torn between the pain in her head and her intense awareness of the proximity of Teague's fingers. She realized that she was holding her breath, knowing that if she inhaled, she would thrust herself against his hand.

"I work my hair during the first morning change." She couldn't think of anything else to do except answer his question. He was beginning to unwind the individual braids now, starting from the bottom and moving upward. Cidra drew a small sigh of relief as the masculine fingers moved to her shoulder. She could risk breathing again.

"Well, you'll have plenty of time on this trip to fool with your hair. How's the head?"

"Better."

"Good. With any luck no one will find those two fake guards for a whole day or two. They won't have any 'gesics to help with the headaches." There was a certain distinct satisfaction in Severance's voice.

Cidra looked up at him as her hair loosened beneath his touch. "Fake guards? They didn't represent port security at Lovelorn?"

"No more than I represent a convention of Saints. Good ID, though. I'm not surprised you bought their story. And they must have had some good connections too. It's not that easy to get hold of an official mail ship bypass."

"Why were they trying to steal your cargo?"

"Those sensors we've got on board are one of a kind gadgets. The latest designs out of ExcellEx labs. The company wants them shipped to their exploration post on Renaissance."

"I've never heard of ExcellEx."

"It's a small outfit run by a tough little guy who left one of the big exploration companies a few seasons ago to start his own firm. His name's Quench. He's shrewd, and he's willing to slit throats when necessary. I've handled a few private shipments for him lately. He seems satisfied. If he can get ExcellEx up and running within the next three or four seasons, he'll own one of the hottest exploration companies in the system."

"And you'll be one of his most trusted mailmen. He'll give you the most lucrative runs. Maybe even employ you full-time so you won't have to scrounge for shipments."

Severance showed his teeth. "Nobody ever said Harmonics

aren't as fast as everyone else when it comes to figuring out a business deal."

"Harmonics have to be fast at analyzing business situations," Cidra informed him demurely. "If they weren't, they'd get eaten alive by unscrupulous Wolves."

"They seem to do all right. Where do you think the phrase 'rich as a Saint' comes from? I don't know of too many poor ones, except perhaps for the young ones who are still doing research or perfecting their art and music."

Cidra shrugged and instantly regretted it as the pain flared back to life in her head. Severance was right. The Harmonics participated in the freewheeling business practices that dominated commerce throughout the Stanza Nine system. Clementia produced and marketed the results of scientific research, as well as fine art, poetry, and music that thrilled the senses. Wolves were a ready market for the talents of Clementia. But when it came to business, Harmonics couldn't rely on the customary goodwill of the general population. Agents who were Wolves, themselves, were used for the often fierce negotiating that took place when a Harmonic product went up for sale. Her own father had made a sizable fortune selling sophisticated investment strategies. Constructing and analyzing complex economic models of the wide-ranging commerce of the worlds of Stanza Nine was a hobby for Garn Oquist. He was a mathematician by training and inclination.

Cidra considered what she had just been told. "So someone else wants those sensors?"

"Looks like it. Since they're supposed to be top secret, that presents an interesting problem." Severance finished untwisting one long braid. He drew his fingers down through it slowly. There was an oddly preoccupied expression on his face as he watched the red highlights hidden in Cidra's hair come to life in the thick stuff.

Cidra, herself, found it difficult to maintain a casual conversational tone as she asked, "If the sensors are so valuable, why weren't they shipped out on a commercial freighter under company guard?" Instead of answering right away, Severance began to work on the second braid. This time his hand seemed to be almost resting on her breast as he began unwinding the strands. And when he spoke, Cidra heard a new harshness in his voice.

"In addition to the fact that it costs three times as much to ship that way, Quench wasn't sure it would really buy him any protection. There's no method of keeping that kind of shipment secret. He was hoping that if he sent the sensors with me on a normal private mail hop, no one would notice. It was a risk, but that's how you make good credit."

"Well, someone did notice." Cidra began to breathe again as Severance's fingers moved upward. A part of her felt strangely disappointed, but another part was appalled at her own sensual curiosity. She had been so sure she had outgrown the very unHarmonic desire for physical knowledge that had tormented her socially as a young girl. "Do you know who?"

"Who knew the shipment was traveling with me? No. I have no idea."

"Those men who came into the ship..."

"Were probably mercenaries. No telling who hired them."

"What did you do with them?"

"Stuffed 'em into a storage locker outside the terminal at Lovelorn." He finished his self-appointed task and sat back on his haunches to survey the effect. Cidra's soft red-brown hair flowed in a cape over her shoulders. He stared at it for a moment, and then his eyes shifted to catch her questioning gaze. "They're lucky I didn't leave them with something more permanent than a killer of a headache."

The coldness in him reached Cidra in a wave, chilling her

to the bone. For the first time since she had left Clementia she allowed herself to remember that murder was not an unheard-of crime among Wolves. A movement around her ankles broke the spell. Grateful for the small interruption, she turned her head to see Fred undulating into a more comfortable position across her legs.

"Fred was quite a hero. You should have seen him go after that one guard," Cidra said with a weak smile.

Severance's attention stayed on her profile. "I saw what he did to the renegade's leg."

"I wondered earlier if Fred might bite. I guess I know now."

"He did a little more than bite the bastard. Fred's got three layers of teeth. When he starts chewing on something, he makes a real meal out of it." Severance stood up beside the bunk. "Think you'll be okay?"

Hastily Cidra nodded. "My head is much better, thank you."

Severance leaned forward, his face suddenly very intent. "It wasn't Fred who was the hero. He was only acting out of instinct. You were the one who had to go against some fairly strong conditioning to try to stop those two renegades. I know Harmonics normally don't get mixed up with safeguards. I owe you, lady."

Cidra realized that she was feeling inordinately pleased by his words. She smiled for the first time since she had awakened with the awful headache but offered the formal response to his praise. "It was as nothing. No sense of obligation is required."

Severance stared at her for an instant and then grinned. "That's a Harmonic for you: Polite to the last drop of blood." He turned from the bunk. "Feel like a cup of coffade?"

"Yes, thank you." Cidra lay back carefully on the bunk, aware that she now missed the comfort of his touch. It said a lot about her weakened condition that she would have liked to have him continue to hold her.

She watched as he dialed open the compact preserver and removed the container of green crystals. He poured the coffade into two mugs and shoved both into the heater. The machine added water and brought the mixture to a quick boil. Severance opened the heater and brought one of the mugs over to Cidra. He held the other one in his fist as he watched her cup her hands around the pleasantly warmed mug.

"When you're feeling better, we're going to have a talk."

She inhaled the fragrant steam. "I realize that. You'll probably want to outline my duties for the next two weeks. I'm really feeling much better already. We can talk now if you like."

"Your duties," he repeated, sounding as if he were repressing a groan. He dropped down onto the bunk beside her, staring at the bulkhead. Leaning forward, he rested his elbows on his thighs, the mug of coffade loosely suspended between his knees. "Yes, there is the little matter of your duties on board. We'll come to that later. There are other things that have to be resolved first. You've never been in space?"

"My parents took me on a commercial freighter once when I was younger. It was more of a sight-seeing trip than anything else. Other than that, I haven't spent any time on a ship."

"Uh-huh." He paused, apparently trying to find the exact words. "You will note that, as I mentioned over dinner, there is very little room in here."

"Don't worry, I don't think I'm claustrophobic. Of course, I haven't spent several days in a confined area before. But I'm sure I'll be able to handle this."

"Claustrophobia is not what I was worrying about." He took a long sip of the coffade. "Let's see if I can put this so that it sounds reasonably diplomatic. Harmonics, as I understand it, are accustomed to a great deal of privacy."

"Yes."

"They are also accustomed to a great deal of personal independence."

"Of course." She waited expectantly, wondering where he was leading.

"There is very little of either on board ship," Severance concluded bluntly. "Small mail ships such as this one are not exactly bastions of democracy. The only way we're going to survive without resorting to violence over the next couple of weeks is if you understand that I'm in charge. I know Harmonics are brought up to question everything. But around here, when I give an order, I am not bringing the issue up for debate. Whenever there is a choice about the way something is done, we do it my way."

Cidra told herself not to be offended, but she knew her voice sounded overly formal. "I assure you I understand the tradition of a captain being in charge of his own ship."

He looked at her in mild astonishment. "You do?"

"I read a great deal," she confided. "I'm a trained archivist. One of my areas of expertise is the fiction written about the First Families and the early explorations."

"Wonderful." His mouth crooked dryly as he took another swallow of the coffade. "I'm sure all that reading will have prepared you to slip right into shipboard life. I've had trouble with the few previous passengers I've had on board, but I can see that won't be the case with you."

Perhaps the residual pain in her head was making her more sensitive than usual. Whatever the reason, Cidra felt a touch of annoyance. "There's no reason to be flippant. If you've had trouble with previous passengers, my guess is it's because you were impolite or abrupt in your manner of giving orders."

"Orders sometimes have a way of sounding rude and abrupt. I just want it clear that the tone of voice in which they are given does not alter the fact that they're still orders. Understood?"

"I have the feeling I've just received the first command. Message clear and comprehended, Otan Severance."

"I've told you to skip the Otan."

"Would you prefer that I address you as Captain Severance?"

"Now who's being flippant?" he drawled. "Use my name. Either name. I don't think the informality will do much damage to the sense of discipline in the remainder of the crew." He glanced at Fred.

"Did Fred ever have any sense of discipline to begin with?" Cidra asked.

"Not a lot." Severance was quiet for a while. "I don't suppose you know how to play Free Market?"

"Harmonics do not gamble."

"I was afraid of that. It's going to be a long two weeks, isn't it?"

Cidra hesitated. But she did want to be as accommodating as possible. "I could learn to play the game," she offered tentatively. "It's not necessary to make wagers, is it? I expect that the game is played the same, with or without credit being exchanged."

"The stakes are what make the game interesting."

"Oh. Well, it's a moot point. I don't have anything to put forth as a wager except perhaps a few novels on data slips. I don't imagine that would interest you." She felt relieved. She had made the offer, and it was obvious that Severance wasn't too excited about it. Cidra felt off the hook.

"I could try teaching you the game first, and then we can decide whether you've got anything worth wagering," Severance said slowly.

A faint thread of wariness unfurled inside Cidra. She studied

Teague's unreadable face. "I've heard that many Wolves are quite addicted to gambling."

"'It's just a way of passing time. A form of recreation. Not to be taken too seriously."

"Then you are not one of the addicts?" she asked cautiously.

Severance smiled, that same grin that showed so many fine, strong teeth and so little real humor. "Of course not. I'm only a casual player."

"Oh, good." She felt vastly relieved. "Well, in that case, I suppose I could attempt to learn to play Free Market."

"We'll give it a whirl after we've had some sleep. I keep standard Lovelady days on board ship." He got to his feet. "Think you can make it up into your own bunk? Or do you want me to carry you?"

Gingerly Cidra started to sit up. Fred moved off her feet with a low, grumbling sound. Cidra ignored him, concentrating on her body's reactions to the movement. Her head still hurt, but the pain seemed distant, a dull threat but not a major disaster any longer. She massaged her temple, aware of a vague sense of weary disappointment.

"What's the matter? Still feel like your head's going to explode?" Severance slid a rough hand under her curtain of hair and began kneading the nape of her neck.

"It's not that. I feel much better. It's just that—" She broke off and moved her hand in a gesture of dismay. "I shouldn't."

"Shouldn't feel much better?"

"Never mind. It's hard to explain."

Severance continued to work on the base of her neck. "Still worrying because you don't have a Saint's catatonic reaction to pain?"

"It's just one more reminder that I have a long way to go before I become a Harmonic. You must understand. I don't want to feel pain. No one does. But every time I do, I'm aware of the fact that I don't react to it in a normal fashion."

"Normal for a Saint."

"That's what I was born to be, Severance," she said with soft insistence. "I remember once when I was very young. I had slipped away from my parents and was trying to climb into one of the plaza fountains in Clementia. They're so beautiful with the light beads mixed into the water. I wanted to go swimming in that beautiful, shining water. That was before I realized that one didn't do that sort of thing," she added hastily.

"Naturally. Very un-Saintlike, climbing into a fountain."

"Yes, well, I slipped and fell, cutting myself. But I was so excited by having gotten into the fountain at last that I didn't pay much attention to the fact that I was bleeding into the water. When my mother found me, she nearly went into shock. Everyone nearby was horrified. Someone came rushing up with a dose of oblivo, and the next thing I knew, I woke up in a med facility. I found out several years later that small wounds such as the one I had gotten in the fountain are treated rather casually among Wolves."

"And you had automatically reacted casually at the time. Because you're a Wolf in Harmonic's clothing." Severance removed his hand from the nape of her neck. "Stop worrying about it, Cidra. We both need some sleep. You want a bath?"

She stood up a little shakily but without kick-starting the headache. "That sounds wonderful." With a sigh she examined her rumpled sleeping robe. "Have you got a fresher on board?"

"Sure. Give me the dress and I'll run it through a cleaning cycle while you hit the lav."

"Thank you." She moved toward the tiny lavatory facility, wondering how she was going to find room even to turn around inside, let alone undress. The ship's lav was nothing like the comfortable facility in her parents' home. When the privacy panel hissed shut behind her, she struggled free of the sleeping surplice with some difficulty. Every time she shifted position she came into contact with some object in the miniature room. Severance knocked on the door just as she finally freed herself of the gown.

"Ready?"

"Here. I appreciate your help." She opened the panel a tiny distance and pushed the black-and-silver robe into his outstretched hand. "How do you move around in here? It's barely big enough for me, let alone someone your size."

"I leave the panel open," he told her calmly. The robe and his hand disappeared.

Never in a million seasons would she leave the panel open, Cidra decided. Turning carefully, she activated the orange controls set in the bulkhead. A wonderfully refreshing hot spray filled the small room. Cidra closed her eyes and gave herself up to the pleasure of it.

It was a long time before she reluctantly deactivated the spray, dried herself with the warm air jets, and plaited her hair into one long braid that hung over her shoulder. Feeling infinitely better and deliciously sleepy, she cautiously cracked the panel.

"Severance? Is my robe ready?"

There was no answer. Pushing the panel open a little farther, Cidra tried again. "Teague?" Still no response. The cabin lights had been dimmed. In the faint glow of the control console she could see the black-and-silver surplice draped over the back of the command seat. There was no sign of Severance. Belatedly Cidra realized that he was in his bunk.

She waited another moment or two, the sight of her robe on the seat tantalizing her. It was obvious that Severance had gone to sleep in the same quick, uncomplicated way he had napped on the flight between Valentine and Lovelorn. The only option she had was to get the robe herself.

Taking a deep breath, she slipped out of the lav and stood poised for a few seconds in the shadows. There was no movement from the lower bunk. Cidra padded barefoot across to the command console and quickly put on the surplice. She relaxed as the garment swirled comfortably around her. Running around naked in front of a strange man and an even odder beast was not her idea of proper decorum. Gathering up the hem of the robe, she went to stand at the foot of the bunks. There was a narrow rope ladder hanging from the upper berth. Presumably that was how one climbed into it.

Experimentally Cidra took hold of the flexible side of the ladder and fit her foot into the bottom rung. After that it was easy. She was safely into her berth a few seconds later. The knowledge that she was truly at the beginning of her quest once again swept over her, making her considerably less sleepy than she had been only moments before. She sat cross-legged on the bunk, closed her eyes, and sought the calming influence of the evening meditation ritual. She was halfway through the elaborate sequence of silent logic when Severance spoke from the bottom bunk.

"Do you always spend that long in the lav?"

Cidra opened her eyes with a start. Instantly visions of herself darting naked across the cabin to retrieve her robe leapt into her mind. "I thought you were asleep," she said weakly.

"I dozed off waiting for you to emerge from your bath. Rule number one on board *Severance Pay* is that passengers don't treat the water supply as if it comes from one of those inexhaustable fountains in Clementia."

"I assumed it was a recirculating, full-recovery system." She was embarrassed and offended.

"No system is one-hundred-percent full-recovery. You lose a little every time you use the lav."

"I understand," Cidra said stiffly. "I will be more careful next time." She gave up trying to meditate and crawled under the covers.

On the bottom bunk Severance folded his arms behind his head and stared thoughtfully up at the bunk above. Chewing out a Harmonic always made a man feel guilty. He'd felt the same way whenever he'd lost his temper with Jeude.

Damn it to a renegade's hell, though—Cidra was not a real Harmonic. There would undoubtedly be ample opportunity to remind himself of that fact during the next two weeks. He allowed himself to dwell for a lingering moment on the sight of her nude body outlined in the dim console lighting as she padded quickly across the room to don her robe.

Small, sleek, with an unmistakably feminine grace. Her breasts were delicately curved, just the way he had imagined they would be earlier when he'd unbound her braids. Nicely rounded buttocks too. Lush and tantalizing. She wasn't a beauty, but she was intriguing on too many levels for his peace of mind. And she was not a Harmonic, regardless of what she thought or wished to be.

For some reason it was becoming important that he make her admit that. Severance realized he wanted Cidra to acknowledge fully that she was a real Wolf, just as he was.

It was a long while before he went to sleep.

The smell of hot coffade and a steaming prespac breakfast brought Severance awake eight hours later. He opened his eyes slowly, letting himself luxuriate in the fragrance. The little fake Saint was obviously up and about. He stretched slowly and climbed out of the bunk. Fred had vacated the premises earlier. He was draped over the back of the console seat, watching

Cidra slip another prespac into the ship's heater. Severance yawned loudly, and Cidra whirled around, smiling. The smile slipped, and her eyes went momentarily quite wide as she absorbed the fact that he was naked. After a startled instant she turned hurriedly back to the heater.

"Good morning, Severance. Are you hungry? I hope you don't mind me digging out the prespacs. I was just thinking, this could be one of my shipboard duties, couldn't it? Getting the meals ready?"

The deliberate chattiness of her voice amused him. He stepped into the lav, leaving the panel open. "I've got news for you. Shoving a food prespac into a heater and pulling it back out again doesn't exactly constitute a full-time job. Now, if we had a grill on board and some fresh food, I might be willing to negotiate."

"Still," she insisted, "it is a task, however small. And we have to agree on something useful for me to do."

He leaned out of the lav, reaching into a storage bin for the trouser portion of his gray shipsuit. "Afraid of getting bored?"

"No. But I definitely want to work my passage, Severance."

He didn't respond to that—didn't *dare* respond. With a grim effort, he forced the panel shut behind him. He had spent too much of the night envisioning exactly how she could make herself useful on board, and Severance knew Cidra would be repelled by the graphic pictures he had formed of her. When he stepped out of the lav a short time later wearing only worn, close-fitting trousers, he said simply, "We'll think of something."

"You keep saying that, but what will we think of?" She set the steaming prespacs on the small serving table and handed him a mug of coffade.

"So earnest and industrious," he muttered as he sat down. The coffade tasted better than usual for some reason. Maybe it was because he hadn't had to make it himself. "Give me some time, all right? I haven't had an opportunity to really contemplate the situation. Everything's happened a little fast since I met you on Lovelady."

She smiled, but he noticed she was having to make an effort to keep from staring at his bare chest. He blinked lazily, set down the mug with a small sigh of resignation, and reached into a bin for a loose, comfortable, wide-sleeved shirt he sometimes wore on board. He shrugged into it but didn't bother to fasten the front seal. Cidra looked relieved.

"Thank you," she whispered. "I'm not a prude, you understand. I have had courses in human anatomy. But Harmonics are generally quite formal in their attire. I'm accustomed to it."

"Yeah, I'm getting that impression. I warned you about the lack of privacy on board."

"Yes." She concentrated on her food. "You did."

"Things on Renaissance are even more, uh, informal."

"I'm prepared for that."

Severance studied her for a moment, taking in the determined carriage of her head. She had her hair back up in the strict coronet, and he wondered how long it had taken her to do it. Her surplice was red, embroidered at hem and cuffs and throat with a delicate purple floss. She was a note of color and restrained elegance against the general gray backdrop of the ship. Quite suddenly he was intensely curious about her.

"What's going to happen if and when you find your magic artifact, Cidra?"

She frowned. "It's not magic. When I find it, I'm sure I will also find a perfectly good scientific explanation for how it works."

He held up a hand. "Sorry. No magic, then. Your scientifically explainable artifact. What will you do with it?"

"Go back to Clementia, naturally."

"Someone waiting there?"

She glanced up, green eyes wary and quizzical. "My parents. My teachers. My friends."

"A lover?" He almost surprised himself with the question—almost but not quite. The hard edge of his words told him more than he wanted to know about his own reasons for pushing in this particular direction. The color that surged into Cidra's cheeks fascinated him.

"That's a very personal question, Severance."

"I know. I'm rude on occasion." He finished his meal and tossed the empty prespac into the disposal unit. He was disgusted with himself.

Cidra smiled tentatively. "I suppose it's just another example of a Wolf's natural interest in sex."

Severance regarded her laconically as he got to his feet and walked over to the control console. "You're a Wolf, lady, whether you like it or not. Don't you have any interest in the subject?"

She quickly cleaned up the remains of the breakfast prespacs, avoiding his half accusing stare. "You must understand that for me a relationship with a man will be much different than it would be between two Wolves."

"There is a man back in Clementia, isn't there? A Saint." He leaned against the console, irritated by the way she was sidestepping the subject.

Cidra turned to face him with quiet reproach. "There is a man," she began very carefully, "but I am not ready for him."

"He thinks he's too good for you because he's a Harmonic and you're not?"

She shook her head. "Mercer would never think such a thing. He is a brilliant, kind, intuitive man. A fine Harmonic who has been both teacher and friend to me. He is in charge of the Archive where I work. I have never told him that I would like the relationship to become more ... more intimate. I would not burden him with that knowledge until I can come to him as a true Harmonic."

"You've just stood in the shadows, pining from afar, is that it? For how long?" Severance didn't even bother to soften the words.

"Three and a half seasons," Cidra admitted wistfully. "We have so much in common intellectually that I just know things will harmonize beautifully between us once I have overcome the barrier of my non-Harmonic mind."

"I think I may get sick."

Instantly Cidra swept forward, concern marking her features. "You're ill? Why didn't you say something sooner?" She took his arm. "Lie down while I get the med kit. Here, I'll help you to the bunk—"

"You do take things literally, don't you? Forget the med kit, Cidra. I'll survive. Come here. I want to show you something." He pushed her gently down into the seat in front of the ship's second computer. "Ever seen one of these?"

"A Consac Four-ten. I've never seen one programmed for use on board a ship, but I'm familiar with the basic model. We use a Consac Sixteen hundred in the Archives." She eyed him uncertainly. "You're not sick?"

"Not the way you mean." He nodded toward the computer control panel. "A Conny is a Conny. If I give you some introduction, you ought to be able to manipulate this one."

"Probably," she agreed with no false show of pride; the simple fact was that she could. "I learn very quickly. What do you want me to do with it?"

"You said you wanted to work your passage."

Her eyes lit up. "Definitely. There's something you want done on the computer?"

"I'd like some advice from someone who's had a good education. Presumably, since you were raised in Clementia, you've had the best."

She smiled. "The best."

Chapter
Five

Fifteen minutes later Cidra shook off her intense concentration long enough to smile up at Severance as he hovered over her and the computer. She understood now what he wanted.

"This is your lucky day, Teague Severance. I told you I'm a trained archivist. I could just as easily have been a microgeologist or a professional poet. And then, while I might have been able to give you some general guidance or advice, I wouldn't have been qualified to really dig in and program a first-class record-keeping system for you. But as it is . . ." She let the sentence drift off as she turned back to the computer.

"As it is," Severance concluded, "this is my lucky day. I should have known. Wonder what I did to deserve having you on board?"

"There you go, being flippant again."

"I think it's more than flippancy," Severance murmured. "I think at times I'm bordering on outright sarcasm. Postmen

77

aren't noted for their social graces." He leaned closer, peering over her shoulder at the screen. "You really think you can get up some kind of workable records and business management program for me?"

"I've been designing and applying records management programs since the day I first set foot in the Archives."

"Yeah, but the stuff you file and retrieve at Clementia is different. I'm not trying to figure out a way to handle a bunch of old slips filled with First Family diaries or middle-second-century poems. I need hard data I can call up on a second's notice, and I'll need it cross-indexed a hundred different ways. I figure that if my plan is going to work, I'll have to be able to access everything from personnel information on company presidents to meteorological details on QED."

"I thought the weather only came one way on QED: dry."

Severance glared at her. "Now who's being flippant?"

"I apologize."

He ignored the formal, self-deprecating inclination of her head. "Weather on QED can be damned tricky when you're trying to land a Class A mail ship in the mountains. In addition to that kind of stuff I'm going to need full payroll capabilities. That means I need to be able to zap credit into employee accounts from anywhere in the system."

"Only the big exploration companies have payroll systems that flexible," Cidra noted. "Just how big are you planning on becoming?"

He lifted one shoulder with seeming negligence, but Cidra saw the glittering determination in his eyes. "I want to build a real organization. Right now private mailmen like me operate on a haphazard basis. Each one of us functions independently with no set schedules. The competition can be cutthroat."

"How cutthroat?"

"Pilots can get killed in this business."

Cidra blinked. "You mean because of the dangers of landing on Renaissance or QED?"

"No, Cidra," he said with patently false patience. "I mean, they can wind up dead because of the stiff competition."

"Murdered?" She felt queasy. "I've heard of some criminal activity among the more aggressive pilots, of course, and occasionally one hears of a landing accident or some such incident, but murder?"

"I don't imagine it makes the newscasts in Clementia. Harmonics probably prefer not to pay too close attention to Wolf news. It isn't always intellectually stimulating."

"You've got a point there." She was beginning to feel mildly irked by his attitude. He was right, it did border on sarcasm. Stepped over the border, in fact. For the first time she wondered if Teague Severance didn't number among the more aggressive in his business. She had just decided not to ask any more questions about the criminal behavior of mail pilots when a thought came to her. As usual she sought an answer without even stopping to consider the consequences. "Do you think those fake safeguards who came aboard at Lovelorn were from a rival mail ship?"

Severance lifted his dark brows. "It's a possibility. It's more likely that they were working for a rival of ExcellEx, though. I'm going to collect good credit for the delivery of those sensors, but I don't think it's enough to get killed over. The shipment has great value to an exploration company in competition with ExcellEx but not to another mailman. I've carried cargo that's paid better than those sensors will."

Cidra decided that she would not ask what that cargo had been. "All right, I think I understand the scope of what you want done. You're going to go into the private post business in a big way. Hire other pilots to work for you. You want to create a computerized inventory system, a payroll system, a general information and retrieval system for business and scientific data, and a personnel file."

"Those are the basics. I want to offer a professionally operated service, one companies and individuals can count on instead of having to take their chances with the schedules and the personalities of whatever independent postman happens to be in port at the moment."

"Don't the commercial freighters already offer that alternative?"

"They're inflexible. The ships are limited to the biggest ports, and they don't offer door-to-door delivery anywhere. And they aren't willing to take risks for a single patron. The reasons the independents stay in business is because they make it a point of honor to do whatever it takes to deliver the mail. My goal is to maintain the versatility the independents offer but add the elements of reliability and dependability."

"What are you going to call this empire?"

"The same thing I call it now. Severance Pay, Ltd."

"That name doesn't allow equal billing for any partners you might decide to take on in the future," she pointed out.

He gave her a hard look. "I don't plan to take on any partners. I had one once. Once was one time too many. Severance Pay, Ltd. is all mine, and it's going to stay all mine."

Cidra smiled. "Another Wolf on the prowl."

"Anything wrong with a little ambition?"

"Of course not. Our whole economy is based on ambition, although I don't think your idea of ambition qualifies as 'little.'"

"Stanza Nine is a big system, Cidra. Lots of room to operate for a man who's willing to work hard."

"And you're willing to work as hard as it will take to build this kind of business?" She held up her hand. "No, forget I asked that. I can see the answer is yes. I do have one other question, though. Most of the systems you want designed from scratch could be purchased already set up and running. Why create your own?"

"I don't want a system anyone else uses or understands. I need something tailored to the way I operate, something unique. I realize that for things like the payroll package I can use the fundamentals of a commercial design, but I'd rather start from the bottom. I can handle changes and modifications to the programs, and anyone with a decent education can program a Conny, but the basic design of a new system is something else. It takes a special kind of ability, a special way of thinking."

"It takes someone who's been thoroughly trained to think both logically and intuitively." Cidra felt some of her earlier assurance slip away. "You'd be better off hiring a true Harmonic, Severance. This is the kind of thing they do so well."

"It's also the kind of thing for which they'd charge more credit than a miner could pull out of QED in a year. I can't afford a true Harmonic, Cidra, but I seem to have someone on board who thinks she's almost a Harmonic. Someone who says she wants to work for her passage. Give me two weeks' worth of basic design work, Cidra, and we'll call it even."

She gave him a knowing glance. "Typical fast-talking Wolf. It will be a little more than even if I give you what you want. You said yourself that this kind of design work costs. I'm not familiar with your postal rates, but I have the feeling that what you want would cost you a great deal more on the open market than the price of a passage to Renaissance."

"Yeah, but this isn't exactly an open market, is it? You've said you want to pay your way. This is what I need. It's the only option I'm offering at the moment. Take it or leave it."

Her head came up proudly. "I'll take it, of course. I'll do the best I can for you, Severance. You have my oath on it."

"The oath of a true Harmonic is solid credit," Severance mused. "But you're not quite a true Harmonic, are you?"

Cidra fought back a rush of anger. She had spent her whole life learning to moderate her emotions. She would not let this Wolf upset the careful balance she worked so hard to maintain. "No, Otan Severance, I am not a true Harmonic. Until I am, you will have to trust me."

"That's asking a lot," he drawled. "I make it a practice not to trust anyone completely."

"I'm aware that among Wolves trust is always a grave risk."

"I suppose you trust your friend Mercer in the Archives?"

"He's a Harmonic," Cidra reminded him calmly. "I trust him absolutely."

"But you wouldn't think of trusting a Wolf that way, would you?"

Was he deliberately goading her? Cidra turned back to the computer. "No more than you would. If I am to design the fundamental approaches of the systems you want, I had better get started. Two weeks is not very long for this kind of task."

"Work hard, Cidra. I want my credit's worth."

Cidra bit back the retort that jumped into her mind. Taking firm hold of the intense concentration the Harmonic educational system had bred into her, she immersed herself in the monumental job Severance had assigned. It would take a lot more than two weeks to do it properly, but she was determined to give him as much as she could. She would not have any Wolf saying that she had tried to cheat him.

Severance worked beside her, describing his needs in detail and explaining the idiosyncrasies of the Consac Four-ten system. Their conversation became businesslike and efficient, but by the time Cidra was ready to break for a meal, she had a new image of Teague Severance. He was a man with a goal, and he was willing to do whatever it took to achieve it. A part of her understood him on that level. She had her own goals. But Cidra couldn't help wondering what Severance would be like by the time he had built his dream. His ambitions were the sort that gave free license to a Wolf's most competitive, combative instincts. The worlds of Stanza Nine provided the kind of anything-goes, make-it-any-way-you-can atmosphere that encouraged people such as Severance. But an unrestrained Wolf was a dangerous creature.

Only after they had eaten what corresponded to the evening meal did Severance again bring up the idea of teaching Cidra to play Free Market. She had secretly hoped he might forget the whole thing. Games rarely interested her. But she forced herself to agree politely. Perhaps accommodating him would insure that his mood remained stable. There had been occasions during the short time she had known him that she had wondered about the reliability of his temperament.

He had been gentle with her when she was recovering from the effects of the Screamer, but he had also been inclined to goad her into responses that would have been impolite and angry. She didn't understand him all that well, which was only to be expected under the circumstances. No one raised in Clementia could always predict the behavior of a Wolf. Wolves weren't very good at explaining themselves. But Cidra sensed a restlessness in Severance that worried her. She didn't want to do anything that would make him snap.

So she reluctantly agreed to learn Free Market.

Severance first poured two full-size mugs of the Renaissance Rose ale he seemed to enjoy so much. Then he set out the markers, the sardite chips, and the three-dimensional playing field that constituted the game of Free Market. Cidra watched the process with a tinge of wary curiosity. She sensed a carefully leashed anticipation in her teacher. His was not going to be the formal, patient style of instruction to which she was accustomed.

"Think of this as broadening your education," Severance said blandly as he straddled the stool across from Cidra. He absently shook the handful of numbered cubes he was holding in his left fist. The small table they used for eating had been set up with the field and playing pieces. "Harmonics are very big on broadening their educations, aren't they?"

"Yes." She watched as he tossed the cubes onto the top level of the playing field. "But games don't generally interest us . . . them."

He smiled, again showing ominously white teeth. "That's probably because they don't believe in gambling."

"It's not a question of not believing in it. More a matter of simply not finding it very interesting or pleasant."

"Cidra, my sweet little would-be Harmonic, you've missed something along the way." He leaned forward. "Now pay attention. I'd just as soon not have to explain anything twice." He pushed half the sardite chips over to her side of the table. "The goal here is to take every last sardite your opponent has."

She picked up one of the dull green chips. "I don't see why. Sardite is neither particularly beautiful nor useful. It's also extremely common."

"Don't give me the innocent-as-a-Saint bit. In a real game each chip represents whatever your opponent is actually wagering, and you know it. Here, count the cubes and check the numbers on each."

"Why?" She removed them from the top level of the playing field and obediently counted them. Then she added up the numbers on each cube.

"Because it's one way you make certain your opponent isn't trying to cheat you."

"I imagine that's an important consideration in a game between Wolves."

Severance's hand closed over the cubes she had just counted. "A very important consideration."

"I won't cheat you, Severance," Cidra promised, offended by the way he was now making a show of counting the cubes himself.

He didn't bother looking up as he checked each cube. "You better believe you won't." He tossed the cubes back onto the field. "All right, let's get started."

He was right about one thing, Cidra decided twenty minutes later: He certainly didn't believe in explaining things twice. She was fortunate she was such an adept learner, for her new mentor was not long on patience. Too many years alone in the confines of a mail ship, together with very little grounding in the rules of etiquette and ritual, Cidra concluded.

By the time Severance had run through an explanation of the basic playing strategy of Free Market, she was still wondering why anyone bothered to play the game. The process of tossing cubes, tabulating the results, and shuffling the playing pieces down through the various levels of the playing field seemed innately dull. There appeared to be an almost endless number of rules, none of which were written down anywhere. So many rules, in fact, that it occurred to Cidra that a few could be added or deleted, and a novice player would never know the difference. No wonder Wolves had to worry about protecting themselves from being cheated. There was skill involved, but winning seemed basically dependent on a combination of luck and the ability to outguess or outbluff one's opponent.

At the end of the basic lesson Severance insisted that they start a game.

Cidra was doubtful. "I'm not sure I've memorized all the rules."

"You'll pick them up as you go along. Easiest way to learn is to play. Take the cubes." He lounged back against the bulkhead, every inch of his long body giving the appearance of a casual, relaxed player about to begin a friendly game.

Thoughtfully Cidra launched the cubes on the field, resolved to do her social duty and play. With any luck she would lose her chips quickly and the game would be over.

As it turned out, she did lose her chips in a very steady, rapid stream. A little too rapid, Cidra decided a short time later as she frowned at the pile in front of Severance.

Severance caught the frown and asked smoothly, "Want to try it again?"

"Perhaps once more. I'm still not certain I have all the rules straight. And there are certain elements of the strategy that I don't fully understand." She reached out to take back half the sardite chips.

"You did fairly well for a beginner." He watched her pile the sardite into neat little stacks. An odd smile hovered at the edge of his mouth.

At least he seemed to be in a good mood now, Cidra thought as she carefully counted the cubes. It was worth playing the game if it kept Severance in a mellow frame of mind. Fred appeared to be enjoying the spate of good temper also. He was lazily draped over his master's shoulder, proving himself to be as good at sprawling as Severance himself. There was no sign of the small button eyes or the teeth. Cidra had long since decided that both Fred and Severance were more comfortable to be around when their teeth weren't showing.

She dropped the cubes into the chute and picked up her playing pieces. Brows drawn together intently, she studied the numbers on the cubes.

The sardite chips disappeared from her side of the table a little more slowly this time, but they disappeared just the same. The ale in Severance's mug vanished relentlessly too. Cidra tried a sip of hers and found the potent brew more interesting than she had expected. She didn't try any more, aware that she needed her full attention to be on the game, but her opponent didn't appear to have any similar concerns. Severance seemed blessed with an endless capacity for Renaissance Rose ale. A very small, unexpectedly churlish part of Cidra hoped at one point that the famous backlash effect of the strong ale would go to work on Severance's playing ability. But the thorn stayed hidden, and Cidra was left feeling ashamed of her unethical thoughts. As if in punishment, she promptly lost the last of her sardite chips.

"I can see there is more to the game than I had realized," she conceded graciously as Severance scooped up the last of her chips. "You play it very well, Severance. I'm afraid I made the winning quite easy for you."

"Like taking nectar from a Saint," he agreed, laconically returning the cubes into their container. "That's enough for now." He picked up a bottle of ale and poured yet another measure into his mug.

Dubiously Cidra watched the process. "Yes," she said. "Enough for now. If you will excuse me, I think I will read for a while."

"Suit yourself." Severance picked up his mug and went forward to drape himself in the pilot's seat. He dimmed the cabin lights and leaned back, mug in hand, to stare out into the endless night that surrounded the ship. Fred clung to his shoulder perch, continuing to doze. Cidra had the feeling that the little rockrug had spent many hours in this way. The runs to Renaissance, QED, and Lovelady were long, and the supply of ale on board was extensive.

Quietly Cidra prepared for bed and climbed up into her bunk with a book in hand. With the aid of the small fluoroquartz reading chip she had brought, she bent her attention to an analysis of a chapter of Argent's *The Role of Ritual*. The familiar passages were still an intellectual challenge to the most expert philosophers of Clementia. Deliberately Cidra lost herself in the deceptively simple writing.

A while later when she finally grew tired and put away her reading, she saw that Severance was still sitting in the command seat, mug in hand, stargazing.

The next three ship days passed in similar fashion as they settled into a routine that, while not always meeting Cidra's approval, was reasonably bearable.

She worked on Severance's computer for a good portion of each arbitrarily designated day-night cycle. Cidra also set aside a certain amount of time to devote to her Moonlight and Mirrors exercise. It was impossible to find sufficient room to develop the full patterns, but she did enough to satisfy herself that she was keeping her body in shape.

Severance's own physical routine consisted of a harsh workout on a compact exercise machine he'd had installed in the bulkhead wall near the cargo bay. It seemed to Cidra that the sweat he worked up during the hour he spent on the machine was excessive. After the workouts she was vividly aware of the rivulets of moisture that trickled down through the hair on his bare chest. His sleek shoulders gleamed wetly, and she could not seem to take her gaze away from the strong contours of his back and the flat, hard planes of his stomach. The scent of his perspiring body would be strong in her nostrils before he stepped into the lav.

After the second such workout in a one-day cycle, Cidra tentatively mentioned the scientific fact that there was a point of diminishing returns in exercise. One session a day on the sophisticated machine should be quite sufficient. Severance responded with a short, blunt splash of temper that left Cidra determined to keep her mouth shut on the subject of exercise. He continued to work out two or three times a day.

After the evening meal Cidra indulged Severance with a couple of games of Free Market. He still won every time, but her stacks of sardite chips disappeared more slowly with each new game. She was getting better, Cidra thought, and was surprised to find satisfaction in that knowledge. When the games were finished, she climbed into her bunk to read, leaving Severance to his lonely vigil in the pilot's seat. She was usually asleep before he finally dropped into his own bunk.

On the morning of the fourth day in space, Severance revealed an interest in something other than exercise and his embryonic business programs. Cidra had spent two hours experimenting with management theory designs, using the computer to do long-range projections and then carefully varying certain factors such as fuel cost and employee problems. Severance had been intently peering over her shoulder as usual most of the morning but was now gone. She hadn't noticed when he'd vanished. After running the fourth viable change in the design Cidra decided she needed a break.

She turned in her seat to find Severance sitting at the command console, a diazite globe in front of him.

"What have you got there?" Rising and stretching, Cidra wandered over to look down into the clear ball between his hands. There was a complex little panel built into the base of the globe. She recognized the object just as Severance answered her.

"A light-painting globe." He did something to the panel, and instantly the inside of the diazite ball began to shimmer.

Cidra leaned closer in pleasurable anticipation. There were

many fine light-painters in Clementia. "Let's see what you've got stored."

"Not much," Severance said coolly. "I rarely record my work. I'm not that good a painter. It's just something I do to pass the time on board."

"What are you going to work on now?"

"I don't know yet. Just thought I'd take a break from watching you run variables." He hunched over the globe as he began to work the controls on the panel. A band of black light appeared inside the diazite, narrowing and changing color as Severance manipulated the controls.

Cidra watched in fascination as the black band became a thin, gray-brown sliver of light. The sliver crinkled into a jagged shape that reminded her of mountains seen from a distance. With a patience that astounded Cidra, Severance called up a new band of color, this one faintly orange, and slowly worked it into the landscape.

"Did anyone ever tell you it's hard to work with someone looking over your shoulder?" Severance asked mildly.

"You've been looking over my shoulder for four days." But he had succeeded in making her feel awkward, as well as annoyed. Cidra went back to the computer. It irritated her whenever Severance provoked a retort or an act of rudeness from her. She should be above that sort of behavior.

During the next few hours she sneaked side glances at the strange landscape forming inside the light-painting globe. She had seen master light-painters at work. The best were usually Harmonics, and the results of their creations were commonplace in Clementia. But the modern schools of light-painting tended to be abstract swirls of color and light blended with infinite care. Most professional light-painters avoided creating exact duplications of scenes from real life. They concentrated instead on prompting an intellectual or emotional response from the viewer with complex, intriguing patterns. The degree of excellence achieved was usually measured by the variety of responses elicited.

But the landscape forming inside Severance's globe was definitely representational. There was nothing abstract about it, Cidra thought as the painting drew more and more of her attention. In fact, it was almost too real.

Inside the globe a brutal landscape of a barren world was emerging. An appallingly desolate expanse of red-orange terrain swept toward distant gray mountains. It was clear that the mountains offered no hope of relief from the barren plains, no promise of vegetation or water, only more endless desolation. The land looked as if it suffered from far too much heat, yet there was a strangely chilled feeling to the scene. Harsh, dry, endless, the landscape provoked no pleasure. Yet Cidra found it harder and harder to look away from it.

"Is it a QED scene?" she asked quietly after a long time.

Severance didn't look up. "Yeah."

"It looks different in your painting than it does in the holo-tapes I've seen," she ventured, trying to understand herself why that should be so. On the surface Severance's painting looked to be a highly accurate representation of a landscape. But she had seen plenty of shots of QED's empty lands and unforested mountains. None of them had made her uneasy the way this light-painting did.

"This is the way it looks to me."

Cidra slipped out of her chair and edged closer. "Have you spent a lot of time there?"

"No more than I can help." Severance straightened, staring down into his creation. He studied it for a moment, and then his hand moved briefly on the control panel. The globe shimmered and emptied.

"You didn't save it!" Involuntarily Cidra reached out to catch his fingers, but the damage was done. The painting had disappeared but not into the memory bank of the light-painting globe. It could never be recalled now. She felt his scarred hand under her palm and hastily withdrew her own hand.

"I told you, I don't save much of my work. It's just a hobby." Severance shut down the globe and stood up to replace the painting machine in a storage bin.

"It's more than a hobby. You have real talent, Severance. I've never seen anything quite like that."

He braced himself with one hand against the bin he had just closed and eyed her steadily. "You like art?"

"Well, doesn't everyone?"

He nodded thoughtfully, appearing to come to a decision. "I'll show you some real art." He paced back to his bunk and went down on one knee to reach into the storage bin underneath.

Cidra watched with interest as he withdrew the metal container she had spotted her first evening on board. A part of her sensed that she was about to see something very personal, something very important to Severance. In spite of her earlier curiosity about the contents of the box, she was suddenly a little uncertain. She moved a hand instinctively, on the verge of telling Severance that she didn't need to see what was in the container. But it was too late. He had already opened it.

Cidra went toward him slowly, half afraid. Then she caught a glimpse and relaxed with a pleased smile, feeling her mood lighten instantly. Not an uncommon occurrence for viewers of the sort of objects housed in the box. The small carvings often had that effect.

"Laughing Gods! They're wonderful, aren't they? Don't tell me you collect them, Teague Severance. Not after all those disdainful comments you made about leftover Ghost junk."

She grinned at him and reached down to pick up one of the exquisitely carved stones.

The object was about the size of her hand and seemed to smile up at her as it lay in her palm, inviting her to smile back. The strangely compelling expression etched into the stone was eons old. No one had yet succeeded in dating the Laughing Gods with any real accuracy. The stone from which they were made was as old as Lovelady and Renaissance. For that matter, no one knew if the creatures were even supposed to represent Ghost gods. Some theories held that the carving might represent individual Ghosts themselves. If that was the case, they had been a very beautiful people, even though they appeared intriguingly alien to human eyes.

Cidra turned the carving over in her hand, admiring the wide, slanting eyes, the vaguely feline profile with its delicate but obviously sensitive nose, lips, and ears. It was difficult to tell what the body was like, because in all the carvings she had seen the Gods wore intricately designed clothing that seemed to float around a slender frame.

It was the smile that bridged the gap between human and alien. The lingering, utterly charming, endearing smile gleamed in the eyes and shaped the full-lipped mouths. There was a subtle, warm laughter in that expression, and on some gut level humans knew that any species that had laughed like that had to be a species with whom communication would have been possible. If the Ghosts had survived and if these carvings were, indeed, representative of them, there could have been contact and perhaps understanding.

"So you don't consider all Ghost finds as garbage, hmm, Severance?" Cidra laughed, handing back the carving she held. "When did you start this collection?"

His expression was unreadable as he stayed on one knee beside the container. "I didn't start it. My brother did. I hung on to it after he died. Once in a while, when I find a good addition, I pick it up."

"I see." She sensed that she had trespassed again, but this time she didn't feel embarrassed or guilty. Severance had more or less invited the conversation. Cidra also sensed a new ambivalence in him, as if a part of him wanted to go on talking about his brother, but another, more dominant, part forbade such openness. She was trying to pick her way through the uncertain situation, wondering if she should ask about his brother, when Severance closed the container without any warning. Cidra blurted out her question.

"When did your brother die?"

"Two years ago."

Intuition made Cidra ask, "On QED?"

Severance shot her a hard look as he rose to his feet. "How did you know?"

She bit her lip. "Something about the light-painting led you to mention the Laughing Gods. Opening the container made you mention your brother."

"Is that a fact? Real Harmonic intuition at work, I imagine."

Cidra flushed, but her eyes were steady. "I'm sorry, Severance."

"Don't be. Did your brilliant Harmonic intuition tell you anything else? Like how my brother died?"

"No, of course not. Please, Severance. I meant no rudeness." She bowed her head very formally. "I'm sorry for your distress. I won't mention the subject again."

"Forget it. My temper is on a short leash these days."

Cidra blinked. "I've noticed. Perhaps you would like another game of Free Market after dinner?"

"Sweet harmony. Always trying to soothe the savage Wolf, aren't you? What I would like after dinner is another large bottle of Rose."

He fit action to words. When Cidra attempted to interest him in a game later that evening, Severance brusquely declined.

"I can't seem to work up any enthusiasm for winning another pile of worthless sardite from you tonight." He uncapped the fresh bottle of Renaissance Rose ale and headed for his familiar evening post in the dim cockpit of the cabin. "Go to bed, Cidra."

She started to say it was too early, but one look at the hard set of his shoulders warned her to keep quiet. She did as she was told, aware that for some reason Fred wasn't assuming his usual position on Severance's shoulder. The rockrug followed her into the lav, fussed around her feet while she changed into her sleeping gown, and then undulated pitifully until she picked him up and carried him into the upper bunk.

"What's the matter?" she whispered. "Don't tell me you're afraid of him tonight? He's just a little tense."

Fred did not appear wildly reassured. He flowed down to Cidra's feet and went to sleep. Cidra closed her eyes and used several rounds of meditation exercises to put herself to sleep. She was as aware of Severance's tension as Fred, and she didn't feel particularly reassured by her own words, either.

She didn't know what woke her a long time later. Nothing had changed in the quiet cabin. The rockrug was still warm and motionless on her ankle, the lights were still dimmed in the cabin, and when she drowsily opened her eyes, she could see Severance's figure still sprawled in his seat. There was a third bottle of the potent ale open beside him. As she watched she realized that he was no longer bothering with the formality of a mug. He was drinking straight from the container. She frowned across the cabin at the ship's clock. Half the sleeping period had passed, and Severance hadn't yet gone to bed.

Cidra experienced a wave of compassion. She knew she should ignore it. She should bury herself in the bedding, go back to sleep, and forget about Teague Severance sitting in the shadows with his ale. But memories of the way he had looked this afternoon when he'd mentioned his brother filled her mind. The images wouldn't let her take the sensible approach.

Cidra slipped out of the bunk, leaving Fred behind. Severance had been increasingly tense for the past four days. She didn't want to think about what his mood would be like by the time they reached Renaissance. He needed less ale and more rest. Perhaps he needed to talk.

Barefoot, she went forward. She didn't think he had been aware of her approach. He hadn't moved. But as she came to within a pace of the seat in which he reclined, his graveled voice stopped her.

"Get back into bed, Cidra."

She hesitated. She had never heard quite that tone from him. It was laced with ale and warning. Firmly she took another step closer. "It's time you, too, were in bed, Severance."

"I'm the one who makes the decisions on board, remember?"

"Severance, please. For your own good. Go to bed."

"For your own good get back into your bunk. I've had a lot to drink, Cidra. And my mood isn't real sweet."

"It's your brother, isn't it?" she asked gently, putting a hand on his shoulder. Severance's muscles were knotted with tension. "You're sitting here thinking about him. Perhaps it would help to talk."

His hand moved, capturing her wrist before Cidra realized what he was doing. When he lifted his head, there was a fierce hunger in Severance's eyes, a hunger that was clearly visible in the shadows, a look made even more intense by the darkness. Cidra reacted to it physically, a small tremor passing through her. For a moment both of them were completely still. Cidra couldn't have moved if she'd wanted to. Her wrist was chained beneath Severance's marked hand.

"Your intuition doesn't seem to be working very well tonight, little Saint." His voice was a husky rasp along Cidra's nerves. "You should have stayed in your bunk."

"Should I?" Her mind-body connection was no longer functioning properly. Cidra knew with absolute certainty that Severance was right. But her brain seemed to be filled with a jumbled collection of thoughts and emotions, reminding her of the inside of a light-painting globe.

Severance's eyes never left her face. Then, abruptly, his fingers released her wrist. "One last chance. Go on, Cidra. Go back to your bunk."

He had released her, but she didn't feel as if she'd been set free. Cidra desperately tried to sort out the conflicting emotions leaping to life within her. There was an element that wanted to offer comfort to this man. Another part of her sought to understand him through the physical act of touching him, something that made no sense at all to her. And there was still another aspect with which to contend: a confusing flare of warmth in the pit of her stomach that seemed to be spreading into her veins.

She didn't move. "Severance?"

His scarred hand closed once more around her wrist, but somehow the strong grip was more gentle this time. "You had your chance, my sweet, false Harmonic. Come here and let me see how much Wolf blood there is in you. Wondering about it has been driving me slowly out of my mind."

He used his grip on her wrist to pull her down across his thighs. Before Cidra could analyze the situation further, Severance's mouth closed over hers.

Chapter
Six

Cidra's first instinct was to free herself. It was an automatic reflex reaction to finding herself so completely off-balance.

She twisted as Severance brought her down into his arms, pressing against his shoulders to try to uncoil herself from the unfamiliar position. But he wasn't paying any attention to her efforts. He cradled her close, his hands large and strong on her thigh and shoulder. His hold tightened as she tried to push away, and with a shock she felt the heavy strength she had sensed lay beneath his lean frame.

But it was the dark, warm, startlingly intimate feel of his mouth on hers that succeeded in stilling her small struggle. She had been kissed before but only in the ritual expressions of affection and greeting that were exchanged between family members and friends among the Harmonics. Those kisses were brief, fleeting touches of lips to cheek, the barest of intimate contact.

This was different, far different, from anything Cidra had ever experienced. She felt her lips urged apart with an aggressive sensuality. She found she couldn't help but respond. Something deep within her seemed suddenly bursting to get out. With a shock she realized that although she had never experienced this kind of thing before, she knew about it. Something that had always lain dormant within her knew everything about this. And the knowledge had nothing to do with what she had always been told about sex.

And, of course, Cidra had been told all about sex by her parents and teachers. They had explained it to her, just as the principles of poetic kinetics and programming theory had been explained. What no one had succeeded in conveying was the sense of anticipation and excitement. No one had told her how her body would grow warm and languid or that there would be a small, curling flame in the pit of her stomach. She shivered, and Severance was immediately aware of it.

"You're a woman under that Harmonic garb, aren't you? A real woman." Severance's voice was husky and textured against her mouth. "Cidra, I need a woman."

Cidra could feel that the tension in Severance was not abating. Rather, she realized that it was being channeled into the physical contact with her. His palm moved on her thigh, exploring the shape of her through the delicate fabric of her gown. She could feel the heat of Severance's body reaching out to envelop her. His fingers tightened on her shoulder as he began to probe her mouth with his tongue. She tasted the ale he had been drinking.

Cidra resisted the intrusion, needing time to adjust to the whirl of new sensations. Severance groaned deep within his chest. His hand under her shoulders shifted, moving upward to capture her head and hold her still.

"Just let me have what I need tonight. I've been going out

of my mind. Should have known better. Too much thinking. Too damned much thinking. Eats a man's soul for breakfast."

The sense of compassion that made her climb out of the bunk and come to him washed over Cidra again in full force. Severance needed her. She had never really been needed by anyone in her entire life. Harmonics needed each other but not in this primitive, fundamental, physical manner. Human need in Clementia was on a higher plane, a matter of deep understanding, friendship, and intellectual communion. Cidra had never been able to offer the telepathic contact that enabled such need between two Harmonics to exist and be satisfied. But Severance was asking her to fulfill another kind of need. The concept was strange and infinitely compelling.

Cidra's hands were still braced against his shoulders. Instead of pushing away from him she began to relax. He felt the change in her and deepened the kiss. Without conscious thought her gilded nails flexed, sinking into the fabric of his shirt and then into the sleekly muscled skin underneath the shirt. When he groaned her name, she shivered again.

She felt him tasting her, sampling her as if she were a new glass of Rose ale. He was moving inside her, touching her tongue with his own, and as she became accustomed to the odd caress, she found herself compelled to explore him in return. The desire was suddenly fierce, and she lifted her palms to frame his hard face. Cidra felt him suck in his breath, and she felt his body tremble with yet more tension.

She probed cautiously, wonderingly. The unique intimacy was delicious but also vaguely alarming. His ready response was a lure she hadn't expected, and it would have been difficult to deny even if she had been thinking of resisting it. She wanted this man to react to her, wanted him to respond with greater and greater need.

His arm moved again, fingers gliding down along her side. She froze for an instant when he touched her breast.

"It's all right, Cidra. You feel so good. So soft and strong and delicate. I like the feel of you."

The pad of his thumb moved lazily over her nipple. The gossamer material of her robe offered only a slight barrier. The sensation was tantalizing, and her body reacted to it with a curious tightening. Cidra stirred, suddenly wanting to feel more of him. As if he could read her mind, Severance cupped her breast completely.

As if he could read her mind. But, of course, he couldn't. No more than she could read his. The sensation of emotion and mental closeness was an illusion. This wasn't the physical extension of an intellectual and emotional communion. This wasn't love the way it existed between Harmonics. This was Wolf sex.

The stray thought cut through Cidra's spinning mind, bringing a note of uneasiness into what had been until now a rising, focused crescendo of emotion. "No . . ."

Severance must have felt the flash of uncertainty. He held her tighter, his hand on her breast becoming possessive instead of tantalizing. He broke the contact with her mouth to mutter urgently against her throat, "Be still, Cidra. Don't panic, my sweet Harmonic. I'm not going to hurt you."

"I know." And she did. The sense of certainty came from within herself. His hand moved gently, coaxingly, on her breast, and then his fingers were sliding inside the surplice, seeking a budding nipple. She was suddenly aware of the straining manhood beneath her thighs and inhaled sharply. Slowly he withdrew his hand from under her clothing and slipped his palm down across her stomach. His fingers rested warmly on her robe, just above the gentle mound.

"I only want to hold you, touch you. It's been a long night. Too many long nights."

Too many long nights spent thinking about his brother? Cidra wondered as tenderness filled her. "I understand," she whispered, stroking her fingertips through the thickness of his hair. "It's all right, Severance. I understand. But I don't think this will buy you the peace of mind you seek," she added sadly.

His hand stopped moving on her body, and he went still. Slowly Severance raised his head to look down at her. "I'm willing to give it a try. I could use a little peace of mind."

"I know," she said gently. "I can feel the need in you. But you're going about it the wrong way."

His eyes were narrowed and gleaming now. "Am I?"

She nodded, smiling tremulously. A part of her wanted to keep quiet and let him take what he thought he needed from her. But that was selfish and dangerous, and it wouldn't give her what she had dreamed of all these years, either. Neither of them would obtain any real serenity.

"You need to talk to a skilled therapist. Someone who has been trained to work with people who have experienced your kind of loss. There are many such doctors, both Harmonic and Wolf, who could help you. You could talk to them, discuss your feelings about your brother. Having sex with me tonight would only buy you a temporary respite."

He stared at her and then swore softly. "Sweet Harmony in hell! I don't believe this. You don't know what you're talking about. Dumb as a torla."

She stiffened under the insult. "Now I've made you angry."

"Well, you sure as a renegade's hell have managed to kill the mood. You thought I needed a little special handling tonight to help me forget Jeude?"

Cidra swallowed unhappily. "Special handling," the mail pilot's slang for quick, easy sex, was not the term she wanted to hear applied to what might have been between herself and Severance. The phrase made it sound light, virtually meaningless. And while she knew intellectually that sex for a Wolf was on a different plane than the communion between Harmonics, she didn't want to think of sex between herself and Severance as being just a little "special handling." But, apparently, that was exactly how Severance saw it.

"I assumed you were sitting here brooding. We had talked about your brother earlier, and there was that light-painting you did. And you've been drinking so much before you go to bed lately." She lifted one shoulder helplessly. "I thought perhaps sad memories were still bothering you."

He closed his eyes in obvious disgust. "I should have known better than to try to take a fake Harmonic to bed." His lashes lifted, revealing a hard, glittering gaze only slightly skewed due to the amount of Renaissance Rose ale in his system. "Let's get one thing understood here, not that it's going to do me any good to explain it. I have not been sitting here getting spaced every night since you've been on board because I'm suffering from deep depression. Jeude was killed a little more than two years ago. I learned to handle that some time back. In fact, I spent one reeting hell of a year as a bonus man on Renaissance, learning to deal with what happened to Jeude. I don't need some damned therapist. Renaissance was my therapist. I do not spend every night drinking myself into a stupor because of Jeude."

"I see." She wondered what a bonus man was.

"No, you don't, but I'm too drunk to explain it to you." He rose to his feet with her in his arms.

Cidra's sense of balance wavered unpleasantly again as Severance staggered a bit, trying to regain his own equilibrium. She clutched at him and tried to wriggle free. "Put me down, please."

"I should." He started toward the tiered bunks. "I should put you down right in the middle of my bed and make love to you until you can't think. I've decided that thinking is part of your problem, Cidra. The Harmonics taught you to think too much. Gave you too much education. Oughta be a law against teaching fake Saints to think. *Therapy.* Saints in hell! The last thing I needed tonight was therapy."

"Severance . . . ?" She realized that he wasn't going to stand her on her feet. Alarm shot through her as they neared the bunks.

"Sure as first-class postage, I'm going to regret this." He halted and lifted her high in his arms.

"Severance!"

Before she could protest further, he dropped her onto the top bunk. Physically it was something of an accomplishment, Cidra had to admit as she tumbled out of his arms and onto the bed. The act of lifting her that high required extensive use of the muscle tone he had obviously been developing on his exercise machine. Considering the fact that he'd been drinking strong ale for hours, it was an even more amazing performance.

Fred awakened with a shudder as Cidra bounced on top of him. She gasped as she felt him move under her leg. For a split second she was afraid that the rockrug might react instinctively, taking a chunk out of her ankle. But he simply slithered to one side in what probably passed for a huff among his species.

Severance glowered at Cidra over the edge of the bunk. "For a while back there you weren't thinking in therapeutic terms, lady. For a while you weren't even thinking in Harmonic terms. For just a short time you were thinking and acting like a real female Wolf. Like a woman. Wonder what the noble Mercer would have thought if he'd seen you with your fancy gold nails digging into a Wolf's neck."

Cidra followed Fred's example and slithered back a few inches. "There's no need to bring Mercer into this."

"You're right. He wouldn't have the vaguest idea what was going on, would he? He wouldn't have known what you were feeling when you were clinging to me like a sexy little snapcat. But I do know, Cidra. I felt what you were feeling."

She flushed under the words, remembering from somewhere that the snapcats found in the central plains of Lovelady's main continent were well known for their almost constant state of being in heat.

"I understand why you're trying to insult me, Severance. You're upset and you've had too much ale. If you have any sense, you'll fall into your bunk and pass out. As for me, I don't have to discuss this sort of thing with you. If you want to talk about it in the morning when you've calmed down and are no longer *spaced*, I'll be willing to sit down and talk. Until then I'm going to sleep."

He shook his head in mock admiration, hands on his hips. "Understanding, intellectual, and formal to the last. A true inspiration to the rest of us lowly mortals."

"Good night, Severance." She turned her back to him, sliding down into the bedding and pulling it up to her throat. She was trembling, but she knew she had to remain quiet and firm. Giving him anything to react to would be inviting more trouble. Severance was obviously spoiling for a fight. All the pent-up tension that he had been unable to release on her body was being funneled into a different sort of release. He was a Wolf looking for combat.

Cidra had had her share of classes in Wolf psychology.

"Cidra!"

She flinched as she felt his hand on her arm. "Please, Severance. Go to sleep. I don't think you're going to want to remember this in the morning."

"You're probably right." His hand fell away. "With any luck I won't."

A small jolt went through both bunks as Severance's full weight hit the bottom one. An unnatural quiet filled the cabin. Cidra's eyes were wide as she gazed at the bulkhead wall. Severance had warned her more than once that the cabin of a mail ship could be a very small place for two people.

"I hope," Severance muttered from the lower bunk, "that you have a lot of trouble falling asleep tonight."

Cidra was quiet for a moment, remembering the feel of his hands on her. She ought to keep her mouth shut, but the question was out before she could stop it. "Severance? How did you get those scars on your hands?"

"Don't you ever stop asking questions?" He paused for a moment, then let out a deep sigh. "I had a run-in with a killweaver once. Their webs leave marks. We can't all have soft, smooth hands like yours, Cidra."

Cidra wanted to ask more questions on the subject, but common sense finally won over to stop her. But she was awake for a very long time trying to analyze the events of the last hour. There was a great deal to assess, but a single, stark fact emerged from all the rest and would not dissolve: She had reacted to Severance's lovemaking with a dismaying intensity. Somehow she needed to deal with that because the discovery of her own desire was a threat to the future she envisioned.

Step by step she reran the scene in her mind. She had gone to Severance initially out of compassion. Very well, that was an understandable, even laudable, motivation. When he had initiated the embrace, she had sensed a raw need in him that she assumed was based on his effort to break the brooding mood caused by thoughts of his brother. Her response to his kiss had again been understandable, if not exactly within normal bounds. She had instinctively wanted to comfort him. It was an extension of the compassion she had felt.

But compassion and the desire to comfort had all too quickly metamorphosed into something else—something dangerous. Ever since she was a child she had learned to keep a tight rein on the emotional reactions that betrayed her Wolf heritage. There was no other way she could hope to fit into Harmonic society.

Severance had a way of shaking loose the grip she worked so hard to maintain, and tonight he'd succeeded in unleashing a very primitive, very Wolf side of her nature.

Bravely Cidra faced the implications. She was a Wolf. But if her quest was successful, she would be able to transcend her status. In the meantime there would be times when her actions would not be those of a true Harmonic. She had known that all her life. Nothing had changed tonight. She could deal with the problem. And in one sense her actions tonight were perfectly comprehensible. After all, she was bound to be curious about certain aspects of her nature. Every thinking human being, Harmonic or Wolf, needed to explore and understand his or her own personality. It was a sign of maturity.

Cidra began to relax as she found the handle she needed to accept her responses in Severance's arms. Like it or not, part of her was still Wolf. That part had a right to be investigated, analyzed, and understood. Someday, when she found the object of her quest, she would be leaving behind the Wolf components of her nature. It only made sense to learn something about those components while she could. No knowledge was to be disdained. And knowledge, she told herself firmly, was all she had been seeking in Severance's arms.

Her response to Severance had been in the nature of an experiment.

* * *

Severance awoke with a headache that must have rivaled the one the Screamer had given Cidra. He opened his eyes with great caution. The smell of hot coffade was wafting through the cabin. Unmoving, he stared up at the bottom of Cidra's bunk.

In a just universe any man who'd had as much Renaissance Rose ale as he'd had the night before would have suffered a convenient lapse of memory. But Severance had learned long ago that the universe was short on justice, at least in the tiny corner occupied by the worlds of Stanza Nine.

'Gesics. He needed a fistful of the fizzers. Slowly Severance sat up on the edge of the bunk, realizing that he hadn't bothered to undress before passing out. A swirl of red materialized at his elbow. Coffade was thrust into his hand. Severance decided he wasn't too proud to take it. First things first, and the noble apologies could come later.

"Thanks," he muttered. "You know where I keep the 'gesics?"

"I'll get you one." The too-cheerful red morning surplice robe moved toward the small locker where the ship's medical stores were kept.

"Several," Severance directed in a soft voice. "I'll need several tablets."

She returned with two. He didn't argue. He wasn't up to arguing. Popping them under his tongue, he waited for the analgesic to hit his system. When the tablets were dissolved, he took a long swallow of the hot coffade. A swollen Renaissance swamp-bubble occupying the place normally filled by his brain slowly began to shrink. It had been close; another few minutes and it would have burst. Severance lifted his head and saw that Cidra had slipped back to the front of the cabin.

"Smart female," he growled. "Give the beast his coffade and 'gesics, and then get out of his way. Where did an almost-Harmonic learn such a practical program of human relations?"

"I keep telling you, Severance, I'm a fast learner." But she smiled at him from the computer console where she had apparently already begun the day's work.

"Learn a lot last night?" Stupid crack. Severance regretted the words as soon as they hit the air.

"A great deal. Feel like eating?"

"No." Her smile annoyed him. "I mean, no thanks. Not yet."

"Let me know when you are. I'll put a prespac in the heater." She turned back to the console.

Severance thought about the situation. "There's something wrong here," he finally announced.

"You're just not feeling well, that's all."

He gritted his teeth. "I mean, there's something wrong in addition to that small problem." He shot her a suspicious glance. "You are not, by any chance, operating under the assumption that I don't remember what happened last night, are you?"

She didn't look at him, her attention on the screen in front of her. "I assume your memory is as good as mine."

"Unfortunately." Severance climbed slowly to his feet. Better to get this part over and done. He held on to the edge of the upper bunk and glared balefully toward his companion. "Cidra?"

"Yes, Severance?" She turned her head with polite inquiry.

"I regret what happened last night," he began in an incredibly stilted tone. "You are a passenger on board this ship. You are entitled to my protection. As the pilot in command, I have an obligation to remain, above all, in command of myself. I assure you that what happened last night will not happen again." He felt both martyred and heroic.

Cidra regarded him for a long moment, her gaze searching and, he could have sworn, gentle. Then she inclined her head in formal acceptance of his apology.

"Thank you, Severance, but there is no need for you to accept the blame for what happened last night. I do not view the incident as anything serious."

He stared at her. "You don't?"

"Of course not." She waved the passionate scene aside with a graceful movement of her hand.

Severance began to feel something besides martyrdom and heroism. He began to feel irritated. "Then you obviously don't know what the consequences could have been."

"I realize what might have happened if matters had gone to the extreme conclusion. I have studied the principles of human reproduction."

Severance's hand tightened on the edge of the bunk. "I keep forgetting your extensive education."

She smiled quite brilliantly. "Precisely. And that is exactly how I view last night's events. They were quite educational. Because, while I have studied the physical interaction of male and female, I have not yet had an opportunity to examine it on a personal level. There are risks involved in such a study, of which I am well aware. But I admit I have enough Wolf in me at this point to be curious about such matters. And I realize that once I have found the object of my quest, I may never again be interested in pursuing this particular line of investigation. Harmonics in general don't seem very interested in sex, as we both know. Once I am one, I will also probably lose interest. In the meantime there is something to be learned, and last night I had a sudden, unexpected interest in learning. You mustn't blame yourself or take responsibility for the risks involved. I was a willing participant. I am, however, also cognizant of the risks, and I give you my word that I will exercise better judgment in the future."

Severance listened to the little speech with a growing desire to break something. "Let me get this straight," he finally said faintly. "You're taking responsibility for last night's little fiasco?"

She inclined her head in that formal, gracious way that was beginning to infuriate him.

"And you view the 'incident' as simply a learning experience?"

"An experiment," she amplified, smiling even more graciously.

"An experiment," he echoed. Slowly he pushed himself away from the bunk. "A scientific experiment." He paced toward her. His headache was breaking through the barrier raised by the 'gesic tablets. He realized that something of what he was feeling must have been showing on his face, because the brilliance in Cidra's smile was fading. A distinct wariness was beginning to take its place. She stood up as he glided to a halt in front of her, but she didn't back away from him.

"Uh, Severance . . ."

He ignored the uncertain tone. Deliberately he reached out, catching her chin with his hand. "Listen to me, my sweet, false Harmonic. I am in charge around here. I told you that the first day. And I am taking full responsibility for what happened last night. You were not conducting a scientific experiment. You were being seduced. Furthermore, you will never conduct scientific experiments with me, is that understood? *I will not be used to further your education.* If we ever wind up in a bunk together, it will be for the usual Wolf reasons. It will be because we've got a hunger for each other that can't be satisfied in any other way. It will *not* happen because you're conducting experiments! Do I make myself clear, Cidra Rainforest?"

"Clear as diazite, Teague Severance."

He hesitated a moment longer, making sure that the last of

the gracious brilliance had disappeared from her expression. Then, satisfied, he released her chin and stalked to the lav.

An experiment. Saints in hell! One thing was for certain, Severance decided as he stood under the spray: He was going to have to keep a lid on his consumption of ale after dinner. The feelings of martyrdom and heroism returned.

But there was another sensation too. A tantalizing, aching, hungry sensation that didn't fade as the ship day progressed. It stirred every time the memory of Cidra's response in his arms flickered through his brain. Severance was afraid he was going to have to learn to live with it, because as long as Cidra was around, his awareness of her was not going to disappear.

Cidra did her utmost to adhere to the normal ship-day routine. The morning's scene stayed fresh in her mind, and she knew that for the first few hours following it she was walking on thin crystal. One false step and everything might shatter.

There was more than one meaning of the term *Wolf*. It referred in part to an ancient, mythical creature reputed to be an extreme carnivore, an animal well adapted to violent survival. The other meaning was just as old. Wolf also meant a discordant, unharmonious chord struck in music, an instance of dissonance. Both meanings suited the general population of non-Harmonics, and Severance was a fine example. But today he seemed as determined as she was to tread lightly, and by the time of the evening meal, things seemed relatively normal.

When Cidra suggested a game of Free Market after dinner, she thought at first that Severance was going to refuse. She saw him glance at the half finished bottle of ale he had started during the meal, and then he seemed to change his mind.

"All right," he agreed, reaching for the playing field.

Anxious to please, Cidra had an idea. "I know the game isn't very interesting for you without real stakes."

He shrugged and set out the cubes. "I'll survive."

She coughed delicately, feeling quite adventurous. "I was thinking," she began cautiously, "that we might try livening up the game for you by making genuine wagers."

Severance's hand paused over the stack of sardite chips. Something gleamed in his eyes and then vanished beneath an expression of polite inquiry. "What sort of wagers?"

"Well, I haven't got much, and it would be foolish to bet anything valuable, anyway, since you're bound to win, but there is the matter of preparing the meals. We've been more or less alternating the task, but we could decide that the loser would put the prespacs into the heater for, say, a full ship day."

Severance lowered his lashes, ostensibly concentrating on counting out sardite chips. "A possibility."

"Well?"

"All right. It's a bet. Whoever loses gets stuck fixing meals for the next cycle."

Cidra felt a strange rush of excitement, an emotion she hadn't yet experienced when she played Free Market. She nodded and sat forward, determined to pay extra close attention to the game. She would probably lose—she always lost to Severance—but perhaps not as badly this time.

It came as an almost overwhelming surprise when she won. At first she couldn't believe it. Cidra stared at the blank spot in front of Severance where his sardite chips were normally stacked. All of the chips were on her side of the table. She was suddenly quite euphoric.

"I won!"

He leaned back in his seat, mouth twisted in a dry smile. "So you did. How does it feel?"

She grinned with unabashed enthusiasm. "Very pleasant. You're going to do all the meals tomorrow?"

"Looks like it."

"You don't mind?" she pressed.

"A man's got to pay his gambling debts." He leaned forward and scooped up cubes and playing pieces. "Want to try another game?"

She did, but there was a problem. "I can't think of anything else to bet."

"How about one of my Laughing Gods against that fireberyl comb you wear?" Severance suggested very casually.

Cidra was shocked. "They're both much too valuable."

"That's what will make the game interesting."

She shook her head firmly. "I couldn't."

"The way you just played, I doubt you'll have any trouble winning again. You seem to have gotten the hang of Free Market."

That much was true. She was obviously improving rapidly as a player. The strange euphoria was still bubbling in her blood. Recklessly she smiled. "All right, Severance, it's a bet."

He smiled too. That smile with all the teeth.

Then he coolly and methodically proceeded to demolish her in the next game.

When it was over, Cidra sat feeling dazed by the loss. She realized belatedly that she hadn't expected to lose. The first win had given her an unnatural confidence in her new skills. It was an unwarranted confidence, apparently. Severance said nothing, waiting for the impact of the loss to sink in. Wistfully she watched him retrieve the last sardite chip from her side of the table, and then she lifted her gaze to his.

"You won."

"Ummm." He sat waiting quietly, with an air of grave expectation.

"I suppose you want the comb."

"It's customary to pay a gambling debt immediately."

"Of course." She straightened proudly, determined to be a

good loser. She fished the beautiful fireberyl comb from her coronet of hair and slowly held it out to him.

He took it from her and examined it. The trapped flames of the polished fireberyl flickered in the light. "It's very beautiful."

"My parents gave it to me when they saw me off on my quest." Memories of her mother's gentle, understanding expression as she had said good-bye to her daughter tugged at Cidra for the first time in days. Her father had been equally compassionate. Their understanding was tempered with the natural emotional distance a Harmonic instinctively maintained with a Wolf. They had both known that this farewell had been coming since the day Cidra was born. Their young Wolf cub had to find her own way. They could offer shelter, but they could not provide a true way of life for her.

Severance looked up. "So your parents know you're on your way to Renaissance?"

Surprised by the question, Cidra hesitated and then admitted, "No. I don't think so. I implied that I would begin my search on Lovelady. They would have had doubts about the wisdom of going to Renaissance."

"Especially as a passenger in a mail ship."

"They might have had doubts," Cidra said firmly, "but they would not have argued with my decision. I am an adult. They respect that status. I simply did not wish to cause them undue concern. Renaissance has a reputation for being very dangerous."

He studied her for a moment. "Your parents don't know you very well, do they?"

"They are kind, intuitive people who saw to it that I had an excellent education and proper training in the Klinian laws," Cidra informed him proudly.

"But no matter what they did, they couldn't make you into a Harmonic. You're a Wolf. So they don't really *know* you."

"You don't really know me, either, Severance, so don't make any judgments," she heard herself retort. "You can't ever get to know me the way Harmonics know each other. Wolves aren't capable of that kind of communication." She got to her feet, aware that she was trembling. Without a word she retreated into her bunk with her precious copy of Nisco's *Serenity and Ritual*.

Severance made no move to stop her. He put away the playing pieces, stashed the field, and then carefully tucked the fireberyl comb into a pouch on the utility loop that was hanging near his bunk. He decided that he, too, would read tonight. He could do without any more ale for a while.

When he finally stretched out to sleep, he had a last mental image of Cidra in his arms. In the fantasy she was wearing nothing except the fireberyl comb in her hair. The flames in the comb were dim compared to the flames in her eyes.

Cidra spent the next couple of days working diligently on her programming project. The tensions of the first week had been far more severe than she could have imagined. Occasionally she had unpleasant visions of how much worse her situation would have been if she had accepted passage with someone such as Scates, the man who had come to her hotel room in Valentine.

There was no doubt that living in close quarters with Teague Severance had its risks and that his mood could be somewhat volatile, but she was learning to manage the unstable atmosphere between them. And she had to admit that Severance was able to deal with the situation. He seemed grimly determined to get to Renaissance without losing his temper or his self-control again. She knew instinctively that he placed a high value on his own sense of control. He was the pilot in command, and the concept was important to him. His sense of responsibility ran deep.

They were four days away from Renaissance when disaster struck in the lav. Cidra had just turned on the spray and was anticipating her all-important evening shower when she realized that something had gone wrong. The spray bubbled briefly from the surrounding walls and then died. She stared at the disappearing drops of water in dismay. Keeping the length of her showers to a minimum was hard enough; to do without a spray altogether was unthinkable.

"Severance!"

He was at the panel in an instant, sounding alarmed. "What's wrong?"

Clutching the panel to shield her naked body, she peered around the edge. "The spray fixture is broken. There's no water."

His alert, concerned expression turned into one of sardonic interest. "Is that a fact?"

"Severance, this is serious! We're four days from Renaissance. What are we going to do?"

"Use a lot of deodorant?"

She glared at him. "This is not a joke."

"I know it's not for you. Anyone who spends a couple of hours a day in the lav probably finds this a full-scale catastrophe."

"I do *not* spend two hours a day in here, and it *is* a full-scale catastrophe. I have never gone one day in my life without a proper bath."

"It's all right. Fred and I aren't overly sensitive to a little sweat. We've learned to take things in stride. I'm sure that after a couple of days we'll all be accustomed to each other."

Cidra was appalled. "I can't possibly go four days without a bath. You have to do something, Severance."

"Such as?"

"Such as fix the spray! You keep telling me you're the one in charge around here. Well, here's your chance to prove it."

He leaned against the bulkhead, arms crossed, and considered the situation. "What's in it for me?"

"A clean passenger."

"I was thinking of something a little more useful."

She eyed him warily. "What do you want?"

"A kiss from my passenger."

Cidra blinked in astonishment. "That's all you want in exchange for fixing the spray?"

"Do we have a deal?"

"Maybe you can't fix it. Maybe that's why you're teasing me like this."

"A deal?" he persisted.

"Can you fix it?" she countered.

"Lady, I may not have your education, but I'm good with my hands. In a situation this critical, a few practical manual skills are a hell of a lot more important than a headful of fancy Harmonic philosophy."

She smiled winningly up at him. "I have great respect for knowledge of any kind."

"A deal?"

Cidra nodded once, very firmly. "A deal."

Severance straightened away from the wall. "Stand aside."

He had the spray working twenty minutes later. Cidra was elated. "You're a magician, Teague Severance. Where did you learn such skills?"

He activated the spray experimentally to make sure it was now functioning properly. "Here and there," he said vaguely.

"I've always had a knack for keeping machinery running. Comes in useful on Renaissance."

"On Renaissance?"

"Yeah. That planet's hell on machinery. The heat and humidity are enough to cause problems on their own, but there are also a whole bunch of corrosive plants and soil materials. A good mechanic can name his own price on Renaissance. Stuff is always breaking down."

"Were you a mechanic for a while?"

"I told you. I spent a year as a bonus man." He gave her a brief, hard smile.

"A bonus man is a mechanic?" she asked.

"In a way. He does whatever he gets paid to do." He stepped back. "Your spray awaits, Otanna."

"Thank you, Severance." She hesitated and then quickly moved close to him. Balancing on her toes, she braced herself against his shoulders and brushed his mouth with her own.

Cidra had disappeared into the lav before Severance could catch hold of her and claim a more thorough kiss. He stood staring at the closed lav panel and tried to tell himself that it was just as well. No sense fueling the ache in his gut.

But a part of him didn't buy that logic for a minute.

Chapter
Seven

Cidra's first impression of Renaissance was that it was too green. As the planet had filled the observation port during *Severance Pay*'s approach, some of that endless green had been broken up by the blue expanse of oceans. But once the ship had touched down, there was little to interfere with the sensation of endlessly lush, dark foliage, stretching forever in all directions.

Port Try Again was merely a drop of nongreen plunked down into the limitless jungle at the mouth of a major river. It would surely vanish at once if its human builders and maintainers ever departed. The jungle looked fully capable of washing over the pitifully frail-looking structures of gleaming triaton and diazite, gobbling up everything in its path and closing up the small wound. The tough triaton was an alloy formed from elemental metals wrested from the small polar regions of the planet. It had proven to be one of the few building materials capable of withstanding the corroding effects of the jungle. Its discovery had been a boon to company exploration teams, saving the firms the cost of importing heavy, expensive materials.

Try Again hardly seemed the major port city of a planet, Cidra decided as *Severance Pay* settled onto the landing strip. It was a small, shaggy boom town, the one place on Renaissance where employees of the highly competitive exploration and development companies supposedly mingled without risk of hostility or outright violence. Renaissance was a tough world, and the people imported by the companies to tame it had a reputation that matched the planet's in many respects. Port Try Again had very few written laws but several unwritten ones. Among them was the understanding that the representatives of the different companies would coexist peacefully while in town. Chief among the written laws was that the town was the one place on the planet where it was illegal to carry a pulser. Outside the gates the sidearm was a familiar sight.

Everyone needed the clearing in the jungle that was Try Again. It was the point of shipping and receiving for the planet, a supply depot, a place where people could relax in safety. The town had been hacked out along the banks of the wide, silty river that offered a green-walled highway into the vast depths.

But even before Cidra had begun to take this all in, she noticed that there was something wrong with the air of Renaissance.

"You'll get used to it," Severance told her.

"It's like breathing soup!" It wasn't that bad, Cidra admonished herself as she followed Severance toward the terminal buildings. But the still, heavy muggyness was a drastic change from the clean, crisp air of Port Valentine and an even greater change from the perfumed gardens of Clementia. With a sense of dismay she realized that the fine fabric of her formal midday surplice was already damp and clinging. The light, gossamer, green material seemed suddenly to have acquired a different texture. Green had been the wrong color to wear, anyway, she decided. There was far too much of it around.

She put the condition of her clothing out of her mind in favor of concentrating on the new and strange surroundings. In spite of the thick heat and the unrelenting backdrop of jungle, she felt a rush of anticipation. Renaissance was the first stop on her journey of discovery. Her quest had begun in earnest.

"Stay in sight while I arrange to have the cargo put in time-lock storage. I'm going to be busy, and I don't want to have to waste time wondering where you are." Severance gave the order somewhat absently as he led her into the air-conditioned terminal building.

Cidra didn't bother to acknowledge the instructions. She was too occupied with observing the jumble of people and luggage surrounding her. A commercial freighter had recently arrived, and the new load of mostly company employees was a mixed lot. The majority were wearing the distinctive uniforms that identified their employers on sight. Here and there amid the spiffy, dashing uniforms was a ship suit of dull gray or brown, similar to the one Severance wore. Independent pilots or a temporarily unemployed worker looking for a job, Cidra deduced. There were plenty of high-paying jobs to be had on Renaissance if a person was willing to work.

Nowhere in the crowd were there any other formal midday surplices. Cidra felt strangely isolated. She was aware that she was attracting a certain amount of polite interest. Harmonics rarely traveled alone on the rare occasions when they left Clementia. They were almost always to be seen in the company of other Harmonics, moving through crowded passenger terminals in small, protected clusters. Her lone status no doubt seemed strange to those around her.

Cidra edged closer to Severance, who was leaning over a desk. He had both hands planted on the surface. Out of the corner of her eye she saw the grim set of his mouth and idly wondered what the young woman behind the desk had done to earn his displeasure. The woman was an attractive creature, Cidra realized. Her long blond hair was loose around her shoulders, framing an elfin profile. She was wearing the uniform of the company that had the terminal operation contract, and Cidra guessed that the outfit had been specially tailored for her full-breasted figure. Becoming interested in the interchange, Cidra turned to study the situation more closely.

"Don't give me that, Gena," Severance snapped. "You know I've got a priority claim on a time locker. Saints know I've paid your company enough for it. I want my mail off-loaded and put into storage within an hour."

"I'm sorry, Severance, but the computer doesn't show any record of your claim. You'll have to get in line behind every other pilot who wants a locker."

"The rest of those pilots can go line up at the nearest lav." He reached into a pouch on his utility loop and removed a strip of plastic. "Shove this into your computer and see if it jogs its memory banks."

"There's no need to shout, Teague."

"I'm not shouting. Not yet. You'll know it when I do. Find my locker, Gena, or I'll pile the mail here on your desk."

Cidra saw the rueful dismay in the woman's eyes. Apparently she believed Severance. Gena took the plastic record-of-contract and fed it into the port computer. There was a pause while the machine scanned the information and tried to correlate it with its records. A second or so later a lush, feminine voice responded to the waiting humans.

"Time-lock storage priority claim acknowledged. Assign locker G17."

Severance smiled faintly in triumph, taking back his strip of plastic. "Thank you, Gena. You're always so helpful. Don't know what I'd do without you."

"Teague, you know you'd get a lot more help from me if you tried a more diplomatic approach once in a while."

"No point in being diplomatic with a computer."

The blonde's eyes widened innocently. "I'm not a computer, Teague. Not a single ounce of cold metal anywhere in my body. And I can prove it." Gena inhaled deeply, filling the specially tailored uniform to perfection. She smiled.

Severance returned the smile, his mouth curving with dry, reluctant amusement. "I'll just bet you can, Gena. The only problem is, I'm not sure I'd survive the experience."

"I'd go easy on you the first time," Gena assured him softly.

"Appreciate that. I'll let you know if I ever work up enough nerve to give it a try." He turned away without waiting for a response, his smile vanishing. He caught hold of Cidra's arm. "Let's go. We've got work to do."

Cidra thought about the smiles she had just witnessed. She had felt uncomfortable during the blatantly sexy bantering. And she was very much aware of Gena's thoughtful gaze following her as she was swept through the terminal.

"What are we going to do, Severance?"

"First we take care of the mail."

Cidra nodded. "The mail always comes first."

"You're learning," he said approvingly. "You can handle the computer manifest while I supervise the unloading."

"And then?"

"Then I'm going to take you to a friend's place and stash you for the duration."

Alarmed, Cidra halted in her tracks. "Stash me for the

duration? What are you talking about, Severance? I must have complete freedom to move around whenever we're in port. I'll need to consult the local Archive computer and talk to people who might be able to confirm some leads I'm following. I will not be stashed."

"Calm down, will you? All I'm saying is that you're going to have to stay someplace while we're in port. You'll be free to do what you need to."

"Why not on board *Severance Pay?*"

"Because I'll be staying on board ship," he told her grimly.

"So what's changed? We've both been sleeping on board for the past two weeks. I don't see why I have to move out for the short time we're here at Try Again."

"Take my word for it, it will do us both good to have a break from each other."

"But Severance, I—" Cidra closed her mouth abruptly as she remembered Gena's smile. And then she remembered Severance's bouts of heavy exercise and even heavier consumption of ale. Most of all she remembered the night he had pulled her down across his thighs and told her he needed a woman. "Oh, I understand."

He shot her a sidelong glance as he propelled her toward the ship. "It's wonderful traveling with an educated woman."

Cidra smiled wryly. "As long as you're going to stash me, why not in a hotel? Why do I have to go to your friend's home?"

"You'll be more comfortable with Desma," he informed her cryptically. "Hotels in Try Again can get a little rough."

Desma Kady was something of a surprise to Cidra. The older woman was large without being fat; she was tall and commanding with pale blue eyes that held intelligence and humor in fairly equal proportions. Her face had once been beautiful and had matured into a combination of features that could best be described as striking and interesting. There was a forceful personality in that face, and Cidra liked it.

Desma met Severance and Cidra at the entrance to a long building fashioned of triaton walls and diazite windows. Cidra knew the diazite had been tempered for extra strength because it had the peculiar yellow cast the process produced. She wondered why the already tough, clear material had needed to be turned into virtual armor for this building. Desma was wearing a one-piece white jumpsuit, the kind usually worn by lab workers.

"Severance! You're back. Bring me my new scope?" Desma laughed engagingly, including Cidra in the welcome.

"Have I ever failed you, Desma?" Severance held out the package he had retained when the rest of the mail had gone into temporary storage at the terminal.

"Never. It's one of the things that makes you so wonderful." She leaned forward and kissed him on the cheek in a motherly fashion, and then she smiled at Cidra. "Otanna, you are most welcome. You honor my home."

The formal greeting was a soothing balm on Cidra's ears. She hadn't realized how much she had missed the small, socially comforting rituals of Clementia. Although she was no Harmonic, this woman obviously knew the ceremonies. With a sense of gratitude Cidra inclined her head.

"You are most gracious, Otanna Kady. I thank you for your generosity, and I regret the inconvenience of my sudden arrival."

"The inconvenience is as nothing. Please do not regard it."

Severance stepped in before Cidra could follow up with the next formal statement. He must have remembered that this could go on for a long time before a ritualistic conclusion was reached. "That's enough, both of you. Desma, this is Cidra

Rainforest. She's not really a Harmonic; she just looks like one because she was born and raised in Clementia. A clear-cut case of an overeducated female. Cidra, meet Desma Kady. She's another female with a lot of education. Mostly in the biological sciences."

Cidra made some quick connections in her mind and then once again inclined her head, this time adding the nuance of deep respect. "Of course. Desma Kady. A most distinguished specialist in the field of bioluminescence. I read your last monograph when I was preparing to enter it into the Archive computers. The one on the Rigor Mortis Mantis."

Desma laughed in delight, dropping the formality. "That's me. The lady who works with bugs that glow in the dark. Where did you find Severance?"

"In a tavern," Cidra said honestly.

"That doesn't surprise me. What were you doing in the sort of place he'd hang out in?"

"Looking for transportation to Renaissance." Cidra smiled proudly. "I'm a member of his crew."

Desma flashed a quick glance at Severance. "Is that right?"

"She's on a crew contract, Desma, not a convenience contract. Mind if we go inside? It's hotter than a miner's temper out here."

"You don't want to come into the lab. It's no cooler in there." Desma looked at Cidra. "Have to keep it at normal Renaissance temperature and humidity. The bugs like it that way. Let's go to the house."

She started off, leaving Severance and Cidra to follow her next door to a smaller, company-built structure that looked much like all the other standard-issue, company-built housing Cidra had seen in Port Try Again. The structure was the usual octagonal design, the rooms inside cut up like pieces of a pie under a convex roof. Deliciously cool air awaited beyond the invisible electronic grid of the deflector screens used to keep out small, flying insects. The invention of the screens was one of the technological advances that had made the exploration of Renaissance possible. When they were constructed along larger, heavy duty lines, the deflectors were capable of warding off most Renaissance wildlife. Huge networks of the screens protected the perimeter of Try Again.

"How long are you going to be in Try Again this time, Severance?" Desma led her guests into a wide, wedge-shaped seating area and punched up a selection of cold drinks from a serving tray. She motioned Cidra to sit down.

"I'm figuring five or six days. Long enough to find a few good shipments to take to some of the company outposts I'll be hitting later." He shrugged, helping himself to a mug of iced Renaissance Rose ale. "Maybe I'll get lucky and pick up some mail for QED. We'll be leaving Renaissance in a couple of weeks."

"Did you want to stay with me while Severance is running around in the jungle, Cidra?" Desma leaned back in a chair and crossed her legs at the ankle as she sipped from a glass of fruit juice.

"Oh, no," Cidra assured her quickly. "I'll be going with Severance when he makes his trips to the outposts. I agreed to a crew contract with him because I want an opportunity to visit as many places as possible."

"Off to see the Stanza Nine system after all those years stuck in Clementia, hm?" Desma was amused.

"Not exactly," Severance answered in a flat voice before Cidra could respond. "She's looking for something. Something she thinks will let her go back to Clementia as a full-fledged Harmonic. Waste of time, but she'll probably learn a lot en route. Cidra's bound and determined to expand her education."

Cidra flushed under the thinly veiled derision. She was

getting used to Severance's remarks regarding her quest, but she was embarrassed that he would make them when others were present. "You must forgive him, Otanna Kady. His manners appear to be very unformed at times."

"I know," Desma said easily, ignoring Severance's scowl. "I'm used to it. Don't be embarrassed for him."

Severance stood up without any warning. "I'll let the two of you dissect my character in private. I've got work to do. I've got to find the local rep for ExcellEx and get his sensors off my hands. Cidra, you're to stay with Desma until we're ready to leave Port Try Again."

"I understand, Severance."

His glare intensified at her meekness. "And stay out of trouble."

"Yes, Severance." She deliberately made her voice even gentler and more acquiescent.

Severance seemed briefly undecided about what to say next. Finally he turned to the older woman, who was watching the exchange with barely concealed amusement.

"Thanks, Desma. I appreciate this."

"Anytime, Severance. Anytime, that is, that you turn up with an intelligent, well-mannered houseguest. I'm sure it won't happen often."

"Sweet Harmony. Why is every female in sight picking on me today?"

"Probably because you make such a good target," Cidra offered far too politely. When he swung around to confront her, she smiled her most brilliant smile. "Have a good time, Severance. I'll be here when you're ready to leave."

"Yeah, that's what I'm afraid of." He stalked to the door and disappeared into the glaring heat. The deflector screens hissed faintly as he passed between them.

A long, speculative silence pervaded the cool room. Through

the window Cidra could see nothing except the row of octagonal houses and lab buildings across the dusty street. The street shouldn't have been dusty. It was paved with an impermeable membrane that was almost as tough as the triaton and diazite of the structures. But there was a general grittiness in the air that hung over the entire town.

Desma Kady took a long swallow of her fruit juice. "Well," she announced at long last, "this is all very interesting, you know. Small towns like Port Try Again tend to thrive on new gossip. And you're bound to create some. I hope you won't mind?"

"I'm rapidly becoming accustomed to Wolf ways," Cidra told her. She tried her fruit juice. She couldn't recognize the flavors but found the drink delicious. "A local product?" she asked, indicating her glass.

"Oh, yes. Like it?"

"Very much." She took another sip.

"I'm very glad to have you stay here, Cidra. My husband is away for several days doing some fieldwork on toxins. It will be nice to have company. But I have to admit, I'm slightly curious. Why aren't you staying on board ship? Severance usually does, and if you're a member of his, uh, crew . . . ?" She left the question hanging delicately.

Cidra adjusted the fold of her midday robe. "I believe Severance wants a little privacy for a few days. The cabin of a mail ship is a small place for two people to share for two weeks. He thought we should have a break from each other."

"Ah."

Cidra looked up, hoping her polite expression hid the faint wistfulness she was feeling. "I think he needs the privacy for other reasons too. There's the matter of his obtaining some, uh, special handling. Wolves are very interested in sex, you know."

"I know," Desma assured her, smiling faintly. "I've been married for some time. Four children, all grown now."

Cidra swallowed fruit juice. "I'm sure you understand the situation."

"So this really is a crew contract you've signed? Not a convenience contract?"

"Definitely."

"This gets more intriguing by the minute. You know, Severance signed a convenience contract once. No one knows for certain what happened, but the contract was terminated by mutual consent by the time *Severance Pay* hit Renaissance. I almost felt sorry for the young woman. She was absolutely enraged, according to those who saw her. Not many did. She never even left the terminal. Severance bought her a return ticket and she left on the next outbound commercial freighter. People said it was a miracle that the woman and Severance had avoided killing each other somewhere between Lovelady and Renaissance."

"He told me the story."

"Did he?" Desma seemed surprised.

"By way of warning, I think. I informed him I wasn't interested in a convenience contract."

"And he took you on as crew? There's a registered agreement?"

"Well, at the moment it's still an informal, verbal agreement, but Severance and I both take it quite seriously."

"More and more interesting," Desma mused. Then she set down her empty glass. "Did you really read that dull piece I did on bioluminescence?"

Cidra nodded eagerly. "One of the advantages of being an archivist. One gets to explore so many different fields. Unfortunately I'm not an expert in any one area, except First Family fiction, which is not exactly on the cutting edge of research. But I can assure you that your article was far from dull. There were many requests for it from Harmonic researchers doing work in related fields."

Desma looked pleased. "Would you be interested in seeing the lab?"

"I would enjoy that very much."

The long lab structure was just as Desma had promised, hot and muggy like the outside air. In addition the heavy atmosphere was overlaid with a distinctive, unpleasant odor that caused Cidra to wrinkle her nose as she stepped inside.

"Bugs," Desma explained cheerfully. "Put a lot of them in one place and they tend to smell. We keep things as clean as possible, but you can't ever escape the odor completely. You get used to it."

"That's what Severance said about the humidity." Cidra looked around with grave interest. Long aisles of cages constructed of clear panels stretched from one end of the lab building to the other. In some cases the panels were of tempered diazite, just like the windows. Cidra contemplated what that said about the creatures housed inside. It took a great deal to cut through tempered diazite.

"Acid," Desma said, pausing beside a yellowed diazite cage to peer inside. "That's the reason for the tempered walls. Some of these critters produce an acid that can dissolve normal diazite or clear silitron."

"Severance said there were many corrosive elements on Renaissance. He said it was hard on machinery." Cidra looked into the cage. "I don't see anything in there."

"Keep looking. There, on that branch. See the eyes?"

Cidra saw the eyes, all right. She gasped and took an automatic step backward before remembering that the malevolent gaze was trapped on the other side of a strong, clear wall. "I've never seen anything quite like it," she breathed, unable to look away now. The eyes were hard, glittering, faceted structures of deep amber. They stared out at her as if the insect brain behind them longed for nothing more than to be able to suck the blood from her body. Huge, folded wings, more delicate-looking than the spun crystal moss of her gown, shimmered with an eerie phosphorescence. Long, spindly legs were bent into a springing position. The creature had been hard to detect for a moment because its general color was the same as its background. It was an uncomfortably large creature, almost a full meter in height.

"Cute little Bloodsucker, isn't he? Raised him from a pup," Desma declared.

Cidra swallowed. "Is Bloodsucker its name or what it does?"

"Both. He sucks blood when he's hungry," Desma said, "which is nearly all the time. Nothing on Renaissance passes up the chance for a meal. No guarantee about when the next one will be coming along. I'm doing some work on the phosphorescent effect produced in the wings. My husband is working on the venom it uses to kill its prey. It's the acid in the venom that can eat through most cage materials." She straightened. "Over here I've got a rather nice assortment of Stoners. Pretty tame compared to the Bloodsucker but interesting all the same. A Harmonic expert in Clementia and I have been exchanging information quite regularly for a year or so. We're going to collaborate on an article soon."

"You're working with someone at Clementia?" Cidra asked.

"Otan Greenlove. Do you know him?"

Cidra nodded. "A most respected teacher. I had a class in bioecological theory with him." She had also had a very un-Harmonic crush on the man that she could only hope she'd managed to conceal at the time. She had found concealing such things difficult when she was in her sixteenth year, but she'd practiced hiding her emotional responses from a very early age. She had known almost before she could walk that strong emotional responses were not viewed as normal behavior among Harmonics.

"He's been a tremendous help to me in my studies. Has access to computer simulation equipment I can't get here on Try Again." Desma leaned down to gaze affectionately at the tiny-waisted insects in the cage. "Handsome as any renegade too. Met him a few months ago. Pity. All those dark good looks wasted on a Harmonic. Ah, well, I'm a married woman." She grinned at her houseguest. "Ready for the rest of the tour?"

With eager curiosity Cidra followed Desma Kady down the long aisles, gazing with fascination at each new horror. Some of the creatures were half familiar to her from her academic work, but most were strange and marvelous. Some crawled on legless bellies, others floated in the air, waiting endlessly for prey. A few hopped around on fragile legs that could be re-grown in the event one was lost. Cold, gleaming eyes of every shape and hue looked out at Cidra, assessing her status as potential food. It was an unnerving experience to be gazed upon with so much malicious intent.

Desma and her husband had combined their fields of expertise, doing a great deal of crossover work and sharing the same lab facilities. They worked for an aggressive research firm that funded the studies in exchange for full rights to anything marketable they produced.

"Our latest success was an interesting new pesticide. It's being tested right now on Lovelady. Doesn't seem to alter the environment or the agricultural product in any way but has an uncanny effect against glitterbugs."

"I read a lot about them in the First Family novels and memoirs. They were a real scourge in the early days. Destroyed countless plantings. They've been just barely under control for years, haven't they? They keep mutating, so don't new pesticides have to be found on a regular basis?"

Desma smiled at Cidra's familiarity with the subject. "With any luck our company will be producing the newest counterassault. Should make a tidy bundle for all of us." Desma moved on. "Over here I've got my current pride and joy. These two beauties were the basis for that monograph I wrote on bioluminescence."

Cidra studied the two creatures behind the tempered diazite. They were a pale, washed-out shade of green, unusually unassuming compared with their more colorful neighbors. Huge, faceted eyes followed her avidly as she moved around in front of the cage. The wings were folded over its elongated body. The back two tiers of legs were clearly designed for long, ground-covering leaps.

"They're smaller than I would have expected," Cidra said. "Considering the damage they're capable of doing." The insectoid creatures were about half a meter in height. "But they're not glowing! In your monograph you said they glowed all over, bodies as well as wings."

"The luminescent effect is selective. They can activate it at will, and they only do so when they've located prey. And they only hunt in the dark. They use the glow to momentarily paralyze the victim."

"That's right," Cidra said, recalling the rest of the monograph. "I remember now about them hunting at night. The eyes are heat-sensing as well as motion-sensing?"

"Definitely. Watch, I'll give you a free show." Desma walked across the room and touched several pads on a wall panel. The light faded, and the windows were sealed with automatic shutters. There was a general rise in the chittering, chattering, clacking sounds from the inhabitants of the cages as sudden darkness descended.

Cidra waited for her eyes to adjust to the lack of light. "They're still not glowing."

"Take a step closer to the cage and act like prey."

With a laugh Cidra stepped closer. "How do I do that?"

"Just breathe. You'll have to get fairly close because the diazite interferes with their normal ability to sense heat. If you touch the cage wall, you'll really get a reaction."

Cidra waited, breathing deeply. Blindly she put a finger on the diazite cage. And quite suddenly she had her answer. The two Rigor Mortis Mantises lit up with harsh intensity, their bodies glowing with a blue-white light that was startling and terrifying. Brilliant eyes locked with hers for an instant, projecting such an inhuman hunger that Cidra's stomach turned to ice. She saw the glowing liquid venom drip from hard mandibles. She had time enough to see the segmented, upraised front limbs poised to seize her throat, and then the mantises leapt. The terror of the moment froze her to the spot. Every nerve in her body was shouting for her to run but she couldn't move. Her mouth was open but no scream emerged. Cidra knew beyond any shadow of a doubt that she was about to become food.

There was a small clicking noise as the mantises struck the tempered diazite, but it took several seconds for Cidra to register the fact that there was a barrier between herself and death. Slowly she tried to regain her self-control, a part of her brain all too well aware that she would have been mantis food by now if there had been no diazite. She shuddered with a sense of genuine horror. The lights came on at once. The mantises went back to being an unassuming shade of pale green. It seemed to Cidra, however, that they looked irritated at having been denied their prey.

"Sorry about that," Desma said, hurrying forward. "Everything okay? It does make for a fairly graphic display, doesn't it?"

"I knew what to expect, but I was still quite stunned when they switched on that glow. I've never seen anything like it, Desma. It's terrifying." With a great effort of will Cidra forced herself to calm down. The adrenaline was still hurtling through her system. "They sensed my body heat through the diazite?"

"They are exquisitely sensitive to heat. But they rely on the prey's movements, as well, to map out the general location of the victim. Altogether a highly sophisticated sensory system, which they need, naturally, because they only attack in the dark."

"Amazing."

"My husband has found that their venom is capable of producing a temporary paralysis in a creature as big as a man. The mantis attacks, administers the venom, and then backs off to wait until the victim has been immobilized. Then the mantis sits down to a leisurely dinner. The paralysis looks a lot like rigor mortis and takes an hour or so to wear off. By then there's usually not much left of the victim."

"I can imagine," Cidra said, trying to sound appropriately academic about the whole thing. Unfortunately she could imagine the scene all too well.

Desma cast her a keen glance. "Field research tends to be a bit raw compared to the work done in Clementia's nice clean labs."

"You can say that again. The labs in Clementia focus on computer modeling and elaborate cell techniques. I've never seen live animals in a research facility."

"Wolves like me do the dirty work in the field and leave a lot of the fancy analysis and application work to Harmonics. It's a good system." Desma grinned at Cidra's pale face. "What I always need after a day in this joint is a good stiff drink,"

Desma Kady announced. "And I see it's getting close to a decent drinking hour. Come on, Cidra, the men are away. We might as well play."

It occurred to Cidra that she should spend the evening in the local Archives pursuing her research. But after two weeks in space with a short-tempered male and the unnerving demonstration of the local fauna, a drink sounded like an absolutely wonderful idea. For the first time she thought she understood the fundamental appeal of alcohol for Wolves.

"I'll change into my evening robe," Cidra said.

Chapter
Eight

One hour and one large mug of Renaissance Rose ale later, Cidra realized that she was enjoying herself very much. She had discovered that one could become accustomed to the heavy, tart ale. Considering the fact that the tavern was crowded, noisy, and only inefficiently cooled, she was interested to find herself having a good time. There were other factors, too, that ought to have hindered her sense of pleasant relaxation. When she had first arrived with Desma, she had attracted a fair amount of covert interest. Initially it had made her uncomfortable.

"We don't get too many Harmonics here on Renaissance. And when they do come, they tend to keep to themselves."

"But I'm not a Harmonic," Cidra had begun to explain with painful honesty.

"You look like one at first glance. Don't worry, they'll lose interest after a while." Desma dismissed the clutter of company uniforms, ship suits, and lab-tech outfits that sat, lounged, or slouched around the smoky room. Not only was the air-conditioning machinery having trouble with the heat, it wasn't doing a particularly good job of filtering the air, either.

Still, by the time she finished the first mug of ale, Cidra didn't really care. When Desma came back from the drink dispenser with a fresh mug for herself, Cidra picked up the conversation where it had been left off.

"There's no doubt in your mind, then, that life on Renaissance shows the same evolutionary and genetic background as life on Lovelady?"

"We've still got a long way to go to be certain, but so far we've found nothing to contradict Maltan's Theory that species on Renaissance are evolved from the same genetic sources as species on Lovelady."

"Which means that the Ghosts must have evolved either here or on Lovelady and then colonized the neighboring planet, taking their flora and fauna with them."

"It makes sense," Desma explained. "We know from the few records that survived the crash of the First Families' colony ship that statistically life is an exceedingly rare event in the universe. The odds are certainly against two planets in one star system developing life independently. And the odds of them developing similar life forms is just astronomical."

"But the creatures you showed me in the lab look so different from the common life forms on Lovelady. Hard to believe they're related. Everything here on Renaissance seems so much more violent by nature."

"Ain't adaptation a wonderful thing?" Desma observed cheerfully. "And believe me, here on Renaissance it's a case of adapt and conquer or die. There are winners and losers here but nothing in between."

Cidra glanced around at the boisterous crowd. "Where do humans fit in, I wonder."

"Right now we're learning to adapt. In some small areas we're even doing some exploiting and conquering. But that could change overnight. We could still run into something here on Renaissance that is capable of flicking us off the planet the way a torla flicks off a scatterbug. We've barely scratched the surface."

"It seems wrong to think in terms of exploitation and conquering," Cidra said thoughtfully. "This is a lush, primeval world. It has its own intrinsic harmonies. It would seem that a more positive approach to exploration would be one that took a different philosophical basis. We should be looking for the underlying harmonic rules, trying to fit ourselves into them."

"Spoken like a true Harmonic." Desma laughed. "The problem is that nature has no qualms about changing the rules on us without much warning. Nature isn't static, and therefore I don't think it's possible to ever be completely in harmony with it. Remember the glitterbugs. No matter what we come up with, they blithely keep mutating—"

"A perfect example of what I'm trying to say," Cidra interrupted happily. She found nothing more entertaining than an intellectual debate. And it was even better, she was discovering, when conducted over a mug of ale. "The glitterbugs mutate in an effort to reestablish the basic harmony humans have destroyed with pesticides."

"Nonsense. The mutation occurs as a means of adaptation in an effort to continue exploiting and conquering. If glitterbugs had a brain and a set of vocal cords, they'd tell you they could care less about harmony. They're out to take over as much of the world as they can get. Just like everything else that's really viable."

"But philosophically that's an approach that leads to a constant state of imbalance, even warfare among various life forms.

It is a destructive theory and leads to a destructive methodology of exploration."

"Maybe that's why Harmonics don't visit Renaissance very often. They can't quite approve of the way we're attacking the planet. The principles of company exploration don't follow the principles of the Klinian Laws. The folks back in Clementia are hungry for new knowledge, but getting it sometimes conflicts with their basic beliefs."

"It can be an uncomfortable quandary," Cidra explained diffidently.

"You bet your Book of Ritual it can."

Cidra smiled. "You've studied it?"

"Had to a long time ago." Desma chuckled. "My husband, Fence, and I were married in a full-scale Harmonic High Ritual wedding ceremony. Well, almost full-scale. We did skip the two hours of meditation and telepathic communion that's supposed to take place in the middle. The guests would have been bored stiff during the meditation, and nobody present was telepathic."

"It's a very beautiful ceremony," Cidra said softly, knowing many non-Harmonics used it to lend solemnity and ritual to the nuptials.

"It's supposed to be a lucky way to start marriage, and I guess it's worked so far for us. I'm still married to the man, although he can be a pain in the rump on occasion."

"Luck? There's no luck involved in a High Ritual ceremony! It's a matter of philosophy and focusing, not luck."

Desma grinned. "Another matter of adaptation. Wolves use the ceremony because they think it's lucky, among other things."

"That's a terrible misunderstanding of the underlying philosophy of the ceremony," Cidra protested.

"Ummm." But Desma was no longer paying any attention to her companion. She was gazing with narrowed eyes at a man who was levering himself away from the bar and starting toward the table occupied by the two women. "Speaking of unharmonious principles," Desma murmured, "did Severance ever tell you he once had a partner?"

"You mean his brother?"

"No. A man named Racer."

Cidra frowned thoughtfully and turned to glance at the man in a khaki ship suit who was weaving his way through the crowd. "Severance mentioned something about a partnership that was dissolved some time back. He didn't talk much about it or about the other man."

"Hardly surprising. The two of them hate each other's guts." Desma leaned forward conspiratorially. "Do me a favor. If Severance ever asks what you did or who you met this evening, don't mention Racer."

Cidra wrinkled her brow. "You want me to lie to him?"

"You will if you're at all interested in maintaining any semblance of harmony in the universe." Desma broke off with a superficial smile as the man halted beside the table. "Hello, Racer. I didn't know you were in port."

"Life," said Cord Racer, looking down at Cidra, "is just one renegade's surprise after another."

Severance stepped out onto the tough membrane that served as pavement on the streets of Try Again. Behind him the door panel of the building that had once housed the offices of ExcellEx snapped shut to the accompanying hiss of the antibug deflector screens. Severance wished that the local ExcellEx rep were a bug. He'd like to see him sizzled by the screen's electronic impulses. Damn Quench, and damn the whole fast-moving ExcellEx corporation.

Severance kept to the side of the street although it wasn't difficult to dodge the few runners and sleds that were zipping from one end of town to the other. Try Again was not big enough to warrant a lot of vehicular traffic. Most people walked from one point to the other.

Above him the night sky proudly displayed Renaissance's twin moons, Borgia and Medici. A record of the words had survived the colony ship's crash two hundred years ago, but the references had been lost. Some research indicated that they were linked to the term Renaissance, and so the names had been attached to its moons. There was a constant hum from the jungle on the other side of the triaton walls. As he walked toward Desma's house Severance batted absently at one or two night-flying insects that somehow escaped a deflector screen. His mind was occupied with the task of telling Cidra that plans had changed.

She wasn't going to be thrilled. She had been counting on at least five days here at Try Again. Time enough to consult local archives and the tall tales of exploration men. She was going to be upset when he informed her that they were leaving the day after tomorrow.

Well, he couldn't help the inconvenience, Severance told himself. Cidra was the one who had insisted on a crew contract. She would just have to learn to accommodate herself to the unpredictable schedules of a mail ship.

He turned a corner, heading down the street that was lined with the majority of Try Again's company stores and taverns. The distant hum of the jungle was a familiar sound, and he tuned it out. After a year as a bonus man he had developed fairly good instincts for Renaissance. A man either learned when to get nervous or he died learning. Companies didn't pay huge bonus credit for ordinary manual labor. Bonus credit was paid for risks, and risks on Renaissance were usually in the life-and-death category.

"Hey, Severance." A man emerging from a nearby tavern

hailed him. "You the one who just hit port with a Harmonic in tow?"

Severance halted. "Hello, Craft. As usual you're up to date. A man would think you're telepathic yourself, the way you always seem to know the latest gossip. How did you know about Cidra?"

Craft chuckled, unoffended. He'd known Teague Severance a long time. "No magic this time. Saw her with Desma Kady 'bout an hour ago. They're in the Bloodsucker." He nodded up the street.

Severance swore in disgust. "Desma took her there?"

"It's not like we got a whole lot of choice when it comes to night spots in this town," Craft reminded him. His faded, friendly eyes assessed Severance in the poor light. "Nothing to get upset about. Looked to me like they were both having a good time."

"You wouldn't think someone raised in Clementia would have developed a fascination for dives like the Bloodsucker, would you? The lady's taste seems to be degenerating." Severance sighed and moved off purposefully. "See you, Craft."

"Sure." The older man nodded, but Severance was no longer looking at him. He was heading toward the Bloodsucker. Craft chuckled again to himself and decided that he could use another drink after all. He went back into the tavern from which he had just emerged. Bound to be some folks inside who'd want to hear about Severance and the little Harmonic. And Cord Racer's presence added a nice extra fillip. Too bad he hadn't had a chance to mention Racer to Severance. No matter. They'd find each other soon enough, and word had it that Racer had already found the little Harmonic.

Desma watched Racer settle into conversation with Cidra. There wasn't much she could do to stop it, short of making a scene and hauling the younger woman out of the tavern. A woman born in Clementia, Harmonic or otherwise, would be thoroughly humiliated at being the object of the kind of attention that would garner.

Objectively speaking, there was nothing wrong with Racer. He was reasonably well mannered, especially compared to the majority of Try Again's population. He was good-looking in an open, breezy kind of way. Red-haired with blue-green eyes and a disarming sprinkling of freckles across his nose, Racer was tall and physically well proportioned. He wore the snug-fitting khaki ship suit and boots with a certain swagger that was not offensive. Women tended to find it endearing, in fact. About the same age as his former partner, Cord Racer was also doing very well for himself as a mail pilot. And he was better educated than the average pilot. Desma had already sensed that for Cidra, intelligence and a good education were vastly more alluring than physical attractiveness in a man. The result of her Harmonic upbringing, Desma supposed.

The only thing wrong with Racer was the hostility that simmered just below the surface whenever he and Severance came in contact. No one, not even that professional gossip, Georg Craft, knew what had dissolved the partnership three planet years ago, but whatever it was, it had been traumatic and probably violent. Everyone was amazed that one of them hadn't made sure the other suffered some sort of unpleasant accident over the years. Perhaps they avoided it by taking pains to avoid each other.

Cidra responded warily to Racer's cheerful conversation. She used formal politeness as a facade behind which she could hide while she analyzed the man. If Severance disliked him as intensely as Desma seemed to think, there had to be a reason. But for the life of her Cidra couldn't find anything particularly jarring or dismaying about Cord Racer. He seemed quite pleasant.

"How long will you be here on Renaissance?" she inquired politely during a short break in the conversation.

"I'll be leaving soon. Got a run for QED. Is it true you're on crew contract with Severance?"

"Quite true."

"Mind my asking exactly what you do for him? I mean, I have a ship the same size and class as *Severance Pay*, and to be honest, they're a one-man operation."

Desma spoke coolly. "The nature of her work on board is hardly any of your business, Racer."

Racer shrugged. "Just curious."

"It's all right," Cidra said quickly, sensing the tension in Desma. "I'm doing some programming work for him. In return he's providing me with free passage."

"Ah, I get it," Racer said easily. "A business arrangement."

"Exactly."

Desma made another attempt to take hold of the conversation. "Cidra, it's getting late. We should probably be heading home."

"You're staying with Desma?" Racer asked, ignoring the older woman.

Cidra nodded, smiling. "That's right. She's been most gracious. I'll be at her place for the next few days while Severance picks up some mail and arranges some delivery contracts."

"Desma, here, is a very nice lady," Racer said agreeably.

"Desma," announced Desma in tones of foreboding as she looked over Racer's shoulder, "may have just made her worst mistake of the season." She smiled weakly. "Hi, Severance. Cidra and I were just about to leave."

"I know." Severance sounded very sure of that fact. He arrived at the table and stood looking down at Cidra. He didn't even glance at Racer. "I came to escort you home. Let's go." He reached out to put his large hand under Cidra's arm and hauled her unceremoniously to her feet.

"Severance, please!" Cidra was mortified by the rudeness.

"Take it easy, Severance," Racer said coolly, climbing out of the chair he'd been straddling. "Maybe the lady isn't ready to leave yet."

Desma got uneasily out of her seat, paying the tab quickly with a credit slip.

"The lady works for me," Severance said, still not bothering to look at Racer. "And I say she's ready to leave. Aren't you, Cidra?"

"There is no need to be so impatient," Cidra hissed, aware of his fingers digging into her arm. "What are you doing here, anyway? I thought you were going to spend the night on board the ship."

"I came to tell you that there's been a change in plans. I'll explain outside." He flicked a glance at Desma. "Are you coming?"

"I'm coming." Desma stifled a groan as she saw the embarrassment on Cidra's face. "You could be a little less heavy-handed, Teague."

"And you could use a little more judgment, Desma."

"Severance!" Cidra was more than embarrassed now. She was shocked. "This is my hostess. You will not talk to her in this way."

"Forget it," Desma advised. "I've heard worse. Let's get going."

Racer stepped closer to Cidra, his blue-green eyes concerned. "Are you sure you want to go with him, Cidra? Just because you're under contract doesn't mean you have to let him ride you this way."

"Stay out of this, Racer." Severance finally deigned to glance at Racer. His eyes were full of warning, and something else. Something that might have been contempt.

"If the lady wants my assistance, she's got it." Racer returned the contempt with a rough hostility.

Cidra realized immediately that she was not the issue. She was the catalyst both men were using to confront each other. The tension in the air was almost palpable. The two Wolves were circling each other, searching for openings and excuses for battle. She had to put a stop to it at once. She smiled tentatively. "It's all right, Racer. I really must be going. It's been pleasant chatting with you. Perhaps some other time?"

"Any other time," Racer stressed, his eyes locked with Severance's. "Any other time you want."

"Don't hold your breath," Severance advised. He turned away, more or less dragging Cidra with him. Desma followed without further demur.

Cidra waited until the three of them were out on the street before she gave way to her feelings of humiliation and anger. Then she rounded on Severance. "I have never been so thoroughly embarrassed in my entire life, Teague Severance. You have the manners of a torla. You should be ashamed of yourself, and if you're not, it's only because you don't have the sensitivity to manage it! How can you possibly excuse such ill-mannered behavior?"

"I won't bother to find any excuses. I don't *have* to find any excuses. I'm your employer, remember? And this is a direct order: Stay clear of Racer."

"You'll have to provide a reasonable explanation for such a ridiculous order."

"As long as you're on crew contract I don't owe you any explanations. Want to terminate the contract right now? Your option."

"Easy, Severance," Desma advised softly.

Cidra threw herself back into the argument. A temper she had never dreamed existed seemed to be bubbling alive inside her. It was as if the hot, humid air of the planet had stirred the heat in her veins. "Don't you dare threaten me, Severance. I demand a full apology for the scene you created in that tavern."

"You're not going to get one. Make up your mind, Cidra. Are you under contract or not?"

"You're not going to get rid of me this easily! I won't let you use a stupid argument like this one to force me to terminate the contract."

"Fine. Then you'll follow orders."

Desma tried again, saying mildly, "Why did you come looking for us in the first place, Severance?"

He glared at Desma and then at Cidra as they arrived at the Kadys' octagonal home. Cidra thought he hesitated for an instant before dropping his bombshell. "ExcellEx has moved its main operations to a field camp upriver. They want the sensors delivered there. I've made the arrangements. We're leaving the day after tomorrow. I've contracted with a guide who's taking some other supplies to the camp."

Cidra blinked, realizing what that meant. "But my research! I haven't even started. Severance, I'm not ready to leave Try Again yet. I have so much to do."

"Then you shouldn't have wasted an entire evening in a place like the Bloodsucker, should you?"

Desma moved toward the door. "If you'll excuse me," she said dryly, "I'm going inside. I've got a squeamish stomach." The deflectors hissed behind her, leaving Severance and Cidra alone on the membrane.

"Severance, is this really necessary, or are you concocting some excuse to leave town because that man Racer is here?"

"Racer is strictly second-class postage. I wouldn't let him

affect anything I do. We're leaving at dawn the day after tomorrow because I'm running a business. I've contracted to deliver the sensors, and that's what I'm going to do. As long as you choose to work for me you stay with me. Understood?"

"Oh, you're doing an excellent job of making yourself clear."

He closed his eyes in brief disgust. "I'm sorry, Cidra. This can't be helped. The potential of more work for ExcellEx is too good to pass up. There'll be other opportunities here for you to search the Try Again files."

She considered the matter. "You could leave me behind while you make the run to the field camp."

Severance's eyes were very steady. "Not a chance. I'm not leaving you alone here. As long as you work for me I'm responsible for you. I want you where I can keep an eye on you."

"It is Racer, isn't it? You don't want me left here near him. Why do you hate him so much, Severance?"

"That subject isn't open to discussion. Good night, Cidra."

"Good night, Severance." She turned stiffly, the hem of her gown swirling around her. "I hope you enjoy what's left of the night."

He caught her arm, spinning her around to face him. She sucked in her breath as she saw the glittering intensity in his eyes. Before she could say anything, he was kissing her, his mouth hard and possessive on hers. She shivered in his grasp, a soft moan echoing far back in her throat. When he lifted his head, Cidra had to put out a hand to steady herself. Wide-eyed, she stared at him.

"I won't, you know," Severance said too calmly.

"W-won't what?"

"Enjoy what's left of the night."

"What's the matter?" she flung back. "Didn't your arrangements for a little special handling work out?"

"No. Fred doesn't take to strangers on board." He released her and pushed her gently toward the door panels. "Go inside, Cidra. I'll see you in the morning."

Cidra was safely through the panels when she realized with a secret satisfaction that Fred had never seriously objected to her presence on board *Severance Pay*.

A muted but nerve-rasping whistle woke Cidra several hours later. The sound seemed to pierce right through her mind, bringing her to a sitting position in bed with a pounding heart. She was gazing at the door to her room, trying to remember where she was when it opened. Desma Kady stood there, struggling into a white lab suit.

"Don't worry, Cidra. It's just an equipment alarm from the lab. Probably means the air filtration system has gone down again. I didn't see any lights when I looked out the window, so it could be that the lighting timer has failed too. Damn. If it isn't one thing, it's another. You have no idea how hard it is to keep machinery in good repair here on Renaissance. The last time this happened we found several kilos of swarming doomlizards tangled in the filtration fans. I'll be back in a few minutes."

"Can I help?"

"Don't worry. This will only take a little while, I'm sure. Stay where you are and get some sleep." She waved absently and left.

Wide-awake now, Cidra went over to the diazite window and watched Desma hurry toward the long lab building. Nights on Renaissance were a couple of hours longer than on Lovelady. She estimated it must be about three hours from dawn. Through the gloom Cidra saw Desma disappear into the lab. She leaned on the windowsill and waited. The thought of going into that long, dark building full of bugs was not a pleasant one, but she supposed Desma was accustomed to her "pets."

Cidra didn't know when or exactly why she began to worry. When the low level illumination she had noticed earlier that evening in the lab didn't come back on soon after Desma disappeared inside, she began to get nervous. Desma had seemed to think the problem was a minor one that could be easily solved.

Minutes ticked past and there was still no sign of her hostess returning from the lab. Perhaps she could use some assistance after all. Cidra put on her delicate emerald-floss slippers and walked down the hall and out into the night. Her black-and-silver gown made her almost invisible in the shadows. The company that had the current contract for street lighting here in Try Again didn't believe in importing too much heavy, expensive fluoroquartz. Most of the buildings on the street were shrouded in darkness, including the lab.

Visions of a long barn full of horrific insectoid creatures were very bright in Cidra's mind when she tentatively opened the door Desma had already unlocked. The fetid smell from the interior assailed her as soon as she stepped inside. It seemed somehow worse in the oppressive darkness. The small, scurrying, screeching, and clacking noises were at full volume as the creatures in the cages went about their shadowy night business.

"Desma?"

There was no response. Cidra took another step inside. Tiny pinpoints of light darted about in the cage to her left. Up ahead she could see another faint, phosphorescent flicker. The natural luminescence of some of the inhabitants wasn't nearly enough to light the aisles in front of the cages. Cidra took another cautious step, letting her eyes adjust to the deep shadows. She could barely make out the entrance to the first aisle.

"Desma? Where are you? Did you find the problem? Want me to get a quartzflash?"

Still no answer. Perhaps Desma was working on the machinery at the rear of the building. Slowly, not wanting to touch the cages she was passing, Cidra moved down the aisle. She knew that if she kept going straight, she would wind up at the back of the room where the control panels were installed. The fact that Desma was not responding was really beginning to alarm her.

When her foot caught on an object in the middle of the aisle, Cidra's first thought was that one of the caged horrors had escaped and she had just become its prey. Her startled, panicked scream was muffled as she lost her balance and sprawled facedown on the metal floor. Frantically she twisted, intent only on getting away from whatever had tripped her. Her hand lashed out to ward off the unseen attacker and came into contact with fabric. Lab-tech uniform fabric. A small object rolled free of the fabric, clattering softly on the floor. It was gone before Cidra could reach for it, disappearing into the thick darkness under the cages.

"Desma!" A new kind of fear assailed her. Cidra groped about, swearing with words she must have learned from Severance. "Desma, what's wrong?" The woman's body was limp, but when she found a throat pulse, Cidra breathed a sigh of shaky relief. Almost at once the fear returned, however. Whichever of the lab creatures had done this was still about, skulking in the shadows under the cages. She had to get herself and Desma out of the building. There was no telling what had bitten or stung Desma, and there was no telling how much time she had left.

Cidra awkwardly found the woman's wrists and was getting to her feet when she realized that there was someone else in the lab. For an instant she froze as she heard the gliding footstep.

There was no possibility of the sound belonging to someone who would offer help. If that had been the case, whoever it was would have responded to her call for Desma. Cidra knew with absolute certainty that whoever was moving down the aisle toward her was the one responsible for whatever had happened to Desma.

Instinct prompted her to release her grip on the unconscious woman. The human hunter was now intent on new prey. Cidra crouched motionlessly, wondering why he didn't simply flick on a quartzflash and pin her in the light. And then she realized what the object was that had rolled under the cages. Desma must have fought back briefly, knocking the flash free from her attacker's hand.

Cidra strained to hear the next footfall above the soft, ominous chittering and chattering. It came after several excruciating heartbeats. She had to get away. Like any wild creature seeking safety, Cidra slipped to one side on her hands and knees, searching for the dark shadows under the cages. She was able to perceive a faint movement in the aisle as she stared out from under a cage. The clicking sound grew stronger, coming from directly overhead now as the creatures above her also sensed movement. There was a flurry of scratching sounds on the diazite, and then, whoever was in the aisle moved on. The insects above settled back down to a normal hum of activity.

Cidra hugged herself, drawing the dark, concealing folds of her sleeping robe around her ankles. She tried to breathe as lightly as possible, using the skills she had learned in meditation practice. One thing was for certain. She couldn't stay here. And she mustn't risk allowing her pursuer time enough to find his lost quartzflash. No one who might be passing on the street outside would hear a scream from the heavily built lab structure. She had to find her way silently to the door.

But now the hunter was between her and the exit. Cidra contemplated that, trying to imagine what he might be thinking. He must have realized that she would try to get out the way she had entered. When she finally lost her nerve and made a dash for the door, he would be waiting. She would probably blunder straight into him. What she needed was an advantage.

In the darkness she needed light. But it had to be light she controlled. Slowly Cidra unwound and crawled out from under the cage. Instead of heading toward the door she began inching her way, still on her hands and knees, down the aisle toward the rear of the building.

Whoever waited for her heard the soft scuffling sounds. Cidra sensed him moving down the aisle, following carefully in the darkness. She stayed low, ready to dart back under the row of cages. As she moved she counted the diazite structures she was passing, trying to remember exactly where she was. The tour of the lab that afternoon had been very thorough, and she had a well-trained memory. What good was an education if you didn't put it to use?

The man behind her was gaining slowly, growing more confident as he followed the soft sounds she was making on the metal floor. When he spoke for the first time, Cidra almost screamed. His voice was a rasping whisper.

"Come on out, lady. Let's get this over with. You don't want to spend the rest of the night with these bugs, do you? No telling when one of them might get free. Why, I could open a couple of these cages myself with this little can opener I brought along. I might just do it, too, if you don't cooperate." He glided closer.

Cidra's heart was hammering as the fear-induced adrenaline ricocheted through her system. Something was wrong with her insides. She felt almost sick. Steadily she moved down the aisle, forcing herself to count each cage. Three more to go . . . two more to go . . .

One more to go. One more, that is, if she had remembered exactly where she was when she had started and if she hadn't lost count. She paused and listened. There was no sound from the inhabitants of the cage overhead. Flattening herself on the cold metal floor, Cidra waited. If she wasn't beside the right cage, she was going to be trapped. She had to let the hunter get close. Too close to allow her to have a chance at escape if she had made a mistake.

She huddled into herself as the footsteps came nearer. He was making no effort to hide himself now. The confidence of the hunter was born of arrogance and the belief that he held the upper hand. Just the same sort of attitude that could get a person into trouble when he was playing Free Market.

The footsteps came to a halt. Now, in the shadows, Cidra could make out a pair of heavy boots not more than two meters away. She drew in her breath and knew he heard the sound.

"There you are, little lady. I told you there wasn't much point in hiding."

Cidra put up her hand and flattened her warm palm against the diazite of what she believed was the Rigor Mortis Mantis cage. For a heart-stopping moment nothing happened. Then the creatures inside reacted with an instantaneous flare of eerie blue-white brilliance, illuminating themselves to the man in the boots facing them on the other side of the diazite.

Cidra was not staring up into the cage. She was waiting for a glimpse of her pursuer's face. It came, the features bathed in blue-white terror as the Mantises switched on the paralyzing luminescence. She had time to note the fear, time to see the pulser grasped in one huge hand, and time to realize that the mantises were very good at their work. Their victim was literally immobilized with shock and horror. He couldn't even scream, although Cidra could see the panic in his eyes as she leapt to her feet.

The mantises had bought her only a few seconds, but that was all the time Cidra needed. She flowed into the deceptively gentle movements of Moonlight and Mirrors.

Chapter
Nine

"I can't let you out of my sight for a minute." Severance slouched as usual in his seat, morosely regarding Cidra. Behind him the green wall of vegetation slipped past at a quick, steady pace as the skimmer, riding just above the water, followed the river into the dark heart of the jungle.

"That's going to make things awkward, isn't it? Because, after that display in the Bloodsucker, I've learned that I can't take you anywhere." Cidra knew she was being dangerously flippant, but the truth was that she was getting tired of the never-ending lectures. They had been going on in one form or another since she had dragged Desma out of the bio lab and called for help. Help had come quickly enough, but so had Severance.

"This isn't a joke, Cidra. You could have been seriously hurt. Maybe killed. You should never have gone into that lab alone. As soon as you opened the door and realized something was wrong, you should have called a company guard. They get paid to go into places like that. You don't. Come to think of it, I probably ought to dock your salary for bad judgment."

"You're not paying me a salary, remember? Just providing transportation and scenic sidetrips such as this one." Cidra's eyes widened slightly as she had a flash of intuition. "I think you're chewing on me as if I were a bite of torla steak because I let him get away."

Severance leaned forward with an abrupt movement and lowered his voice so that it was only barely audible above the hum of the skimmer's power cells. "If you really believe that, then you're functioning on fewer brains than a novakeet."

The image was not a pleasant one. Novakeets, with their splashy orange-and-red plummage, were pretty enough creatures, but on Lovelady nature seemed to have decided that such beauty didn't need a lot of brainpower. Cidra cast a quick glance toward the front of the skimmer where the pilot was safely out of earshot inside the diazite cabin. Then she glared at Severance.

"Why are you so angry with me, Severance? You've been this way since you found out what happened."

"I'm angry because you came so damn close to getting yourself hurt, you little idiot!"

She searched his fierce gaze for a moment. "Desma was the one who got hurt."

"I'm aware of that. Just promise me that next time you're on the threshold of a situation that looks serious, you'll go get help, not try to handle things yourself."

Cidra considered the request. It seemed reasonable. "All right. I promise." She was silent for another moment. "Do you think I'm likely to run into many such situations while I'm traveling with you?"

"Not if you do as you're told." Somewhat mollified,

Severance leaned back in his seat again. "Saints in hell, you gave me a scare."

"Believe me. It was nothing compared to the scare that intruder got. I've never seen anyone's face twisted in such a way. It was as if he were wearing a mask. Which is why I had so much difficulty describing him later to the company guards."

"They know he was carrying a pulser, at least. That's illegal inside the walls. Did you knock it out of his hand when you went into your Moonlight and Mirrors routine?"

Cidra closed her eyes, trying to remember those awful few moments. "I don't know if I disarmed him or if he simply dropped the thing in his terror. He was quite frozen with fear for a few seconds. And I wasn't far behind. Even though I wasn't looking at the creatures and I knew something of what to expect, that eerie brilliance they produce is very hard on the nerves. In the darkness the man couldn't see the diazite between him and the mantises. Even if he knew that logically speaking they were probably in a cage, his mind reacted first to the terror. When they leapt toward him, he saw them move. The next thing he knew, he *felt* me attacking. In his fear I think his mind mixed up the two sensations and assumed that the Rigor Mortis Mantises actually had hold of him. He didn't try to fight me as if I were merely a human being. He screamed and fled. Which is why I was not successful in detaining him. His terror gave him a great deal of strength."

"And you're just damn lucky he didn't use it against you."

"Severance, if you say another word along those lines—"

He held up his hand. "I know. It's just that I'm still recovering from shock. Thank Sweet Harmony that you and Desma are both all right."

"I just hope Desma's not in any danger now that we're gone." Cidra still felt uneasy about leaving her new friend behind in Try Again, even though Desma had displayed no such concern.

"She's hardly alone," Severance said bluntly. "Her company will be giving her and the lab full-time protection now that they know someone has his eyes on one of the products she's on the verge of producing."

"She thinks the intruder was after some record of the results of her work on a new pesticide," Cidra murmured. "Apparently it would be worth a great deal to a rival firm."

"All the more reason for her company to take care of her. She and the lab both qualify as company property." Severance's mouth lifted slightly in the first trace of amusement Cidra had seen since he'd shown up after the incident in the lab. "And you come under the heading of company property yourself. Right now you belong to the firm of Severance Pay, Ltd. It's my responsibility to keep track of you. So you will stay in sight so I can do exactly that."

Cidra withdrew into the remote, polite facade that she was learning served her well during times when she wished to halt a conversation with Severance. She was careful to maintain a serene expression so that he couldn't accuse her of sulking. There were advantages to some of the Harmonic tricks she'd learned over the years.

She turned her attention to the wide swath of river that served as a highway for the skimmer. Occasionally they passed the mouth of one of the many tributaries that fed into the main stream. The network of rivers was extensive, and many of the smaller ones still had not been fully explored. The water passing under the skimmer was a murky color, thick with the sediment it had picked up on its meandering journey. She couldn't see more than a few centimeters under the surface. The vegetation grew right to the water's edge and into it. Huge leaves of an impossible green hung over the banks. Occasionally Cidra caught a splash of movement as some river denizen leapt out of the water to snatch a tasty morsel that had made the mistake of journeying too far out on a broad leaf.

At one point she thought she had seen a set of reptilian eyes just above the water, watching the skimmer sweep past. When she had pointed them out to Severance, he had shrugged and said she had probably seen a river dracon.

"I'm not familiar with river dracons," she said. "What do they look like?"

"You don't want to know," he told her.

"Nonsense. All knowledge is good."

"Even knowledge that gives you nightmares?"

She let that pass. She hadn't slept easily the previous night. Images of huge bugs shining with unnatural light had invaded her dreams.

Tough reeds and floating flowers that were almost a meter wide battled for living space near the banks of the river. Beyond them the jungle was a wall of green that discouraged any attempts at penetration. The companies involved in exploration work had soon learned that it was easier to use the rivers as roads than to try to rip out the vegetation and pave the jungle floor. There were one or two other small settlements similar to Try Again where a mail ship or small plane could land on the continent, but for the most part, field camps and outposts were accessible only by river skimmer.

The skimmer rode a short distance above the water, sinking back down onto the water when the engines were cut. It was a lightweight boat, made to carry small amounts of cargo and passengers. The crew usually consisted of just one individual who also acted as guide. In this case the pilot's name was Overcash. He wore the uniform of the ExcellEx company. If Overcash had a birth name in addition to the one he'd chosen, he hadn't bothered to dispense it when he had been introduced to Cidra. It hadn't surprised her. She was growing accustomed to the lack of formality among Wolves. She was also getting used to the fact that outside Try Again, people were armed. Overcash and Severance both wore pulsers strapped to their thighs, the small, personal weapon the lab intruder had held. Pulsers were blunt, ugly instruments that would kill.

The skimmer had a clear, enclosed cabin in which the navigation instruments were housed. There was room inside for the pilot and one or two passengers to shelter in the event of a storm. Since they had left Try Again, however, Cidra and Severance had been sitting in the stern of the craft, which was open. That had suited Cidra just fine because she was fascinated with the scenery. The river seemed to have its own scent, a distinctive combination of vegetation and water thick with life. Unfortunately Severance had utilized the privacy afforded in the back of the skimmer to continue with his endless commentary on the events in the bio lab.

Cidra shifted slightly, vaguely uncomfortable in her new clothes. She had never before worn anything but one of the formal Harmonic surplice robes, and she felt odd. The tough fabric of the trousers and long-sleeved shirt Desma had insisted she wear were rough against skin that had only known the touch of finely spun crystal moss. The garments were designed in the manner of the functional uniforms worn by most people on Renaissance: snug trousers and a cool, loose-fitting shirt. The fabric was heavy and largely insect-proof, although it wouldn't be much help against something the size of a Bloodsucker. There was a hood that could be drawn over the head in the event of bad weather or a swarm of flying creatures such as the stinging bandini Desma had described. When she moved around, Cidra was aware of a sensation of being partially undressed. It seemed to her that the trousers and shirt defined her body too revealingly. More than once she had caught Severance eyeing her in the new clothes. He seemed especially fascinated with the shape of her buttocks.

In spite of the excitement in Desma's lab, Severance had seen to it that he and Cidra had left on time that morning. The mail must go through, Cidra thought humorously, especially when it was COD. At least she'd had a chance late yesterday afternoon to query the official Try Again Archive computer. The company in charge of maintaining it had charged a fee for access. Cidra was learning that the competitive free enterprise system that was so much a part of the worlds of Stanza Nine was especially fierce on Renaissance. Nothing was free here.

There hadn't been time to do a thorough search, and she hadn't had time to study what she had copied onto data slips, but she had the slips with her and fully intended to read them during the journey. Overcash had said that they would arrive at the ExcellEx field camp in two days' time. He would be returning as soon as he had dropped off the supplies, and Severance had promised Cidra that they would be going back with the pilot to Try Again.

"Four days of sight-seeing on this river is more than enough," he had said with a touch of grimness.

Cidra had agreed with him initially because she was so anxious to continue with her research. But now, as she watched the awesome scenery sweep past, she wasn't so sure. She was familiar with holotapes and data slip reproductions of Renaissance, but nothing could convey a true picture of the incredible, overly lush tangle of vegetation. Nor could any holotape duplicate the startling quantity of animal life. Four days wouldn't be nearly enough to drink in this amazing world, Cidra decided.

When the skimmer rounded a sweeping bend in the river and started up a long, straight stretch, Overcash locked the guide stick and came out of the cabin to join his passengers. He was a big man, taller than Severance and built along heavy, chunky lines. Cidra suspected that the chunkiness wasn't composed of much fat but was just muscle. His face was deeply tanned, made up of blunt features carved with a heavy hand. He had all the assurance of physical strength one would want in a guide in this wild land. Overcash stood with one thumb hooked into the utility loop he wore and nodded at Cidra.

"Enjoying the scenery, Otanna?"

She inclined her head, surprised by the polite title. "It's fascinating. But please call me Cidra."

Overcash nodded agreeably. "Ever been to Renaissance before?"

"Never."

"Kinda overwhelming at first. But you get used to it. There's a thousand different fortunes to be made here. Maybe ten thousand if you're willing to work for bonus credit." His narrowed gaze swept along the passing riverbank. "Assuming a man survives to make his haul."

"I understood that statistically most workers are safe now, as long as they follow the company rules and safety regulations," Cidra noted. "I thought the accident rate had declined sharply during the last few years with the invention of the deflectors."

Overcash laughed, a big booming sound that echoed along the water and caused a stir of activity in a tree on the bank. Something with a wingspan that seemed much too wide lifted into the air, its long, toothed beak outlined evilly against the sky.

"The statistics are probably accurate. Any renegade who wants to work hard and follow the rules can make a nice salary and probably stay out of trouble. But that's not how you make real credit on this planet. The companies all have what they like to call bonus plans. Take a few risks for your firm and you're guaranteed a bonus. 'Course, you got to survive to collect the bonus. I'm not sure how many bonus men who don't come back make it into the statistics. Companies got a way of doing things to statistics."

Severance threw a glance at the pilot. "And Renaissance has a way of doing things to bonus men."

"Yeah, well, it's like Free Market. Got to take a risk now and then, or it's not worth playing the game. You know that, Severance."

Cidra's mind winced at the philosophy. Having not played Free Market since *Severance Pay* had set down at Try Again, she had deliberately forgotten some of her odd, increasing enthusiasm for it. Severance obviously hadn't forgotten, however. He grinned wickedly.

At least he was smiling at her, even if he was showing his teeth. It was far more pleasant than being chewed on. Cidra looked down over the side of the skimmer. The thick water was ruffled on the surface from the effects of the skimmer's lift thrust. As the skimmer swept past she thought she saw another set of cold, wide-set eyes hovering a few centimeters under water. In that brief moment Cidra glimpsed the outline of a frighteningly long body. Perhaps Severance was right; getting a close-up view of a dracon might not be very pleasant. The eyes she had seen reminded her of some of Desma's lab creatures.

"Everything here on Renaissance seems to be out to eat everything else," she remarked.

"Just don't decide to trail your fingers in the water when we stop for the evening," Severance advised.

"I won't." She glanced at Overcash. "Do we stay on board the skimmer tonight?"

"No. Some dracon or a skater might decide to get playful. Skimmers are safest when they're in motion. We'll stay on shore."

"Is that any safer?"

Overcash chuckled. "Sure. We've got the heavy-duty deflectors and the armor tents. No problem. If something does decide to come looking for a midnight snack, we'll have plenty of warning. Not much can get through a deflector. Severance, here, wouldn't have brought you along if there was any real danger."

"On the contrary," Severance informed him, "I *had* to bring her along because she digs up the worst trouble when she's on her own."

They turned off the main river later that afternoon, swinging into a tributary that wasn't quite as thick with sediment as the first waterway had been. This river was also narrower than the first, and the walls of vegetation on either side seemed to loom higher and closer. But that might be just a trick of the waning light, Cidra told herself. She realized that she wasn't looking forward to camping out this evening.

As if he sensed her uneasiness, Severance became more talkative. He gave her a dissertation on how effective the big deflector screens were and how they had revolutionized field camps on Renaissance. The invisible grids they produced were based on the same principle as the Screamer. They were set to repel any creature with nerve impulses different than those of human beings.

"I get the feeling that some things out there haven't even got nerves." But Cidra made the observation with a smile to show Severance that she wasn't really worried. Wonderful what Harmonic training could do when it came to covering up one's true feelings. Or perhaps she was so adept at it because she had been covering up the Wolf side of herself for so many years.

Overcash chose the campsite just as the shadows along the river became uncomfortably long. With the instinct of a good guide he managed to find a rare break in the undergrowth. Carefully he slowed the skimmer, letting it sink down onto the water. The craft rocked slightly in the lethargic current while the pilot made it fast. A flexible landing plank emerged when Overcash activated a control panel.

"I don't see enough room here to erect a couple of tents," Cidra observed, eyeing the bank. The vegetation was thinner along this stretch of bank, but it was still fairly spectacular to her eyes. She watched as a small, wriggly creature flashed on the bank and slid into the water. Cidra had a mental picture of it sliding just as easily into a tent.

"Don't worry, we'll make a little space for ourselves." Overcash went into the cabin and came back with a long-barreled machine that had a squat base.

"What's that?" Cidra asked.

"A crisper." Overcash switched on the machine, and a narrow band of white flame jumped out, searing the vegetation it touched. With a few sweeping movements the guide cleared a relatively large area along the bank. The undergrowth that had fallen into the path of the crisper smoked for a moment, wilted, and then disintegrated.

"I guess that's one way of dealing with too many weeds." Cidra was a little appalled by the small devastation.

"Too bad this thing hasn't got a longer range," Overcash remarked, stowing the machine. "It would make a useful weapon."

The deflector screens were hauled out next. They were charged on the skimmer's power cells and then carried ashore. Severance helped the pilot set them up so that they produced a grid that completely encircled the campsite. Occasional tiny hissing noises gave notice that the screens were working. Inside the protected area the light metal tents were erected—two of them, Cidra noticed. Severance moved his and Cidra's small travel packs into one. Neither he nor Overcash seemed to have any interest in how Cidra felt about the sleeping situation. It was apparently a foregone conclusion that she belonged in Severance's tent. She shouldn't have been surprised. Among Wolves it was clear that when a man and a woman spent time together, it was assumed that they had a sexual relationship.

Well, she thought bracingly, she'd already lived with him for two weeks in the confines of a mail ship. This wasn't much more intimate, all things considered. She just wished she had a proper sleeping robe. It occurred to her that she might be expected to undress before she climbed into the air-cushioned sleepers. The thought of sleeping naked was more unnerving than most of her other recent experiences. She couldn't do it.

The background clamor of the jungle changed perceptibly as the night shift took possession of the premises. The deflectors had no effect on the sounds that permeated the shadows, and Cidra found the clickings, clackings, screams, and cries disturbing. Severance had had the forethought to insure that some vegetarian prespacs were on board the skimmer, and she flashed him a look of gratitude when hers came out of the portable food heater. He had also made sure a few containers of his beloved ale were on board.

It was going to be a long night.

Hours later, Severance lay awake in his sleeper, aware of the tension in the woman lying next to him. Her body was insulated from his by the plastic fabric of the sleepers, but Cidra was lying so still, she was clearly wide-awake.

He had said nothing when she had crawled into the sleeper wearing her clothing. She clearly had not felt comfortable in the trousers and shirt all day, so he had resisted the urge to tell her what a sweet, sassy little rear she had. Harmonic males undoubtedly did not say things like that to their women. Harmonic males didn't even think in terms of "their women."

But Wolves did think in such primitive terms, Severance was discovering. Like it or not, he was starting to think of Cidra that way. "Company property" he had called her, but she hadn't seemed to realize just what he was saying. His feelings of possessiveness were stronger than ever, yet he hadn't even had her in his bed. He wondered how he would ever get as far as QED without trying to seduce her. The only option he had—terminating her crew contract—was not one he wanted to consider. She would fall into the path of some piece of second-class mail like Racer.

Severance turned onto his side, watching Cidra's too-tense outline. The movement made him aware of the second pulser he had stowed under his sleeper. The Screamer was in the utility loop that hung within reach, and he could put out his hand and touch the first pulser, the one he had worn strapped to his thigh during the day. He'd had the second one in his travel pack and, as a general precaution, had decided to sleep on top of it. Renaissance was a dangerous planet, and not all the hazards were from its natural flora and fauna. Some of them were man-made.

Seeing Racer two nights ago had made Severance remember just how dangerous the human species could be. A part of him still burned with a frozen flame of anger as he recalled the emotion that had shot through him when he'd entered the Bloodsucker and seen Racer sitting with Cidra. There was no way he could have left Cidra behind on this trip. She might have been reasonably safe from the perils of Port Try Again, but she wouldn't have been safe from Racer. Every gut-level instinct had warned Severance that Racer would have found a way to use Cidra.

"Severance?"

The quiet whisper of her voice made him jump. "What is it, Cidra?"

"Are you awake?"

"No, I'm just making conversation in my sleep." He smiled to himself as she wriggled around in the sleeper to face him.

"Do you hear those weird clanking sounds?"

He could barely see her face in the shadows, but he sensed the genuine tension in her voice. "I hear them. Probably zalons. They've got shells as hard as armor. And they like to fight a lot. Sometimes you can hear the clanking for several kilometers. They're huge, but they eat only plants."

"Why do they fight?"

"Male zalons fight over female zalons. Mating rituals. They mate frequently."

"Everything on Lovelady and Renaissance seems to mate frequently," she said, almost to herself. "Desma told me she has four children."

"That's a small family by Wolf standards. Last I heard, the average number of children was over five per family."

"I can't even imagine having brothers and sisters. When I was growing up, there were hardly any other children in Clementia."

Her voice trailed off but not before Severance picked up the unspoken inference. He knew without being told that those other children hadn't provided much in the way of companionship for the little Wolf born among Harmonics.

"My family was smaller than average too. I only had one brother," he heard himself say.

"The one who was a Harmonic?"

"Yes." He was quiet for a while. "Jeude was a late bloomer in a sense. We didn't realize he was a Harmonic until he was in his late teens. Just thought he was a little different—quiet and thoughtful. A bit eccentric in some ways. My parents had just begun to acknowledge that he might be Harmonic when they were killed."

"Oh, Severance," she said gently, "what happened?"

"They were geologists with a big mining company on QED. There was an accident. An explosion." He sensed her movement, and the next thing he knew, she was stretching out her hand to touch his. "Jeude took it hard. Very hard. And he refused to be separated from me after that. He wouldn't hear of being sent to Clementia."

"So you let him run mail with you?"

"He was good at it. Very determined. Once in a while I let him take a ship out alone while I made deliveries and arranged contracts here on Renaissance or on Lovelady. He liked going to QED by himself with just Fred along for company. Said it gave him a lot of time to think. I knew I should have insisted he go to Clementia for training, but he kept resisting the idea and I just didn't have the heart to force him. He got killed because of my lousy judgment."

"Was he killed on that red plain? The one you light-painted on board ship?"

She might not be a Harmonic, but there were times when the lady was too damn intuitive. "He went straight into the ground answering a distress signal in a QED sandstorm. Nothing that flies can survive one of those storms. The only thing a pilot can do is run from them. But Jeude didn't run." Severance felt his hand clench into a fist under the sleeper cover. Very deliberately he forced himself to flatten out his palm. "Fred survived. The rescue crew found him wrapped around Jeude's leg when they arrived. The ship was destroyed, pieces of it scattered over a wide area. They never did find all the cargo."

"I'm so sorry, Severance."

"I know." He didn't doubt it for a moment. Cidra's compassion was as real as her ability with Moonlight and Mirrors. Sweetness and light were her inner core of strength. He shook off the brooding feeling as he thought about the conflicting image. "It's in the past, Cidra. I wish I hadn't mentioned it." Severance rubbed his eyes wearily, thinking that he hadn't talked about Jeude to anyone for a long time.

She didn't press him. Her hand slipped back into her sleeper, and she turned on her back to stare at the low ceiling of the tent. Another distant clanking sound echoed in the night, and a small scream split the air close to the camp.

"Overcash is right. Renaissance is somewhat overwhelming," Cidra said quietly.

"Frightened?"

"No, of course not. I understand about the security systems and the deflectors and all. There's nothing to worry about."

"Cidra . . ."

"Too bad they haven't come up with some way of blocking out some of the night noises, though. It's very hard to sleep with so much jungle racket."

Severance said again, "Cidra."

She ignored him again. "I hope Fred is enjoying his stay with Desma. He certainly seems to like her. He'll be in for a shock if he wanders into the lab, though, won't he?"

Severance unfastened the opening of his sleeper. "Cidra, come in here with me. There's room for two."

Her head snapped around. "Severance, no, I don't think that would be a very good idea."

On one level he agreed with her. But he couldn't spend the rest of the night listening to her tension. "Then relax. I'm not about to fight my way through those trousers you're wearing. I'm just offering a little human comfort."

"I'm not a child."

"Did anyone ever hold you until you fell asleep when you were a child?"

There was a long silence. "Harmonics don't touch each

174

other, except when they're in full telepathic communion. My parents were never able to experience that kind of bond with me."

He heard the careful explanation and then reached across to unfasten her sleeper. "Come here, Cidra. I'll hold you until you fall asleep."

"Really, Severance, that isn't necessary. I'm just fine the way I am."

He sat up and pried her gently out of the sleeper. She resisted slightly at first, and then, with a warm, scrambling rush she was inside his sleeper, curved against his body. She lay still for a moment, and then he felt her begin to relax. The distant clank of zalon armor sounded again, but this time she didn't flinch. The lumbering warriors continued to fight their battle in the darkness while Cidra gradually ceased to be an unwilling audience.

Some time later, when he was absolutely sure that she was asleep, Severance allowed himself to cradle Cidra more intimately. His hand drifted to her breast and rested there as he yawned deeply. She felt good nestled into him this way, her firm buttocks tucked against his thighs. He liked the relaxed way she was finally sleeping. It made him feel good to have her trust him, even on an unconscious level. She was so concerned with trust, so convinced that she could never establish it completely with a man until she was a Harmonic.

Cidra wasn't born to be a Harmonic. Severance knew that with a certainty that burned deep. He wondered how long she would pursue her fruitless quest. It wasn't in her to acknowledge defeat. The only thing that would deflect her from her goal was if she, herself, changed her mind. And from what he knew of her that wasn't likely. She was a stubborn woman.

He allowed himself the luxury of resting his hand on her breast and decided that he could be just as stubborn as any false Harmonic. With that, Severance finally slipped into sleep himself.

It wasn't the clanking of zalons or the screams of another jungle denizen, but the sound of human voices and the hum of a river skimmer that awakened him the next morning. For a moment Severance lay still, considering the coincidence of another skimmer having chosen this tributary to travel. It wasn't very likely an accidental event. According to what Severance had been told, only the ExcellEx field camp lay along this tributary, and Overcash was the only skimmer pilot supplying that base. He yanked on his trousers.

Overcash's greeting boomed out over the water. "Hey, come ashore for some hot coffade. We're just about to eat."

"Sounds good," came the response. "I'm coming in."

Severance heard the answering voice and reached for his pulser holster.

"Severance?" Sleepily Cidra blinked and looked up at him. "What's wrong?"

"Nothing yet." He finished strapping on the pulser and slid out of the sleeper.

"Then why are you . . . ?"

"Racer's here."

"Racer!"

She sat up, startled. Her face was flushed and her braid half undone as she stared at him in astonishment. Severance wished he had the freedom to get back into the sleeper with her and conduct an intimate discussion on the merits of human comfort. But that option wasn't open to him.

"It's one renegade hell of a coincidence that he's running the same river with us. I don't trust him any farther than I can ship him without postage."

Severance stepped out into the dawn to find that Racer was already on shore, his skimmer bobbing lightly behind him on the water. The man's blue-green eyes followed Severance as he emerged from the tent.

"Spend a pleasant night teaching new tricks to the Harmonic, Severance?" Racer smiled and lifted the pulser in his hand until it was pointed at Severance's bare chest. "Maybe before this is all over I'll take the opportunity to add to her education. But for now, drop the pulser, Severance. I'm here to do a little business. Bonus business."

Chapter
Ten

"What's the matter, Overcash? ExcellEx bonus money not good
enough for you? Think Racer's going to pay more? You're in
for a surprise. Racer's not all that reliable. Take my word for
it. I've had firsthand experience."

Inside the tent Cidra listened in shock to Severance's cool,
contemptuous voice. She shoved aside the feathery light sleeper.
As she struggled with the awkward boots that went with her
new outfit, she could hear the three men very clearly. Their
rough, tense tones sounded infinitely more lethal than the noises
of the jungle morning.

"Shut up, Severance," Racer said. "We're just going to
conduct some business. After which we'll leave you in peace.
Where are the sensors, Overcash?"

"In the skimmer's cargo hold."

"Get 'em out. Load them onto the skimmer I brought."

"But why?" Overcash sounded honestly confused. "I thought we were going to take both skimmers back with us."

"I've changed the plans slightly."

Severance interrupted mildly. "He does that a lot, Overcash. Racer's changes of plans have a way of leaving a man holding a lockmouth by the wrong end."

"I've told you to shut up, Severance. Call the little Saint out of the tent. You can't hide her in there forever."

Cidra was already stepping through the iris diaphragm opening. She spoke very softly. "I'm here, Racer. There's no need to shout."

"Stay where you are, Cidra," Severance ordered without turning to look at her. "Don't come any closer."

Obediently Cidra halted, taking in the scene with a quick glance. Overcash was transferring the carton of ExcellEx sensors from his skimmer to a second craft that had been made fast alongside. While he labored Cord Racer kept a pulser trained on Severance. The pulser Severance had been wearing was missing from its holster. Racer had taken it.

Severance stood with his customary ease. If there had been a chair nearby, he probably would have sprawled in it as usual. Nothing except the contempt in his expression gave any indication of his tension. But Cidra sensed the leashed fury in him so clearly, she thought for an instant that she had almost read his mind. The sensation was disconcerting.

Racer showed his tension much more visibly. It radiated through his body as he faced Severance. His eyes were narrowed, and the hold he had on the pulser seemed far too tight. When his gaze flicked briefly to Cidra, she knew he had already dismissed her as a source of trouble. She knew that in his mind she occupied the status of a "harmless Harmonic." And at the moment she did feel harmless. The frustration was enough to push aside some of her fear and allow anger to take its place. But as she stood silently beside the tent Cidra kept all of her emotions sheltered behind a serene facade.

"We'll make this short and sweet, Severance," Racer said. "Wouldn't want to take up too much of your valuable time. You're going to need it to try to walk out of this jungle by sunset."

Overcash finished loading the cargo and jumped to the bank. "There's no way he can walk out by sunset. I made sure we came far enough yesterday to make that impossible for anything but a zalon. Want me to collapse the tents?"

"No need," Racer replied. "They won't do him any good. That lightweight armor isn't enough to do any more than keep the bandini off him. And I don't want to waste time. We've already wasted too much as it is."

Severance looked at him with idle interest. "Those were your men at Lovelorn? The ones who posed as port security?"

Racer shrugged. "A couple of incompetents. But I didn't have time to be too choosy. Quench moved unexpectedly when he commissioned you to make the run with the sensors. I'd been expecting him to delay for another few days. As it was, I barely got word of it in time to make any kind of try at all. I'd like to know what you did to those guys, Severance. They were almost incoherent when I finally found them."

"You should have told them that coming aboard *Severance Pay* without an invitation wasn't going to be a simple slide-in, slide-out job."

"I figured two of them could handle it. Especially with you running around Lovelorn trying to pick up some extra credit from one more patron. A good postman like you couldn't resist just one more commission, could you?"

Severance nodded. "I wondered about that deal at Lovelorn.

Especially yesterday, when I couldn't find the man who was supposed to be waiting so eagerly for the case."

"Good help is hard to find," Racer drawled. "And getting harder all the time. Didn't have much luck with the renegade I hired to pick up Cidra the other night, either. After I met her at the Bloodsucker it occurred to me that she might be a handy sardite chip. Thought if I had her, you might be more amenable to a little bargaining."

For an instant Cidra felt her outward control slip. "That was your man in the lab? The one who hurt Desma?"

Racer gave her a short, wry glance. "He wasn't after Desma. But he figured she would head for the lab when she got the malfunction alarm. The idea was that you would be alone in the house. Easy pickings."

"But she followed Desma to the lab instead," Severance said.

Racer shrugged. "It still would have worked if one of those bugs Desma keeps as pets hadn't gotten loose. The way Payne told it, he was lucky to escape alive. This time I decided I'd better handle things myself. My clients are getting impatient."

"I'll just bet they are," Severance murmured. "You've missed twice so far. What makes you think you're going to have any more luck this time around?"

"In case you haven't noticed, Severance, my luck is running very high today. Thanks to some advance planning." Racer spoke over his shoulder to Overcash. "Is the skimmer I brought ready?"

"All set. I'll take the deflectors."

"No, we'll leave those behind along with the tents. The screens have already been used all night, haven't they?"

"Sure, but . . ."

"Then they haven't got more than a few hours' charge left.

Without the skimmer's fuel cells there's no way to recharge them."

"What are you going to do with the skimmer I brought?" Overcash demanded.

"It's going to be in a severe accident. And that's what this whole scene will look like in a couple of days. An unfortunate, but not untypical, Renaissance river accident. Skimmer sinks and the crew is left on shore with failing equipment. By the time another skimmer heads up this far, there won't be much left. Renaissance will see to that for us."

"You're a fool, Racer," Severance said wearily.

Overcash moved uneasily, his hard face knotting into a frown. "I don't know, Racer. Might be better to make sure of 'em before we leave."

Racer shook his head. "Too much chance another skimmer will be along in a couple of days. If we use the pulser, there'll be evidence. I've heard too much lately about that renegade named Quench who runs ExcellEx. He's trying to build a reputation as a company owner who looks after his own. If he hears that his handpicked mail pilot got shot trying to deliver the sensors, he'll demand an investigation. And he's getting big enough to force one. Hell, he'll pay for it out of his own pocket if he gets really mad. No, this has to look like an accident." A terrifying screech sounded from the jungle followed by a bitten-off scream. Racer smiled. "Come on, Overcash. We're not leaving anything to chance. No one spends a night in a Renaissance jungle without equipment and lives to tell about it. Everything will be over by morning."

Overcash looked unconvinced, but he obviously wasn't going to argue. He turned and jumped on board the second skimmer and made ready to loosen the moorings. Twin dracon eyes emerged briefly in the river as if curious. They disappeared again with barely a ripple.

Severance studied Racer as if he were looking at the man through a microscope and didn't like what he saw. "Think it will work this time?"

"It'll work," Racer said roughly.

"Maybe. Maybe not." Severance gave every appearance of being only mildly interested.

"Tell you what," Racer said, glancing at Cidra, who was still standing motionless in front of the tent. "I'll do you a favor. I'll take Cidra with me."

Cidra started, growing cold inside. "No."

Severance was watching Racer. "And do what? Throw her in the river when you've finished with her? She might as well stay with me."

Racer grinned, sensing that for the first time he had a handle on the situation. He seized it, motioning at Cidra with the pulser. "Get on board the skimmer, Cidra. You don't want to stay behind. Something in this jungle is going to have your shipmaster for dinner tonight, and you'll be dessert if you're hanging around."

"No," Cidra said again. She looked to Severance for some support, but he was quiet, almost thoughtful. "I'm staying here."

"She's a Harmonic, Racer. If the right people find out you've hurt her, there'll be a reckoning. You know that."

"I might not have to get rid of her," Racer temporized, "if she has the sense to keep her mouth shut. Do you, Otanna?" He made the formal title a mockery.

"I don't understand." Cidra's tone was aloof, but her heart was beating much too quickly, and the palms of her hands, folded serenely in front of her, were damp. This was as bad as facing the intruder in the lab had been.

"Sure, you understand. Harmonics are real good at understanding, aren't they? They're also real good at keeping their promises. I'm going to take you with me. At the end of the trip you'll have a choice. Give me your word as a Harmonic that you'll keep quiet about what happened here this morning and I'll put you on the next freighter to Clementia. Refuse and I'll feed you to a dracon."

"Why don't you simply leave me here with Severance?"

"Because knowing you're going to be warming my bunk for a couple of nights will eat him up inside. I want to give him something to think about while he's waiting for the deflector screens to fail."

Cidra understood. Racer thought that she and Severance were lovers. He thought he could use her to twist the blade in Severance. She knew in that moment that there was far more between the two men than was obvious. This kind of hatred went back a long way. She shivered and unconsciously stepped closer to Severance.

"Go with him, Cidra."

She was stunned at Severance's soft order. "I will not go with him. I work for you. I'm staying here."

"Cidra, with him you've got a chance. Take it."

"No."

Overcash snarled. "How long are we going to stand here and chat, Racer?"

"No longer." Racer lifted the pulser slightly. "Get on board the skimmer, Cidra, or I'll kill Severance and be done with the whole thing."

He would do it. Cidra looked into Racer's face and knew he had been pushed far enough. Any farther and Severance would die. He wouldn't even have the hours until nightfall that the deflectors could provide. She was trained to analyze a situation and react logically. Without a word she stepped past Severance and walked toward the skimmer.

Racer visibly relaxed, a satisfied expression in his eyes.

"They always say Harmonics are bright. Be interesting to see how good one is in bed. The next couple of nights are going to be amusing. Think about them while you're waiting for the deflectors to run out of power, Severance."

"You know what'll happen if I make it out of here, don't you, Racer?" Severance asked very softly.

"We both know you'll never make it out, so there's no need to worry about it. If I were you, Severance, I'd stop wasting breath on threats and start thinking about how long those deflectors will last without a recharge." Racer backed to the boat, keeping the pulser trained on Severance.

When he was on board, Overcash slipped the last tethers holding the skimmer in place and moved into the cabin. Cidra stood in the stern, her eyes on Severance as the skimmer's fuel cells hummed to life. The power packs glowed green beside her in the rear of the boat. She was cold and sick inside. When Severance met her gaze and smiled faintly, she felt an unfamiliar stinging sensation behind her eyes. Her hands tightened in front of her.

"I'll take the wheel," Racer said as the skimmer moved away from shore. "This next little surprise has got to be timed properly." He holstered the pulser as Overcash stepped out of the cabin.

Cidra tensed as the skimmer drifted farther from the bank. Severance was walking back toward the tent. He seemed in no hurry, but Overcash frowned and palmed his own pulser. The base of the weapon glowed red. "What's he doing?"

"There's nothing he can do," Racer told him from inside the cabin.

"I don't like it."

"You don't have to like it. In another couple of minutes the skimmer will go to the bottom and, with it, any chance he's got of getting out of this in one piece."

Cidra listened to the exchange, aware that in typical Wolf fashion both men had assumed that she was incapable of being a threat. They were right. She could not hope to use her Moonlight and Mirrors on both of them at the same time. Not when each man was armed with a pulser. But their attention was not on her, and this was the only opportunity she was going to get. She edged toward the high gunwale of the skimmer. It would be better if she could take off the boots, but that was not possible.

"He's disappeared!" Overcash yelled. "I think he's inside the tent. I can't see what he's doing."

"This will bring him out in one renegade hell of a hurry." Racer activated the control of the small instrument he was holding in one hand. "Watch. I rigged your boat for you, Overcash, before you left Try Again."

There was a muffled roar. The skimmer left floating near the bank seemed to shudder, and then it imploded with a sickening crunch of diazite and metal. Slowly but inevitably the boat crumpled in on itself and sank into the river. Cidra waited no longer. This was the best chance she was going to get.

Overcash was staring in fascination at the disintegrating skimmer when Cidra went over the side. She launched herself in a smooth, flat arc, aiming for the shallowest possible dive. The last thing she wanted to do was go any deeper into the river than was absolutely necessary. Behind her she caught part of Overcash's outraged yell.

"She's gone over!"

"Forget her," Racer yelled back. "She's dead meat."

"The renegade bitch!" Overcash raised the pulser.

Cidra was on the surface, stroking strongly toward the bank. Her main concern was trying to keep from getting any of the muddy, brakish river water in her mouth. It was Severance's shouted order that stilled her movements in the water.

"Cidra, stop swimming! Float, damn it. Just float. Don't splash. Don't make a sound. Keep yourself on the surface."

She obeyed, glad that the awkward boots seemed bouyant in the water. With practiced ease she floated while she turned toward the shoreline to spot Severance. She didn't notice if he was there or not; instead she found her gaze locked with a pair of malevolent eyes between her and the bank. A dracon was cruising toward her.

Cidra had never known this kind of terror. Only instinct kept her moving her hands in smooth, gentle sweeps around her midsection. The small movements were sufficient to keep her afloat. But compared to the fear that engulfed her as the dracon approached, drowning seemed a pleasant alternative. She could not yet see anything other than the eyes, but she sensed the vastness of the creature moving toward her. More terrifyingly she sensed its relentless, endless hunger. It wasn't certain yet whether she constituted a potential meal, and dimly Cidra realized that it was probably because she was floating on the surface like a log rather than behaving like normal prey.

Another set of eyes surfaced to Cidra's right. She wanted to give in to the panic and have done with it. Anything was better than waiting for the dracons to leisurely start sampling her arms and legs. Perhaps they wouldn't even bother with a sample. Perhaps one of them would simply swallow her in a single gulp. Still she floated, vaguely aware of Overcash's agitation in the skimmer. Racer hadn't thrown the boat into motion yet. He kept it hovering behind Cidra, and she knew that he and Overcash were waiting to see how long it would take the dracons to move in on her.

"I'm going to draw some blood," Overcash announced. "It'll get things over with a lot sooner." Standing in the stern of the skimmer, he raised the pulser and aimed it at the floating Cidra.

Everyone's attention was on Cidra and the dracons. No one

noticed Severance when he stepped around the tent, the pulser he'd slept on during the night now in his hand. He aimed the weapon at Overcash and gently squeezed the trigger.

Behind her Cidra heard a man's scream. A second later there was a loud splash and then, with blinding speed, the dracons were in motion. She closed her eyes, waiting for the horror to engulf her. A pair of eyes passed within inches, and she felt the brush of a huge, scaled body against her leg. But there was no tearing sensation. Another set of eyes flowed past, also ignoring her. Cidra didn't stop to question fate. Using all her strength to keep her body as much as possible on the surface, she stroked again for the bank.

There was another scream behind her, but Cidra didn't pause to glance back. She heard the thrashing sounds in the river and, slightly louder, the hum of the skimmer as it was shoved urgently into high speed. The bank seemed very far away.

Then Severance was there, wading into the river and reaching for her. He caught her wrist and dragged her the rest of the way to shore. Cidra wanted to scream as he pulled her up beside him. She automatically turned to see what was happening in the river. There was a flash of a huge, obscene shape that seemed to be made entirely of teeth. And there was something between its jaws, something that had once been human.

"Don't look." Severance forced her head against his shoulder. "It'll all be over in a minute. Just don't watch."

Cidra stood shuddering in the circle of his arm, trying not to think of what she had seen and trying even harder not to think of how it might have been her own torn and mutilated body held fast in those fearsome jaws. In the distance she heard the skimmer's hum fade.

"Racer's gone," she gasped, more for something to say than anything else.

"Racer's good at leaving a friend in an awkward situation.

Not that he could have done much for Overcash. Once the dracons sensed blood, nothing on this planet could have stopped them."

"He was going to shoot me. I heard him say a little blood would get things over more quickly."

"He was right."

"You killed him to stop him from shooting me," she said into his damp shirt. She wasn't certain which stunned her more, Severance's killing Overcash or Overcash's willingness to kill her. Cidra felt dazed.

Severance hesitated. "I would have shot him even if he hadn't been trying to wound you. I needed something to feed the dracons. In another minute or two they would have decided you were prey, after all."

"Oh." She couldn't think of anything else to say.

"I would have preferred feeding Racer to the river, but I couldn't get a clear shot at him. Overcash was in the way."

The awful thrashing sounds died away. Slowly, still afraid to turn and look toward the river, Cidra lifted her head. She realized that she was leaning heavily on Severance, seeking strength in him. "It's over," she whispered.

"No," he answered, gently freeing her to look down into her stricken face, "it's just beginning. Why did you jump overboard, Cidra?"

"I had no choice. I couldn't go with him."

"There was a chance he would have believed you really are a Harmonic, and a chance he would have let you go eventually if you'd given him your promise to keep quiet."

"Which I would never have done, so there's no point discussing it, is there?"

"Cidra..."

"Stop it, Severance." She pushed away from him, still looking anywhere but at the river. "I could not go with him, and that's all there is to it."

He touched her cheek, his finger rough on her wet skin. "You would have survived rape, Cidra. I'm not so sure about the jungle."

A sudden, fierce rage welled up in her. "I would not have survived rape. He would have had to kill me before he succeeded in raping me. Haven't you ever heard of death before dishonor?"

Severance looked at her. "Not lately."

"It would have been utterly degrading for me to have submitted to that man in exchange for my life after he'd left you to die. And it would have been equally dishonorable to have given him my promise not to tell the company authorities what had happened."

"That's a little extreme under the circumstances."

"I work for you, Teague Severance. Have you forgotten our contract? I have sworn my loyalty to the firm of Severance Pay, Ltd. It would have been a breach of that act to have let Racer use me. He only wanted to add to your suffering, you know," Cidra explained, lowering her voice. "And it would have bothered you greatly. Not because I was your lover but because you feel responsible for me. Racer didn't seem to understand that I am merely your employee."

"Lately I've had trouble understanding that myself." Severance reached out and wrapped his palms around the nape of Cidra's neck. He pulled her close and kissed her with a quick roughness that betrayed the tension he had hidden so well all morning. "Sweet Harmony in hell, Cidra Rainforest. I've never been so scared in my life as I was when I saw that dracon eyeing you. Don't ever, ever do that to me again."

She smiled mistily as he freed her. "I'll make a note not to go swimming in the near future."

He stared down at her for another long moment, as if he wanted to say more. Instead he released her and turned toward the tent. "I guess I'd better get moving."

Surprised, she stepped after him. "What are we going to do?" A sloshing sound reminded her of her wet boots. Gingerly Cidra sat down on the charred ground and removed them, shaking out the river water.

"I'm going after Racer." He spoke from inside the tent.

"Going after him? But, Severance, he's got a skimmer. He's long gone."

"He's got a skimmer that's in trouble, although he may not realize it yet. It's going to take a while for the fuel cells to start losing power." Severance reappeared outside the tent carrying his travel pack. He put it down on the ground, crouched beside it, and began going through the contents.

Cidra watched him. "Why should the fuel cells fail on his skimmer?"

"After I shot Overcash, Racer ducked into the cabin. I had a clear view of the engine section of the skimmer. And I got in a couple more shots. One cell was glowing yellow when the skimmer took off up the river. Yellow means that the charge was already starting to diminish. Racer will realize what's happening when he calms down and has a chance to check his controls."

"Then what will he do?"

"Panic, I hope. He tends to lose his nerve when the sardite's down. I'm counting on him losing it this time too."

"You speak from past experience with the man?" Cidra asked carefully.

"This isn't the first time we've tangled."

"You said he was once your partner."

Severance removed a thin blade from the travel pack and slipped it into his utility loop. "The partnership dissolved the day he left me to fight my way out of a sinkswamp here on Renaissance."

Cidra sucked in her breath. "He's tried to kill you before?"

"Not exactly. We had a mail run into a field camp that was doing some work in the swamps up north. There was trouble with the sled. Always something going wrong with machinery on this damned planet. The sled started to slip into a sinkswamp with both of us on board. When we realized what was happening, we managed to attach a wire line to a tree. The plan was to use it to climb to safety. Racer went first. When he reached the tree, the line broke. He was getting set to toss me another one when he saw the killweaver. The things live in the swamps, and this one apparently decided to investigate the activity going on over its nest. It surfaced beside the sled. Big ugly thing with very unappealing pincers. Racer took one look and fled."

"Leaving you behind?"

"Guess he figured I didn't have much chance, anyway. He made it to the company's field camp a couple of hours later and somehow neglected to mention that he had left me behind in the sled sitting on top of a killweaver's web. I think he was busy realizing just how convenient the whole setup was. In one fell swoop he was now sole owner of the ship and all our equipment. It was somewhat disconcerting for him when I wandered into camp an hour behind him. We've made a practice of avoiding each other ever since."

"How did you get away from the . . . the killweaver?" Cidra struggled with the dim recollection of a holotape she had once seen of a huge spider shape. Another typical Renaissance horror. Even the wild parts of Lovelady seemed tame in comparison to this planet.

"It's a short story. The trick with dracons and killweavers is to distract them with a convenient meal."

Cidra shuddered. "What did you find to feed the kill-weaver?"

"Something equally mean and ugly." Severance got to his feet, having removed several small objects from his travel pack.

"But you didn't find this, uh, distraction until after the web had burned your hands?"

"It never pays to be slow on Renaissance." He dropped the travel pack and checked the contents of his loop.

"Are we leaving already?" Cidra asked.

"I'm leaving. You're staying here."

She shot to her feet. "Severance, no!"

His face softened. "You'll be all right. There's enough charge left on the deflectors to last until nightfall. I'll be back by then. Just stay inside the screens and don't wander outside for any reason. Understood?"

"I refuse to stay here alone while you take off into that jungle!"

"I'll be staying close to the riverbank. Don't worry, Racer won't get far. When he realizes that the fuel cells are faltering, he'll bring the skimmer into shore, set up the deflector screens, and call for help. I intend to arrive long before help does."

"I don't like this," Cidra began earnestly.

"I'm not especially thrilled with the mess we're in, either. But since I'm the one who got us into it, I'd better start fixing things. Once the fuel cells start to go, the skimmer won't have enough power to stay afloat, but there'll still be enough of a charge left in them to keep the deflectors and a comm unit going for quite a while. I can float the skimmer back down the river if necessary. Relax, I'm supposed to be the one whose good with his hands, remember?" He walked toward her, coming to a halt a short distance away. "Don't look at me like that, Cidra. It's going to be all right. This is my fault and I'll take care of it."

"It's hardly your fault!"

"I'm the pilot in command. The head of Severance Pay, Ltd. That makes it my job to clean up the situation. Besides, even if I wanted to delegate the responsibility, this is a very small firm. I don't see any convenient vice-president standing around to send after Racer."

"There's me."

"You've already done more than your share to defend the mail and the firm. It's my turn. I'll be back before the screens fail. Believe me? I spent the year after Jeude's death getting to know this jungle very well."

She chewed helplessly on her lower lip and then nodded once. "I believe you, Severance." And she did. If he didn't come back before the screens failed, it would be because he couldn't come back. She didn't want to think about that possibility.

"I'll see you before nightfall, then."

"And then what?" she challenged. But she knew even as she spoke that she had accepted the inevitable. There was no choice but for him to leave. Taking her with him would slow him down far too much.

"When I come back, I'll bring the skimmer and a fresh set of screens. If we can't repair the skimmer, we can still use the communications equipment to call for aid."

She drew a deep breath. "What about Racer?"

Severance didn't look up as he adjusted the utility loop. "What about him?"

She searched his face. "You're going to kill him, aren't you?"

"Don't think about it, Cidra. Racer is my problem." He leaned down to brush his mouth over hers. When he lifted his head, he was smiling again. "I've got to stop doing that."

She touched her lips with her fingertips, realizing how accustomed she was becoming to his brief, intimate gestures. She remembered how she had felt when she'd stood in the stern of Racer's skimmer and watched as she was dragged farther and farther away from Severance. Then, in a wordless rush, she threw her arms around his neck.

"Be careful, Severance. Please be careful."

"I'll be back for you before nightfall." He held her, his arms closing with bruising fierceness around her slender body. Then he released her and moved through the screens without glancing back.

Cidra watched until he was out of sight. It didn't take long. The undergrowth closed behind him, and it was as if he had never been standing there with her at all. Out on the river all was once again placid, giving no hint of the living hell that cruised just below the surface.

Cidra was staring at the spot where the skimmer had floated when she caught sight of something shiny out of the corner of her eye. It was a container of Renaissance Rose ale that had apparently survived the explosion of the skimmer. It was caught in the reeds near shore. Cidra risked a quick trip through the deflectors to rescue the container. Severance would appreciate the ale when he returned.

Holding the Renaissance Rose as if it were a talisman that could somehow guarantee Severance's safe return, Cidra slipped back into the safety of the deflectors.

Chapter
Eleven

He had to get the deflectors and the skimmer's communication equipment. And he would probably have to kill Racer to do it.

Severance didn't try to fool himself. There was an outside chance that Racer would allow himself to be dragged back to Try Again and turned over to the company authorities, but it wasn't likely. He had too much to lose. He was far more likely to force Severance's hand, counting on what he knew of his ex-partner to keep him from getting killed. Deep down Racer was probably convinced that Severance wouldn't have the guts to kill him.

Severance moved through the undergrowth along the riverbank, trying to make as little noise as possible. There was no chance that Racer would hear him, but there was every chance something else might come to investigate the strange movement. Without the deflector screens a man with a pulser and a utility knife was among the more poorly armed of Renaissance's inhabitants.

Severance knew that all of his senses were on full alert. He had reached that unpleasantly acute state of awareness he had come to know well during the year after Jeude's death. It didn't take much to translate awareness into panic. There were a lot of things that could kill on Renaissance, but panic was one of the surest methods. Severance let his eyes and ears and the hairs on the back of his neck do their job while he thought about Racer.

Racer, who had once been his friend. Racer, who in some ways he knew better than any other living man in the universe. Racer, who had tried to take Cidra as a battle prize while he left his former partner to die.

A band of dark green slithered through the light green river grass ahead of Severance. Automatically he brought the pulser up and trained it on the wedge-shaped head. But the green slicer apparently had better things to do than sample a jungle boot. It moved out of the way, shivering iridescently in the morning light. Behind him Severance heard a startled squawk that ended with telling abruptness. The green slicer had found another meal.

Severance kept moving, using the utility knife when the tangled vines became too thick to push aside. He tried to calculate how far Racer could get with a failing set of fuel cells. The second and third pulser shots this morning had done real damage; Severance was sure of it. But it was difficult to tell how far the craft would go before it started sinking toward the water line. As long as Racer ran the skimmer at top speed, the end was bound to come quickly. And he was certain Racer would force the craft as far as he could at the highest possible speed. Racer was the nervous type under pressure. He tended to panic.

That tendency was a side of the man few people would ever know. Only when you had worked with a man in a high-pressure situation did you learn his real weaknesses, the ones that could get you killed. Severance had learned them the hard way. Finding yourself facing a killweaver alone had a way of making a lasting impression.

So he'd learned his lesson. Never trust anyone—except perhaps a Harmonic—completely. Severance's partnership with Racer had dissolved. Life went on, and Severance saw to it that he and Racer rarely came into contact. Racer had been cooperative in that respect. Severance also avoided any more attempts at forming a partnership. Severance Pay, Ltd., he'd decided, would take a slightly slower route to success.

There was a flurry of black wings up ahead. Severance paused and gave the flying reptile the chance to get off the ground with its prey impaled in its toothed beak. Then he started moving again, circling a stand of suspicious-looking flowers. Anything as beautiful as those flowers had to be deadly on this planet.

A pair of eyes watched him from the river. Severance didn't look at them. For the rest of his life, whenever he saw dracon eyes, he would think of those sickening moments when Cidra had been the center of dracon attention. The memory made his hand tighten on the grip of the pulser. Deliberately he forced himself to relax. A too-solid grip made the weapon more difficult to aim properly.

Cidra had floated. The image of her hovering quietly in the water as the dracons moved closer was still a source of amazement to Severance. Doing so had been her only chance, of course. She had bought him the time he needed to find the monsters another meal. But the terror would have overcome most people, *should* have overcome a gently raised lady from

Clementia. Most people would have panicked. But Cidra had heard his desperate instructions and she had obeyed them.

Racer had put her to that savage test and nearly gotten her killed. And it was Racer who had tried to carry her off, knowing with a man's sure instinct that Severance's helpless rage would be a worse torment than the knowledge that the deflector screens were going to fail by nightfall.

Severance had half convinced himself that Cidra might be better off with her captor than left behind to face the Renaissance night, but that belief had been his rational, thinking side speaking. His emotional side hadn't come close to seeing that logic. His guts had been twisted with fury at the thought of Racer trying to rape Cidra. And it would have been rape. Cidra would never willingly submit to Racer. She would have seen it as a betrayal of herself and of Severance.

"Death before dishonor." He wondered where she'd picked up that phrase. Probably from those First Family tales she was so fond of reading. No telling where the First Family writers had picked up the concept. Must have been a part of the folklore they had brought with them to their new world.

Even though he had feared for her life when she had dived from the skimmer, Severance acknowledged that a part of him had been exultant. Cidra belonged to him, and on some level she had acknowledged that. He didn't know any other woman who would have chosen to stay behind with him in a Renaissance jungle when the alternative was some hope of survival.

He swore silently. He was getting as primitive in his reactions as everything else on this planet.

The time slipped past. Severance heard no distant hum from the skimmer. But he did perceive a change in the atmosphere, a lengthening shadow from the heavy, bloated clouds building high overhead. Just what he needed, Severance thought—a storm. Renaissance did thunderstorms the way it did everything else—on a grand scale.

Heavy rain would have no effect on the deflector screens surrounding Cidra, and she could stay reasonably dry in the tent, but the storm was bound to be unnerving for her. And it could slow him down. He had to get back to Cidra before the deflectors went down. With common sense, a certain amount of knowledge, luck, and a pulser, a man might survive Renaissance during the day. Night was another story. The only consolation was that the storm would also slow the failing skimmer. Maybe Racer would start to panic sooner than he might otherwise.

The cloud shadows had nearly blocked out the sunlight entirely when Severance detoured around a broad-leafed tree that was as thick in the trunk as a small building. Suddenly he realized that he could hear metallic sounds. Not the hum of a skimmer—for an instant he thought he might have had the unbelievably good luck of happening across someone else camped on the riverbank.

He slowed, using the thick foliage for concealment, and edged toward the sounds. Severance saw the skimmer first. It had been pulled into shore and made fast. Racer had apparently used the crisper to carve out a small clearing on the bank. He wouldn't want anything sneaking up on him while he was occupied with the skimmer, and from the hot, sweaty look of him, he had already been working on the machinery for quite a while. He had left the engine panel in the stern open and was bent over the controls inside.

Seeing Racer, Severance felt a wave of seething fury sweep through him. He grimly waited for it to pass. It would only cause his hand to shake and his brain to function on partial power. It wasn't the way for a predator to confront prey. And, this time around, Racer was the prey.

Severance gave himself another moment or two to control the anger, and then, pulser raised, he stepped out into the open.

"Don't waste your time on it, Racer. You won't be needing transportation."

Racer's head came up with a hard jerk that betrayed his nervous state. For a second he simply stared at Severance from the stern of the skimmer. There was desperation in his face, something Severance had never seen in him before. He stepped closer.

Racer threw himself down onto the deck of the skimmer. Severance fired the pulser, not at the empty stern but at the diazite cabin wall. The wall crackled and exploded, sending a shower of jagged shards down onto the man hiding behind the gunwale.

There were several startled screams and a brief scurrying in the vegetation behind Severance as a few of the local inhabitants opted to vacate the area. He knew that while some fled, others would be big enough and hungry enough to indulge their curiosity. They would come closer to investigate.

But the diazite shower had had the desired effect. Only something as powerful as a pulser could break up diazite, but when it did fracture, the shards were like jagged blades. Racer didn't wait for the next wall of the cabin to be splintered. Pulser in hand, he leapt over the side, using the craft as cover while he waded the short distance to shore. He risked a shot over the bow, driving Severance behind the house-sized tree, and then ran for shelter at the edge of the small clearing he had made with the crisper.

"It's all over, you renegade bastard," Severance called. "Did you really think I'd let you get away with it?"

"You don't stand a chance without the skimmer and screens, Severance. Throw down the pulser and I'll consider a deal."

"You don't have anything to bargain with. I'm claiming the skimmer."

"You'll never get close to it. From here I can cut you down before you get aboard." Racer wasted a pulser shot demonstrating his line of sight. A small vine that had been missed earlier by the hurried crisping job fizzled, smoked, and died. "Won't do you any good, anyway. You really did a job on those fuel cells. The only thing working on that damn boat is the communication equipment. I was just about to put in a call. We're both stuck here, Severance, until I make that call."

Severance listened as Racer moved uneasily on the other side of the clearing. "I was always better with equipment than you were, Racer. Remember?"

A pulser shot was the answer. Overhead several huge leaves crumpled. The angle of the shot was different. Racer was trying to edge around the clearing. Severance slipped away from the shelter of the tree trunk, paused to let a small creature with oversize antenna scurry out of the way, and then padded quietly to a different position.

"Be careful, Racer. You never know whose mouth you'll step into out here. Maybe something like a killweaver. Something that takes its time sucking a man dry."

There was a silence from the other side of the clearing. Too much silence. Severance could guess what Racer's imagination must be doing to him. He knew damn well that his own imagination was operating in high gear. Grimly he clamped down on it, refusing to let himself see fangs in every trailing vine. That kind of thinking wasn't going to get him far. Slowly he worked deeper into the vegetation. Racer would stay close to the clearing's edge while he tried to find Severance.

There was a flash of movement at Severance's right shoulder. He froze. A long, forked tongue emerged from between jaws that could grind rocks. The tongue tasted the air and then delicately extended to taste Severance's sleeve.

There was no way he could lift the pulser and fire it before the scaled head struck. Severance didn't move, hoping the fabric of his sleeve wouldn't taste very good. Beyond the tongue, two small eyes that looked like bottomless pits stared at him. The tongue touched the sleeve and flicked about in confusion. Severance didn't move.

"I'm willing to talk, Severance. We can deal. We were partners once. For old time's sake I'm willing to make a deal."

Racer's voice came from somewhere behind Severance. He didn't dare turn around. He would have to rely on the vegetation to conceal him while he waited for the tongue to finish sampling his sleeve. The death that lurked in the creature's eyes was closer and more certain than the death in Racer's weapon.

At the sound of the voice from another location the tongue darted about in more agitated confusion. Finally it disappeared back into the rock-crunching jaws. With another flash of movement the baleful eyes vanished too. Severance began to breathe again. Turning slowly, he listened to Racer. The other man was only a few meters away now, but he couldn't yet be seen.

"You'll need my help to get back to the camp. You left your little Harmonic there, didn't you? If you don't get back by dusk, she'll be food. Come on, Severance. You don't want that. The longer you play this hunt-and-stalk game, the weaker those deflectors are getting."

Severance said nothing. He was too close. He caught a glimpse of clothing as Racer edged forward in the undergrowth. The other man slipped past within arm's reach.

"I'm going to call for help, Severance. Another skimmer can get here by midday tomorrow. You want that distress call put in as much as I do."

Severance waited a few more seconds and then glided forward until he was directly behind the other man. "Drop the pulser or I'll end this now."

Racer went still, but he didn't drop the weapon. "You won't kill me, Severance. You need my help. And I'm willing to give it."

"I need you about as much as I need a visit from a dracon. Drop the pulser."

"Bastard!" Racer broke, diving into the tangled vines and leaves to his right.

Severance raised the pulser but held his fire as he listened to the other man charging wildly through the undergrowth. Racer was in full flight, and he was in a panic.

The scream that echoed through the jungle a moment later was almost anticlimactic. Severance tensed, waiting for it to be cut off with the usual deadly abruptness. He didn't want to think about what had gotten Racer.

But the scream didn't die. It kept reverberating, chilling Severance's nerves. He would have given a great deal of credit to have it cease. But there was no escape from it. Racer kept screaming.

There was no walking away from that kind of human fear and despair. No man deserved to die that slowly. Severance worked his way toward the terrified cries. He kept the pulser in front of him, dreading what he might see. The sound wasn't shifting direction. Whatever held Racer was confident enough not to bother carrying its prey back to its lair.

Severance edged around a leaf wider than he was tall and stared at the predator that held the screaming man. It was a flower. The most spectacularly beautiful flower he had ever seen. Huge, lacy petals shimmered gold and purple and red, the colors flowing into each other. The whole thing was twice as big as Racer.

He had blundered into the very heart of the flower and was

now held fast by a sticky center. The huge, lacy petals were just beginning to fold shut, enclosing their prey. Racer's pulser lay on the soft, musty ground.

"Severance! Severance, save me! Stop it. You can't let this happen. You know you can't. You'd never be able to live with yourself. You were always so big on doing things by your own damned code. Let me die like this and your reeting honor won't mean a thing. And you'll know it. You'll know it, even if no one else does. For the rest of your life you'll know it. You'll have to live with it the way I've lived with it. Waiting. Always waiting for someone to find out."

Severance looked at the flower, fascinated by the lethal beauty. The edges of a couple of the lacy leaves had just begun to cradle Racer as if he were a lover. Racer screamed again as he felt their touch. He tried to pull one hand free from the sticky substance and failed. His face was a mask of growing terror.

"Severance, it's starting to eat me. I can feel it. Stop it. You've got to stop it!"

"I'm trying to think of one good reason." Severance waited. "Come on, Racer. Give me one good reason. After what you've done . . ."

"It was an accident," Racer screamed. He was almost incoherent now. "I never meant to kill him. He wasn't supposed to die. How did I know he'd follow that signal into the ground? Do you hear me, Severance? I didn't intend to kill Jeude."

Severance felt as if a giant shock wave had caught him and hurled him to the ground. He was still standing, but there was something wrong. He wanted to scream too. Not in fear but in rage. Slowly he raised the pulser and took aim at the base of the flower. He squeezed the trigger. It took three shots to eat through the tough fibers of the deceptively graceful stem.

The flower, severed from its base, fell limply to the jungle floor. Racer was still trapped inside. He was weeping uncontrollably when Severance reached him. Carefully Severance pried open the lacy leaves, using the pulser once or twice. Then, avoiding any contact with the sticky, hairy heart, he reached down and pulled Racer free.

It was hard work. The flower, even dead, did not willingly he raingive up its prey. When Racer at last rolled free, Severance saw that his clothing had already been dissolved in places and that there were bright red marks on the skin that showed through the holes.

"Get up."

Racer crouched at Severance's feet, still weeping.

"I said, get up."

Racer shook his head, brushing his eyes against his sleeve. "You'll kill me. I knew you would. I figured you'd rather do it than let that . . . that *thing* do it once I told you about Jeude. A pulser's better than being eaten alive."

"Why, Racer? Why couldn't you just stay the hell out of my way? Why did you have to kill Jeude? Why did you try to take Cidra? You should have just come after me, Racer. You should never have gone after them."

"This time I figured I had you too," the kneeling man whimpered. His voice broke into a hoarse whisper. "I couldn't stand it any more."

"Couldn't stand what?"

"The way you look through me as if I weren't worth a single credit. I knew what you were thinking. I kept wondering when you'd decide to have a laugh and tell someone else what really happened that day in the sinkswamp. You knew what it was doing to me. Never knowing when you'd decide the game had gone on long enough. You were just biding your time, waiting for a really good moment to tell everyone how I'd left you to face that killweaver. And after you'd made your announcement

I'd never have worked as a mail pilot again. No one would have trusted me. I couldn't let you hold that weapon over me forever, Severance."

"Why did you go after Jeude?" Severance realized that his hand was trembling. He ached to pull the trigger.

"It was supposed to be you," Racer said bleakly, staring at the spongy ground. "It was supposed to be you in that ship. I didn't know you'd stayed behind until afterward. All I wanted was the cargo. I wanted to make it look like you'd sold the cargo to a higher bidder. But the sandstorm came up so quickly. Jeude didn't stop following the distress beacon. He just kept riding it."

"Right into the storm and then into the ground. I should have left you in the flower, Racer."

"You wouldn't," Racer said. "You couldn't. That's the thing about you, Severance. You're soft in some ways. Too soft." He climbed slowly to his feet, more assured now. "I don't think you're going to use the pulser, either. You'd have done it by now if you were capable of killing me in cold blood. You'll take me back for a nice, neat legal trial, won't you?"

"Sorry, Racer. I've got better things to do than see you get that kind of justice. Besides, a good trial costs credit." Lowering the pulser, Severance walked around the man, heading back the way he had come.

"Severance!"

Severance ignored him. He didn't trust himself to turn. It would be so easy to use the pulser. The memory of Jeude and the image of Cidra filled his head. The pulser grip was warm in his hand. Too easy. Racer didn't deserve it that easy.

"Severance, you can't leave me!"

There was a scrambling sound behind him. Severance heard it and knew instinctively that Racer wouldn't risk tackling him, which left only one other explanation for the frantic, scuffling movements. Racer was going for the weapon he had dropped when the flower had caught him. Severance swung around and fired just as Racer, kneeling, raised the pulser he had found. He gave only one short, chopped-off cry. The familiar, horribly abrupt scream of one more Renaissance victim.

Severance lowered the pulser. Too easy. Jeude's killer should have died more slowly. He had wanted Renaissance to execute the sentence in its own inevitable, fearsome manner. The fact that neither Jeude nor Cidra would have wanted that kind of end for Racer was immaterial. They had nothing to say about it. Severance was the judge, the jury, and the executioner.

The rain broke out in a torrent. Severance holstered the pulser and raced for the skimmer. Water would be filling the engine housing already. Racer had left the panel open when he had been surprised. Renaissance was so good at destroying equipment.

The rain caught Cidra by surprise. She had watched the clouds build up all afternoon, but the sudden, drenching downpour had begun without any warning drops. The skies of Renaissance simply opened. She dashed for the tent and was thankful to find it dry inside. Huddled on a sleeper, she went back to doing what she had been doing since Severance had left: she waited and thought.

A great deal went through her mind as she sat in a position of meditation. Thoughts of Clementia's tranquil gardens, memories of the games of Free Market she had played with Severance, and a desperate curiosity to know what was happening between Severance and Racer all crowded her head. The one thing she didn't allow herself to think about was the amount of time left on the deflector screens. She had checked the controls before escaping into the tent, and she knew the charge was already beginning to weaken.

The rain was a steady roar on the curved shell of the tent. At least the drumming was a change from listening to the screams, clickings and occasional thrashing noises that were a part of normal jungle life. Cidra tried meditating and found it impossible to concentrate. She consoled herself with the thought that even a true Harmonic would have had trouble meditating under such circumstances.

That thought only led her to the next, inevitable bit of logic. She was farther than ever now from being a true Harmonic. Everything from her interest in gambling to her growing hunger for Severance's brief, possessive kisses was ample evidence that she had too much Wolf in her. She had to face the possibility that even if she found the relic for which she searched, she might never be entirely free of her Wolf heritage.

And if Severance did not succeed in finding Racer, neither of them would be free of this damned jungle. Surprisingly she wasn't as worried about that as she ought to have been. She discovered that she had a great deal of faith in Teague Severance's abilities. She also knew that when he found Racer and secured the skimmer, he would be back for her. She knew it with the same certainty as she knew the deflectors were going to fail by nightfall.

Cidra was not at all so sure of what would happen to Racer when Severance found him. Or perhaps she simply didn't want to think about it. What would it do to Severance if he killed a man? Perhaps he had killed in the past. She had no way of knowing. She had seen so much violence already during her short visit to Renaissance. The planet seemed to inspire it. Only a true Wolf could survive here. Cidra didn't want to imagine what would happen if a group of Harmonics was abandoned on Renaissance.

The steady roar of the rain became hypnotic. Gradually Cidra stopped thinking about what might be happening to Severance. She sat quietly and just listened to the rain, which sounded as if it would come down forever. On and on it poured, the sound driving out all other thought. Cidra drifted in her mind, staring at the curving wall of the tent.

The first, gentle call passed by her almost unnoticed. Cidra became vaguely aware of a feeling of curiosity. For some reason she was suddenly interested in exploring the world outside the tent. She shook off the odd thought. It was utterly impossible. There was no point in getting soaking wet again today. Drying off after the swim in the river had taken long enough. She dismissed the strange curiosity and went back to drifting in her mind. The rain continued to beat down on the metal tent. Outside, the charge on the deflector control panels went down two more levels.

Another soft tendril of thought curled in her head, beckoning pleasantly. Not all of Renaissance was violence and death. This was a beautiful world that had once been under control.

Cidra lifted her chin from where it had been resting on her folded arms and stared, puzzled, at the tent wall. Under control? She wondered where that thought had sprung from. She shifted position, wishing there was something constructive she could do. This business of waiting, knowing nothing of what was happening to Severance, seemed to be affecting her brain. She wondered if he could even move in the skimmer in this rain.

There seemed to be a slight altering in the steady beat of the water. Cidra waited until she was reasonably sure of the change in intensity and then unsealed the iris opening. It did appear that the rain was lessening. The knowledge brought a measure of relief. One less obstacle for Severance to surmount.

The rain passed slowly but surely, leaving in its wake a jungle smelling fresher than usual. Cidra was surprised at the almost pleasant fragrance. Also, the squeaks and screams seemed to have faded as everything took shelter. There were a few calls from the creatures living high in the trees but no close screams. Cidra unsealed the iris closure completely and stepped outside.

The ground was muddy, but in general, the water had drained off quickly into the river. Overhead, the clouds were already breaking up. Unfortunately the sunlight was not returning with reassuring warmth. Stanza Nine was already sinking slowly over the green horizon. Cidra listened to the occasional hiss of the deflectors and shivered. She didn't want to examine the control panel again.

She was standing near the edge of the bank, staring out over the river when she caught sight of the skimmer. Incredible relief swept through her, even as she realized that there was no accompanying hum of the craft's engines.

"Severance!" Belatedly she realized that he was poling the floating skimmer, using a long, thick limb to keep the craft away from the bank. In complete silence the skimmer glided toward her. Cidra saw that two of the cabin walls were shattered. Frantically she scanned Severance's body as he jumped into the shallows and pulled the craft into shore. Diazite tinkled on the deck of the boat. Cidra knew what it must have taken to shatter the tough material.

"It's all right, Cidra. I've got the screens." Wearily he made fast the boat and turned to face her.

Cidra took one look at him and knew what had happened to Racer. "Oh, Severance." She ran forward, throwing her arms around him. He was hot and sweaty, and there was a feeling emanating from him that she could only describe as hard and bleak. It made her want to cry. Instead she hugged him even more fiercely. "I've been so frightened for you."

His arms went around her. "It's all right. It's over."

She didn't ask about Racer. Instead she helped him finish securing the boat, and then she carried the screens ashore as he handed them to her from the cargo hold. The deflectors were the first concern. The old ones were stored in the skimmer as the new ones took over.

"There's not enough power left in the fuel cells to get the skimmer off the water, but there is enough to keep the deflectors charged. I've stopped the fuel leak. Be careful of the diazite," Severance added as Cidra stepped into the craft.

"I wanted to see if there are any prespacs on board." She walked carefully forward and opened the galley bin. There were several prespacs containing meat and two containing vegetables. Gratefully she pulled out two packages—one for her and one for Severance—and shoved them into the tiny skimmer heater. Food was what Severance needed.

When she brought his heated prespac into the tent, she found him sitting on a sleeper. He looked up without much interest as she handed him the food.

"Thanks."

Cidra reached down and found the container of Renaissance Rose ale she had rescued and held it out to him with a tentative smile. He raised an eyebrow in surprise, and then his hand wrapped around it. Without a word he downed a good portion of the brew.

"You know how to welcome a man home," he said. Then he slipped back into his bleak silence.

They ate without talking for several minutes. Cidra was aching to ask questions but afraid to interrupt whatever thoughts were going through Severance's head. He seemed very remote this evening. More distant than she had ever seen him. When he finally spoke, it was to give her a few facts.

"The communication equipment has to have a chance to dry out completely. It's housed in the engine compartment, and that got flooded. We won't be able to make any calls until morning." He went back to chewing methodically.

Cidra hesitated and then asked, "What if the comm equipment doesn't work when it's dried out?"

"The worst possible case is that we have to pole the skimmer down the river the way I did this afternoon. It's slow going and there are some risks, but it works. We'll do it that way if necessary." Severance lapsed back into silence.

Cidra could think of nothing to say, no way to break through the barrier that existed between them. In silence they prepared for bed, crawling into separate sleepers. For a long time Cidra lay awake, aware that Severance was staring into the darkness.

"Severance?"

"What is it, Cidra?"

"You had to kill him, didn't you?"

"I killed him." The words were flat, final.

Cidra lay in silence, wondering what to say next. Severance needed comfort, and she knew he would never ask for it. She wasn't even sure how to go about offering it to him. But then she felt that trying was pointless. He would reject it.

But after another long silence Cidra shifted in the darkness. She unfastened her sleeper. And then she reached out to unfasten Severance's sleeper.

"Are you scared again tonight, Cidra?" He didn't move as she slipped in beside him. She could feel the tight tension in him.

"Yes," she whispered. But not of the jungle outside, she added silently. She was frightened by the remoteness in him, terrified by the memories he must be rerunning in his head. He cradled her against him, and she felt the taut muscles in his arm. He hadn't even begun to relax, but she knew he must be thoroughly exhausted.

"Go to sleep, Cidra."

"I won't be able to sleep until you do."

He turned his head to look down at her as she lay in the circle of his arm. "Then you're going to be awake a long time."

"I know." She put her palm on his bare chest.

"Cidra, I think you'd better go back to your own sleeper. I'm not feeling normal. I'm not feeling in control."

"It's all right, Severance." She nestled closer.

"I want you."

"I know."

"You don't understand," he said roughly.

"I understand." She waited.

Severance shuddered, then turned suddenly and pinned her beneath him. His mouth came down on hers with the urgency of a man who is running toward the promise of safety in a wild and uncontrolled land.

Chapter
Twelve

Cidra was startled by the sudden intensity of hunger she felt in him. Severance overwhelmed her. She had thought him exhausted, in need of comfort and human warmth; she had wanted to offer him gentleness and relaxation. But he was gathering her to him as if what she had to offer was life itself. As though he would feed on her in some manner.

"Sweet Harmony in hell, Cidra. I need you."

His urgent mouth tasted her, following the line of her jaw to the curve of her throat. She flinched in surprise when she felt the edge of his teeth and then shuddered from the excitement of the sensation. Her gilded fingertips sank into his sleek shoulders, and she turned her head into his throat. He groaned when she touched him first with her lips and then tried out her own sharp little teeth. The shudder that went through him was reward enough to tempt her further. Cidra's arms slipped higher, curving around his neck.

"Yes. Tighter. Hold me as tight as you can, Cidra."

She obeyed, her uncertainty fading as a new wave of feeling took its place. His mouth locked on hers, in an intimate contact that enthralled her. She parted her lips at his urging, allowing him inside. Severance didn't hesitate. In his hunger he would take everything she gave. His tongue tangled with hers. Cidra moaned softly as the wealth of sensation poured through her. She closed her eyes and let herself edge closer to a whirlwind she could not yet name.

Severance's hands had been cupping her face, holding her still for his heavy kisses. Now his palms slipped down, seeking the fastening of the shirt Cidra wore. He raised himself a little bit away from her, and she shivered when his fingers parted the material. Then he pushed aside the fabric and lowered himself back down on top of her. Cidra's soft breasts were gently crushed beneath the unyielding hardness of his chest. It was a strangely satisfying kind of pressure, and she instinctively moved beneath him.

"Cidra, my sweet, strong Cidra. You're so soft." The words were a dark murmur against her skin as Severance shifted his weight.

Cidra felt his hands gliding over her shoulders and down to her breasts. When his fingers found one budding nipple and began to stroke it, she whispered his name far back in her throat.

The small cry seemed to please him. It also fed the physical urgency in Severance. He lowered his head, taking the taut nipple between his teeth. Cidra shivered as excitement unfurled deep in her body. Her leg moved languidly, sliding over his. The fabric of their trousers was an unnatural barrier, one she no longer wanted.

Severance took instant advantage of her small, unconsciously enticing movement. He pushed his leg between hers, letting her feel for the first time the waiting heat in his lower body. Even through the clothing Cidra was made fully aware of the straining male power in him. She wanted time to grow accustomed to the physical changes going on in herself as well as in him. But Severance seemed driven now. He went to work on the unfastening of her trousers.

"Lift up, Cidra. Hurry, sweetheart. I can't wait much longer for you." His hand was under her buttocks, raising her slightly so that he could force the pants down her legs.

His hand followed the clothing as she pushed aside the trousers. She felt his fingers curling into her hips, her thigh, and her calf. Then the trousers were gone and she lay nude beneath him. Her lashes lifted, and she found herself looking deeply into his shadowed gaze.

There was a drawn harshness in his face that brought back some of her earlier uncertainty. This wasn't how she expected a Wolf to look when he made love. She had always imagined that there would be more gentleness, a kind of lingering tenderness.

She felt very vulnerable. At the same time there was a heated excitement flowing through her that even the uncertainty couldn't quell. This was Severance. Everything was all right with him. Tentatively Cidra drew her palms down his back, feeling the strong, muscled contours.

His hand flattened on her stomach, and he stroked her as he whispered rough words of desire against her throat. She responded to the words as much as to the touch, trembling a little as his hand moved lower. When his fingers tangled in the dark nest of hair above her thighs, she gasped.

"It's all right sweetheart. It's all right. It's going to be so good. I swear, it's going to be good. I need you so much. Let me touch you. Just relax and let me touch you."

Under the soothing onslaught of his words she parted her

legs, allowing him an intimacy that left her feeling dazed. His hand slid lower, fingertips drawing strange, curling patterns over a part of her that had become unbearably sensitized.

"Severance?"

"You're so hot and damp." He seemed awed by the response he was evoking. "So welcoming and ready. I want everything, Cidra." He rested his head on her breasts. "I know I should take this more slowly. But I can't. . . . You don't know how it's been for me. I want you so damned much."

She laced her fingers into the depths of his hair. "I want you, too, Severance." The whispered confession startled her. But as soon as the words were out, she realized that they were nothing less than the truth. All thought of dispensing comfort or human warmth had vanished. She ached for something else now. There was a growing need to have him closer. His hand moved again between her thighs, and this time she knew she wanted more. She lifted herself, pleading silently for even more intimacy.

He pulled away from her with a muffled groan, fumbling with the trousers he still wore. In the shadows she saw the strong shape of his thighs, the flat planes of his hips and stomach. There was an alluring strength in him that made the blood sing in her veins. Cidra felt at once light-headed and heavy. When Severance came back down beside her, gathering her close again, she was aware of the strong, hard thrust of his manhood pressing against her.

"Open yourself for me, my love." His hand was on her inner thigh, gently but firmly pushing apart her legs. She clung to him as he slid into the warm place he had made for himself.

"Severance, it feels good. So strange, but good."

"I know. Sweet Harmony in hell, I know."

She felt him move closer, felt the blunt, probing shaft at the gate of her femininity. He was moistening himself with the dampness he had brought forth there. She moved, savoring the promise of even more intense sensations.

"Now, Severance?"

"It has to be now. I'll go crazy if I wait any longer. Look at me, Cidra." She opened her eyes and saw the barely controlled desire in his narrowed gaze. "I want to see your eyes when I take you. I want to see if you really understand this."

"I understand."

"I'm not talking about the kind of knowledge you've known before from books. I want to know you understand what this *means*." He groaned deep in his chest. "Ah, hell, I can't explain it and I can't wait. Hold on to me, Cidra. Just hold on and whatever happens, don't let go."

She obeyed, her hands on his shoulders as she felt him surge against her. The short, sharp pain took her by surprise, and she opened her mouth to cry out. But he covered her lips with his own, drinking the small, startled sound as he continued to push forward in a single, strong thrust. Only when he was embedded in her did he stop and give her a chance to adjust. She felt a shudder go through him as he fought to control himself.

But Cidra wasn't at all sure she could adjust. Her body had tensed instinctively at the moment he had entered her, and now, instead of the deliciously satisfying feeling she had been anticipating, she was aware only of feeling invaded.

"Easy, sweetheart. Don't fight it. Trust me. Can you trust me, Cidra? Give me a chance to show you what it's supposed to be like."

Her tongue touched the edge of her parted lips. Her breath was coming in quick little gasps as she met his eyes. "I trust you."

He muttered something she couldn't quite catch, nestling

his head beside hers as he slowly, carefully, began to move within her.

Cidra waited, unsure of what to expect next. But the too-tight sensation faded beneath a compelling rhythm that gradually became far more important than the initial discomfort. Slowly she began to echo the pattern Severance was establishing, lifting to meet his heavy thrusts. One of his hands slid down to cup her buttock.

"That's it, sweetheart. You feel so right. So perfect."

She tightened her arms around him as her body began to eagerly seek each new surging thrust. Each time he withdrew slightly, she sank her nails into his skin, pulling him back with a fierceness that seemed to deepen his desire. The driving strokes filled her until she thought she would burst.

"Ah, Cidra, I can't stop. I can't wait."

She wasn't certain what he meant, but she tried to reassure him, anyway. "Severance, it's all right. It's all right," she whispered, unconsciously using the same words he had used earlier.

"*Cidra!*" He drove deeply into her one last time, and his body shuddered heavily. There was an exultant shout caught somewhere in his throat, and then slowly he collapsed along the length of her.

For a long time Cidra lay still beneath him, her palms tenderly stroking the damp skin of his back. She felt him recover his breath, felt his heartbeat return to normal, and then he slowly lifted his head to look down at her. In the shadows his gray eyes were dark and unreadable. He touched her mouth with his fingertip. She smiled tremulously. He didn't respond. Instead he searched her face.

"Are you all right?" he finally asked.

"I think so." Her smile widened. "What about you?"

He bent his head and brushed her lips with his own. "I'm

much better than all right. I feel normal again. Better than normal. I feel good. Very tired and very good. Because of you, Cidra." He cradled her head in the curve of his arm. "Go to sleep, sweetheart. Next time I promise it will be better for you."

She stretched a little and nestled against him, inhaling the musky scent of his body. "I can't imagine it being any better. I felt so close to you, Severance. I've never felt that close to another human being in my life. Maybe that's why Wolves are so interested in sex."

He chuckled sleepily. "Maybe. I wish I could show you how really good it can be for you. Next time. I promise you that next time I won't be so damned exhausted and so out of control."

"Go to sleep, Severance. It's been a long day."

"You can say that again," he said, the words fading as he closed his eyes and slipped into deep sleep almost at once.

Cidra stayed curled in his arm, wondering why she wasn't equally sleepy. For a long time she lay still, thinking of the jumble of emotions and physical sensations she had experienced during the day. They had all culminated tonight in Severance's arms. His lovemaking had left her feeling dazzled and dazed. She wasn't quite certain what to make of the experience. It had been, as she had anticipated, a very physical act, and yet there had been so much more. The feeling of oneness, the sense of closeness, had been totally unexpected, and it added a whole new dimension.

Dreamily she listened to the usual cacophony of night sounds from the jungle. A curious lethargy stole over her, but she was no nearer sleep than she had been earlier. It wasn't Severance who was keeping her awake now. In the darkness she could make out the hard lines of his face. They didn't appear any softer in repose than they did when he was awake. Cidra wondered what he would say to her in the morning. And then she occupied several long minutes wondering what she would say to him.

The first words after a night like this ought to be significant, she thought. But she wasn't sure in what way. The knowledge that their relationship had been fundamentally altered was vaguely disturbing. It had been easier when she had been able to consider herself simply a temporary member of his crew. Now she wasn't sure what category she fit into.

The night sounds didn't seem as harsh tonight. After a while Cidra realized that she wasn't hearing very many of the usual chopped-off screams. That was a relief. It made one think of what this planet might have been like if it hadn't evolved along such violent lines. It might have had some truly beautiful places in it, places that offered a green and welcoming tranquillity. Places where even a Harmonic might feel at home.

There were such places here, Cidra thought with sudden certainty. And they weren't far away. The jungle outside wasn't as dangerous as it seemed. A person simply had to understand it. Humans were always struggling to subdue it, and, of course, the jungle had to fight back. But if a woman simply walked into it looking for the tranquil places, she would find them. They were so close.

Slowly Cidra slipped away from the shelter of Severance's arm. He didn't stir. She sat up, listening. The night noises were definitely quieter and less threatening this evening. The twin moons would be shining, illuminating a path through the thick foliage. It would be an easy matter to follow that path to the gentle, tranquil spaces hidden in the jungle.

Her compulsion to follow the moonlit path grew. Moonlight and Mirrors. She knew how to chase moonlight in mirrors. The jungles of Renaissance were open to her. All she had to do was walk into them.

Cidra got up and pulled on her trousers. Then she reached for her shirt. She found her boots near the tent entrance. When she had them on, she opened the iris closure and stepped out into the night.

She had been right. The twin moons were shining very brilliantly tonight, revealing a path through the jungle. Borgia and Medici weren't their true names, she decided. They had once been called by other names, names that she couldn't quite say. The words were strange in her head. Without any hesitation Cidra turned toward the path.

Severance came awake with the startling certainty that something was wrong. He turned on his side and realized that Cidra's warm weight was no longer pinning his arm.

"Cidra?"

When there was no response, a flare of panic reared up within him. He got to his feet. She was not in her own sleeper.

"Cidra!" Memories of her in his arms flooded his mind. And along with those memories came others. She wanted to be a Harmonic more than she wanted anything else. After tonight she would feel farther than ever from her goal. How would she react to that? He felt slightly sick as he reached for his boots. Surely she wouldn't do anything rash just because she had been forced to face the fact that she was a true Wolf. It had hardly been rape, for Harmony's sake. He'd seen the passion in her eyes, felt the throbbing, moist warmth between her legs. She had clung to him with a woman's stirring need.

But what if she hadn't been able to accept her own desires afterward? Severance thought wildly. He ignored the rest of his clothes and activated the tent opening with a savage twist of his hand. An instant later he was outside.

He saw her almost at once and breathed a sigh of relief. Then he realized that she was on the other side of the deflector screens, heading into the wall of vegetation.

"Cidra! Come back here. What in a renegade's hell do you think you're doing?" Severance raced through the screens, reaching for Cidra as she started into the mass of night-darkened greenery surrounding the campsite. He caught her shoulder and spun her around.

"Severance?" She smiled, but she didn't seem to be quite focusing on him. She waved her hand gracefully at the jungle. "Isn't it beautiful tonight? I never realized how beautiful it was."

"What's the matter with you? Are you out of your mind? If you think I'm going to let you walk into that green hell just because you finally discovered sex, you're dumber than a no-vakeet." He yanked her back toward the safety of the screens.

"But, Severance, it's not a green hell. That's what I'm trying to tell you."

"You're dreaming on your feet. Why didn't you ever tell me you walk in your sleep?"

"I don't walk in my sleep. Severance, there's no need to hide behind the screens anymore."

He ignored that, pulling her through the invisible safety net. There he turned to confront her. The moonlight seemed to shine in her eyes as she looked up at him. Something was wrong, and he couldn't figure out what it was. He tried shaking her gently. She blinked and some of the moonlight seemed to fade from her gaze. He got the impression that she was starting to really see him. He clasped her shoulders firmly and tried another small shake.

"Cidra, listen to me. I don't know what you think you're doing, but I'll be damned if I'm going to let you do anything stupid because of what happened tonight. You're coming back into that tent with me. In the morning everything will be all right. You'll see."

She frowned slightly, almost thoughtfully. "I'd rather not go back into the tent with you, Severance."

"You haven't got any choice, damn it!" He picked her up and carried her back to the opening. He stepped through and set her down on his sleeper. Methodically, he began stripping off her clothing.

"Severance, listen to me."

"Why? So that you can give me some illogical reason for trying to commit suicide?"

She seemed genuinely shocked. "I wasn't trying to commit suicide."

"You're upset because of what happened between us." He tugged off her boots. "I can understand that. First time around, sex is a little upsetting. Like everything else, it improves with practice. I know I wasn't the greatest lover between here and QED tonight, but I'd had a tough day. That's no excuse for you to start thinking in terms of death before dishonor. I didn't rape you, Cidra."

"I know that," she said gently.

He sat on the edge of the sleeper and yanked off his own boots. "Furthermore, you liked it. Or at least you liked most of it." He bore her back down onto the sleeper, sprawling across her so that her legs were pinned beneath his. "This time around I'll see to it that you like all of it. I swear it."

Before she could protest, he sealed her mouth with his own. Beneath him he felt her stir, and the movement of her naked body began the chain reaction that led to the hardening in his groin. Severance forced himself to stay under control. He was going to make it right for her. If he satisfied her completely, maybe she would be able to accept her normal passions. She had to accept them. Damned if he would let her kill herself because he'd made love to her.

Clamping down on his rioting reactions, Severance delib-

erately began to stroke and coax the response he wanted from
Cidra. After a brief struggle that seemed to stem more from
her surprise and confusion than any real desire to fight him,
she stopped resisting. Her arms went around his neck, and he
knew a vast sense of relief. It was going to be all right this
time. He could make her want him.

"Say it, Cidra. Say you want me." He probed between her
legs, finding the nubbin of exquisitely sensitive female flesh.
He flicked lightly with his fingers and felt her react almost at
once. "Say it, sweetheart."

"I want you," she whispered, arching against his hand.

He kept up the light teasing between her thighs while he
lowered his head to draw first one nipple and then the other
into his mouth. She shivered in his hold, and another wave of
satisfaction went through him. Relentlessly he kept up the
tender assault, even after she was trembling under his hands.
She responded to him the way a flower responded to sunlight,
opening herself and welcoming him.

"Severance. Please. I can't stand any more." Her eyes were
squeezed tightly shut, her head arched back over his arm.

But he didn't stop, and he didn't move to cover her. This
time he would make sure everything went right. Slowly he
began working his way down her body, tasting her with his
tongue, nibbling at her until she cried out for more. All the
while he kept his fingers moving on her and in her. She twisted
and writhed in his hands, and he gloried in it.

When he dropped an intimate kiss into the triangle of hair
at the apex of her thighs, she cried out again and clutched at
his shoulders.

"That's it, sweetheart. That's it."

The scent of her was dark and spicy, the essence of her
femininity. Severance thought it would surely drive him over
the edge. Still he maintained his self-control. He touched the

nubbin with his tongue and felt Cidra's whole body tighten convulsively.

Deliberately he deepened the passionate caress. The little cries in her throat were the most beautiful songs he had ever heard. He felt her nails digging into his shoulders and knew another lightning jolt of satisfaction.

"Severance!"

"Let go, Cidra, Just let go!" He parted the pliant opening with his fingers, and she whispered his name again. He loved the tight, husky, aching way she said it. He slid two fingers gently into her, his tongue still curling around the bud of throbbing flesh.

She tensed again, breathed his name again, and this time a thousand tiny shivers flooded her body.

"Severance. Sweet Harmony, *Severance!*"

"That's the way I want to hear my name." Intoxicated with the knowledge that he'd brought her complete satisfaction, half spaced with his own anticipation, he flowed back up along her body and slipped between her legs. He drove into her before the tiny convulsions had ceased. The last of them pulled him deeply into her. A moment later it was Cidra's name that was filling the tent and his body that was shuddering in completion. And then he went still on top of her.

When he finally came back to his senses, he was aware of Cidra's fingers moving languidly in his hair. Severance decided he liked it. He moved his head a little closer.

"I wasn't trying to kill myself, Severance."

"You were upset. Scared, maybe."

"Scared of what?" she asked.

"Scared of what's happening to you. To us."

She appeared to give that some thought. "It's confusing, but I don't feel really frightened."

"Good. We'll talk about it in the morning."

"I'm wide-awake," she told him. "I wouldn't mind discussing it now."

He opened his eyes and found that his line of focus took in the peaks of her breasts. It was a pleasant view. "You need the sleep, Cidra. And so do I. We've got a long day ahead of us tomorrow."

"I feel strange, Severance."

"You'll feel better in the morning."

"I don't feel bad," she emphasized. "Just strange."

"I'm sure it's a normal reaction."

"I don't know." She sounded genuinely puzzled. "I also feel a little sore."

He winced guiltily. "I'm sorry, sweetheart. You'll feel better in the morning. And next time you won't feel sore afterward."

She yawned. "You sound very sure of everything."

"I'm the pilot in command, remember? I'm supposed to sound sure of everything." He lifted himself up on one elbow and looked down at her. "Cidra?"

"Hmmm?"

"You swear you weren't thinking of doing anything rash because of what happened tonight?"

"Why would I want to kill myself after enjoying such pleasure?"

He smiled and kissed her. "That's the true Wolf outlook."

"You know what the best part is, Severance?"

"What?"

"Feeling so close to you. It's very nice."

"Very," he agreed.

As he drifted back into sleep Severance decided that Renaissance wasn't such a bad place to stake his claim on Cidra. He hadn't intended to rush things. He had wanted the right time and the right background. During those two weeks on board *Severance Pay* he had fantasized more than once about the perfect setting. In his mind he had constructed a picture that included good ether wine, Harmonic music in the background, a wide, lush bed, and all the time in the world.

Here in the middle of a Renaissance jungle he'd had none of those props, but it didn't seem to matter. There was something primitive and new about the jungle, and it fit in well with the way he felt about Cidra. The more he thought about it, the more appropriate the setting became. She had been right earlier when she had tried to tell him that the jungle wasn't really a green hell. It was an exotic, exciting, primitive world, not a hell.

A man could survive in the jungle without deflector screens and crispers, Severance decided. Hadn't he survived today? There were places in the jungle that were soft, green refuges. In such places he could make love to Cidra beneath twin moons with strange names all night long. It would be good to see her soft, slender body bathed in moonlight. He fell asleep with that last image in his mind.

When he awoke again, he knew it was nearly dawn. Lazily he turned, feeling for Cidra. Then he sat up with a jerk. She was gone again. This time Severance didn't feel the rush of fear he had felt the last time he had awakened and found her gone. She hadn't had time to get far, he thought as he pulled on his clothing. And she would be safe enough. The jungle was safe for her. And for him.

He stepped out of the tent, fastening his shirt, and glanced around. There was no sign of Cidra, but he was curiously unconcerned. He sensed the direction in which she had gone, and he set out to follow. He was just about to step through the deflector screens when a niggling sense of unease stopped him. For a moment he couldn't figure out what the problem was. Then he thought about the pulser and utility loop he had left behind in the tent. It wasn't like him to go anywhere on this planet without either. He felt undressed without them. Habit was hard to break.

Shrugging, Severance walked back toward the tent. He wouldn't need a weapon, but since he seemed uncomfortable without it, he might as well get it. Inside the tent he strapped on the holstered pulser and reached for the utility loop.

With the familiar weight of the pulser and the utility loop in place, he walked back outside and through the deflectors. A strange impatience was beginning to eat at him now. He wanted to catch up with Cidra. She might be quite a way ahead of him by now. He pushed his way through the underbrush, deciding not to worry about what sort of creatures might be hiding in the vicinity. Hadn't he already realized that the jungle was not really a hell? It was a good place, a natural place, one where a man could feel in harmony with nature. Perhaps this was how Harmonics had always felt. If so, he could understand Cidra wanting to become one. Poor Jeude. He'd never had his chance to become a trained Harmonic.

Severance frowned and then relaxed, pushing thoughts of his brother aside. Jeude had been avenged. His memory could be put to rest. Renaissance was a good place to do that too. It was a planet of rest. Gentle, green rest.

He kept walking, not bothering to question his absolute certainty of direction. After all, he'd always had a good sense of direction. The jungle didn't fight him. Why should it? It was expecting him.

He stepped through a wall of trailing vines and saw Cidra. She was only a short distance ahead of him, right where he had known she would be. Severance smiled, quite pleased with himself. But he didn't call out to her. That seemed unnecessary. Instead he simply moved a little more quickly.

She glanced at him when he caught up with her. Her eyes had that slightly unfocused expression again, but that was all right. He knew what she was thinking of now. There was no need to communicate. He was thinking of exactly the same things she was. The shared knowledge was pleasant.

Green hell.

No. Green shelter. Peace. Tranquillity. Rest.

It all waited up ahead. Not far now. Severance was sure of it.

So was Cidra. She moved unerringly in the right direction, following the gentle, guiding call. It wouldn't be long now. The safehold was very near. All the answers were very near.

She and Severance stepped through the last wall of tangled vines and leaves and into the clearing. Cidra halted, drinking in the sight of the safehold bathed in the last of the night's moonlight. Severance stopped beside her, equally enchanted.

It was a graceful, airy thing. The Ghosts had had a light, perfectly balanced touch when it came to architecture. And the safehold had been designed with special care, for it housed important secrets.

Even as Cidra and Severance watched, walls of a translucent stone caught the first light of the morning dawn and glowed with it. The vaulted doorway was open wide, an invitation that could not be denied. The structure seemed lighter than air, circular in shape, and yet it rested firmly on the green velvet of the clearing. It was not a large building, not much bigger than Desma Kady's octagonal living quarters. It appeared to have been carved out of a single huge block of stone. The roof was arched, revealing delicate veins in the material. Through the vaulted entrance nothing could be seen, but it was obvious that light was passing through the stone to gently illuminate the interior.

Cidra stepped forward eagerly, and Severance followed more slowly. For a moment just before she entered the safehold, Cidra had time to realize that it was unusual to find anyplace on Renaissance where nature was not in a constant state of combat. Yet here the green velvet underfoot was obviously not having to compete with other foliage. No stray shoots of vines had encroached from the surrounding jungle. There was no sign of any wildlife within the protected circle. Not even insects. In the clearing all was tranquil and serene. A small brook emerged from the jungle on the far side of the protected clearing, bubbled through it, and disappeared into the foliage on the opposite side.

"Just like a garden in Clementia," Cidra breathed as she came to a halt in front of the entrance. "Smell the air, Severance. It's so soft and fragrant."

"I know," he said, glancing around curiously. Some of the feeling of quiet sureness was receding in him. "Maybe too soft and fragrant, Cidra."

"Nonsense. This is how the Ghosts lived. I know it. When they were here, the jungle was a place of harmony. Just like this clearing. Come on, Severance. Let's go inside."

He hesitated, struggling now with something in his mind. Severance's eyes were vaguely troubled as he looked down at her. "Cidra, I'm not sure . . ."

"I'm going inside." She stepped through the entrance.

Severance shook his head, trying to clear it. Then he realized that there was no need to clear it. All was in order. All was serenely in order. He followed Cidra through the open gate.

Chapter
Thirteen

The first thing Cidra noticed was the silence.

"Like the inside of a grave on QED," Severance said.

"No. Like the Hall of Archives in Clementia." Cidra stood just inside the entrance and glanced around. The curving walls allowed sufficient light into the room to see a floor that was made of the same white stone. The far end of the circular room was in soft shadow. There were no lines of joining between walls and roof or walls and floor. "It's that kind of quiet, Severance. A place where something has been stored for the ages."

"But there's nothing here." He reached out to touch the translucent stone wall. "Perhaps long ago it was a..." He hesitated, struggling for the right word. "A safehold."

"Yes."

"Cidra. What's a safehold? We don't have any facilities called safeholds. Where in hell did I get the word?"

"From whatever led us here."

"I don't like it."

She was surprised by the underlying resistance in his voice. "You don't like what?"

"Having words put in my head. I don't like being led through the jungle by something I can't see. Something in my mind."

"Why did you come, then?" Cidra asked.

"I don't know. Seemed like a good idea at the time."

"Severance..."

He turned to her, anger and growing concern in his face. "I said it seemed like a good idea at the time. But it wasn't *my* idea."

She put out her hand, touching him lightly. Cidra smiled wistfully. "Calm down, Severance. This place is good. It's safe. It's in control of the jungle, can't you tell? The Ghosts could deal with the jungle. And that feeling of having something or someone communicate with you mentally?"

"What about it?"

"That must be what it's like to be a true Harmonic, Severance. It may be as close as I'll ever come to knowing that feeling."

He shook his head. "That wasn't communication, Cidra. That was an act of control. We didn't consciously decide to come here. We were pulled here. We could have been killed at any point along the way by anything from a green slicer to a lockmouth."

"No. I think that whatever led us to this place of safety had the strength to make the path here safe too."

"I wonder if it will bother to make the path back safe or if it only works one way." Severance took a few more paces into the dimly lit room. "All right. We're here. Now what?"

"This may be all that's left." Cidra began moving along the wall, following the curving surface to the far end of the room.

As she walked she trailed a hand along the warm stone surface. It was pleasant to the touch. "But once there was something more here."

"How do you know so much about this safehold?" he demanded. He was moving behind her, unwilling to let her get too far out of reach, even though he could see nothing that looked dangerous.

"I'm learning about it because I'm willing to *listen*. I'm open to it. You must be able to listen, too, Severance. After all, you were able to follow the call. Stop being so wary of it. Be still a moment and let yourself absorb it. Do you really feel anything wrong here?"

"Yes and no."

She swung around, her eyes full of amusement. "Yes and no? Come now, Severance, you're not usually so ambivalent."

He shrugged, scowling. His hand was resting on the butt of the pulser. "I can't explain it. I didn't feel anything wrong on the way here, although I should have, and part of what I feel now is acceptable, I guess you'd say. Strange but not dangerous. But there's something else that I don't like. It's just a feeling."

"Perhaps just a sensation of alienness. After all, this is the first complete Ghost structure ever found as far as I know. There are records of hundreds of fragments of their buildings but nothing complete and in good condition like this."

"Have any of those records of the fragments mentioned this kind of building material?" Severance eyed the gently glowing stone.

"None that I've come across," Cidra admitted. "This is truly unique. Perhaps it's newer than the others. If so, then it might help us date the Ghost civilization. Severance, this is such an important find. We're so lucky to have discovered it."

"We didn't discover it," he said flatly. "It discovered us. There's a difference, Cidra."

She decided to ignore him. He was obviously going to be difficult. Cidra started walking again, curious to see the far end of the hall that lay in shadow. She was aware of Severance reluctantly following. "I think there's something back there." Excited by the possibility, Cidra hurried forward.

"Cidra, wait. Hell, the floor is changing color!" Severance stared down as the white stone began to shade into a pearlescent pink. "We're getting out of here." He grabbed Cidra's arm, jerking her to halt.

"I want to see what's at the back of the room." She tried to pull free, but his hand was clamped around her arm like a manacle. "Severance, please. This is what I've been looking for. Don't you understand? What's here could be the source of the legends I'm following. This place might hold the key I need to go home."

"I don't care if this place holds a lifetime supply of Rose ale. We're not hanging around any longer." Roughly he hauled her toward the entrance.

But the floor was changing color quickly now, shimmering from pink to red and then to violet. Other colors were filtering to the surface, and even as Severance watched, the shifting colors bled upward into the walls and ceiling. Then, without any warning, there was something more than colors. There were shapes. Shapes that weren't restricted to the two-dimensional surface of the walls. They seemed to be stepping out into the room.

"The Laughing Gods, Severance. Look at them. They were real. Just look at them."

Stunned, Severance came to a halt in the middle of the room, still holding Cidra with one hand. His other hand hovered above the holstered pulser. He heard the wonder and excitement in Cidra's voice and knew that he felt the same sense of awed anticipation. The feeling of alienness was gone. What filled him now was a magnificently amplified version of the serenity and quiet pleasure he got when he handled his collection of stone carvings. The Laughing Gods were everywhere in the safehold. They surrounded Cidra and Severance, but it was clear that they had no substance. They were an illusion, something like a holotape projection but far more perfectly reproduced. It was like being in the midst of Ghosts.

Mesmerized by the reality of what he was seeing, Severance continued to stand still. Cidra didn't move beside him. There was no sound, only the shifting images on the ceiling and walls and in midair.

"It's a record," Cidra whispered. "I was right. This place is an Archive. These are the Ghosts."

"They look different than they do in the carvings."

"I don't think so. It's only their clothing that's different. That would make sense if these are images of them at a later period in their development."

The drive to get out of the safehold was gone. Severance felt relaxed again. Cidra stopped struggling to free herself when she realized that she wasn't going to be hauled forcibly out of the room. They stood quietly, watching the shifting images that filled the room. The Ghosts had been a handsome people. The vaguely feline features expressed a deep intelligence and an awareness that was obvious even to people whose ancestors had come from another solar system. They moved with a lithe grace, walking on two legs. Their clothing was more simply styled in these images than the clothing worn by the statues. The portions of the body not shielded by the simple robes were furred.

As Cidra watched, the crowded figures began to fade.

Unhappily she watched the swirling images disappear. "Severance, they're going."

"The picture is just fading. They were never really here to begin with."

"But I need answers!"

"There's no reason to expect any," he said gently.

He was right. She knew that, but a part of her wanted to cry out in protest. There was so much to learn, so many questions she wanted to ask. Above all there was the mystery of how she and Severance had been led here in the first place. "Damn it. I wanted to know."

"We've already seen more than any Harmonic archaeologist has ever seen."

"I realize that, but it's not enough. I need to find the key." She stopped talking as she realized that not all the graceful images had disappeared. Five Ghosts remained, shimmering between her and the doorway. "Look, Severance. There's more."

He said nothing, watching as the five robed figures coalesced in midair. In addition to the simple white garments, these Ghosts appeared to have a golden band around their furred wrists. Long, delicate fingers tipped with curving nails reached out.

For a wild moment Cidra thought that the creatures were gesturing toward her, and then she realized that the gentle, slanting eyes were not really seeing her. This was still only a projected image. But there seemed to be a purpose to the gestures. When all five Ghosts pointed toward the wall to their right, she automatically followed the tapering hands.

A new series of pictures sprang into existence on the curving wall and began flowing out from it. More Ghosts appeared, moving through a wild jungle setting that could only have been Renaissance. But the hands of these Ghosts were tipped with long, dangerous-looking claws, not well-trimmed nails. There

were crude weapons worn on leather belts. Very little clothing
was evident, but there were quite a few pieces of primitively
ornate decorative items on furred throats, wrists, and ankles.

"The Ghosts' ancestors?" Cidra asked.

"Could be. I get the feeling there's a lot of distance between
those cats with the claws and the five guys standing in the
middle of the room."

Even as Severance spoke, it became obvious that the scene
evolving around them was a hunt. The handful of Ghosts were
prowling. There was no doubt about it. They moved with a
menacing care, and it wasn't long before the object of the hunt
came into sight. A horned animal stood on six legs nibbling
leaves off a tree. Severance thought the creature resembled a
modern-day Renaissance mannator.

Cidra swallowed as the Ghosts attacked. The six-legged
animal went down amid a flurry of thrown knives and scrab-
bling claws. As it struggled, its throat was ripped out. The
fine quality of the illusion made the blood look very real. She
was sure that what was happening was a simple and necessary
hunting operation, but the violence of it was sickening. It
brought back memories of feeding dracons. When she glanced
briefly at her companion, she saw that he wasn't particularly
affected by the gory scene.

The lifelike mural continued, showing the Ghosts engaged
in other activities besides the hunt. Cidra became interested in
what was apparently a religious ceremony. Five Ghosts conducted the proceedings from behind an altar made of stone.
The observers were seated cross-legged on the ground, swaying
to an unheard beat. The fact that there were five leaders was
interesting because that was how many Ghosts had appeared
a few minutes ago in the room. Cidra tried to see if there were
gold bands on their wrists but got distracted when a large,
scaled animal was thrown down onto the altar. Too late she

realized what was about to happen. She didn't manage to look away in time to avoid seeing the knife dragged across the belly of the sacrifice. Again she felt nausea welling up, threatening to choke her for a moment.

Averting her eyes from the bloody scene, Cidra glanced back toward the middle of the room. The five Ghosts in white robes continued to stand pointing toward the moving illusion. Reluctantly she looked back.

"This is getting awfully gory, Severance. I don't understand. It isn't how I imagined the Ghosts would be."

"You don't think it was easy surviving on Renaissance, do you? Nothing that becomes dominant on this planet is going to be sweet-natured."

"But the carvings show a gentler nature. And those five standing over there, they couldn't have been like this."

"Wait and see."

The images continued to shift, fading in and out of the walls. They moved more swiftly now, slowing only to show the details of a scene of weaving, the preparation of a meal or the carving of stone. It became clear that there was an element of time and progress involved. Clothing changed, becoming more elaborate. The design of structures altered. The early images showed the Ghosts sheltering in huge, wide-limbed trees. As the scenes progressed, however, shelters were created out of rocks and vines.

"It's moving too quickly." Cidra wanted to slow the images and savor each nuance of information contained in them. "There's too much to see."

"Maybe the Ghosts weren't sure how long a visitor's attention span was going to be."

"How can you make a joke out of it? This is the most important find of the century. Perhaps the most significant discovery since the First Families arrived and found the first Ghost relics."

Severance thought for a moment. "There's another possible reason why the scenes are moving too swiftly."

"What reason?"

"It could be because there's a great deal of history to be conveyed. We could be dealing with several thousand years, here. Or a million, for all we know."

"The rise and fall of a whole species?" Cidra watched as a scene of a village being built between the jungle and the sea took shape. "It looks like an alien version of Port Try Again. Right down to the walls built to hold out the jungle."

It was clear that every inch of progress was a struggle. The Ghosts of Renaissance paid a high price for their growing civilization. Images of Ghosts being attacked by huge, fanged snakes and other horrendous forms of wildlife flickered on and off the walls. Pictures of tiny villages being trampled by lumbering, armor-plated animals were common.

"Zalons," Severance told her. "Or at least an earlier version of them. The horns look slightly different, and the ears are smaller."

"You said they were vegetarians."

"They are. But that doesn't make much difference to something smaller than they are that happens to get in their way. Zalons are a little clumsy."

There were other kinds of difficulties. Volcanic eruptions, flooding rivers, intense storms. Then came the even more unsettling pictures of warring tribes. Cidra couldn't watch the battle scenes. Such violence between Ghosts didn't fit the mental image she'd always had. Severance watched with intent interest.

Regardless of the setbacks, natural disasters, and war, the Ghosts continued to expand as a species. They grew in numbers. In fact, Cidra noticed at one point that there were a great many images of children in the mural. Scenes of them playing, practicing with weapons, and going about their daily lives were frequent.

It was clear that the Ghosts were holding their own and beginning to thrive in the jungles of Renaissance. Small mechanical devices appeared. Technology began on a small scale. After that the little villages grew into towns. Gradually the jungle was tamed. It was never wiped out, but in the regions where Ghosts lived, it was under control.

Scenes shifted more and more rapidly, showing towns growing into cities. And then came the leap into space. The colonization of Lovelady was easy for a people who had tamed a jungle world. QED and Frozen Assets were also featured briefly, although it was obvious that they had never been fully colonized. The spaceships never left the Stanza Nine system as far as Cidra and Severance could tell. It was as if the explorers ran out of interest or energy.

Eons passed. How much time, Cidra had no way of knowing. But gradually things began changing again. The technological trappings of civilization began to fade in the scenes. They were replaced with pictures of translucent structures such as the one in which Cidra stood. The jungle was controlled now without obvious technology. Quiet, serene clearings were common, and in them, quiet, serene Ghosts went about their daily business. These people no longer had the undeniably aggressive element that had been so common in their ancestors.

"They're changing," Severance said.

"Evolving. They're developing mentally now instead of technologically." Cidra was sure of her analysis.

"There's something different about these pictures."

She frowned. "What do you mean?"

"Where are all the kids that were always running around in the earlier scenes?"

He was right. Cidra searched the new pictures, looking for some sign of the laughing, playing, practicing young Ghosts. Once or twice a youngster appeared, but it was becoming increasingly rare. As rare as a child in Clementia. She did see more of the gold wristbands, though. They were becoming a common form of jewelry. Almost all the Ghosts wore them.

The interaction between the Ghosts had changed too. There was no longer evidence of hostility or rivalry, no more open warfare. A sense of peace and gentleness pervaded the mural.

"It's beautiful, Severance. They became a people of harmony and grace."

"Two worlds full of Harmonics. Must have been kind of dull."

"Damn it, Severance! Why do you have to be so cynical?"

"It's in the blood. I'd still like to know what happened to all the children."

"Maybe they developed a very long lifespan and had to control their population."

"Or maybe, like Harmonics, the Ghosts simply lost interest in sex and the results thereof."

Cidra shifted uneasily, the memory of her own recent interest in that field plaguing her for a moment. Severance was studying the graceful illusions closely.

"I think there's more than just a few kids missing here," he finally said. "The whole population seems to be declining. There aren't as many Ghosts as there were earlier. No sense of huge cities or bustling economies. Just more and more of these quiet little parks."

Cidra felt a sharp pang of regret. "What's happening, Severance? Do you think we're coming to the end?"

He nodded slowly. "The population level is falling. No

evidence of children being born to replace their parents. Fewer and fewer towns."

"Maybe species just get old and die the way individuals do," Cidra suggested. Her pang of regret was turning into a pervasive sadness.

"Or maybe this particular species took a bad evolutionary road."

"At what point?" For some reason she felt defensive.

"When they stopped spreading outward and started turning inward. When they stopped having children. When they became more interested in mental and spiritual development and stopped worrying about keeping the species alive physically."

"You don't know what you're talking about, Severance. We're only looking at pictures. We can't know what really happened. We can only draw inferences." Even as she argued, the images were fading. It was obvious that the civilization they depicted was fading too. The last picture was of a circular building carved from a single block of translucent stone. In it five Ghosts sealed the history of a species and then clasped hands. The golden bands they wore on their wrists glowed in unison for a moment. Serenely, effortlessly, without any sign of struggle or regret, the five died. When the image on the wall vanished, so did the five figures who had been projected into the room earlier. Cidra wanted to weep.

"That last structure was this place," Severance observed as the image flickered and faded into the wall. "You were right. This is an Archive. Saints in hell. We're going to be rich."

Cidra was astounded. She brushed the moisture from her eyes to glare at him. "Rich? What are you saying?"

"We can sell the location of this place to any number of research companies or to the Harmonics. There's enough in here to keep investigators happy for fifty years." He swung around to face her. "Don't look so shocked, Cidra. What did you plan to do with the information we've found here?"

She hesitated. "I suppose it will have to be turned over to some company to analyze. But it seems wrong to sell it. This is a precious discovery."

"Damned right. We'll find out just how precious when we put it up for sale." He glanced at the chronometer on his utility loop. "Sweet Harmony. We've been in here for hours. It's already the middle of the afternoon. We've got to get going."

"Wait, Severance. I want to see what's at the back of the room."

"Later. I don't know how I lost track of time so completely. Hours. *Hours*. We should have called for help early this morning. As it is, it might be another full day before a skimmer can reach us. That means we'll probably be spending another night here in the jungle. Damn it to a renegade's hell. How could I have let this happen?" As he berated himself he was hustling Cidra toward the door.

"Still playing pilot in command, Severance? Why can't you just calm down and admit that we've found something absolutely extraordinary. We're safe enough for the moment. We've got time to explore further. If we have to spend another night in the jungle, we might as well spend it here. It's obvious that nothing violent from outside ever enters. This is one of the last refuges. A safehold."

"We have no way of knowing just how safe it really is."

They were almost at the entrance. Cidra resigned herself to being force-marched back to the campsite. "All right, stop dragging me along like a sack of mail. I'm coming with you."

He shot her an assessing glance and decided that she was going to be cooperative. Severance unholstered the pulser.

"What's that for?" Cidra asked.

"Just in case we don't get the same guided tour out that we

245

had coming in. Stay close to me and don't touch anything you pass if you can avoid it."

"I'm sure we'll have no trouble. Whatever protected us on the way here will probably protect us as we leave."

"Uh-huh." Severance checked the charge in the pulser. He obviously didn't believe in the lingering protection of the Ghosts. "All set?"

Cidra reluctantly started through the door and then screamed at the sight of the huge Bloodsucker blocking the entrance. She stumbled backward, frantically trying to put distance between herself and the facet-eyed monster. It was far bigger than the Bloodsuckers she had seen in Desma's lab.

"Severance!"

His hand closed on her shoulder, spinning her out of the way. The pulser came up, and he fired twice. Nothing happened. The Bloodsucker moved forward on its long spindly legs. The mandibles clicked together. Severance fired again, backing slowly. None of the shots were registering. It was as if they passed right through the creature.

"Get back, Cidra. Move toward the back of the room." Slowly Severance edged backward himself, covering Cidra's escape.

"They're not supposed to be that big," Cidra gasped.

"Maybe you'd better remind it." He raised the pulser again and aimed carefully at the braincase. Once more the charge passed straight through without doing any damage. "Either this thing is absorbing the charge with no effort or it's an image, just like the ones we've been watching."

"Nice theory. How are we going to test it?"

The Bloodsucker was still approaching. Cidra and Severance kept backing toward the far wall. Cidra glanced behind her.

"There are some stones back here."

"Toss one toward this Sucker and see what happens."

Cidra quickly examined the large triangular-shaped pile composed of five perfectly round stones. Each was slightly bigger than a human head. Experimentally she lifted the top one. It was pleasantly warm to the touch.

"It's heavy," she gasped, struggling with the weight of it. "But it'll roll." She dropped the stone to the floor and shoved with all her might.

The stone rolled right through two Bloodsucker limbs with no sign of any resistance. The creature didn't appear to notice, either. It raised its forelegs and reached for Severance.

Cidra shouted, trying to yank him out of the way. Severance swung his arm out in a reflexive movement. The hand holding the pulser passed through the lowering head of the Bloodsucker as if it weren't there.

"It *is* just an image, Cidra. Let's go." He reached around to catch her wrist with his free hand.

Cidra wanted to scream and claw free of that hold. The Bloodsucker was too terrifyingly lifelike. She had known that the moving mural of the Ghosts was an illusion from the start. But this thing seemed far more real. Its forelimbs were waving around in the air now, seeking the prey in front of it. But she followed Severance as he warily circled the image, tugging Cidra with him. The creature lunged at them, and Cidra shut her eyes, convinced that in another instant she was going to find herself just another victim of Renaissance.

Nothing happened. When she opened her eyes again, Severance had pulled her halfway back toward the entrance. The Bloodsucker had winked out of existence. They were almost at the door when an unnatural light filled the formerly dim room. This was no pale, translucent, filtered sunlight but a searing blaze. Instinctively Cidra closed her eyes, wondering if she'd been blinded. She felt Severance stop and knew it had affected him the same way.

"I can't see," Cidra whispered.

"Neither can I. It's probably another illusion, but I can't see the door. Let's find the wall. We can follow it around to the entrance."

Cidra hooked her fingers into his utility loop, and together they groped blindly for the solid wall. The chamber was still filled with the searing light. Whenever Cidra risked a glance through slitted lashes, the unnatural brilliance overwhelmed her. She felt Severance pull up short and mutter a short, expressive oath.

"The wall," he said grimly. "Now we'll try following it."

A rush of screaming noise crashed into existence around them. Cidra reeled, feeling Severance stagger under the impact of the wild sounds. She let go of his utility loop to clutch at her ears, but it did no good. Once before she had tried to block out such noise. Frantically Cidra tried to remember when, but she couldn't concentrate on anything but the agony in her head.

"Don't open your eyes, Cidra!" She heard Severance's voice without realizing how she could over the strange cacophony.

"The light?"

"It's still there, but it's full of things."

"I can't stand it, Severance. I can't stand this!"

He didn't answer, and Cidra knew with a terrifying certainty that he wasn't faring any better than she was. They were both helpless under the bombardment of sensations.

And then the crawling began on her skin. She sensed it first on her legs. Something had gotten under the fabric of her trousers. Something with white-hot pincers and venomous fangs. Screaming, she slapped at her legs. She could feel nothing under the fabric, but that knowledge didn't lessen the pain.

Suddenly she remembered when and where she had faced this kind of assault.

"The Screamer," she choked, stumbling against Severance. "It's like the Screamer."

"Something's playing on our nerve endings. All of them," he agreed.

He fumbled with his utility belt. Cidra didn't risk opening her eyes, but she could feel him trembling as he fought to master himself. "What are you doing?"

"I'm going to see if the Screamer can jam whatever is jamming us."

Another burst of white-hot noise cascaded through the room, and Cidra groaned under the weight of it. The force of it drove her to her knees, and she was aware of Severance hunched down beside her. She sensed that he had the small Screamer remote in his hand. He leaned against her, assuring that their bodies were touching, and activated the remote.

The riot of sensation altered suddenly. For a few seconds everything disappeared—the noise, the light, the physical sensations, even the chamber itself. Cidra found herself in a gray limbo. She drifted mindlessly in the wonderful silence, drinking in the pain-free void, and then it was over.

A new kind of whirling terror shot through her. This time she recognized it. This was what the Screamer had done to her on board *Severance Pay*. She clamped her hands over her ears in agony, and then chaos faded back into grayness again.

There were a few seconds of peace before the white light and noise started to build again.

"We'll have to move during the short periods when the Screamer wipes out the other stuff," Severance said tensely. "I can only buy us a few seconds at a time. If I keep it up too long, the Screamer goes into effect."

"I understand. The wall?"

There was a burst of blinding noise as the seconds of gray-ness faded back into violent sensation. She waited agonizingly for the next burst of grayness.

"The wall," Severance agreed. He was already up and moving, keeping a hold on Cidra so that the Screamer's effects worked on both of them.

It was a painful tightrope of a journey. Between bursts of staggering sensation Cidra and Severance found the curving wall and doggedly followed it to the entrance of the chamber. Cidra lost all track of time, just as she had when the murals had been in motion. But when she tumbled through the vaulted opening, all of the mind-numbing noise and light disappeared. The relief was awesome. Almost frightening.

She lay on the soft, green velvet ground cover of the protected circle and tried to regain her breath. Severance sank down beside her and dropped the Screamer back into the utility loop. They huddled together, knees drawn up, heads cradled on folded arms, and waited to regain some sense of normality. For long moments neither of them spoke. They stayed close, seeking silent comfort from each other while their nerves adjusted to the standard range of stimulation on Renaissance.

"I never thought Renaissance would look 'normal,'" Cidra finally said.

"After what's inside that chamber, anything would seem normal. At least we're not suffering too many aftereffects. It could have knocked us out the way the Screamer usually does when it's used for more than a few seconds."

"Mostly I just feel exhausted, as if I've been running for hours."

Severance glanced at the sky and then at his chronometer. "We've lost more time. We've spent nearly a whole day in that damned place."

"I'm aware of that. My body is starting to remind me that the facilities don't include a lav." Wearily Cidra got to her feet. "I'll politely turn my back if you'll turn yours."

Severance managed a brief, amused grin. "It's a deal."

"I hope the Ghosts don't mind us using their magic circle as a lav."

"As far as I'm concerned, they deserve it." Severance turned his back to her.

Cidra felt on the defensive again. "I can't believe the Ghosts were responsible for all those awful illusions and that wall of noise and light."

"Any other bright suggestions?"

"No," Cidra admitted. "It just doesn't fit, that's all. By the time they built this place they were a peaceful, gentle people. It doesn't seem in their nature to build such traps."

"There's a lot we don't know about their nature, Cidra, and don't forget it." Severance turned around. "Ready?"

She nodded. "Uh, I've just thought of something."

"What?" He was checking the pulser.

"A minor point. Do you know how to find our way back?"

"You should have worried about that last night when you went for your joy walk." Then he saw the look on her face. "Stop worrying, I can find the way back." He pulled a small instrument out of his loop. "We didn't come that far according to this."

"What's that?"

"A directional system. Everyone who works on Renaissance carries one. It'll home in on deflector screens, a skimmer's comm unit, or anything else that puts out a man-made signal." He walked to the edge of the protected area and peered ahead. Then he glanced at the small instrument in his hand. "Okay, let's try this one more time, shall we? Remember what I said. Stick close and don't touch anything."

They got no more than two meters outside the Ghosts' serene, sheltered circle before the lockmouth attacked.

Chapter
Fourteen

If he'd ever been given a written guarantee that the universe played fair, Severance would have sued now. It was all too much. He was too exhausted, too slow, and too anxious to get back to the safety of the deflectors. And the lockmouth was too hungry and too fast.

The clawed feet ripped downward as the scaled head that was twice as large as a man's opened its cavernous mouth. A reserve of sheer, blind instinct, not nimble, clever resourcefulness, threw Severance backward at the last possible instant. The claws, each as long as his fingers, slashed across his chest and shoulder instead of his throat.

He heard Cidra shout something as she struggled to pull him out of the way. He thought about telling her that it was too late to run. But there wasn't time to explain just how fast and vindictive a cheated lockmouth could be. Severance shoved at her, sending her sprawling.

The long, evilly shaped creature with the oversized head was already plunging down out of the nest of vines where it had been waiting for unwary prey. The mouth opened wide. Lockmouths could swallow a human being whole. They did it slowly. Once the locking mechanisms in the powerful jaws were closed, the only way to free whatever was trapped inside was to cut off the huge head. By then, there wasn't much point.

The lockmouth crouched briefly, preparing the final spring. This time it wouldn't miss. Severance decided he'd better not miss, either. On Renaissance there were very few second chances, and he'd already used up his quota for a year. He was sorely tempted to fire the pulser straight into the creature's gaping mouth but resisted and aimed for the eyes. Behind them resided whatever the creature had that passed for a brain.

The pulser withered one huge, glassy eye, and the lockmouth jerked spasmodically. Severance used the second's grace to edge backward. He heard Cidra breathing quickly into the sudden, hushed silence, but she said nothing.

That was the thing about Cidra, Severance decided as he fired again. She knew when to keep her mouth shut.

The lockmouth jerked once more and then crumpled heavily to the jungle floor. The jaws slammed shut, locked for the last time in death.

"Severance, you're bleeding."

"I know. It's one of the dumber things a man can do on Renaissance." The pain was lancing through him now as the short-term anesthetic effects of adrenaline and fear wore thin. He looked down at where the lockmouth's claws had ripped through the tough fabric of his shirt as though it were made of spun crystal moss. There were three savage scrapes across the tough hide of the rantgan leather utility loop. The loop had kept the lockmouth from ripping up his chest as well as his shoulder. Warm blood of an interesting shade of crimson had already dampened too much of the shirt. It was running down his arm and dripping on the ground. A small, innocent-looking flower suddenly spread its petals to absorb the moisture.

"The Ghost circle." Cidra stepped forward, clamping a hand solidly over Severance's bleeding wound. Blood seeped between her fingers but began to slow as she applied pressure. "We'll be safe there while we bandage your shoulder."

Severance didn't argue. He was feeling strangely dizzy already and was alarmed. He couldn't afford the luxury of any picturesque wounds. He had to get Cidra back to the safety of the deflectors; had to put in the call for help. Damn it, he should have been faster back there when the lockmouth attacked. Being exhausted and a little slower than usual were not acceptable excuses on Renaissance.

"I guess this answers the question of whether we're going to get the same escorted tour back to the campsite that we got coming here." He tried to seat himself calmly on the rich green ground cover inside the perimeter of the magic circle and wound up collapsing, instead. Not a good image for the crew, he chided himself. The one in charge was supposed to look as if he really were in charge. He hadn't done too well in that area recently.

"I don't understand," Cidra said. She studied Severance's shoulder with a grim intensity while she kept up the steady, blood-slowing pressure with her hand. "Why doesn't the protection work both ways?"

"Who in a renegade's hell knows? Maybe we got here through pure luck the first time. Or maybe the signal, whatever it is, has grown too weak to work well. Or maybe it never was designed to work both ways." He flinched and gritted his teeth.

"You've been badly hurt, Severance."

"Yeah, well, I wasn't going to call it just a small flesh wound." He groaned, more in frustration than from pain. "No wound on Renaissance qualifies as a minor flesh wound, unfortunately. Any amount of blood draws too much interest." At the edge of the circle there was a flash of movement. Fangs gleamed for a moment and then vanished. "See what I mean? Thank Sweet Harmony this circle seems to be holding." He fumbled with the utility loop. "There's some emergency stuff in here somewhere. The antiseptic is the most important thing."

He cursed, a soft, sibilant sound, as he withdrew the small spray vial. Cidra took it from him, maintaining her pressure hold on his shoulder.

"I think the bleeding is slowing," she said.

He scanned her steady face. "It doesn't seem to be making you sick to your stomach."

She glared at him. "Nothing has made me sick to my stomach so far. Why should this?"

"Getting cocky, are you, little Wolf?"

She saw the affectionate amusement that briefly replaced the pain and frustration in his eyes. "It isn't blood that bothers Harmonics. It's knowing someone else is in pain that bothers them. I don't have to worry about that, though, do I? You're doing an excellent job of playing the stoic hero."

"Fool, not hero." He closed his eyes as she peeled away the torn fabric of the shirt. Wordlessly he handed her the small utility knife. Cidra looked at him in horror. "Don't worry. I'm already ripped up enough as it is. You don't have to do any cutting except on the shirt."

"Oh. For a minute there I thought I was going to have to perform minor surgery."

"Just spray the area with the antiseptic, and then we'll try bandaging it."

"Perhaps I should wash the wound first."

"Get some water from that stream. I've got a bag you can

use to collect it. And there are some standard-issue purification drops somewhere on this damned loop."

"But I'm sure any water flowing through this circle would be clean and pure," she protested.

"You've got a hell of a lot more faith in the Ghosts than I do. Have you forgotten that last set of illusions inside that safehold?"

"No, but I'm sure there's an explanation for them."

"I'm sure there is too. Just like there's an explanation for everything on this planet. The trouble is, it may not be one we want to hear."

Cidra said nothing, collecting water in the clear plastic bag from the cheerful little stream. She added the chemical drops and waited while the water turned a strange shade of purple. Then she carefully bathed the wound, relieved to see that the bleeding was under control. When she was done, she reached for the antiseptic.

"Ouch!"

She stopped spraying antiseptic and glanced worriedly at Severance's face. "Does that hurt?"

He set his teeth. "No. Not a bit. What makes you ask?"

"Severance..."

"Finish spraying. I'll work harder at playing the stoic hero."

She hurried, aware of his growing pain. When she was finished, she dropped the spray back into his loop. "What do we use for bandages?"

"A mailman is always prepared. Try the small pouch near my other shoulder. I've got some plastic adhesive in there."

She applied the liquid adhesive with quick strokes and watched as it hardened into a strong bandage. "I think that's stopped the last of the bleeding. How do you feel?"

"I still feel like a fool." He looked down at her handiwork.

257

There was a lot of blood and gore on his arm, but the adhesive seemed to be holding.

"This was hardly your fault, Severance." Cidra leaned back on her folded knees. "The responsibility for getting us into this mess is mine."

"I'm the one who set off on a midnight garden walk through the jungle with you instead of dragging you back to the tent, remember?"

"Yes, but . . ."

"But, nothing. I'm the one who screwed up." He held up a hand to keep her from arguing further. "The subject is closed for discussion. We'll reopen it later when I feel more like fighting with you. Right now I haven't got the energy."

She subsided, not liking the pallor on his tanned face. "If you're not up to fighting with me, Severance, then you probably aren't up to trying to make it back to the deflectors."

"Trust a Harmonic to grasp a difficult situation the first time out."

"I'm not a Harmonic."

"Hush, Cidra." He paused for a moment, eyes closed. "It looks like we're stuck here for the night. I'd say we had to try for the deflectors if this weird circle didn't seem to be working, but it does, so I guess our odds are better staying here than trying to hike back. It's going to be dark soon." He swung an assessing glance around the perimeter of the circle. "Let's move over to the wall of the safehold. That should protect our backs just in case."

Cidra tried to help him as he staggered to his feet. He was shakier than he wanted to admit. He looked down at her supporting hands.

"You're stronger than you look, aren't you, Cidra?"

She ignored that. "At least we'll be warm enough."

"Food," he announced succinctly, "will be our next problem."

She glanced at him as she eased him down with his back to the translucent wall. "Any ideas? Can we eat any of the vegetation around this circle?"

Severance leaned his head back, taking a few seconds to gather his strength. Cidra crouched beside him. When he opened his eyes again, she breathed a small sigh of relief. His gaze was steady, not showing any signs of disorientation. He gazed at the jungle growth that ringed their shelter. "I'm no botanist. Any of this stuff could be deadly or simply inedible. The safest thing to eat on Renaissance is what most everything else eats: Meat. If you can kill it before it kills you."

Cidra felt her stomach lurch for the first time. She cleared her throat. "Actually, there shouldn't be more than a few hunger pangs if we simply wait until we get back to the campsite tomorrow. No harm in going a day without eating."

He looked up at her through slitted eyes. "Personally I'm starved. Neither of us has had anything since yesterday, and we've gone through a lot of our stored energy since then. Renaissance has a way of doing that to a body. By tomorrow we could be light-headed. That's not a good condition to be in when we make another try for the campsite."

"I understand." She said no more. This was a matter of survival. There was no obligation to follow the Klinian dietary restrictions under such circumstances. Vegetarianism was a luxury she could not afford tonight. "What do we do?"

He unholstered the pulser. "We sit here very quietly and wait for the crowd to arrive."

"What crowd?"

"The guests who will be sitting down to dine on the late, unlamented lockmouth. Sooner or later something will pass by on the way to the meal. I'll try to get it before it realizes we're a threat."

Cidra nodded, quelling her stomach with a stern effort of will. She sat huddled in silence beside Severance as the darkness descended. Before long, the dinner guests began arriving. The first indications were eyes. Far too many eyes. They flickered and flared in the shadows.

Next came the sounds of scufflings and one or two piercing screams. This was not a well-mannered crowd, Cidra decided. And some of the guests had just become entrées themselves. She shuddered at the thought and stayed very still.

The unwary, overanxious diner who passed too close to the circle was a small four-footed hopping creature that had fur instead of scales. Cidra had been rather hoping for something with scales. It was easier to dislike scaled things. A totally irrational, even primitive reaction, but one she couldn't shake. She shut her eyes when Severance brought up the pulser and fired in a smooth, sure movement.

"Get it," he snapped, "before something else does."

Cidra leapt to her feet and dashed to the edge of the circle. The little hopper lay dead less than a meter away. It looked very cuddly and pathetic until she saw the fangs in its mouth. She reached out, grabbed it by the fluffy tail, and hauled it into the safe area. Her heart was pounding, and her insides again moved uncomfortably. Huge, dead eyes gazed up at her in mute reproach.

"I'd better clean it on the edge of the circle." Severance made his way painfully to the perimeter and pulled out the utility knife. He removed the miniature quartzflash he carried and set it on the ground to light the hopper. "Ever do any dissection work in those biology classes you're always mentioning?"

She swallowed. "No. Everything was demonstrated with

holotapes. I wasn't going to be a biologist, so there was no need to actually do dissections."

"This isn't going to look like any neat, clean holotape. Why don't you start the flamer while I take care of this?" He handed her the tiny can of instant fire he had removed from his loop and turned back to the hopper.

Cidra looked away, busying herself with igniting the emergency flamer. She had it going quickly and adjusted the wide flame to a reasonable level. The fire was very comforting here in the middle of the jungle, she discovered.

Severance was tiring very rapidly. Cidra kept a wary eye on him as he washed his bloodied hands in the bubbling stream. But she said nothing as he doggedly roasted sections of meat on the narrow point of the utility knife.

Cidra listened to the hissing of animal fat and tried to close her nostrils to the smell of roasting meat. When Severance handed her a portion, she took it without a word.

"Careful, it's hot." He bit hungrily into the hindquarter he was holding.

Cidra stopped breathing as she took a tiny bite. She'd never eaten meat in her life. Closing her eyes, she chewed woodenly, trying not to taste. On the other side of the small flamer Severance chewed vigorously and watched her. Under his steady gaze she forced herself to swallow the first bite, trying to think of it as medicine.

"We're very lucky you remembered to bring the utility loop and the pulser with you," she remarked, trying for light dinner-table conversation. In the shadows the other diners weren't being nearly so fussy. Their conversations consisted of squeals, growls, hisses, and shrieks. She hoped they would finish quickly.

"It was probably instinct more than luck. It certainly wasn't careful, foresighted planning. I wasn't thinking clearly at the time. I just remember feeling undressed. Wearing the loop is second-nature to me. And carrying a pulser on Renaissance has gotten to be an unconscious action." He finished gnawing on a leg. "How are you doing?"

"Fine," she said tightly, and forced down another bite.

"You look a little green." He scrutinized her in the flickering light. "Sure you're okay?"

"Yes."

His expression softened. "Poor Cidra. Just one new experience after another these days, isn't it?"

"This trip has turned out slightly different than I had anticipated."

"What an understatement."

She felt obliged to hold her own. "But thanks to your unorthodox way of doing things, I might have discovered a shortcut to my goal." She glanced behind her into the darkened entrance of the circular chamber.

"You think whatever drew us here is the source of the legend you're chasing?" His eyes were unreadable now in the firelight.

"It's possible. There was definitely a telepathic sensation involved, don't you think? I felt the first trickle of it yesterday afternoon while I waited for you. I wonder if the failing deflector screens allowed the call to get through. Maybe deflectors normally block it."

"But last night the screens were working at full strength."

"True," Cidra mused. "But by then the mechanism responsible for projecting the call might have had a fix, so to speak, on our location. Maybe it can't compete against other distractions, but in the quiet of the night it was able to touch us."

Severance shrugged and said nothing as he spitted another chunk of hopper and held it over the flame.

Cidra continued, trying to reason out the logic of the situation. "If one or two others in the past have felt that call, they might have told the tale to their friends. Over the years the stories would have grown more involved and complex."

"Until they reached the point where they made it into the Archives? It's possible. But if others have heard that call and followed it, why hasn't anyone discovered this safehold?" Severance asked in a reasonable tone.

"I don't know."

"Perhaps they heard the call but didn't follow."

Cidra frowned. "Why wouldn't they follow? We did."

"We were camped in the vicinity for two nights. The others might have merely caught traces of the call as they went by on a skimmer. The odds are no one's ever camped in that particular spot before. It might take a while for the call to focus in on a mind and become strong enough to draw someone to this place. If it's a mechanical device, it might have to tune itself."

She nodded. "That makes sense."

"There's another possibility. Someone may have found this place before but not lived to tell about it. If a man thought that he'd get the same protection going out as he got coming in, he'd be in for a rude surprise. I wasn't expecting protection, and I was still rudely surprised. Your Ghosts have a nasty sense of humor."

"I don't think they would have set a trap to lure intelligent beings here, show them their history, and then leave them unprotected. Perhaps they assumed that whoever found this place would be smart enough to protect themselves on the way back."

He groaned. "Never make assumptions. Case in point sitting right here in front of you."

She was shocked at her own words. "Oh, Severance, I never meant to imply that you . . ."

"That I'm not very bright? Don't worry. You don't need to imply it. Facts speak for themselves."

"Are you always so hard on yourself when things go wrong?"

"Only when they go wrong badly enough to get someone killed."

"Neither of us has been killed, Severance."

"I'll cling to that thought."

He stood up again and walked back to the stream to wash the grease from his hands. He needed rest very badly, Cidra thought as she unobtrusively put down the uneaten section of her meat. She didn't think she could swallow any more. Something was very wrong in the region of her stomach.

"Let's try to get some sleep. Since we don't know for certain just how reliable this circle is, we'll take turns keeping watch."

"I'll take the first watch," she volunteered.

He shook his head. "I'm liable to feel worse later on tonight. I'll need the rest then. I'll take the first watch while I've still got some energy left." Severance sank down onto the ground with his back to the curving wall. "Turn off the flamer. Don't want to waste fuel. We'll use the quartzflash for light."

"I think the circle is very safe. Nothing has even tried to cross the boundary." Cidra was only absently aware of what she was saying. Her attention was on the growing nausea that was simmering in her stomach. She was swallowing rapidly now, and her forehead felt damp from something other than the local humidity.

"Cidra?"

"It's all right, Severance. Just give me a minute." She kept her back to him and walked slowly to the edge of the circle, just beyond the range of the quartzflash.

"Cidra, come back here. What do you think you're doing?"

At that moment she lost the battle with her stomach. Her first meal of meat exited the way it had entered, leaving Cidra shuddering with unpleasant convulsions. She felt Severance's good arm around her even before she was finished.

"I'm sorry," she whispered. "I guess eating meat takes a little practice."

"I'll admit you don't seem to be taking to it as readily as you do to other Wolf ways." Gently he led her over to the stream, purified some water for her, and started to bathe her face.

"I'll do it." Embarrassed, she took the bag of water from him and knelt to finish washing her face and rinsing her mouth. "I'm all right, Severance, honestly. You must be careful not to start that shoulder bleeding again."

"Yes, Otanna."

She shot him an uncertain glance and realized that he was smiling laconically. Hastily she finished washing herself. Then she joined him at the wall where he was trying to settle into a reasonably comfortable position with the pulser resting on his drawn-up knee. His other leg was stretched out in front of him. Slowly she sank down beside him.

"You'll call me when it's my turn?" she asked.

"I'll wake you. Try to get some sleep, Cidra. Put your head down on my leg."

Carefully she obeyed, intensely conscious of the long, smooth muscles of his thigh as she used it as a pillow. She couldn't think of anything appropriate to say under the circumstances, so she lay very still, listening to the sounds of the darkness and trying not to think of the previous night's lovemaking. After all, she lectured herself, this was neither the time nor the place to dwell on the emotional and physical intimacy she had found in Severance's arms.

His arm moved, draping across her shoulder and breasts with casual possessiveness. Cidra flinched and then relaxed. His touch was comforting, she decided, not sensual. She went back to trying not to think of what she had experienced with him.

But she was very much afraid she would never forget that time of pleasure and passion. There had been a raw, primitive response coursing through her last night that had nothing to do with serenity and calm ritual. It was an emotion totally pegged to the man who had held her, and Cidra knew that a lifetime would not be long enough to dim the memories. Severance kept telling her she was a Wolf, like it or not, and last night he had proved it.

"Go to sleep, Cidra. Stop thinking about it." His hand stroked her arm with reassuring gentleness.

She knew for a fact that he couldn't read her mind. "Stop thinking about what?"

"Last night."

She grimaced. "How did you now that's what I was thinking about?"

He chuckled softly. "It was either that or else you were thinking of what you had for dinner. Since you weren't showing any signs of getting nauseated, I decided it was probably sex that was keeping you awake."

"Your ego at work, no doubt."

"No. Actually it was a lucky guess based on the fact that I was thinking about the same thing."

"Oh."

There was a pause before Severance said gently, "It changes everything, you know."

"I don't see why it should." But she was lying and she knew it. He was right. Everything had changed.

"Sweet liar." He bent his head and brushed her cheek with his lips. "You're picking up all sorts of new habits, aren't you? I'll bet you never told a single lie all the time you lived in Clementia."

The truth of that observation was disturbing. "I didn't make this journey to become a Wolf, Severance."

"I know." The brief amusement faded from his voice. "I know. Go to sleep."

She closed her eyes and was surprised to find that she could obey.

When Severance awakened her a few hours later, Cidra stirred stiffly, sitting up slowly and yawning as he shoved the butt of the pulser into her palm. She blinked sleepily, realizing vaguely that in the light of the flash his face looked more drawn and exhausted than it had earlier. She didn't think his eyes appeared quite as clear, either.

"How are you feeling?"

"Lousy. But I'll live till morning. Know how to use the pulser?"

"I know the theory, yes." She was surprised by how cold and heavy it felt in her hand.

"Shoot first if something crosses the edge of the circle. Believe me, I'll be awake shortly thereafter." He stretched out along the side of the wall, pillowing his head on her lap as if it were the way he bedded down every night. His eyes closed immediately.

Tentatively Cidra rested her arm on his chest. It seemed to her that he felt very warm. Too warm. She hoped the antiseptic spray she had used earlier was doing its job.

Staying awake with a pulser in one hand proved to be a formidable task. Cidra decided that she had never given enough credit to the heroes in the First Family novels who spent so much time standing guard. The problem was boredom.

Behind her back, the wall of the safehold continued to radiate the warmth it had collected during the day. Rather than being uncomfortable, it was rather pleasant, although by rights the balmy air should have been sufficiently warm. Beyond the edge of the circle, night things moved about their deadly business. Cidra occasionally got disconcerting glimpses of prowling eyes. Fortunately, for her peace of mind, very little else was visible. The circle was holding. The knowledge made her wonder again why the mind call had not provided a safe path back to the campsite.

That thought led to another. She realized that she was totally unaware of any lingering call in her mind. Having served the purpose of drawing the visitors to the safehold, the telepathic lure had dissolved. And with it, perhaps, had dissolved her chances of discovering the truth behind the legend.

If this safehold was the source of those small hints and uncertain promises she had set out to track down, she might be at the end of her quest before it had even properly begun. Furthermore the results of that quest showed every sign of being useless. A faded mind call left by a people who had long since passed into the shadows held little hope of being converted into the magic elixir that would make her a true Harmonic.

There was always the possibility that the mind call was not what had prompted the legends, however. If this safehold had survived the centuries intact, who knew what else might be hidden on Renaissance? She let her mind drift back to the history she had seen in the safehold. The ending bothered her. It wasn't just a sense of sadness she felt for the passing of a great civilization. Cidra realized that she also felt anger. Deep inside she hadn't wanted the Ghosts to fade away without a struggle of any kind. Unconsciously she had wanted them to fight back against their fate, not bow serenely to it.

Severance shifted slightly, not waking. She touched his forehead and found it dry and hot. Anxiously she examined the wound. As far as she could tell, no blood was leaking through the plastic adhesive. The flesh around it was swollen and red, but that probably wasn't unusual under the circumstances. Cidra rested her head against the safehold wall again and stared out into the darkness. Renaissance had a way of forcing a person to view things in fundamental terms. She found maintaining a belief in wispy tales and legends difficult when she was constantly being faced with so many real-life monsters and challenges.

Sooner or later she was going to be forced to decide how far to follow her personal dream. Every step with Teague Severance had an odd way of moving her goal farther from her grasp. Yet she could think of no other method of pursuing her quest. The thought of dropping the search altogether left her feeling shaken. She had dreamed for too many years.

Memories of the twinkling fountains and perfumed air of Clementia drifted up to tease her, reminding her of what she sought. But the delicate fragments of her visions kept getting demolished by the more powerful memories she was accumulating with Severance.

Even as she said his name in her mind he stirred again on her lap. She touched his forehead again and began to worry in earnest. He was far too warm. The wound must be infected. That thought left her feeling helpless. There was no way she could guide a wounded, sick man through the jungle. They would be easy prey.

Perhaps Severance carried other medicine in his utility loop. Trying not to disturb him, she began going through the pouches one by one. The contents were varied and curious, covering everything from the utility knife to a spare set of Free Market cubes. Sometime she would make a point of asking him why he carried the extra cubes. The explanation, Cidra was sure, would prove interesting.

She found a packet of tablets that had long since lost its label. No point speculating on what they might be. But other than the antiseptic and the adhesive bandages, there was nothing else that appeared medicinal.

Severance turned on his side, clearly fretful and uncomfortable in his sleep. Cidra hesitated and then decided to get some water from the stream. She could soak his shirt in it and use it to cool him down somewhat. Gently she lifted his head off her lap and pillowed him on the ground cover. She opened the lightweight bag and hurried to kneel beside the stream. The water felt cool against her hands, and she hoped it would have the same effect on her patient.

She was getting to her feet when she realized that Severance was trying to stagger erect. Alarmed, she went back to him. In the moonlight she could see that he wasn't focusing on her. His eyes were fevered and restless.

"Lie down, Severance. I'm going to cool you off." She tugged coaxingly on his arm.

He reacted as if he weren't even aware of her. Pulling free of her grasp, he leaned against the wall of the safehold and began making his way along it toward the entrance. Cidra suddenly realized where he was going.

"Severance, no!" She raced forward and caught his arm again, this time much more firmly. "You can't go in there. Lie down. You'll feel better when I bathe your face. Lie down, Severance."

Again he shook free of her and started toward the entrance. Cidra became frantic. If he got inside and activated the illusion trap, she would never get him back out, not in his present condition. There was no telling what the terrifying images would do to him while he was burning up with fever. They were hard enough to deal with when one was feeling normal.

He was almost at the entrance when Cidra acted out of desperation. Smoothly, swiftly, she moved against him with the dancing patterns of Moonlight and Mirrors. Given his current condition, the motions should have folded him gently to the ground.

But when he felt her touch, Severance reacted as if he were under attack. He swung around, blocking her with a swift, violent throw that caught Cidra totally off-guard. She was flat on her back before she even realized what had happened.

"Severance, wait!"

It was too late. He had vanished inside the safehold.

Chapter Fifteen

Severance slid out of the head with eyes that told Cidra that he was in shock. Deep fear of another attack had kept the Sweep at bay. Driven by it, easily field-stripping the wellbred inner man with his deft, feral, warrior-trained muscle reflexes.

She pulled herself up carefully to be readied, fought her own fear and monitored the walk-world. But, for the moment, ran into the crackling flash of uncertainty. If someone touched the cold key inside her all. Tracy did not allow him to pass through them during the greatest of illumination during starlight. There was a war of what positions turned in for the moment.

"Severance? Cmn it in. Please. Please. Let me know."

In the distance, Cidra stirred and watched back toward the walk-world was no answer. Cidra dared over to where the walk-world had gone far. She pulled at the flicked at, sat

Chapter
Fifteen

Severance was out of his head with fever. But even as she reached that conclusion, Cidra had to wonder where he had gotten the strength to toss her aside so easily. The next question was what had made him, even in a delirium, want to go back into the safehold?

She scrambled to her feet and raced to the vaulted entrance. There she braced one hand on the wall beside her. Touching something solid as she leaned into the chamber gave her a small sense of security. Inside, she could see nothing at all. The walls that allowed light to pass through them during the day produced no illumination during the night. There wasn't any sign of either the Ghost narrative or the illusion trap.

"Severance? Come back, Teague. Please. You don't want to be in there. Turn around and walk back toward me."

When there was no answer, Cidra darted over to where the quartzflash had been left. She picked it up, flicked on full power, and swung the beam around inside the safehold entrance. The light fell on Severance almost at once. He was crouched beside the heavy stone Cidra had tried to use against the apparition of the bloodsucker. His large hands were curved around the smooth surface.

"What is it?" Cidra asked, cautiously taking a step into the safehold. She had to talk him out of here if she could. If both of them got trapped inside by the illusions, she wasn't sure she would have the strength to lead him out. "Tell me what you've found, Severance."

He was totally oblivious to her. His whole attention was on the stone. Cidra took another step inside, wondering at what point the illusions would be activated. Perhaps not until she tried to turn around and walk out. She studied Severance's crouching form in the light of the quartzflash and knew she wasn't going to be able to talk him out of the safehold. She was going to have to lead him forcibly back to safety.

Counting her steps in the hope that she could retrace them even through a hail of illusion, Cidra advanced slowly into the darkened safehold. Her cautious movement didn't trigger any images. When she reached Severance, she touched his shoulder. This time he looked up at her. Cidra was shocked to see the raging fever in his eyes. She put her arm around him, and her voice instinctively slipped into the gentling, hypnotic cadence Harmonics used when they sought to soothe one of their own.

"Come with me, Severance. All is safe with me. Let me lead you to safety. Outside, the air is cool and calm. You'll feel better outside. Come with me and be safe. Outside, all is serene."

She felt him tremble and sensed that somewhere in his fevered mind he was trying to understand. Cidra also had the impression that he was torn between conflicting needs. She saw the way his hands rested on the stone.

"Is it the stone you want? Bring it with you, Severance. Pick up the stone and bring it with you. Let's go outside where it's cool and clear."

His shoulder muscles flexed beneath her arm, and he picked up the stone. Cidra straightened, relieved when he stood up beside her. When she tugged on his arm, he followed her docilely. Warily she guided him toward the doorway, fully expecting to find their exit impeded by anything from a giant bloodsucker to a wall of light.

Nothing happened. Using the quartzflash, Cidra made it back outside with her patient in tow. Breathing a sigh of relief, she guided Severance to the wall and eased him down onto the ground. He was still astonishingly docile, willing to go where she led as long as he had the stone.

"What is it about the rock, Severance? Why do you want it?"

He clutched it protectively. "Warm. Feels good. Feels warm. I'm so cold."

"You're already burning up," she whispered, knowing that he didn't really hear her. "Lie down and I'll see if I can break that fever." She pushed him down onto the ground. He curled around the stone and closed his eyes.

He did seem calmer, Cidra decided as she began bathing him. Perhaps the stone was having some beneficial effect. She couldn't imagine what it could be, though. When she touched it, the hard, smooth sphere felt faintly warm. Perhaps it carried a residue of the heat it had collected during the day.

The hours dragged on toward dawn. With one eye on the small movements that occasionally occurred around the edge of the circle, and another on Severance, Cidra kept watch and worried about the fever. The pulser was never far from her hand, although she no longer had any fear of something cross-ing the unseen boundary of the circle. She kept the pulser close primarily because Severance's last, clear instructions had been to do so. He was still the pilot in command, she thought as she filled the water bag for the fifth time. And she was still the one and only member of his crew.

As dawn filtered slowly through the tangle of overhead leaves and vines, Cidra decided that the stone wasn't doing Severance much good. He still clung to it, but she didn't like the way he seemed to have become dependent on it. The fever wasn't abating, and the added warmth of the stone might easily be doing harm. Kneeling beside him, Cidra tried to remove it from his grasp.

"No." He reacted sharply, protecting the sphere with both arms. For a moment his eyes opened, staring at her with fierce resistance. "Don't touch it," he said very clearly.

They were the first clear words he had spoken all night. Cidra tried to reason with him. "It's warm, Severance. You need to be cool. Give me the stone. You can have it back later."

"Don't touch it." His eyes closed again, but his grip on the stone didn't loosen.

Cidra gave up on the task and went back to trying to cool him down with stream water. Around the perimeter of the circle the shift from night to day was taking place. A few choked shrieks marked the efforts of a few lingering hunters. She was getting used to the sounds of the jungle, Cidra realized dis-passionately. She was amazed at how many things she was becoming accustomed to seeing, hearing, and doing these days.

As the day began to warm, Cidra became aware of a slight dizzy sensation. The light-headedness Severance had warned her about, she assumed. She wasn't sure what to do about it. She didn't dare risk eating any of the plant life. Severance had been convinced that there was too much possibility of being poisoned. Without the proper equipment she couldn't test for toxins.

For a while she tried to convince herself that she could go another day without eating. After all, she had fasted more than once for a day or two in a secret effort to open her stubborn mind. It had been a long time ago, back when she had still believed she might be able to catapult herself into Harmonichood by sheer willpower. The exercise hadn't worked, although it had produced a light-headed feeling that for a while convinced her she might be onto some useful technique.

The problem today was that she simply couldn't afford to be light-headed. Not with Harmony-knew-what prowling around outside the circle and a sick man on her hands. She had to maintain her strength, both physically and mentally. And that meant she was going to have to find something to eat.

She glanced toward the perimeter of the protected ground, looking for the remains of the hopper Severance had skinned and cleaned the previous evening. He had pushed the entrails outside the circle. There was no sign of anything, not even the head. Renaissance had taken care of the garbage in its own sure fashion.

Not that she wanted to eat whatever was left of the poor hopper. Cidra's stomach grew queasy again just at the thought. She went back to the endless task of bathing Severance and tried to put food out of her mind.

But when she stumbled a little on a trip to the stream, she began to worry. She had no idea how long she was going to be trapped inside this circle with Severance. Common sense dictated that she not let herself grow weak. She was going to have to eat. Just existing on this planet seemed to take a lot of inner energy. Cidra eyed the pulser and wondered how hard it would be to hit something such as the hopper.

Surely the principles of aiming and firing a weapon couldn't be fundamentally different than the task of collecting and focusing a mind for deep, concentrated study. Harmonic philosophy taught that all things could be assessed and comprehended. In addition to focusing and concentration, she would need a certain amount of coordination, Cidra supposed. She had that from her training in Moonlight and Mirrors.

Picking up the pulser, she went to the edge of the circle and sat cross-legged. It could be a long wait until something edible wandered close enough to assure her a clear shot. She took the time to slowly clear her mind of extraneous thought. If she was going to do this, she would do it quickly and cleanly. Using the techniques of meditation, she willed herself to an outer and inner stillness. She would become one with the weapon, not a fake Harmonic holding a foreign instrument of destruction. She must make the pulser an extension of herself.

Deliberately she fused herself and the pulser into a single entity. It wasn't particularly difficult once she had cleared her mind of the ramifications of what she was about to do. In some ways she was merely applying the methods she used for programming a computer or writing a poem. The underlying philosophical harmony of all tasks was the same.

Time passed, bringing nothing into range except a slithering green snake that didn't look very edible to Cidra. She waited. Behind her Severance was quiet, still wrapped around his precious rock.

When the small hopper flitted into view, Cidra's hand came up and her finger squeezed the trigger without any hesitation. It was what she had been waiting for, and her body responded accordingly. The hopper flipped over, quivered for a second, and then went limp. Cidra lowered the pulser.

Slowly she got to her feet and shook herself out of the trance. As she stared at the dead creature all of her natural revulsion to eating meat returned in a sickening wave. This time she kept her stomach under control. She stepped cautiously out of the circle, caught the hopper by the ears, and yanked it back to safety.

For a moment she simply looked at her catch, wondering how she was going to find the nerve to cut into it. She had almost talked herself out of making the effort when she experienced another wave of unsteadiness. There was no point in waiting any longer. Resolutely she went over to where Severance lay and reached into the utility loop for the knife.

The job was, as Severance had said, not neat and tidy like a holotape of a dissection. Twice Cidra had to stop long enough to let the racking heaves pass. Both times she recovered and went back to the task. She knew the theory of what needed to be done. She'd had a very thorough education. When she was finished, she pushed the entrails and the head outside the circle.

She washed the hopper's blood from her hands and let her stomach have its way one more time. Then she switched on the flamer and spitted a hindquarter on the point of the knife. Ignoring the hissing of crackling fat, she roasted her kill. She stilled her mind and her body before she took the first bite by repeating the familiar words that preceded a Harmonic meal.

This time the food stayed down. It took an effort of will, and there were a few seconds when Cidra wasn't sure she was going to win the contest with her stomach, but in the end she did. Slowly and methodically she ate the entire hindquarter. Then she roasted the second hindquarter and carried it over to Severance.

"Try to eat," she coaxed, letting him have a whiff of the meat. He didn't respond. When she tried to insert a bite between his lips, he spit it out. With a sigh Cidra sat back on her heels and wondered what to do next.

An hour later she happened to glance across the circle and saw that the remains of the hopper were gone. Another Renaissance meal was concluded, bones and all. Nothing went to waste on this planet.

The day progressed with painful slowness. Twice Cidra dozed, snapping uneasily awake each time. Perhaps it would be better if she slept during the daylight. If she didn't, she was bound to drift off to sleep tonight. The circle seemed so safe. The third time her eyes closed, Cidra allowed herself to drift into sleep.

A faint cracking sound woke her some time later. She opened her eyes slowly and realized that dusk was settling on the jungle. She and Severance had spent another whole day here. The thought of her companion made her glance automatically in his direction. He was still sleeping soundly, curled around the stone.

She heard the cracking noise again and roused herself fully, reaching for the pulser in her lap. She climbed to her feet and peered around the circle. Nothing stirred near the edge as far as she could see. When the sound came a third time, she suddenly realized where it was coming from and whirled around toward Severance. She saw the rock he was holding shiver in his grasp.

"Sweet Harmony!" Cidra edged closer, trying to see what was happening. Severance was still huddled around his possession, but the stone seemed to be quivering in his arms. Even as she watched, a distinct crack appeared in the black surface. Unaware of what she was doing, Cidra brought up the nose of the pulser and stepped forward. This time she would take the stone away from Severance by force. Surely, after all these hours of fever, he was no longer strong enough to stop her.

There was a sharp splintering sound from the rock just as Cidra reached for it. Severance groaned and hugged it closer. She succeeded in pushing one of his hands out of the way and had just gotten a grip on the sphere when it cracked completely open.

She heard the savage hissing before she saw the damp reptilian head emerge from the broken stone. Frantically Cidra struggled to pull the rock away from Severance before whatever was inside escaped. Fragments of the shell came free in her hand. The head whipped out, snapping at her hand with a mouthful of tiny sharp teeth.

Cidra yelped and yanked her fingers out of the way. The creature turned immediately toward Severance's midsection, its blue, leathery body uncurling from the remains on the shell. With a sudden shock of logic Cidra realized what was going to happen. Severance was intended as the hatchling's first meal.

She didn't dare fire the pulser at this range. She would surely kill Severance as well as whatever was trying to eat him. Furiously she banged the nose of her weapon against the creature's snout. The blow managed to get its attention away from Severance. The creature hissed again and struck at the offending pulser. Its teeth closed around the metal and then released it as it apparently realized that the pulser couldn't be eaten.

Frantically Cidra slammed the weapon against the leathery blue head once more. Again she got the creature to snap at the muzzle of the pulser. This time she jerked upward and out. With its mouth still locked around the metal mouth of the pulser, the blue reptile was carried with it. The creature released its hold in midair and fell to the ground in a hissing coil. It struck at Cidra as if realizing that she was the source of the problem.

Cidra raised the pulser and fired with the same unthinking sureness she had used to bring down the hopper. The reptile jerked twice. It writhed horribly on the ground, attempting even in its death throes to get back to its intended meal. Cidra fired again, and at last it went still.

Behind Cidra Severance groaned sharply, still not waking. He moved restlessly and spoke in a slurred, hot tone. "Cidra. *Cidra.*"

She ignored him, her attention still on the dead stone creature. She wanted it out of the circle. It was wrong here. Dead or alive, it had no business in this place. She kicked at the body with the toe of her boot. It flipped over, revealing four appendages on the iridescent light blue belly. The front pair terminated in projections that looked too much like human fingers for Cidra's peace of mind. She kicked at the dead body again, intent on getting it out of the circle. The sense of wrongness was almost overpowering now. She knew for certain that she didn't want to touch it with her hands.

Three more kicks brought the stone creature's body to the edge of the circle. Cidra swung the toe of her boot one more time and pitched the remains into the thick greenery on the other side of the magic perimeter. There was a stir of activity almost at once. She got a glimpse of a furred tail as something pounced and then heard the crunch of jaws on a blue, leathery body. Renaissance would take care of the problem. Cidra hurried back to Severance.

He was more restless than ever. The front of his shirt was ripped where the creature had taken a bite out of it, but there were no marks on his skin. Cidra breathed a sigh of relief and knelt beside him. His stirred under her hand.

"So hot. It's so reeting hot. I can't stand it." He tore at his shirt with his hands.

"Stop it, Severance." Firmly she pulled his fingers free of the shirt. "I'll cool you down. I promise." She reached for the bag and poured water over his head, throat, and chest, dampening the shirt. He shivered and quieted. Lapsing back into an unintelligible mumble, he curled up again and appeared to be about to go back to sleep. Cidra wetted him again and waited. The delirious mumbling halted finally, and Cidra decided that he was asleep. She sat back and tried to think.

The first thing that came to mind was the memory of the four black stones that were piled in the safehold. She had to destroy them. There was no telling when Severance might decide to make another trip inside and carry one out. Furthermore, there was no telling when one of those awful eggs might hatch of its own accord. The thought of four of the dark blue reptiles wandering out of the safehold seeking food was more than Cidra wanted to contemplate.

Wearily she got to her feet again and went to stand at the entrance of the safehold. From the walls came a faint glow, illuminating the interior now. At the far end of the room the four stones rested in shadow. Cidra tried to decide what she would do if she went into the room and accidentally triggered the illusions. She would need the Screamer. She went back to Severance and removed it from his loop. Then she tightened her grip around the pulser and stepped inside the chamber.

Nothing happened, just as nothing had happened the first time she had entered. Staying close to the wall in case she needed to use its surface as a point of reference, she walked slowly around the room. She reached the small group of eggs at the back without having touched off either the Ghost history or the horrific illusions. Facing the eggs, Cidra took aim and systematically shot each.

At first nothing happened. The tough stone casing around the creatures seemed to absorb the energy of the pulser. She stepped closer and fired again. This time one of the shells cracked. When it fell apart, Cidra could see that the reptile inside was dead. She used the pulser to break open the rest of the shells so that she could assure herself that all the creatures were destroyed.

A part of her wanted to clear the remains out of the safehold, but she didn't feel up to the task. She would have to content herself with knowing that the eggs were no longer a menace. Cidra turned back toward the entrance, one palm still flattened on the curving wall, and trotted quickly toward the sunshine.

Expecting a wave of illusions to block her path, she didn't realize she was holding her breath until she stepped outside without incident. It occurred to her that perhaps the illusions were somehow tied to the eggs. Perhaps a protective device. With the eggs destroyed the trap might not work any longer. As for the Ghosts' history projection, perhaps it was simply so old that it had faded into oblivion after one last showing.

There was no point speculating on either possibility. She had her hands full, tending Severance. For the next two hours she kept up the cooling baths. He slipped in and out of a troubled sleep, muttering occasionally and once in a while knocking her hands away in restless irritation.

At the end of the two hours of bathing his fevered body, Cidra thought she detected some improvement. He seemed to be cooling down at last. She peeled off the bandage and examined the wounds. They were red and swollen but not alarmingly so. She sprayed more antiseptic on them and then covered them again with the plastic adhesive. Severance opened his eyes just as she was finishing the task. His gaze was clearer than it had been for hours.

"Did I hurt you?" Cidra smiled, relieved to see something besides fever in his eyes. He still looked dazed and uncomprehending, but she could see him struggling to identify her.

"How could you hurt me? You're from Clementia."

Cidra shook her head at his logic and touched his temple. "You're on the mend, Severance. Your fever is breaking."

"I didn't take care of you. I almost got you killed."

"No, Severance. You saved my life. More than once."

He moved his head in restless denial. "Just like Jeude. Almost got you killed, just like Jeude."

"Hush," she soothed. "You didn't kill your brother."

"Should never have let him go to QED alone. He was too soft. Too gentle. Followed a distress signal right into the ground. Never realized he'd been tricked."

Cidra frowned. "Be easy, Severance."

"Had to kill Racer. Racer set up the signal. Racer tried to take you from me. He would have hurt you, Cidra. He wanted to hurt you to hurt me."

"I know," she whispered, wondering about what he had said earlier. "Racer drew your brother to his death with a fake distress signal?"

"Racer murdered Jeude. Said he hadn't meant to, but he did. And I never even knew until . . . until—" He broke off, clearly groping for some sense of time.

"It's all right, Severance. It's all over. Everything's over. Racer is dead."

"All my fault," he muttered again. "I put you in danger. Just like I put Jeude in danger."

"Severance, listen to me. It is not your fault. You've taken care of everything. Racer is dead."

But he wasn't listening. The gray eyes looked up at her with unnatural intensity. "I let Jeude get killed, and I almost let you get killed. You're like him. I'm supposed to protect you. You and he both belong in Clementia." His voice faded as his eyes began to close. "You're like him."

Cidra stared down at his hard face as he drifted back into sleep. "No, Severance. You're wrong. I'm not like Jeude." Her eyes fell on the pulser that lay close at hand on the ground. "I'm not at all like Jeude."

She bathed him once more, but now she was certain that he had turned the corner. The fever was definitely subsiding. A damp, healing sweat filmed his skin. Cidra concentrated on getting Severance to drink plenty of water. Toward nightfall she stationed herself near the edge of the circle, slipped into the trance that made the pulser a part of her, and waited for another unwary hopper. Now she was amazed that anything as stupid as a hopper survived on Renaissance. The food chain was a complex thing. Right now she was sitting at the top of that chain: a reasonably well-adapted predator.

For someone who had never before eaten meat, doing so was a major change. But, then, everything else in her life was changing, so her eating habits might as well also. A flicker of ears caught her attention. The hopper made a dash through a relatively open area of vegetation, and Cidra killed it in mid-leap.

This time she didn't throw up when she cleaned the carcass. Cidra wasn't sure if that was an improvement or not. It seemed to her that part of her should still be fastidious enough to get sick at the thought of killing and butchering food. On the other hand, a steady stomach was proving much more convenient than an unsteady one.

When Severance awoke long enough to eat some of the roasted meat and drink more water, Cidra stopped worrying about her weakening vegetarian ethics. She was too busy being grateful that she had managed to get her patient to eat.

After dinner she settled herself against the wall of the safe-hold and cradled Severance's head in her lap. Fingers wrapped around the grip of the pulser, she leaned back against the wall and wondered if she would be able to stay awake all night. Probably not. She was exhausted. She could only hope that the ring of safety would protect both herself and Severance during the times she was unable to keep her eyes open.

She slept off and on during the long night. Every time she awoke she could tell by the chronometer on Severance's loop that she had only been napping for fifteen or twenty minutes. the usual screams and cries of the jungle went on all around the edge of the circle, but nothing encroached.

Severance slept soundly, pillowed in her lap. Cidra could tell that the fever had left his body. With any luck he would be feeling much better in the morning. She still wasn't sure how long he would need to recover enough to risk the trip back to the campsite, but at least he was on the mend. If need be, they could spend another couple of days here in the circle.

Once or twice Cidra awakened during the night to discover Severance burrowing closer to her, his face turned into her midsection as if he sought comfort from her warmth. She wrinkled her nose as she caught her own unbathed scent. In the morning she would clean herself at the stream. Never in her life had she gone so long without a bath. She fantasized for quite a while about having unlimited access to one of Clementia's elegant bathing rooms.

The night passed without incident. When dawn filtered once more through the green canopy, Cidra yawned and gently eased Severance's head out of her lap. She left him sleeping while she undressed and knelt beside the sparkling stream. The water looked clear and pure, and she could no longer resist it.

The liquid felt wonderfully cool and bracing in the morning air. She even undid her frazzled braids and washed her hair in the bubbling stream. She arranged it loosely around her shoulders to dry in the sun. By the time she was finished, Cidra decided that she felt like a new woman. She put her trousers back on but decided to rinse out her shirt. Leaving it to dry on the green carpet, she picked up the pulser and walked to the edge of the circle to look for breakfast. Carefully she put herself into the trance that enabled her to become a hunter.

Severance yawned and stretched, distantly aware of an ache in his shoulder. He flexed it irritably and felt the pull of bandages. Slowly memory returned. He was stiff, and his head no longer felt nearly as comfortable as it had when he'd been sleeping in Cidra's lap.

Cidra's lap.

The thought opened his eyes. He saw the curving translucent wall rising above him, felt the green cushion under his back, and wondered how in a renegade's hell he'd been so stupid as to let himself get used for target practice by a lockmouth.

Reluctantly he rolled onto his side, looking for Cidra. He saw her rise from the edge of the stream, her slender body nude from the waist up. Her sweetly curved breasts looked perfect in the primitive morning light. The dark brown fire of her hair gleamed damply in the sun. Severance stared at her in silence, absorbing the sight of her, and then he winced at the direction of his thoughts. He was definitely feeling better, Severance decided.

He was about to speak when he saw Cidra bend down, scoop up the pulser, and walk to the edge of the circle. At first he thought she had seen something to alarm her, and then he saw her sink down into a cross-legged position. She went very still, her slender back elegantly straight. Before long, there was a flash of movement in the bushes. As calmly and coolly as a lifelong huntress she squeezed the trigger. A hopper flopped to the ground within easy reach.

Severance stared at the scene with a sense of shock that quickly changed to admiration. He sat up as she reached out of the circle to catch hold of the hopper by its ears.

"Is this the same lady who can't look a torla steak in the eye?"

"Severance!" She whirled around, the hopper in one fist, and gazed at him in delight. For an instant, relief and happiness lit her whole face, and then she remembered that she wasn't wearing her shirt. A tide of pink flowed into her cheeks and throat. She dropped the hopper and made a dash for the damp garment she had left beside the stream. "How are you feeling?" she asked as she turned away from him to put on the wet shirt.

"Like I've been hit with a freight sled."

She turned around as she finished fastening the shirt and peered at him. "You look much better. I've been very worried, Severance. You were quite feverish from the wound."

He shrugged his injured shoulder, assessing the pain critically. "I think I'm going to live. How much time have we lost?"

"We've spent two nights here in the circle." She came forward slowly. "Do you remember any of it?"

He smiled. "Some. You have a very nice lap." He started to get to his feet. Something sharp on the ground dug into his leg. He reached down and picked up a small, jagged object. "Where did this come from?"

Cidra glanced at the scrap of shell. "Now that," she said, "is a very interesting story."

"You can tell it to me while I clean the hopper."

Her eyes brightened. "Do you feel up to cleaning it? I can't say I like the job."

He grimaced. "How many have you cleaned?"

"Two."

Severance shook his head wonderingly. "Incredible. You've become a real carnivore."

She made a face. "I prefer not to think about it."

He held out his hand. "I can handle the pulser again too. Maybe not quite as well as you seem to be doing, but it would make me feel useful."

She glanced down at the weapon in her fingers. "I've grown used to having it around."

Severance realized that her reluctance to give him the pulser was real. Gently he took it from her and examined the charge window. "How many shots did it take to get the first hopper? The charge is way down."

"Oh," she said easily, "I've been shooting a lot of things besides hoppers."

Her words sent a distinct jolt through him. A fleeting glimpse of a nightmare cropped up from out of nowhere. There had been something evil and dangerous in his fevered dreams, something that had demanded his help. The image flickered and died, leaving behind an unpleasant taste.

"I think you'd better tell me what I've missed," Severance said.

Chapter Sixteen

"Eggs, Severance. Those stones were some creature's eggs. Really nasty little renegades too. The one you were clinging to tried to eat you alive the second it hatched. Don't you remember anything at all about going back into the safehold to bring out one of the stones?"

Severance concentrated on the task of butchering the hopper. "No." Then he hesitated, his jaw tightening. "There were some dreams, though."

"Dreams?" Cidra waited, aware that he was struggling with himself. She couldn't decide if he was trying to remember or trying to forget.

Severance paused with the knife in his hand and stared unseeingly into the jungle. "I remember having to do something. It was important. No, it was *imperative*. Something's life depended on it. And if I obeyed, I would stop freezing. I was so damned cold. That's all I remember."

Cidra wasn't sure she believed him, but she did believe that was all he wanted to remember. "You insisted on going back into the safehold. I tried to stop you with my Moonlight and Mirrors routine. I might as well have been trying to dance with you."

His head came around quickly, eyes alarmed. "Did I hurt you?"

"Knocked me flat," she assured him cheerfully. Seeing the expression on his face, she relented. "Don't worry about it. I'm fine. You weren't out to hurt me, you just wanted to be left alone. The interesting part about all this is that when you went inside the safehold to get the egg, you didn't trigger the illusions."

"How do you know? Perhaps I was too far gone to know what I was seeing."

"I know because I went in after you, and I didn't see a thing."

"You went in after me?" He sighed as if in resignation, but he didn't launch into a lecture. "Go on."

She told him about the hatching of the egg and her decision to destroy the rest of them. "The illusions didn't stop me when I tried to leave the safehold after finishing off those eggs, either. I think they were tied to them somehow. A protective device. I wouldn't be surprised if the idea was that the illusions trapped the prey close to the eggs."

"Food for the hatchlings?"

"And perhaps a source of warmth for them. No telling how long those eggs have been in there. It wasn't until you curled around one that it hatched. What kind of creature could it have been, Severance? From everything we've seen nothing else on this planet except us has crossed the boundary of this circle or gone into the safehold."

"Except the Ghosts themselves," he pointed out.

"I refuse to believe that those blue things are related to the Ghosts in any way."

"You're the well-educated member of the crew, Cidra. You should know by now that refusing to believe in something doesn't mean it doesn't exist."

"Those egg creatures are something out of a nightmare," she insisted. "The Ghosts were a gentle, civilized people."

"Who at one time conquered this very ungentle, uncivilized planet. They might have become soft at the end, but they sure as hell weren't at the beginning."

"I'm not going to argue with you about it. I just know that those blue things aren't related to the Ghosts."

"Maybe they were watchdogs for the Ghosts," Severance suggested thoughtfully. "Guardians for the safehold?"

"I don't think so. There's something wrong about those eggs and the creatures inside them. They don't fit in here on Renaissance."

At that comment Severance laughed shortly. "Anything that can kill its own food and eat it raw fits in just fine here on Renaissance."

Cidra folded her arms across her chest, pacing restlessly around the circle. "It wasn't just that they were vicious and ugly. Lots of things here seem to be vicious and ugly. But even the worst of them, that lockmouth for instance, seem to belong in some way I can't explain. Those eggs don't. Or didn't. Remember when we first went into the safehold, you said there was a feeling of alienness?"

"Yeah. You didn't agree, though. You were too wrapped up with Ghost stories."

"It wasn't the Ghosts who felt alien. But the presence of the eggs might have bothered your instincts on some level."

"My instincts are fairly basic, Cidra. Chiefly focused on staying alive, eating, sleeping, and, uh, one or two other fundamental matters. They're not the elevated, intuitive instincts of a Harmonic. I don't see why I would have sensed the eggs in some special manner."

She stopped pacing at the edge of the circle. "Well, whatever they were, they're gone now."

He stood up, leaving the skinned hopper on the ground near the edge of the circle. Coming up behind Cidra, Severance said softly, "Thanks to you. I'm not sure I'm paying you enough. I've never had a crew member quite like you, Cidra Rainforest. Loyalty and resourcefulness above and beyond the call."

She turned, aware of a deep feeling of pleasure. She dipped her head formally. "It is as nothing, Teague Severance. Do not concern yourself. All is serene."

He grinned, a brief flash of teeth that disappeared quickly as his eyes grew serious. "Still a few remnants of Harmonic ways left, hm? Amazing. How are you handling the transformation, Cidra?"

Her flush of pleasure faded. She thought about killing hoppers and little blue monsters. Memories of trying to stay awake with a sick man lying in her lap and a pulser in her hand flooded her mind. "There has not been a great deal of choice in the matter."

He looked at her oddly. "No, there hasn't, has there? I haven't given you much choice." Abruptly he turned away to set up the flamer.

Sensing his inner withdrawal, Cidra stood quietly, watching his efficient manners. "Your arm seems much better this morning."

"Yes."

"Severance, while you were delirious you said I was like Jeude. But I'm not, am I?"

He studied the flame he had started before answering slowly.

"Jeude had great courage. He would have done what had to be done. But it would have torn him apart."

"It hasn't torn me apart." She made the observation almost to herself.

"You shouldn't have had to face what you've faced since you shipped out with me. You weren't raised to confront murderers and monsters. I should have followed my instincts that first night and packed you off to Clementia."

"You didn't have that choice, Teague Severance. I make my own decisions."

"Let's argue about it after we get back to Try Again."

She wanted to argue now. Cidra lifted her head proudly, prepared to defend herself and her rights. But she stopped cold as her eye caught a flash of movement at the edge of the circle.

"Severance!"

He was on his feet at once, the pulser in his fist. "What is it?"

"The hopper. The one you just finished cleaning. It's gone."

He swore, striding toward the spot where the carcass had lain on the ground. "I left it inside the circle."

Cidra's eyes widened. "I know. Something with a long orange tail just reached into the circle and grabbed it. Severance, in all the time we've been here nothing has come inside that circle."

"Either there's something else besides us that's immune or . . ." He dug the toe of his boot into the invisible line of protection. A small worm slithered to the surface and disappeared again. Until now there hadn't even been any worms inside the protected area. "Or the circle is shrinking."

"Why would it start shrinking now?"

"How should I know? It might have been a lot bigger once than it is now. It might have been gradually shrinking all along but at such a slow rate that you haven't noticed."

"Or perhaps it started fading when the mind call was activated one last time. It's probably all connected." Unhappily she stared at the edge of the circle. "I hope everything we've found isn't going to disappear. There's so much to learn here, Severance. So much to be explored."

"We can worry about that later. Right now we've got another problem."

"What problem?"

He absently massaged his shoulder. "I was thinking of spending one more night here and leaving in the morning. But if this circle is shrinking, I don't want to risk it. The whole reeting thing could disintegrate in the middle of the night, and we'd be left in what would definitely qualify as an awkward situation. We'll have to start back to the campsite today."

"Do you feel up to making the journey?" Cidra asked anxiously.

"My shoulder's stiff, but I feel fairly normal."

"I would have thought that the fever would have left you feeling exhausted."

"I know. But maybe the fever wasn't caused by the wound," Severance said thoughtfully. "Maybe it had something to do with what happened in the safehold. If I've been as sick as you've said, I shouldn't be feeling this good so soon. But my shoulder feels the way it should after two days of that antiseptic. And I'm not weak the way I should be after spending several hours in a delirium."

"You think the eggs caused the fever? I wonder. What if they were capable of sensing your weakness after the lockmouth clawed your shoulder? Perhaps they sensed the blood and somehow focused on you. Something drew you back into that safehold. And when you came out, you wouldn't let go of that stone."

His mouth tightened. "I think our luck here is running out.

We'll be better off making a try for the campsite than sitting here waiting for the circle to collapse. This time around I'll make it a point to stay alert on the trip out. Let's get our stuff together."

Cidra obeyed, collecting the water bag and the knife as Severance repacked the utility loop. She paused when she spotted the stone shard on the ground. "I think I'll take this back to Desma. She'll find it interesting." She dropped it into her pocket.

"All set?"

Cidra nodded, glancing back at the safehold. "I hope it lasts until someone gets here with a holotape set to record the history stored inside."

"Even if the circle doesn't hold much longer, it will take quite a while for that safehold to be reduced to rubble, even here on Renaissance. Let's go."

"Does it strike you, Severance, that you're always asking if I'm ready to go?"

"You'll get used to it." The pulser was gripped in his right fist as he started back into the jungle. The utility knife was in his left hand.

Cidra smiled to herself and followed.

One hour and two dead green slicers later, Severance called a halt. He tapped the face of the directional indicator and sighed. "We've got a problem."

Cidra battled at a small buzzing creature intent on landing on her cheek. "You're thinking we didn't walk for much more than an hour that first night?"

"I see that the thought has crossed your mind too."

"We might have been totally unaware of the time," she offered.

"It was dawn when we reached the safehold. I think we left

the campsite just shortly before dawn. No more than an hour before."

"What does the directional gadget show?"

"That we're within a few meters of the skimmer."

Cidra looked around at the heavy vegetation surrounding them on all sides. "I don't see a river."

"Neither do I."

"Perhaps we're just a few meters away." Tentatively Cidra shoved at a hanging vine. "This stuff is so thick, we could be a short distance from the river and not be able to see it."

"We should be able to smell it."

She remembered the unique scent of the muddy water. "You've got a point. Okay, fearless and respected leader, what next?"

"We'll give the beacon another ten minutes. If it hasn't led us to anything familiar by then, we'll backtrack."

"Is that why you took a whack out of the tree with your knife every couple of meters? So we'd have a trail to follow back to the circle?"

He lifted one shoulder negligently. "You can't be too careful on Renaissance."

"So I've noticed. How are you feeling?"

"Fine. The shoulder's stiff, but it's not getting in my way."

"Want me to wear the utility loop for a while? I imagine it gets a little heavy. You've got so many interesting things packed inside." She stepped close, reaching for the closure of the rantgan leather loop. "I was going to ask you a couple of questions about what you carry around with you, Severance." As she moved, the edge of her skirt brushed against Severance's arm.

"Forget the loop. I said I'm fine. I'll feel naked without it." He was staring at the directional device as she stepped back. "Do that again, Cidra."

"Do what?"

"Come close."

She saw the direction of his attention. "Something wrong?"

"Just brush up against my arm again."

Uneasily she did as she was told. When she started to move back, Severance caught her wrist and held her close. "What is it?" she asked.

"Look at the signal," he muttered. "It's going crazy."

"You mean, I'm causing it to go crazy?" Cidra's mouth felt very dry.

"Or something you've got on you. I don't understand. These things are virtually fail-proof."

"Desma says mechanical stuff is always breaking down on Renaissance."

"Empty your pockets. Hurry!"

She reached inside her shirt, and the first thing her hand touched was the stone shard. Slowly, with a feeling of doom, she brought it out and held it toward the directional device.

"Sweet reeting hell." Severance jerked the shard from her hand and waved it back and forth across the surface of the device.

"I'm sorry, Severance." Cidra stood in dismay, bearing the full weight of a heavy guilt. "I didn't realize it would cause trouble."

He tossed the shard as far as he could into the undergrowth. "Neither did I, although I suppose we should have made an educated guess on the subject. I wonder what it was about that slice of eggshell that could screw up the signal on this thing."

"How does it read now?"

"It says the skimmer is west of us and not very close. We've got a long walk ahead." He looked up and started to say something else.

Cidra held up her palm. "Don't say it. I'll say it. Let's get going."

A reluctant smile edged Severance's mouth. "You're learning." He started forward with Cidra close behind.

They hadn't gone more than a few paces when Cidra saw the glint of black stone. "Severance, there's the shard. But I thought you threw it much farther."

He turned to glance back. "I did. And I threw it in a different direction. That's not the shard." Cautiously he used the knife to push aside the heavy mass of creeping vines. A black, curving surface glinted in the dappled light.

"Sweet Harmony in hell. It looks like a giant version of one of the stones."

"Severance, we've got to get out of here!" Cidra tugged at him frantically, but he shook off her hands. "If it's another egg, it's a huge one. Anything that hatches from that thing isn't going to be stopped very easily. You saw how much of the pulser charge it took to destroy the little eggs."

"If it's an egg, it's already cracked."

"What?" She peered around his shoulder to see what he was looking at. The huge sphere was crumpled and jagged on one side, revealing a gaping hole. Inside there was only darkness. Cidra edged back, trying to pull Severance with her. Everything within her that had felt wrong about the eggs was reacting violently to this discovery.

"It's not made of the same material as the egg, although it's the same color." Severance touched the black surface. "It's a metal of some kind. Like nothing I've ever seen." He dug out the quartzflash and shined it into the dark hole. He sucked in his breath. "It's a ship, Cidra. Some kind of vehicle. It's got to be!"

She stared at the array of mechanisms revealed in the light

of the flash. The shapes were oddly distorted to her eyes, unfamiliar and strange. "Not a human ship."

"You can say that again." Severance stepped closer, clearly fascinated. "Not a Ghost ship, either. At least nothing in here appears designed to fit one of the creatures we saw in that history lesson we got in the safehold. Their hands were similar to ours, and anything mechanical they built would have had similar gripping surfaces. The height of everything is wrong too. Some of it's too high and some of it's too low. Everything's made out of this same black metal."

"Severance, it looks too much like one of those eggs. The same color, the same shape, and it was that shard in my pocket that drew us here. I told you those blue things were alien to this planet. Let's get out of here."

But he was already moving closer to the gaping black hole. It occurred to Cidra that any man with Severance's natural aptitude for keeping machines in working order was probably going to be overcome with a fascination for this alien gadget.

"Whatever was once in this thing is long gone, Cidra. If it survived the crash, it probably stepped outside and became a meal for one of the natives."

"No," she said with quiet certainty. "First it carried its eggs into the safehold. Maybe it was following the same mind call we followed. Maybe the call draws anything above a certain level of intelligence to it. Perhaps that's how it screens out the rest of the jungle life. It was meant as a record for another intelligent species to find. Whatever was in this ship must have found it. The safehold probably looked like a good place to leave the eggs."

"You're assuming that the ship and whatever was inside was alien to Stanza Nine."

"I know it was," Cidra said stubbornly. "There's something wrong about it, I keep telling you."

"It will take a full-scale scientific investigation to find out the truth. Perhaps another intelligent species developed on this planet."

"No."

He waved the quartzflash around inside the ship. "You can't be sure of that, Cidra."

"Severance, please come away from there. After what I saw of those eggs, we've got to assume that the ship is dangerous. Maybe it's protected the way the eggs were."

"Just a minute. I want to get a closer look at this stuff. Doesn't look like this metal has had the corrosion damage most metal gets on Renaissance." He whistled soundlessly between his teeth, his eyes gleaming with barely suppressed excitement. "We've got to be able to find this ship again." Severance punched a code into the directional indicator. "Between this thing and the safehold, I'm going to make enough credit to launch Severance Pay, Ltd. in a big way."

"Is that all you can think about? Selling this information? You've got a one-track mind, Teague Severance! This is the find of the century, ultimately maybe far more significant than the safehold. And all you can talk about is how much you'll get when you sell the location."

"Yeah, well, a man has to keep his eye on the main chance." He edged closer, shining the flash around the edge of the jagged metal. Suddenly they heard a sharp hiss, and something with a long tail and four short legs leapt from the darkness. Severance ducked, and the disturbed inhabitant of the ship disappeared into the trees.

"What was that?" Cidra took a deep breath.

"A roacher. They like caves. That one must have thought he'd found a really nifty home when he came across this thing." He wrinkled his nose as he leaned forward again. "What a stench. The roacher's been living here a while."

Cidra stepped closer, caught a whiff of the rancid odor, and nearly choked. "Are you going inside that ship?"

"I just want to take a quick look around."

"I don't think that's a good idea, Severance."

"I'll be just a minute." He stepped over the jagged edge. "Stay here in the opening where I can keep an eye on you."

Reluctantly she moved closer, aware of a deep curiosity that was at war with her instinct to put as much distance as possible between herself and the ship. The ramifications of the discovery were endless. She could certainly understand Severance's fascination with it. But Cidra didn't like the feel of the whole thing any more than she had liked the feel she'd gotten from the eggs.

The quartzflash moved around inside the ship, falling on banks of alien machinery that stood silent and blank. There was a lounge that might have been a seat or a bed for a body the size of a man, but it was shaped oddly. Cidra had a passing mental image of one of the blue monsters, grown to the size of a man, lying on that lounge, and she shuddered. The creatures from the eggs were bad enough when they were hatchlings; she didn't want to imagine what the adult version looked like.

"Look at this, Cidra." Severance shone the light along the surface of a long, sealed case. It was made of the same black metal as the hull of the ship, but the top was fashioned of a clear material, perhaps a hard plastic. There were scratch marks on the clear portion, as if something hungry had tried to get inside. Whatever it was had not succeeded in prying open the case.

"What do you think it is?" Cidra asked.

"Some kind of storage facility probably. I can't see what's inside. The cover looks clear, but it's not when I shine the light down through it. Too much dirt and grit caked on it. Maybe I can get it open."

"Don't, Severance. It looks too much like a coffin. Let's leave it for an exploration company that's got equipment and time. We don't have either right now."

He paused as if a part of him realized the truth of what she was saying, but Cidra saw his eyes drift back to the long case. She realized that getting him out of the ship wasn't going to be easy. She remembered all too clearly how stubbornly he had insisted on fetching the egg from the safehold. Cidra decided to try a drastic approach to breaking the spell the ship seemed to have on him.

"I'll just be another minute or so, Cidra." He ran his hand along the line on the metal case where the clear section joined the black portion.

"Fine." She swung around determinedly. "I'm leaving."

"Cidra! Don't be a fool. You can't leave without me."

"Want to bet?" She was sure of herself, absolutely convinced that she had to get him out of the ship. The same sense of wrongness was permeating her senses as she had experienced when she had kicked the blue reptilian carcass out of the protected circle.

"Damn it, Cidra, come back here. That's a direct order."

"No. You'll have to come with me if you don't want me to leave alone." She paused, about to shoulder her way through a wall of vines, and glanced back. "Severance, I mean this. I'm leaving and I— *Severance!*"

His name was a scream on her lips as she looked back and saw him silhouetted in the doorway. Behind him a deathly black light flashed inside the ship. But light couldn't be black, Cidra thought in horror. For a timeless instant everything seemed frozen. Energy crackled from the depths of the round ship, flickering around Severance's body as he stood poised with the pulser in his hand. For a few seconds he stood staring out at her, his face a mask of agony, and then he collapsed backward, out of sight. The black glare flashed again and then died out.

Cidra caught her breath in fear and raced forward, slamming to a halt at the opening in the ship. "Severance, where are you?" She could see nothing. The quartzflash no longer shone in the darkness. He was dead, Cidra thought in a flash of hysteria. No, it wasn't possible. She refused to believe it. Frantically she started to scramble over the torn hull. She had one leg swung over the edge when she heard the heavy scrape of claws on metal.

Cidra froze. She knew with sure instinct that the long coffin-like case had opened. The shock of that knowledge was enough to make her feel dizzy. Clutching at every ounce of willpower she possessed, she started to edge back out of the ship. Slowly, her eyes never leaving the jagged opening, she backed away from the horror that lurked within. But her body seemed to be moving in slow motion. It was like a dream in which she was trapped, knowing that she should flee but finding herself unable to make her body respond.

The blue, leathery body appeared in the opening of the ship. Cidra was mesmerized by the shock of its size. As tall as a man but far heavier. Standing erect, its pale, iridescent blue belly looked obscenely shiny. The head was massive, built to hold the teeth of a predator. Red eyes gleamed with the flat, lethal, unemotional expression of a true reptile. The little appendages she had seen on the hatchling were indeed sickeningly handlike. One of them held Severance's pulser.

The jungle was safer than what waited in the alien ship. Cidra whirled to run.

"Racer!"

Stunned to hear Severance's voice, Cidra glanced over her

shoulder. There was no sign of him. The alien lifted one massive clawed foot over the edge of the jagged metal. It was coming after her. Frantically Cidra tried to peer around it.

"Severance, where are you?"

"Damn you to hell, Racer. You're dead. This time you'll stay dead." The blue reptile raised the pulser it was holding, aiming it at Cidra.

The voice was coming from the mouth of the alien. Disoriented, Cidra reached out to grab a tree limb to steady herself. The creature moved closer. "Severance, if you have any control over that thing, make it stop. Don't let it come any closer."

"Stop talking with Cidra's voice, damn you. Where is she? What have you done with her? You're already dead meat, Racer. Tell me what you've done with her or I'll make it slow this time."

"No!" With a staggering sense of disorientation Cidra began to realize what must be happening. "Severance, listen to me. Can you hear me?"

"Cidra, where are you?" The six-foot reptile swung its scaled neck, searching the vegetation. The pulser didn't wave.

"Severance, is that you holding the pulser?" She was trembling with the force of will it took to stay where she was, instead of fleeing into the jungle.

"Of course it's me. Where are you?" The huge mouth moved as if having trouble shaping the words, but the voice was definitely Severance's. "Come out, Cidra. It's all right."

"I'm standing right in front of you. Severance, it's another illusion trap. I must look like Racer to you, and you look like a monster to me. Please put down the pulser." She took another step backward and found herself with her back to a thick tree.

"An illusion? It can't be. It's too damn real."

But he was staring at her, the hideously unemotional gaze full of a deep, savage hunger. In spite of her analysis of the situation, Cidra was terrified. Even if she was right and the creature facing her was Severance, she might not be able to convince him of who she was before he pulled the trigger of the pulser. "It's me, Severance. Please believe me. It's only another illusion. Saints know we've seen enough of them lately."

The creature took another ponderous step closer. "An illusion? Prove it. Take my hand, Cidra." One of the clawed palms was extended toward her. The pulser was still aimed at her breast.

"Don't touch me!" She was certain that what she was seeing was only a bad dream, but her instinct for self-preservation was stronger than her logic. She pressed herself tightly against the tree.

The creature that claimed to be Severance took another step forward, holding out the handlike appendage that wasn't gripping the pulser. "Cidra, if it's really you, prove it. Take my hand. Don't look at me like that."

"Stay away from me until I figure out what's going on. We've got to break the illusion."

"I'll know it's you if I touch you. Nothing on this planet could feel quite like you feel."

"Please stay away from me." She was trapped against the tree, and the creature took another pace closer. The eyes raked her. If she was wrong, she was already dead.

The reptile halted. The hand holding the pulser came up with a swift, sure movement, aiming at her head. Cidra closed her eyes. There was no time to run. It would be better to go like this than to have her head snapped off between those fierce jaws. "Severance," she whispered.

The creature triggered the pulser. Cidra waited for the withering shock, wondering what it would feel like, hoping it would be quick. There was a sharp movement in the tree beside her. She opened her eyes to see a mouthful of fangs fall past her head and land at her feet. The fangs were connected to a sinuous, mud-colored body. She stared at it in dazed astonishment. Whatever it was, it was dead. Hesitantly, she raised her eyes. The blue reptile still held the pulser, but it was no longer aimed at her.

"Come away from the tree, Cidra. You never know what's hiding behind trees around here." Once more a blue, handlike appendage was held out to her.

Slowly Cidra moved away from the tree, her eyes never leaving the awful mouth that spoke with Severance's voice. "Are you sure it's you, Severance?"

"From the way you look at me I admit that I've got my doubts. But I know Racer is dead. He has to be dead. A little trust is all we've got to work with, so we'll take it from here." He continued to hold out the appendage.

He was right. A little trust and some common sense was all they had to work with at the moment. Uneasily Cidra touched the leathered palm. The unhuman fingers closed around hers. She closed her eyes, waiting for disaster. Then, slowly, the universe seemed to right itself. The hand holding hers felt warm and familiar. She relaxed slightly.

"You're right," Severance said, sounding wearily relieved. "Whatever it is, it's just an illusion."

"Yes," she agreed shakily. "But it's so real. I'm afraid to open my eyes."

"Try it. As long as you're holding my hand, you can keep telling yourself who I am. Believe me, you don't look like Racer any longer."

Slowly she risked a glance through slitted lashes. When she saw Severances's familiar face watching her with narrow-eyed concern, she breathed a sigh of relief. "You're back to normal," she told him.

"Says who?" But he grinned briefly.

"What happened to you in there? I saw a strange flash behind you, and you fell backward. When I got close to see what had happened, you came toward me looking very blue and very hungry."

"I don't know. I felt a sort of shock that knocked me down. I lost the quartzflash. When I got up again, you were screaming but you looked like Cord Racer. I feel all right. Do I still look okay to you?"

She nodded, afraid to let go of his hand for fear that he would turn back into a monster. "I've about had it with things messing around with my head."

"I thought you were the one who was so convinced that mind link was the ultimate form of orgasm."

She was outraged. "I never said any such thing!"

"I beg your pardon. My misunderstanding."

"Harmonic mind link is a beautiful, creative, sensitive experience. It is not an . . . an orgasm, and it is not made up of horrible illusions."

"How do you know? You've never experienced it, remember?"

"One doesn't have to have experienced something to have an understanding of it."

"I keep forgetting about your educational accomplishments." Severance headed back to the gaping hole in the ship. "Yell if I start turning into a blue monster again."

"I'm going to start yelling right now. Severance, I think we ought to get out of here."

"I agree. I just want to see if I can find the quartzflash first, though." He used the flame for illumination as he leaned back inside the ship and scanned the interior. "There it is. We'll need it tonight. Stay here while I get it."

"The last time you went inside, you came out wearing an

ugly blue suit. I'm not sure I could stand it a second time around."

He was already inside, scooping up the flash. He flicked it on one last time. "Look, Cidra. If I hold the light just right, I think I can see into that case." He used his fist to scrub off some of the dirt. "Sweet Harmony, I think it's a skeleton."

Leaning through the opening of the ship, Cidra caught a glimpse of a huge skeleton mouth through the murky case cover. She shuddered. "Look at those teeth."

Severance grinned briefly. "Definitely a carnivore."

Cidra glanced at his own rather feral smile. "His teeth remind me of yours. Damn it, Severance, if you don't come out of there, so help me, I'll—" A flash of black light at the end of the case interrupted her words. Once more energy sizzled, although it seemed weaker this time. "The light! Severance, that's what happened before!"

Severance felt the same tingling shock he had experienced earlier. Energy clawed him, not as strong this time, but enough to force him to his knees. With both hands he gripped the pulser and aimed for the source of the eerie light. He squeezed off one shot and then another before a small explosion rocked the shattered ship. He heard Cidra call his name, and then everything went still.

Slowly he got back to his feet, watching as the light flickered and died at the end of the long case. "Cidra?"

"I'm all right, Severance. So are you. What happened?"

He examined the charred metal fixture that had produced the crackling energy and the light. "Whatever it is, it's useless now. Tough to keep machinery working on Renaissance."

Chapter
Seventeen

The hike through the jungle to the river's edge was without
further incident. Cidra was exceedingly grateful. When the
campsite came into view, looking very much as it had when
they left, she smiled with relief and headed for the tent.

"I can't wait to change these clothes. This habit Wolves
have of wearing one set of clothes all day long is bad enough,
but to be stuck in the same set for three days is very annoying."
She plucked at the fastening of the oversize shirt as she walked
through the silent deflector screens.

"Wait a minute, Cidra. Let me make sure nothing has decided to take up residence in the tent. The deflectors have been
off for at least a full day." Severance caught her arm.

She stopped short. "Yes, of course. Details."

"Paying attention to details is supposed to be one way of
staying alive on this planet." He stepped around her and cautiously opened the tent, pulser in hand.

"If you ask me, sheer luck has a fair amount to do with staying alive around here."

Satisfied with the tent search, Severance turned to give Cidra a laconic glance. "I didn't know you believed in luck."

"I've learned a lot lately." She sauntered past him as he waved her into the tent. "What I'd really like is another bath."

"I don't know how you survived without your usual two hours a day in a lav."

"'A clean body aids in the development of a harmoniously tuned mind,'" she quoted from inside the tent.

"One of your Klinian Laws?"

"A minor but important one." She stuck her head outside the tent and smiled winningly. "Feel like fetching some water for me?"

His mouth kicked up at the corner as he took in the blatantly coaxing expression. "You're not the only one who could use a bath. I smell like the inside of that egg-laying spaceship. I'll rig up something."

"You always manage to rig up something." She ducked back inside the tent.

There were more important things to worry about first, however. Severance stepped into the skimmer and critically scanned the instruments and the innards of the powerhouse. There was still sufficient power to recharge the deflectors. He snapped the power pack out of the pulser, replaced it, and then got the deflectors operating at full strength. When he was satisfied with the security of the campsite, he put in the call to Port Try Again. The comm set worked after a bit of relatively minor tinkering.

"Where in a renegade's hell have you been, Severance? I've had ExcellEx reps yelling at me for two days. Seems they're expecting some sensors. Where's Overcash?" The security official sounded short-tempered and inclined to be abusive.

"Overcash became a meal. So did Racer."

"Racer? He was on a run upriver to the Masterson field camp. How did you connect with him?"

"It's a long story. I'm requesting a skimmer and pilot to pick us up."

"Who's us? Oh, you've still got the little Harmonic with you? If Overcash and Racer wound up feeding the local wildlife, how did she make it?"

"She's tougher than she looks. How about the skimmer?"

"Give me your coordinates. I'll get someone out to you as soon as possible. Can you make it through another night?"

"Yeah, the deflectors are working, and we've got a pulser."

"I'll have a skimmer out to you by midday tomorrow."

"Thanks," Severance said, and waited for the inevitable final question. Nothing came for free on Renaissance. Or anywhere else in the Stanza Nine system for that matter.

"Who's picking up the tab for the rescue run? ExcellEx?"

"No. Charge it to my account," Severance said.

There was a short wait while his account was pulled up from the computer. "Good enough," the security officer said. "Your credit is still first-class. Looks like you always pay your bills."

"Always," Severance murmured, and switched off the comm set. He sat for a moment in the gently rocking skimmer and idly watched a pair of dracon eyes that were watching him.

Nothing came for free. There was a price on everything. How much of a price had he forced Cidra to pay in order to survive? He'd had no right to subject her to the events of the past few days. He should have taken better care of her. His job was to protect her.

Instead she had taken care of him. He remembered the comfort she had given him when he had been swimming in and out of his fever. In addition to the hazy nightmares he saw fleeting images of her gentle touch, the cooling baths, and the soft warmth of her lap as she cradled his head. She had come aboard *Severance Pay* as a delicate, cultivated creature accustomed to the finest manners and the most elevated of lifestyles. This morning he had awakened to find a young huntress rising from the edge of a stream to bring in the day's meat. Because of him she had been forced to become a carnivore. That seemed unpleasantly symbolic to Severance.

She had learned other things from him too. He'd had no right to teach her about passion. But even as he berated himself, Severance knew deep in his gut that, given the chance, he would have repeated the lesson. The woman pulled too strongly at his senses and his mind. The two weeks on board *Severance Pay* alone with her had been sweet hell at times. He had known then that if she stayed with him on the run to QED, she would end up in his bunk. As long as he was anywhere near her, he would have no peace unless he knew he could possess her. He could not allow her a choice. She affected him too fiercely, made him ache with need, filled him with the desire to put a claim on her. At the same time he was aware of a violent desire to protect her. The possessiveness and the protectiveness went hand in hand, seeming natural and inevitable until the twin goals foundered on the ultimate dilemma. How could he protect her from himself?

Everything he did for her and to her took Cidra farther and farther from the one thing she wanted most in life. Because of him her goal of becoming a true Harmonic was more distant than it had ever been. He had forced the Wolf in her to the surface after she had spent years struggling to suppress that part of her nature.

As he watched, the dracon eyes disappeared under the water. Severance continued staring unseeingly at the point where the creature had vanished. It seemed to him that Cidra had given him more than he'd had any right to take. She had welcomed him in her arms, drawn him into her with an honest, sweet passion that had taken away his breath. She had given him an intense loyalty, the kind he had learned not to expect from anyone since Jeude had been killed. Severance could not imagine any female of his acquaintance who would have thrown herself into a river full of dracons rather than have allowed herself to be carried off and used against him. But Cidra offered more than loyalty and passion. She radiated a sense of rightness, a quiet certainty that he didn't fully understand.

"Severance? Where's the water?"

He shook off the bittersweet mood and got to his feet. She was standing on the bank, gazing curiously into the shattered wall of the skimmer's cabin. He grinned. "I'll have something ready in a few minutes." He opened the skimmer's cargo hold. As she had said, he was good at rigging things. Fixing a bathing apparatus for a fastidious lady from Clementia shouldn't be an impossible assignment.

In reality the job wasn't difficult, given the contents of the skimmer's cargo hold. He was cutting a length of plastic tubing when he noticed the carton of sensors. The bright red COD seal was still in place. Mail still waiting to be delivered. He looked at it for a long moment and then went back to work on the bathing arrangements.

When he was finished, he handed the bucketful of water and the plastic tubing to Cidra. "Try this. When you're done, I'll use it."

She eyed him critically. "Do you have any depilatory cream left in your travel pack?"

"Don't worry, Cidra. You'll look just as cute with hairy legs."

"My legs are fine," she informed him. "The cream I use lasts for a month. It's your beard that needs work."

Severance touched the side of his face, felt the stubble, and grimaced. "Oh." For some reason he was oddly embarrassed. The knowledge annoyed him, and he frowned. "There'll be a skimmer out from Try Again at about midday tomorrow."

She nodded, seemingly content as she examined the bucket and hose she was holding. "What about your ExcellEx delivery?"

"Funny you should mention it. I was just thinking about that myself. As late as it is, I'll be lucky to collect for it."

She looked up, alarmed. "If ExcellEx doesn't pay for it, don't give it to them."

"It's better for Severance Pay, Ltd.'s reputation if I deliver late rather than not at all. Besides, I'm getting tired of people trying to steal those reeting sensors. Let ExcellEx worry about them."

"Severance," she said sternly, "you are not going to simply hand them over without getting paid for them. Not after all we've been through to protect them."

His gaze narrowed in faint amusement. "You're beginning to sound like a real member of a mail ship crew."

Her chin lifted proudly. "I *am* a real member of the crew. I don't know why you insist on forgetting that fact when it suits you. You certainly had no trouble remembering it the night you came into the Bloodsucker and announced that we were leaving on this little joy run up the river."

She was right. "I should have left you behind after all."

"Nonsense. Racer would have gotten hold of me one way or another and used me as a hostage or something. He was a very determined man, wasn't he?"

"Yes," Severance said, thinking about it. "He was."

"As long as you were alive, you were a constant reminder to him. He couldn't forget his actions that day in the sink-swamp, and he never knew when you might tell someone else about them. On top of that he was the one who got your brother killed. He must have known that if you ever figured it out, you wouldn't rest until you'd settled the score. It must have eaten at him for ages before he finally decided to take care of the problem permanently."

"You're a very perceptive woman at times, Cidra Rainforest."

She smiled. "I've been trained to be perceptive. Now turn around, Severance. I want to take my bath."

He hesitated, wanting to ask her how she really felt deep inside about the fact that he had killed a man. Then, deciding it might be better not to know the answer, he turned his back and went to work foraging in the skimmer's cargo hold for other useful items.

"I've been thinking about that skeleton back in the alien ship," Cidra said later as she finished eating her vegetables. She had been tremendously relieved to find a prespac that contained something besides meat. She didn't think she would ever grow to actually enjoy the taste of meat. Severance had no such qualms, naturally. He was into his second full prespac meal. Wolfing it down, as it were.

"Don't think about it. It'll give you nightmares," he advised.

"I wonder if that creature was the pilot of the ship," she persisted, ignoring his advice.

"That sphere didn't look big enough to house two monsters that size. Whatever it was must have been traveling alone."

"Except for the eggs."

Severance paused, chewing thoughtfully. "Yes, the eggs. That's going to give several biologists a lot to think about. I wonder if the ship was a small colony vessel."

"Maybe we humans aren't the only ones who have started

settling other worlds." Cidra had a sudden thought. "What if that ship was just one of many, Severance?"

"If there were others, we have to assume that they didn't fare much better than that one did. No one has recorded a sighting of anything like that blue monster. At least, I'm not aware of any such sightings."

"It's a big planet."

"True. But an aggressive, intelligent species would have probably made its presence known by now. We've been here for several decades."

"They did appear aggressive, all right." Cidra shuddered. "Didn't do them much good, though. They didn't survive."

"Thanks to you."

Cidra allowed herself to absorb the shock of his simple observation. All by herself she had destroyed the only known members of an intelligent, space-faring race. She was unnerved by the thought.

Severance saw the look on her face and hastily changed the subject. "I wonder how old those eggs were. The skeleton in the case wasn't exactly fresh. It could have been lying in the ship for hundreds of years. But the eggs were ready to hatch."

"They might have been capable of staying viable for years in the shell until the right conditions occurred for them to hatch," Cidra pointed out. "Perhaps the pilot of the ship was wounded in the crash. He followed the mind call and left the eggs in what appeared to be a safe location. Apparently that telepathic call works on any sort of intelligent mind. He set up his own protective device to insure that eventually something would wander into the safehold and become food for the eggs. Then he went back to die in the ship. The case in which we found the skeleton might have been some sort of medical facility."

"Which failed."

"As people keep observing, it's hard to keep machinery working on Renaissance." She smiled. "You seem to do a fairly good job of it, though."

He shrugged. "I told you, I've always been good with my hands."

"We make a good team, don't we? My brains and your brawn."

He gave her a sardonic glance. "I may not be a near genius like your friend Mercer, but once in a while I manage to think my way through things. I can still take every piece of sardite you have in a game of Free Market."

At the mention of Mercer, Cidra flinched. She hadn't thought about him or about Clementia for quite a while. The humor faded from her eyes as she grew pensive. "Yes, you're still better at Free Market than I am."

Severance swore somewhat viciously and asked himself what in a renegade's hell had made him mention her idol, Mercer. Cidra was right. He might be good with his hands, but he wasn't always the fastest thinker in the universe. Severance slowly finished the last of his prespac, aware that Cidra had slipped off into her own thoughts.

She was thinking of Clementia. He knew it, and the realization hit him in the gut: Clementia and a lofty relationship unsoiled by a Wolf's passion and need. Severance asked himself bluntly what he had to offer compared to the wise and distant Mercer. The cabin of *Severance Pay* was a far cry from the formal gardens and glowing fountains of Clementia. Hardly the sort of place in which a gently bred woman would want to set up housekeeping with a man who occasionally drank too much ale and who would frequently reach for her with a hunger he couldn't disguise as platonic love.

"Are you going to give up your search, Cidra?"

She blinked herself back to an awareness of him and smiled

wanly. "I think I've had enough of alien mind-tapping. Perhaps one has to be born a Harmonic to feel comfortable with the idea of someone or something else inside one's head."

"It doesn't seem right somehow," he agreed. "I didn't like being manipulated by either the good guys or the bad guys during the past couple of days."

"We learned to control the manipulation to a certain extent," she reminded him.

"I still don't feel comfortable with the whole idea of mind communication." Severance set down the prespac and leaned back on his elbow, gazing into the flamer. "I never will."

She followed his gaze. "As I said, perhaps one has to be born a Harmonic to have mind-touch feel natural and right. I wasn't born a true Harmonic."

"But you were raised as one."

"Yes."

"Cidra," he began with a rough edge in his voice that he couldn't control, "you can go back to Clementia, can't you?"

She raised her eyebrows in surprise. "Of course. No one kicked me out. I left of my own accord. It's my home. I can go back whenever I wish."

"And work in the Archives?"

"I'm a good archivist, even if I'm not a Harmonic," she said firmly. "Besides, I'm the only archivist they've got who's bothered to make a speciality out of First Family tales. I have virtually a whole field to myself."

"What would they do without you?" He tried to make it a joke but didn't think he pulled it off. She took the question seriously.

"They'd relegate First Family tales to the bottom of the pile of acceptable literature. No big deal. It's already on the bottom of the pile. I did get Mercer to admit once that the sociological implications of some of the first traditions were interesting, but that was about all."

Severance stared at her grimly. She could and would go back. He had nothing to offer her to induce her to stay. Nothing to put up against all that Clementia could offer. She would go home and take with her all the tenderness, companionship, loyalty, and passion she had brought into his life. Severance's hand tightened into a frustrated knot on his thigh. Coolly he forced himself to relax. He would take her back to Port Try Again, put her on a freighter, and never see her again. Something knotted up again, this time inside. *Never see her again.* The years stretched out ahead of him, as empty as the farthest reaches of the galaxy.

"We'd better go to bed. We've had a long day." He got to his feet and began the small ritual of checking the deflectors. Out of the corner of his eye he saw Cidra obediently pick up the remains of dinner and dispose of them. A few minutes later she disappeared into the tent. He kept himself busy for as long as possible, thinking of her crawling into her own sleeper and fastening the closure. When he could delay things no longer, he went into the tent.

She had blanked the light, and it took a while for his eyes to adjust. Severance peeled off his shirt and yanked off the boots. Unconsciously he put the pulser and utility loop within easy reach and fumbled for the opening of his own sleeper. Deliberately he kept his eyes off the other portable bunk. If he allowed himself to look at Cidra in bed, he knew he would crawl in with her, regardless of whether or not she invited him. He was selfish enough to take what memories he could. Hell, he was *Wolf* enough to take what he could.

He took a deep breath and a savage grip on himself and turned to slide into his sleeper. His hand touched a bare female shoulder before he realized that the bed was already occupied.

"Cidra! What are you doing in here?"

She smiled up at him in the shadows. "Waiting for you. What took you so long?"

"You shouldn't be here."

"Going to throw me out?"

"Sweet Harmony, I haven't got the strength." He unfastened his trousers and stepped out of them, leaving them lying on the floor of the tent. With a heavy groan he crawled into the sleeper and found Cidra naked and waiting. He buried his face against her breasts, aware that his body was hardening already with a fierce desire. "I doubt that I'd ever have the strength to throw you out of my bed."

"I'm glad." Her fingers laced through his hair as her body stirred against his.

He felt her soft leg moving along his thigh, and the tight ache in his loins became a fire almost instantly. She had such a powerful effect on him that he would have been alarmed if he hadn't been so excited. Severance stroked her, savoring the curve of her hip and the smoothness of her belly. At this moment he easily convinced himself he had a right to this night. She would be gone all too soon from his life.

Hungrily he sought and found her lips, drinking the taste of her into his veins. He would never forget the sensation of probing the sweet warmth of her mouth. Her small tongue darted around his a little anxiously at first and then with greater boldness. Her body arched, opening to his touch. When he drew a palm across one breast, he could feel the nipple tighten. The response sent a wave of excitement through him.

She was his. The need and the longing roared through him, swamping the knowledge that soon he would have to send Cidra back to Clementia. The primitive certainty that she belonged to him and no one or no place else was too strong in that moment. Severance forgot about the morning and what it must bring in the way of reality. Tonight was his, and he was going to take all he could get.

"Cidra, you feel so good. Do you know what you're doing to me?"

"I'm learning."

He moved one hand lower, threading his fingers through the wonderfully soft tangle of hair below her stomach, and then he could feel the gathering moistness between her legs. The sensual dampness dazed him, almost overwhelming him with a sense of anticipation. He probed gently, and when she gasped, he probed again. He could never get enough of her soft cries of excitement. "Touch me, Cidra. I want to feel your hands on me."

He caught her hand and guided it down to his throbbing manhood. When her fingers closed tenderly around him, he shut his eyes and forced himself to take a calming breath.

"What's wrong?" She sounded anxious.

"Nothing," he told her, his voice tight. "You have the damnedest effect on me, little Saint. Touch me again. I'm a glutton for punishment."

"Like this?"

He nipped her shoulder as she obeyed. "Yes," he muttered as she gently used her nails on him. "Yes, sweetheart. That's exactly right."

He gloried in the feel of her, moving his hand beneath her lushly rounded buttocks and finding the dark cleft between them. She flinched at the unfamiliar caress, and he held her more tightly until she relaxed again and let herself respond. When he had her straining urgently beneath him, he let his hand rove elsewhere. He teased the parting folds of flesh that guarded the entrance to her warm, fragrant core. She moved pleadingly under the touch, closing her thighs around his hand as if she would draw him further into her.

"Do you want me?" he asked, his voice harsh with his own need.

"I want you. I want you, Severance."

"Not half as much as I want you." He lifted himself, sliding her into position under his heaviness, and then lowered himself along the length of her. "Wrap your legs around me, love."

She did. He had been poised on the threshold, and when she lifted her legs to clasp his thighs, the movement forced him into her. He heard his name on her lips and felt her shiver as he thrust forward, taking her completely.

Then she was clinging to him, her breasts soft beneath his chest, her body strong and supple as she held on to him with all her might. He would never be able to get enough of her, Severance thought fleetingly. Not even if he had her all to himself for the rest of his life.

She accepted the rhythm he established, augmenting it with her own inner muscles. The resulting harmony sent both of them spiraling upward to an inevitable conclusion. Severance lifted his head to watch her face as he felt the beginning of her joyous release. He wanted to watch her expression forever, but already the sight and feel of her satisfaction were driving him over the edge of his own. He sucked in his breath and surged forward one last time, sinking himself into her until all sense of separateness was gone. The two of them felt like a single entity. And then he just held on, clutching her more tightly than he would hold on to a pulser in the middle of the jungle.

"Cidra."

It was a long time before either of them surfaced in the darkness of the tent. In mutual silence they lay listening to each other's breathing and to the sounds of the night beyond the deflectors. At long last Cidra stirred, stretching luxuriously in a movement that brushed her breast along Severance's rib cage.

"Good night, Severance." Her voice was soft and sleepy as she curled into him.

"Good night, Cidra." He felt her drift off to sleep, a bundle of feminine contentment in his arms. Then he lay awake for a long time and thought about the future.

Cidra awoke the next morning feeling decidedly stiff. The sleeper could accommodate two people in a pinch, but it wasn't really designed for the extra crowd. Tentatively she moved her leg and felt Severance turn in response. His arm, which was lying across her breasts, tightened. He yawned in her ear.

"Do you think your bunk on the ship is going to be big enough for both of us, or will you rig up something to connect the upper and lower berths?" she asked drowsily.

"My bunk? Do you mean on the ship?"

"Uh-huh."

"I hadn't thought about it."

"Well," she announced grandly, "you'd better, hadn't you? You're the one who's always worrying about little details."

He stilled for a moment and then slowly levered himself up on one elbow to gaze down at her searchingly. She smiled smugly, wondering why he was looking so serious.

"You're talking about staying on *Severance Pay* with me?"

"I'm a full-fledged member of the crew, remember?" She reached up and toyed with his tousled hair. He ignored her.

"You're going back to Clementia."

"Nope. I'm going to QED to help deliver the mail." She tugged at a lock experimentally. He didn't seem to notice. The first faint trickle of alarm passed through her. "Severance?"

"You have to go back to Clementia, Cidra." His voice sounded raw.

"Why?"

"Because that's where you want to go."

She shook her head with grave certainty. "No. Not anymore. I want to be with you."

"But you belong in Clementia. It's your home. Your work is there. The people you care about . . ."

"I care about you now."

He drew a deep breath as if preparing himself for an unpleasant task. "You have to go back."

His dogged stubbornness began to make an impression. "Why do I have to go back? Just because you say so?"

"Yes, damn it!" He sat up abruptly, pushing aside the cover of the sleeper. In the muted morning light that passed through the tent screen, the muscles of his shoulders and back were set and rigid. "You have to go back to Clementia because you've been saying all along that you belong there. Your life's ambition is to be a Harmonic."

"I'm not a Harmonic. I never was one and I never will be one. I know that now."

He looked at her. "But you can live like one. You can change your fancy gown four times a day, practice all the rituals, study the philosophy and the laws. Part of you is Harmonic, Cidra. Hell, Harmonics aren't an alien race living among humans. Some part of every human being is Harmonic. You can indulge that part of yourself. All you'll lack is the telepathic ability. You were born into that world, and you can't possibly know for certain that you want to leave it permanently."

"I do know for certain," she said calmly. "I'm ready to leave it permanently."

"Get one thing straight, Cidra. If you do leave it to come with me, you can never go back. I wouldn't let you go back. Do you understand what I'm saying?"

"Do you want me to come with you?" she countered.

He closed his eyes for an anguished instant. When he opened them, his gaze was very hard. In that moment he was all Wolf. "Sweet Harmony, yes. Yes, damn it, I want you to come with me. But not unless you're absolutely sure it's what you want too."

"I'm sure."

"Cidra, you can't possibly know that. It's too soon."

She tilted her head as understanding dawned. "You don't trust me, do you?"

He was startled. "What do you mean, I don't trust you?"

"It's true. You don't trust me. You're afraid I don't know my own mind. Well, that's one thing about being a Wolf, Severance. You have to learn to trust the hard way. You have to take a chance."

"I'm not going to take a chance on this. It's too important. And don't give me any lectures on what it means to be a Wolf. I'm the Wolf here."

"So am I."

"Only because I made you into one!"

Cidra began to get angry. "Don't go taking all the credit for everything, Teague Severance. You're always so anxious to assume responsibility, to be the pilot in command, that you tend to forget I'm capable of free will and clear thinking too. I've got news for you, this is a decision I'm making all by myself."

"Be reasonable, Cidra. You've only been away from Clementia for about three weeks. So much has happened to you in that time that you can't possibly be thinking clearly."

"I was trained to think clearly under all circumstances!"

He eyed her. "You're starting to lose your temper."

"Astute observation. I'm getting very angry, Severance."

"Cidra, all I'm asking is that you consider this in a calm, rational manner. You've been under a great deal of strain lately."

"Strain? I've been seduced, assaulted by wild beasts, attacked by alien illusions, obliged to eat meat, and taught to gamble. Yes, I've been under a strain. But that doesn't mean I can't think straight. It's Wolves such as you who get muddle-headed in emotional circumstances. And the fact that you are presently in just such a circumstance is the only reason I'm making allowances for your behavior at the moment. I'm the best crew mate you ever had, Teague Severance. I'm loyal, trustworthy, and intelligent. If you had any sense, you'd realize just how lucky you are and get down on your knees in gratitude!"

He stared at her as she sat up in the sleeper, her long hair spilling around her shoulders and dancing across the tips of her breasts. Her eyes were full of fire and daunting determination. He felt himself wavering in the face of it. Summoning all his fortitude, he stood firm. "Cidra, I know you think you mean what you say."

"I do mean what I say!"

"But this decision is too important."

"To whom?"

"To me, you little idiot. Will you listen to me? I'm trying to do what's best for both of us."

"You're just trying to protect yourself," she retorted.

He started to argue and then halted abruptly. "Maybe I am." He looked away from her. "I couldn't bear it if I took you with me and you changed your mind a season or two from now. I couldn't bear to watch you pining for the gardens of Clementia and the love of a man who will never want to make love to you. It would destroy me, Cidra."

She heard the gritty truth in his words and knew her first sense of genuine uncertainty. She didn't doubt her own feelings for a moment, but she had to acknowledge that Severance had a right to be unsure of her. From the moment he had met her

327

she had talked mainly of finding a way to go back to Clementia. She couldn't blame him for doubting her change of heart and mind.

"What about a compromise?" she asked softly.

He swung around to face her. "What kind of compromise? I'm not going to be a visiting lover for you. I won't agree to just drop in and sleep with you occasionally when I happen to be near Clementia."

Her head came up proudly. "I'm not interested in such a ... a thin relationship, either. For the record I won't be a convenient resource for a little special handling when you're between mail runs."

"I know that."

"Very well, then, why don't we try a more or less platonic association for a while."

"The way we did for two weeks on the hop from Lovelady to Renaissance? You're out of your tuned mind. I'd never survive. Talk about strain!"

"Then you suggest something," she shot back.

His face hardened. "All right, I will. Go back to Clementia...."

"But, Severance..."

"Go back to Clementia while I finish the run to QED. When I get back, I'll come to Clementia. If you're still sure you want to come away with me, I'll take you."

She drew a breath. "It's six weeks from here to QED and then eight more to get back to Lovelady. That's a long time, Severance."

"Long enough for you to be sure of what you're doing."

Cidra felt her stomach tighten as she saw the determination in him. "You really don't trust me to know what I'm doing, do you?"

"I think you need time."

"What if you don't come back for me, Severance?" she asked softly.

"You'll have to trust me to come back, just as I'll have to trust you to be waiting."

"Wolves have a very hard time with trust, don't they?" she whispered sadly.

"Yes."

Chapter
Eighteen

"It's amazing how sophisticated and cosmopolitan Port Try Again looks after a few days in the jungle." Cidra grinned across the table at Desma Kady, who was halfway through a meat stew. "Renaissance has a way of giving one a new perspective on things."

Desma chuckled. "I know what you mean. But cosmopolitan as we may be, you're still drawing a few stares. Most of these renegades wouldn't blink at a charging zalon, but they've blinked several times at that beautiful dress." She inclined her head to indicate the other diners in the restaurant.

Cidra glanced down at her yellow-gold early evening gown. "I didn't mean to cause a scene. It's just that it felt so good to get back into my own clothes." She added quickly, "Not that I didn't appreciate your advice on the practical clothing for the jungle. I don't know what I would have done without the trousers and shirt."

"I doubt Severance would have allowed you to go trekking off without the right gear. He's usually very conscious of details such as that. I wonder where he is."

"Attending to more details." Cidra grimaced. "He's negotiating a deal with two of the biggest scientific firms who have representatives here at Try Again. He's been at it ever since we got back last night."

"When it comes to business, that man has the tenacity of a lockmouth," Desma observed. "He deserves a break like this. He's worked hard to build Severance Pay, Ltd. into one of the most reliable of the small mail runners. The stake he gets from selling the information you two discovered will go a long way toward helping him set up a major business operation." Desma's eyes glowed. "Sweet Harmony, what a find. Absolutely fantastic. I just hope my firm makes the high bid. With any luck I'll get a piece of the project."

"I'm sure Severance will sell to your company," Cidra said politely. "He knows you'd like to be involved."

"He'll sell to the highest bidder. Period. When it comes to something this big, Severance isn't going to let sentiment interfere. How are the veggies?" Desma peered at the pile of greens and tubers on Cidra's plate.

"Wonderful. To be quite honest, I don't care if I never have occasion to eat meat again."

"Poor Cidra. This whole thing has been quite an adventure for you, hasn't it? Starting with that night in my lab when you drove off the intruder."

"I take it he hasn't turned up?"

Desma shook her head. "No, damn it. I'd give my last research report to get my hands on him. The company guards have circulated the description, but I'm afraid it wasn't very useful."

"I know." Cidra's mouth curved wryly. "The one look at

his features that I got wasn't very good. He had such an expression of horror and fear on his face and the light from those bugs was so bizarre that I doubt I'd recognize him again myself."

"Well, if he knows what's good for him, he won't come near enough to you to let you have a look. Severance would feed him to a dracon." Desma stopped short at the look on Cidra's face. "What's the matter? Did I say something wrong? It's just an expression."

"I know," Cidra assured her hurriedly. "I'm still getting accustomed to Renaissance colloquialisms." She blanked out her mental image of the last meal Severance had fed to the dracons and grimly went back to work on her greens.

"You'd better get used to the local slang," Desma said cheerfully. "Severance spends a fair amount of time on Renaissance." Her friendly eyes narrowed. "I take it you will be traveling with him for a while?"

"I'll be traveling with him. As soon as he gets through behaving in his current stubborn, authoritarian, dictatorial manner." Cidra's smile thinned. "He's insisting that I return to Clementia until he gets back from the run to QED."

"Interesting," Desma murmured. "Is that connected to the reason why he spent last night in the ship and you're rooming with me again? Somehow, when I saw the two of you yesterday, I got the feeling that certain matters in your, uh, partnership had been resolved."

"We don't have a partnership. I'm just a member of his crew." Cidra stabbed at a golden-skinned tuber. She was getting better at using a knife on food. "What do you make of the alien ship, Desma?"

"From what you've told me it could be almost anything from a lone scouting foray that went astray to a colony ship. Assuming it is an alien vessel. There's still the possibility that the point of origin is somewhere in the Stanza Nine system. We may never know."

"There were only five eggs. Hardly enough to colonize a new planet."

"Perhaps there were several small ships headed somewhere else, and this one went off course."

Cidra chewed her lower lip. "I hope this was just a lone ship. I would hate to think of facing a large number of those blue monsters."

"The hatchling's behavior when it emerged from the egg seemed entirely instinctive?"

"Oh, yes. All it wanted to do was eat. I think there was some kind of homing device built into the shell. Probably designed to lead it back to the ship eventually. Who knows what's stored in that ship? Perhaps the equivalent of an Archive. Perhaps once led back to the ship, the young would discover their heritage. I imagine Renaissance looked like paradise to whatever piloted them here."

"Well, it didn't prove to be a paradise," Desma observed coolly. "The machinery broke down and the hatchlings fell victim to the first intelligent predators who found them."

Cidra swallowed uncomfortably. "Don't remind me. Do you have any idea what it's like to know you've wiped out the five surviving members of an intelligent race?"

"Don't start feeling guilty. From what you've told me the first hatchling was going to eat Severance for lunch. Probably would have turned on you next."

Cidra nodded gloomily. "You know, it was strange, Desma. There's no sense of alienness about the Ghosts. They're different from us and we're fascinated by them, but we're more or less comfortable with the idea that they belonged in this system. It wasn't the same with the blue creatures. They felt wrong, somehow. I hated that hatchling on sight."

"Small wonder. You've still got your primitive human instincts, Cidra, even if you have been reared in Clementia. I'm sure those instincts were working at full strength when you saw the egg crack. Your primary reaction was to protect Severance."

"And a brilliant reaction it was too," declared a new voice.

Cidra glanced up in surprise as Severance grabbed a vacant chair, shoved it near hers, and sank down onto it in his usual sprawl. He looked extraordinarily pleased with himself. He signaled for a mug of Renaissance Rose ale and leaned back to smile smugly at the two women.

"I take it," Desma said, "that you have concluded a successful negotiating session?"

"Right. And you'll be happy to know that your firm coughed up the necessary credit to get first crack at the ship."

Desma's eyes gleamed. "Fantastic. Who got the safehold?"

"Vinton Archaeology."

Demsa nodded. "They'll do a first-class job. When do you show them their new finds?"

"We leave at dawn tomorrow. It's a big event. Four skimmers and two research crews. After I've helped them locate the safehold and the ship, I'm going to take one of the skimmers on up the river to the ExcellEx camp. I've still got those reeting sensors to deliver. You don't mind if Cidra stays with you for a few days?"

"Of course not."

"She'll be returning to Lovelady on the next commercial freighter. But it doesn't leave until the end of the week."

Cidra cut savagely into another tuber. "How much, Severance?"

He gave her a sidelong glance. "How much what?"

"Credit. How much did you get in exchange for the locations

of the safehold and the ship?" She didn't look at him. Her whole attention was on her meal.

"Five hundred thousand."

Cidra nearly dropped her knife. "Five hundred thousand? Sweet Harmony, that's a fortune."

"I know." The ale arrived, and Severance took a healthy swallow. His eyes were glittering over the rim. "A very nice stake."

"Five hundred thousand." Desma's tone was awed. "Congratulations, Severance."

"I'll want a recorded contract for my share, naturally," Cidra said. "Two hundred and fifty thousand."

Severance set down his mug with great care. "I beg your pardon?"

"You heard me." She continued eating the remains of the tuber. "I'll want a contract. Properly sealed and recorded. And I'll want it before you leave tomorrow morning. We'd better find a contract office tonight."

Severance's gray eyes slitted. "Why do you want a recorded contract?"

"You know the answer to that. Remember all those games of Free Market, Severance? The one lesson you drilled into me was that you can't trust a Wolf. Always count the cubes before you start play. In the case of a two-way split of five hundred thousand, I'll want to get it on tape and get it recorded."

The frozen silence at the table was broken only by the sound of Cidra continuing to eat the tuber. Desma stayed very still, watching the other two from under her lashes. Severance just stared at Cidra, his gaze brooding and malevolent.

"You don't need a contract and you know it," he finally said.

"How do I know it? You're taking off for QED as soon as

you get back from this little jaunt up the river. After QED, who knows where you'll go and what you'll do? I may never see you again." She smiled grimly. "I have to protect my share of the profits."

Severance continued to glare at her for another moment, and then he turned on Desma. "Did you put this idea in her head?"

Hastily Desma put up a hand. "Not me. I had nothing to do with it."

"I," said Cidra calmly, "thought of it all on my own."

"This is ridiculous." Severance's voice was tight. He took another large swallow of ale.

"A woman alone can't be too careful."

"This is a form of retaliation, isn't it? You're madder than hell because I'm sending you back to Clementia."

Cidra waved her fingers in a graceful, airy gesture. "I'm merely putting into practice all the things I've been learning recently."

"Yeah?" He leaned closer. "And what else that you've learned recently are you planning to put into practice?"

Cidra smiled gamely even though she was fully aware of the newly erratic nature of her pulse. She had to struggle to control her breathing. Severance could be very intimidating when he chose. "You needn't concern yourself with anything except the details of splitting the credit."

"Why, you little . . ." He made an obvious effort at regaining control of his own temper. Then he slammed the half empty mug down on the table and got to his feet. "You want a recorded contract? All right, you'll get one. We'll take care of the details right now."

"But I haven't finished my dinner."

"We do it now or not at all." He turned to Desma. "You," he informed her, "can act as a witness."

Desma struggled to hide her amusement. "I'll be happy to do so." Quickly she paid for the meal and stood. "Ready when you are."

The deed was done in almost total silence. By the time her signature had been recorded and her voiceprint used to verify it, Cidra was almost shaking. Severance was furious. He scrawled his name beside hers, barked into the voiceprint recorder, and escorted her out of the contracts office in a chilled silence. He didn't speak until he had deposited the women at Desma's door. Severance stood in front of Cidra, feet braced slightly apart, one thumb hooked in his utility belt. He was the very picture of a man scorned.

"I'll see you when I get back." His words sounded more like a threat than a promise.

"Fine." Cidra hung on to her poise with sheer willpower, wrapping it around herself like an early evening gown. "I trust you will have a swift, safe trip."

"Thank you for the kind wishes." The heavy irony in Severance's tone was enough to dampen any further gestures of reconciliation. "Just one more thing."

"Yes, Severance?"

"You are now officially a very rich young woman. As long as my name was the only one on the credit account, no one would have bothered you. But as of tonight you've become a prize."

"A prize?"

"Any reeting renegade who thinks he can talk you into bed and out of your credit will probably try."

"I'm not that naive, Severance."

"You'd better exercise some common sense while I'm gone. If I get back and find out you've done something foolish, I'll—"

"You'll what?" she challenged.

"I'll feed whoever succeeded in seducing you to the river. And when I'm finished with him, I'll tear several long and painful strips off your soft hide."

Uneasily Cidra tried to outglare him. "You have no rights over me."

"Don't bet on it. Officially you're still a member of my crew. And I'm still the pilot in command." He stepped closer and seized her by the shoulders, pulling her against his hard body. "Good-bye, Cidra. Behave yourself while I'm gone or there'll be hell to pay when I get back. I promise you." His mouth came down on hers, quick and hard. Then he turned on his booted heel and started down the street.

"Severance!"

He halted and glanced back, his face set in forbidding lines. "What?"

"Don't you dare give away those sensors. You make sure you get paid for delivering them, do you hear me?"

"I can hear you just fine. So can everyone else in the vicinity." He vanished into the night.

Cidra awoke the next morning to find Fred collapsed across her ankle. She opened one eye and tentatively wriggled her foot. "Up and at 'em, Fred. You can't sleep all day."

The rockrug wriggled into a more comfortable position. He had been as happy as a rockrug could be to see both Severance and herself when they had returned, although Desma claimed that he had made himself at home in her household. So much at home, in fact, that he had munched two of her valued exhibits before someone discovered he'd wriggled into a cage. The huge flutter moths inside hadn't stood a chance. Fred had been discovered with a wingtip still draped rakishly from one corner of his mouth.

Cidra worked free of the rockrug's light weight and headed

for the large, comfortable lav. It was a joy to spend as long as she wanted under the invigorating spray without worrying about Severance reading her a lecture on conservation.

The thought of Severance sent Cidra into a reverie that lasted for nearly half an hour. The spray pummeled her as she considered her parting argument with the self-proclaimed pilot in command. He hadn't been pleased by her lack of trust.

"Well what did he expect?" she demanded at Desma at breakfast. "Sometimes he makes me very angry. He's being so arbitrary about packing me off to Clementia."

"So arbitrary that you felt compelled to get even?" Desma poured coffade and savored the aroma.

Cidra winced. "I don't know what came over me. I hadn't planned to insist on a contract for my share of the credit. Severance would never have cheated me. But when he came into the restaurant looking so smug and in charge last night, I couldn't stand it."

"There's nothing wrong with insuring your half of the deal."

"Except that I insulted Severance in the process. I think he sees himself as having some obligation to protect me. He's got a very overdeveloped sense of responsibility, Desma. That's the real reason I'm being shipped back to Clementia. Severance feels obligated to give me a chance to make up my own mind about the future. He feels guilty for having pushed me into everything that happened here on Renaissance."

"The decision to come to Renaissance was yours, wasn't it?" Desma looked at her searchingly.

"Oh, definitely. But that doesn't seem to keep Severance from assuming the responsibility."

"Maybe it's because you remind him of Jeude. He's always felt responsible for what happened to his brother."

"Well, I'm not Jeude. What's more, I've learned that I never will be a Harmonic. The truth is," Cidra added slowly, "I

339

wouldn't want to be one now, even if someone could wave a wand and turn my mind into a harmonically tuned brain."

"Because of Severance?"

"Because of a lot of things. Severance is the main reason, but there are others." Cidra paused, remembering the scenes in the safehold. "Wait until you see the tapes of the Ghosts' history, Desma. It's very sad. From what I can tell they were once a strong, aggressive race that managed to control Renaissance. Then they moved on to populate Lovelady and QED. But they never went any farther. Something happened. It's hard to tell from the visual record, but it looks as though they simply stopped expanding and started turning inward. For a while toward the end of the history, everything appears idyllic. The architecture is beautiful, the faces are serene, the life-style looks gentle and harmonious. But it doesn't last long. There are no children in the later images, just fewer and fewer Ghosts, gradually fading away until the jungle swamps them. I realized later that it made me angry to see them just give up and die out. I wanted them to go on living, to fight back, to expand. Instead they became so serene and so passive, they lost the will to survive as a species. It made me think of what might happen if all humans suddenly became Harmonics."

"You don't think they'd survive?"

"I think they'd go the way of the Ghosts," Cidra said bluntly. "The truth is, Harmonics are not really constitutionally built to survive under adverse circumstances. Do you know that my mother had to be totally unconscious for hours before I was born? The trauma of childbirth is enough to kill a Harmonic female, even if there are no complications. That's one of the reasons why it's such a major decision when a Harmonic couple decides to have a child. Desma, I don't want to be that weak. I've learned a great deal about myself during the past few days. Given a choice, I'll fight. I think, under the right circumstances, I could actually kill another human being. And I've already proven that I can kill other creatures."

"Does the knowledge scare you?"

"A little. But I've accepted it. I don't want to retreat to Clementia. Harmonics are a luxury for the human race. They are valuable and to some extent they are our conscience. But I'd rather be a survivor than a luxury." Cidra's mouth curved. "And I'd rather fight with Severance than go back to Clementia and worship Mercer from afar."

"Who's Mercer?"

Cidra grinned. "Another Harmonic on whom nature wasted a pair of gorgeous shoulders and the darkest eyes you've ever seen. For ages I told myself I loved him for his mind. I lied."

Desma burst out laughing. "Does Severance know about him?"

"Ummm. Irritates the hell out of him. But I think Mercer worries him too. Severance is afraid I'll start dreaming of the perfect platonic relationship somewhere between Renaissance and QED."

"I never could imagine Severance being very good at a platonic relationship with you," Desma mused.

"He's not. Oh, he tried hard for a while. Inspired by his noble sense of responsibility, no doubt. But it didn't last. Now I'm the one who's worried. He's shipping me out on a commercial freighter, the same way he shipped out that woman with whom he once signed a convenience contract. What if he doesn't come back for me, Desma?"

Desma smiled reassuringly. "You've got a contract with him to split the credit from this trip, remember? Nothing like a business agreement to tie two people together."

Cidra brightened a bit. "That's true."

* * *

Severance had been right about one thing. During the next two days Cidra was aware that she was attracting more than merely curious attention. "Friends" of Severance materialized out of nowhere, professing eager interest in Cidra's health and welfare. Most were concerned that she enjoy herself in Port Try Again while Severance was gone. Cidra was frequently stopped on the street, and Desma was prevailed upon to make introductions. Cidra handled the new attention with classic Harmonic politeness.

"It would be humorous if it wasn't for the fact that all this interest in me merely proves Severance was right one more time," she told Desma at one point. "I've had three invitations for dinner this evening, four for tomorrow night, and half a dozen offers to buy me a drink. One very nice man asked if I was interested in playing Free Market. I got the feeling that I was going to be encouraged to put up my contract as a bet."

"Severance would explode if he found out."

Cidra smiled a little savagely. "Yes, he would, wouldn't he? What's happening to me, Desma? I never used to be vindictive or . . . or irrational and emotional."

"You're scared," Desma said gently.

"I'm afraid so. I have no real hold on Severance. A couple of nights in his bed and a shared adventure. That's all. It's pleasant to think that the contract ties us together, but it won't. Not really. Not the way I want it to hold us."

"He's said he'll come back for you."

"I know. But he's a Wolf."

Desma frowned. "You're afraid he won't keep his word?"

"I'm afraid he'll change his mind; that perhaps when he made the statement, he didn't really know his own mind."

"You're a Wolf too. You might change your mind or fail to keep your word. You might not be waiting for him several weeks from now when he returns from QED. Perhaps the gardens of Clementia will hold more appeal than you remember."

"No." Cidra spoke with conviction, aware of her inner decision. "I won't change my mind. If he comes back for me, I'll be waiting."

"He has no way of knowing that for sure."

"He shouldn't put us to the test."

"Severance is looking for reassurance, if you ask me."

"It's odd, isn't it, Desma? We've trusted each other with our lives more than once during the past few days. Yet we're afraid to trust each other's feelings."

"I imagine things are much simpler in Clementia."

"Yes," said Cidra. "They are."

Severance silently sent up a word of thanks when the holotape crew managed to trigger the Ghosts' presentation inside the safehold. He had been mentally holding his breath, afraid that the showing he and Cidra had seen had been the final one. If that had been the case, he would have had to take a penalty cut on the contract he'd signed with the company. The safehold, itself, was still valuable but not nearly so valuable as the contents. The mind call itself was no longer functioning. Either that or the conditions weren't right for activating it. When Severance and the exploration crew had finally located the safehold by a process of quartering all the terrain within an hour's walk from the river, he had seen at once that the protected circle had shrunk. It was obviously fading, and that meant the valuable scenes inside were probably about to disappear also.

"I'm not sure we'll get it to trigger again," the crew chief announced, "but we've got it down on holotape." He looked pleased. "A hell of a find, Severance. When you stumbled across this, it was really your lucky day. Enough history in here to keep half of Clementia busy for years."

Severance stood in the vaulted entrance of the safehold, gazing at the bubbling stream where Cidra had been bathing the morning he'd awakened from the delirium. The stream was still barely inside the protected area. "My lucky day," he agreed softly. He forced himself out of the reveries as a crew of technicians bustled past. "Any sign of a mechanism to explain how all this operates? We could use the secret of keeping the terrain clear. Whatever the Ghosts used, it's more efficient than the deflectors."

"Nothing so far. We've picked up no energy readings and no indications of any hardware hidden in the safehold walls. We may never find the answer. Might not be able to comprehend it if we do find it. This is damn sophisticated stuff, Severance."

He nodded thoughtfully. "They had the ability to survive. But in the end they just gave up."

"Never even made a try for space travel beyond the local system," the crew chief said. "Doesn't make any sense. So much technical expertise gone to waste. Other things became more important, I guess."

Severance looked at him. "What could have been more important than the survival of the species?"

"I don't know. What's more, I don't think I want to know. When are you taking the Vinton crew to the home of the big blue monsters?"

"Now. Shouldn't be as hard to find as this was. I got a fix on it with a directional indicator." He also wanted to try another shard of one of the shells to see if it still had a homing effect.

The Vinton crew was elated with their find. The shard worked as a directional device but not because of mechanical reasons.

"The shells are naturally attracted to the metal of the ship," one technician announced. "Like magnets that work over long distances. No wonder you had trouble with your signal." He ducked into the floodlit hole in the ship where uniformed men scurried around with great caution. "What the hell happened to that gadget on top of the long case? The damage looks fresh."

Severance ambled in after him and scrutinized the results of the pulser on the device that had activated the illusions. "Had a little trouble with that." He looked into the case. "Going to open it?"

"No. Not here. It'll have to be done under controlled atmospheric conditions. Don't want the skeleton dissolving into dust."

"Do you think it's that old?"

The technician shook his head. "No. But we don't know how it will react to the atmosphere once the case is opened."

Severance hung around for the rest of the day, assuring that his clients were satisfied. When the teams headed back toward the river to spend the night, he made his decision to leave for the ExcellEx camp in the morning. The sensors were long overdue.

"Hey, Severance, stop worrying about the mail," Rand Bantforth said during dinner. "You're making enough off these discoveries to let you forget whatever ExcellEx was going to pay for the COD delivery."

"It's the principle of the thing," Severance growled.

"Yeah, well five hundred thousand is a lot of consolation for a principle."

Another man spoke up as he helped himself to ale. "Severance isn't making five hundred thou off of this. He's only getting two hundred fifty. His lady gets the other half. That's one interesting female you left behind in Try Again, Severance. She's got enough credit to her name to buy a man his own mail ship. If I were you, I wouldn't wait too long to get back to her, or somebody else will take on the job of keeping her amused."

"Cidra's not naive enough to fall for some fast-talking renegade's line of torla manure." Severance swallowed his ale and hoped to hell he was right.

"I don't know," the other man offered. "It's hard to figure women."

Severance thought about that. He had figured Cidra out almost completely. But he needed her to be sure of herself and she hadn't had the time and the distance to do that. She had been through too much, too quickly, thanks to him. He owed it to her to give her time and the peacefulness of Clementia in which to make her decision.

"Hey," said one of the holotape technicians, "I brought along a Free Market playing field. Anyone interested?"

Severance smiled. "I just happen to have a set of cubes on me."

As he crawled into a lonely sleeper that night Severance was aware of the same sense of heroic martyrdom he had experienced on board ship when he'd managed to refrain from seducing Cidra. He had discovered then that the feeling wasn't much compensation for denying himself her warm, sweetly willing body. Tonight he decided that heroic martyrdom didn't improve with practice.

Fear gnawed at him as he lay staring at the curved ceiling of the tent. What if she was drawn back into the safe, serene world of Clementia? He was taking such a stupid risk by sending her back home.

But he had to be sure of her.

Chapter
Nineteen

"I'm scared, Desma. That's what the problem is. I'm just plain scared." Cidra gazed morosely into her half empty mug of ale. Around her the patrons of the Bloodsucker went about the business of enjoying themselves amid a canopy of smoke and the occasional clatter of Free Market cubes. A big commercial freighter had arrived in port today, and the normal tavern crowd was augmented by the shipload of newcomers. The freighter was due to leave the following afternoon, and Cidra was scheduled to be on it.

Desma eyed her friend with affection. Cidra was wearing her early evening gown, and her hair was done in its traditional, neat coil of braids. Cidra was her old, elegant self this evening, except for one thing: she was on her third mug of Renaissance Rose ale. Desma found the process of watching Cidra drink interesting. Desma kept waiting for the effects to show. Surely the fine manners and the gentle grace would start disintegrating at any moment. The fact that neither had faded so far only went to show how strong a force good breeding could be. Desma was fascinated.

"If you're really scared, Cidra, you're certainly using a traditional means of overcoming the fear."

Cidra gazed at her mug. "Severance likes this stuff."

"I know."

"He should have been back yesterday, Desma. He said he'd be back in three days. This is the fourth day."

Desma sighed. "I realize that. Renaissance has a way of making folks change their plans in the field. You know he's all right. He checked in with Security this morning. He's not in trouble, Cidra."

"He's deliberately delaying his return so he can avoid having to see me again before I leave."

"You're getting paranoid."

Cidra considered that. "Do you think so? Harmonics never get paranoid. Everybody likes Harmonics. No reason to be paranoid. But I'm not a Harmonic. So it's okay for me to be paranoid."

"That's a wonderful string of logic. Have some more ale."

"Thank you," Cidra said with grave politeness. "I will." She sipped reflectively and then said with an air of great insight, "He's a loner. That's the real problem. I think he likes me, but he's basically a loner. He doesn't want to allow anyone, especially a woman, into his life on a permanent basis. The cabin of a mail ship is very small, you know."

"I know. But the two of you got here from Lovelady without murdering each other."

"And now he's sending me away."

"He's the one who's scared, Cidra. He knows he can't offer you the things you'll have if you go back to Clementia."

"Hah. Severance could have used that excuse before he

negotiated five hundred thousand in credit for the safehold and the alien ship. It won't wash now. He's rich."

Desma's mouth curved wryly. "Don't forget he's only got two hundred and fifty thousand."

Cidra flushed guiltily. "He annoyed me. That's the only reason I made him give me a separate contract. I was very irritated."

"The fact is, even if he had all five hundred thousand, he'd spend every last credit on Severance Pay, Ltd. This time he's determined to make his plans a success. He's seen everything fall apart on him at least twice already."

Cidra frowned. "What are you talking about?"

Desma shrugged. "He went into partnership with Racer because Racer had some capital and wanted to be a wheeler and dealer. Racer had the credit but not enough business sense to make it work."

"Severance had the business sense?"

Desma nodded. "Severance had the ideas and the ambition. But the partnership didn't work out."

"It's a little difficult to continue in a partnership with someone who's willing to leave you in a sinkswamp with a killweaver," Cidra said.

Desma arched one brow. "Is that what happened? Interesting. Everyone knew something catastrophic had happened, but no one knew exactly what."

"Don't tell him I told you," Cidra said urgently. "I think I might have had a bit too much ale. I seem to be babbling."

"Don't worry, Cidra. I won't say a word. As I said, after the partnership was dissolved, Severance was left with only his ship and virtually no capital. He and his brother started building things up again, and just as they were beginning to see some progress, Jeude went down on QED."

"I know." Cidra swallowed a wave of sadness. "It was very hard for Severance to handle."

"The emotional trauma was only part of it. The other half of the story is that the loss of the ship sent Severance Pay, Ltd. back to circle one. For a year Severance took some awful risks as a bonus man here on Renaissance for some exploration companies. ExcellEx was one of the firms he worked for during that period."

"Do you think he took the risks because he just didn't care anymore?"

"I don't know. People take risks for different reasons. I know he was a bitter, angry man for a long time. He spent more time in the jungle than he did in Try Again. But when the year was over, he seemed to have pulled himself together. In the meantime he had accumulated enough bonus money to finance *Severance Pay*. He's been working his way back for a third try at the big time ever since."

"And now he's got another crack at it." Cidra sighed. "I suppose I shouldn't get in his way."

"But are you going to get in his way?" Desma asked perceptively.

"I prefer to think of myself as a useful and extremely valuable member of his crew." Cidra took another sip of ale. "Now all I have to do is make him see me that way."

"Hey, Severance, how much will you take for the little lady?" Craft grinned cheerfully as he helped make the skimmer fast to the dock. He examined Severance's dusty boots and sweat-stained shirt, which were revealed under the marina's bright lights. It was obvious that the past four days had been hard and long. But, then, most days on the river and in the jungle were.

The balmy night air was thicker than usual, heralding the

approach of a storm. Borgia and Medici were quickly being veiled by clouds. Severance and the skimmer's pilot had made it back barely in time. Skimmers avoided travel by night if at all possible, especially when a storm was in the offing. But Severance had pushed for the unorthodox travel that afternoon because they were so close to Try Again and Cidra was due to ship out the next day. The thought of not seeing her before she left had led him to give the skimmer pilot an extra fifty in credit for traveling after dark. Folks were always on the lookout for easy bonus money on Renaissance.

"You haven't got enough credit to buy her, Craft, and you know it." Severance jumped onto the dock, his stained travel pack slung over one shoulder. "Even if I decided to sell, you'd have one renegade devil of a time trying to collect. The lady's got a mind of her own."

"She's also got two hundred and fifty thousand of her own from what I hear." Craft chuckled as he reached down into the skimmer to take a container the pilot was handing to him. "A lady like her draws a considerable amount of attention in a place like this."

Severance, about to walk down the dock toward shore, glanced back. "Anyone been making too much of a nuisance of himself?"

"Why? You going to feed him to the river if he has?"

"After I separate his head from his neck. Let's have it, Craft. What's been happening?"

"Calm down, Severance. She and Desma haven't been seen apart since you left. Saints know a few hopeful types tried to get Cidra interested in a nice steak dinner or something, but no one had any luck."

"She doesn't like meat." Severance readjusted the travel pack and stalked off toward the bank.

"Maybe that's why she's drinking ale at the Bloodsucker

tonight," Craft called after him. "A lot of protein but not much meat in a glass of Rose ale."

"One of these days, Craft, someone's going to accidentally push you into the river." But Severance didn't pause this time. He headed away from the dock facilities and up the dusty street, driven by a sense of urgency. He had so little time left with Cidra.

She must have gotten very bored to have gone to the Bloodsucker for a drink. Maybe Desma had talked her into it. Cidra never did more than sip elegantly at a glass of wine or ale. At this late hour she was probably tired of killing time in a tavern. She wasn't really cut out for spending her evenings that way. At least there was no Cord Racer around to cause trouble that night. Severance decided he wouldn't chew Cidra out for spending a couple of hours in a tavern. After all, there wasn't much to do in a place like Try Again. Besides, from what Craft had said, it sounded as if Desma was doing a good job of playing chaperon. He paced more quickly along the street, anticipating the pleasure in Cidra's eyes when she saw him again.

It was Desma who saw Severance come through the door. She glanced up, took in his dusty, stained appearance and the intensity of his eyes as he scanned the room, and then she smiled at Cidra. "He's back."

Cidra blinked. She had just finished the last of her third mug of ale. "Who's back?"

"The love of your life."

"Oh, him." Eyes narrowed to help her concentrate, Cidra looked around and saw Severance starting toward her down an aisle of tables. She smiled wistfully. "Isn't he wonderful, Desma?"

"He's interesting, I'll say that for him."

Cidra's smile congealed into a frown as Severance reached the table. She glared up at him. "You're late," she announced.

Severance tilted his head to one side, studying her as he let the pack slide to the floor. "You're drunk."

"I have been drowning my sorrows. Ask Desma."

Severance slid a grim glance at Desma. "How the hell did she get into this condition?"

"I did it all by myself," Cidra answered.

"I can see that. Why is it that every time I leave you on your own you get into trouble?"

"I'm not in any trouble. You're the one in trouble. Did you give those sensors away to ExcellEx?"

Severance leaned down, planting his hands on the table, to confront her. His eyes were glittering with a mixture of masculine irritation, desire, and possessiveness. "No, I did not give the sensors to ExcellEx."

"Did you get full credit on delivery?" she demanded.

"Yes, Otanna Rainforest, I did. Satisfied?"

"No. You should have gotten hazardous duty credit on top of the agreed-upon fee."

"I got a contract for another shipment instead. Does that please you?"

Cidra's severe expression changed back into a warm, approving smile. "Oh, Severance, that's wonderful."

"Thank you." He looked at Desma, who was smiling. "How much has she had?"

"Three mugs. Holding it very well, I might add."

"She's spaced out of her little mind."

"She's been waiting for you," Desma said simply. "Today she started worrying that you wouldn't return until after she left."

"She should have known better. That's no excuse—"

"I," Cidra interrupted grandly, "don't need any excuses. I am a financially independent woman who can do as she likes."

"Too much education and too much money. It's a bad combination in a woman." Severance straightened. "Are you ready to leave, Cidra?"

"Yes, please. Where are we going?"

"Someplace where there's a bed." He reached down to take her arm.

"You need more than a bed, Severance. You need a shower." Desma grinned up at him. "Why don't you take her back to my place? I won't be home for a while yet. You're welcome to spend the night. Fred's waiting there too."

"I appreciate the offer, Desma. I'll take you up on it." He started to tug Cidra out of her chair.

"Now wait just one spaced second." Cidra lifted her chin. "I have decided that this relationship of ours is based entirely too much on bed. It's too physically oriented. We need to talk. We need to explore the intellectual side of this whole thing. Then we need to discuss the business aspects of it. You'd better sit down, Teague Severance. We have a lot to discuss."

Severance regarded her politely. "The thing is, Cidra, you're not in any condition to carry on an intellectual analysis of our relationship. You're spaced, Otanna Rainforest. Drunk as a renegade on a bonus spree."

"Oh. How interesting. I hadn't realized."

"It's all right," he assured her, hauling her to her feet. "Just leave everything to me. I'll handle it." He scooped her up and slung her easily over one shoulder. Cidra's yellow-gold gown swirled around his stained shirt.

Cidra examined the floor from her upside-down position. Then she steadied herself by grasping his utility loop. She smiled reassuringly at Desma. "It's all right. He always handles things. Pilot in command, you know."

"I understand," Desma said gently. "Good night, Cidra."

"Good night, Desma."

Desma spoke to Severance. "The door's keyed to Cidra's voiceprint."

"All I have to worry about is getting her to say something coherent when we get to your place. See you in the morning, Desma. And thanks."

Severance clamped one hand firmly around Cidra's thighs, plucked the travel pack off the floor, and started toward the door. He ignored the interested attention of the tavern crowd. He was out on the street, striding toward Desma's before he realized that Cidra was humming contentedly.

"I didn't know you were musical," he growled.

"I can do a great many things. Excellent education."

"I'm going to put you in a bed and let you show me what you do best."

"You don't think we're placing too much emphasis on the physical side of this relationship?" Cidra asked with both whimsy and worry.

"I think," Severance told her, "that memories of you wrapped around me are all I'm going to have to keep me warm for a long time."

Cidra sighed. "You shouldn't send me away, Severance."

"I have to send you away."

"I know. I've thought it all out. I know you have to do it. But I'm scared, Severance."

"So am I."

Cidra lapsed into silence for the remainder of the trip. When Severance stopped at Desma's door, she obediently said her name into the voicelock and then felt herself being carried into the house. Severance walked into the bedroom she had been using and stood Cidra carefully on her feet. She circled his neck with her arms and smiled wistfully up at him.

"I've missed you."

"Not half as much as I've missed you." He pulled her close, feeling her gown whip lightly around his legs as he did so. She lifted her face for his kiss, and he took her mouth with a hunger he knew he would be feeling frequently during the days and nights to come. For a long moment he simply helped himself to the promise of her, drinking deeply of the nectar that was waiting. She melted against him the way he had remembered, and Severance wondered how he would last without her during the long time ahead. The thought that she might not be waiting when the ordeal was over filled him with a dangerous tension. He realized abruptly that his kiss was growing rough and heavy. She was such a soft little creature.

"I don't want to hurt you."

"You're not hurting me." She framed his face between her hands.

"I should get cleaned up first."

"Later," she murmured. "We have so little time."

"Cidra, do you know what it does to me when you look at me like that?"

"Like what?"

"As if you want me so much, you'll dissolve if you don't get me."

"I might."

His fingers were trembling as he undid the delicate fastenings of the yellow-gold robe. It slid to the floor, a heap of treasure around her feet. Severance decided it was nothing compared to the treasure it had concealed. He unhooked the utility belt and draped it on the table beside the bed. Impatiently he tugged off the rest of his clothing. When he was finished, he reached out to touch Cidra. It occurred to him again that he should get under a hot spray before he claimed such a sweet-smelling woman, but he couldn't seem to stop himself. Already he was pushing her backward onto the bed.

"Watch out for Fred," Cidra said.

"Where is he?"

"I don't know. He's usually in here somewhere."

Severance looked up and saw three rows of teeth grinning at him from the window ledge above the bed. "Hello, Fred. Go back to sleep."

The three rows of teeth winked out of sight. Severance gathered Cidra into his arms. He heard her soft sigh, felt the warm, eager welcome in her arms, and wondered how he could let her go in the morning. Then he stopped thinking of the future entirely. All that existed for him was the present with its promise of passion and satisfaction. On Renaissance a man took what he could get.

He made love to Cidra with the burning need of a man who knows he's going to go hungry for a long time.

Severance didn't know what brought him up out of sleep later that night. He came awake the way he usually did on Renaissance: with a sudden alertness that kicked his system into full gear. He lay listening to the shadows, unmoving. One arm was wrapped securely around Cidra as if even in his sleep he were afraid of losing her. Her rounded rear was nestled intimately into his thighs, and he could feel the curves of her breasts under his palm.

But it hadn't been Cidra who had awakened him. She was sound asleep. He listened intently, and then he heard a faint movement on the window ledge. Fred was awake too. Perhaps he had only heard the sound of his movement. The rain had begun, pouring down outside with enough force and noise to mask any sounds from the street. Severance wondered if it had been Desma's return to the house that had brought him up out of sleep. But he could hear nothing from the hall.

Then he heard another sound, and this time he recognized it: the hiss of a deflector screen as a man moved through it. The faint noise was coming from the deflector that guarded the window across the room, Severance slitted his eyes and turned his head a few fractions of a centimeter. A shadow moved on the other side of the diazite pane. On the window ledge over the bed Fred shifted again.

Severance reached up and touched the rockrug. Fred went still, his body still and alert. Satisfied that the creature was going to obey the silent command, Severance reached for the knife in his utility belt. Logically, whoever was outside the window shouldn't be able to open it. The diazite was locked. But there were ways around locks. Too many ways.

Severance wasn't very surprised when the diazite pane swung inward without a sound. The figure coming through the window was holding a pulser. He got no more than one leg hooked over the windowsill. Severance came to a sitting position in a smooth rush of movement, launching the knife in his hand with the full power of his shoulder and upper arm.

The heavy-duty utility knife caught the intruder in the right side of his chest. The pulser dropped to the floor as the victim yelled in pain and rage. The force of the blow sent him spinning backward, out of the window and onto the ground.

"Severance!" Cidra came awake with a startled gasp, clutching at the sheet. Rain was pouring through the open window. "What happened? What's wrong?"

But he was already out of bed and leaning out of the window. An instant later he was through it and crouching on the ground outside. Cidra heard Fred moving agitatedly on the ledge above her, and then she felt him undulating down onto her shoulder and along the bed. He was moving almost as fast as Severance had moved. The rockrug crossed the room and wriggled onto the other window ledge. Cidra wasn't far behind both of them.

"Severance? What are you . . . Sweet Harmony, it's him!" She stared at the man lying flat on the ground in the pouring rain. Severance was hunkered down beside him, his nude body gleaming sleekly from the steady downpour. "It's him," she said again, dazed. "The man who attacked Desma and me in the lab."

Then she saw the blood mingling with the rainwater that was running down the man's chest. The hilt of the utility knife protruded from his rumpled clothing. She caught her breath. "Is he . . . is he dead?"

"No. My aim was a little off. It's hard to get an accurate shot from a sitting position. Especially when you're in a hurry." Severance was examining his victim. "You're sure it's the same renegade?"

She stared at the stricken man, whose face was twisted in a grimace of pain. It was an expression that wasn't all that different from the one of fear she had last seen him wearing. "It's him. What's he doing here? Everyone assumed he'd disappeared."

"Since he's still alive, we'll be able to ask him a whole lot of interesting questions. See if Desma is home yet. If not, use her comp-phone to get company Security out here."

Cidra hesitated, deeply aware of the pain the intruder must be feeling. "We've got to stop the bleeding, Severance."

He looked up at her as she stood framed in the window. For the first time Cidra saw the expression on his face. Rain washed over his hard features, revealing a grim, hollow stare that shook her to the core.

"I'm almost sure he came through that window to kill you," Severance said much too softly. "I don't give a damn if he dies right here and now. Go wake Desma."

She still had far to go yet before she became completely accustomed to Wolf ways, Cidra thought as she went in search of Desma. There was no sense fooling herself. In some respects she would never become a true Wolf. She wondered if it was that weakness in her nature that made Severance wary of taking her with him.

Severance watched the window as Cidra disappeared and wondered if she could ever accept the part of him that was capable of this kind of violence. Then he looked down at the man on the ground and felt like slitting the renegade's throat. The temptation to finish the job he'd begun with the utility knife was strong. Not only had the intruder represented a threat to Cidra, he had given her one more glimpse of Severance as a man who was about as far from being a Harmonic as it was possible to get.

Cidra stood in the departure lounge the next day waiting for Severance to confirm her reservation. She was wearing her embroidered green midday robe, and her hair was in its usual coronet. Her hands were clasped in front of her in the formal position of patience. Around her the hustle of passengers and crew flowed unheeded, not touching her either physically or emotionally. She felt isolated and intensely alone, her eyes following Severance as he verified her flight. As he turned to make his way back through the crowd she searched his face, hoping for some sign of a reprieve.

There was none. Severance had made up his mind, and she knew better than to expect to change it at this late hour. Cidra felt a rush of anger and resentment at the midnight intruder, not because he had come through the window with the intention of killing her so that she couldn't identify him, but because he had succeeded in ruining what was left of her last night with Severance. The man had been questioned by company security immediately after he had received medical aid for the knife wound. Then Severance and Cidra had both been obliged to give statements. It was all cut-and-dried as far as the legal aspects went. Violence within Try Again was dealt with severely. Renaissance couldn't afford to encourage it inside the one safe zone on the planet. Bad for business. The intruder was under computer lock, but no one could give Cidra back the rest of her night with Severance. Morning had arrived all too quickly.

"You're all set. I upgraded your cabin. This way you'll have more room."

She inclined her head in formal thanks.

"Bigger lav too," he added in a deadpan tone. "You can bathe to your heart's content. You'll be able to spend the whole trip under a spray if you feel like it."

"It was very thoughtful of you. I am in your debt."

Severance winced. "Could you cut out the ritualistic good manners? Sometimes lately I've had the feeling that you use them when you want to be sarcastic. I'm never sure how to take them."

"I'm sorry, Severance," she whispered unhappily. Nothing was going right. Severance had been short-tempered with her since he had used his knife against the man who had tried to kill her. Time was running out, and they seemed to have less and less to say to each other. Cidra was aware of a sensation of panic waiting to swamp her.

Severance ignored her soft apology, took her arm, and guided her over to a quieter section of the lounge. "I've got something I want you to do for me."

Cidra's heart lifted for the first time that morning. "Of course," she said simply, but her eyes were shining.

He handed her a credit plate. "Take it."

She stared at it in dismay. "But it's for your account."

"I've had it opened for you. You can use that card to access it."

"But, Severance, I don't need any credit. I have plenty of my own, remember? What is this all about? I don't understand. If this is some gesture of warped responsibility on your part, you can just forget it. I don't want your share of the stake!"

"Cidra, try not to get hysterical on me over a little thing like this. I am not exactly giving you the entire contents of my credit account."

"Then what are you giving me?"

"Access to it. I'm going to be stuck on board *Severance Pay* for the next several weeks. On board, communications are limited. You know that. I don't have the facilities to do research or make investments from the deck of a mail ship. On the other hand, you're going to be running around Clementia with access to the best information sources on three planets. I don't want my two hundred and fifty thousand sitting still in a credit account. I want it working."

"You want me to invest it for you?"

"Something short-term and highly profitable," he said bluntly. "You're the one with all the education. Do something useful with it and with my stake. Take good care of it, Cidra. Lose my capital for me and I'll—"

"I know," she said. "You'll take it out of my hide." She was gazing up at him with a palpable glow as she clutched the credit slip tightly in her palm. "I'll take care of your stake for you, Severance. I swear it."

He smiled crookedly. "I know you will. I trust you."

Not with his heart and not yet with his future, but he trusted her with his credit. It was a hopeful sign, and Cidra clung to it. She dropped the credit slip carefully into the concealed pocket of her robe. It was a bond between herself and Severance, one that would surely draw him back for no other reason than to find out what she had done with his capital. Any kind of trust at all from a Wolf like Severance was a small miracle.

"You will be very careful, Severance?"

"I'll be careful." He touched the tip of her ear. "You'll go straight home to Clementia and stay out of second-class taverns and dives?"

"I promise."

"Cidra—" He broke off as if uncertain about what to say next.

Cidra touched his hand. "It's all right, Severance. I understand. It has to be this way. This is the only way you can be sure of yourself and of me." She stood on tiptoe and kissed him lightly. Then she stepped back. "I'll be waiting for you." She turned and was gone.

Severance felt his gut twist as she walked into the crowd of departing passengers. Her slender, green-robed figure was lost amid the hulking uniforms and standard-issue Renaissance jungle garb. For an instant he almost gave into the sense of panic that was clawing at his insides. She was out of reach already. The panel doors of the boarding gate were sealing shut, cutting her off from him, perhaps forever.

He had been a fool. He should have taken his chances, should have risked the odds and kept her with him. He'd taken so many risks in his life; why hadn't he been able to take this one?

But he had no right to try to make up her mind for her. She needed time and the peace of Clementia. Only then could she be sure of what she was doing.

Severance reached into a small pouch on his utility belt and let his fingers close around the fireberyl comb. The feel of it seemed to soothe the gnawing uncertainty that he knew was going to be a close companion during the long weeks ahead.

Chapter
Twenty

QED looked different on this trip, Severance realized as he oversaw the unloading of the mail. The endless vistas of orange and red dust were as barren and forbidding as ever, but the sight of them no longer made his stomach tighten or caused his mind to beat at him in angry frustration.

Revenge was exactly what he had always suspected it would be: calming and satisfying. It hadn't taken away the old pain or allowed him to forget his own sense of responsibility for what had happened to Jeude, but it had quieted him inside. The pain and the feeling of being partially responsible were things he had already learned to live with during the past two years. Time diluted the self-recriminations and would continue to do so. But exacting a measure of justice had eased him inside in a way that time would never have succeeded in doing. Racer's death had paid not only for the threats to Cidra but also for Jeude's death, and it had balanced some internal scale.

QED was never going to be his idea of the ideal vacation spot of the Stanza Nine system. The planet would always hold memories of the deaths of his parents and his brother. But Severance could view the raw, boomtown of Proof and the outlying orange hills with a sense of perspective now. It occurred to him that it wasn't simply revenge that had enabled him to gain perspective. He had learned something from Cidra too. Her gentleness had also eased something inside him.

This was an ore- and mineral-rich land. Companies and individuals were wresting fortunes out of the ground with the assistance of the ubiquitous spidersleds. Severance was obliged to step out of the way of one of the mobil metal monsters as he crossed the landing field to the port office. Its long, insectlike legs, so useful for covering rough terrain, narrowly missed his boot.

"Hey, up there," he yelled to the man in the driver's seat, "if you can't operate that thing properly, someone's going to show you how it's done the hard way."

"Don't need any advice on how to do it the hard way," the middle-aged ex-miner rasped. "I do it that way all the time. Back again, huh, Severance? Miss the local fun spots?"

"The only thing I've missed is taking your loose credit in a game of Free Market, Tanner." Severance stopped beside the spidersled as the man halted it. "You interested in trying to take back some of what you lost last time I was in Port?"

"Sure, if we can use my cubes." Tanner grinned hugely, his weathered face crinkling into a hundred creases.

"The day I let you use your cubes is the day I'll be too spaced to play."

"Don't trust anyone, do you, Severance?" Tanner observed with mock admiration.

Severance thought about it. At one time his answer would have been a ready no. "Maybe one woman I know."

"Severance, you're a damn fool if the one person you decide to trust is female. I do believe you've got a problem."

"I'm coping. See you this evening. And I'll bring the cubes." He moved away from the spidersled as it lurched into motion.

One night was all he would be spending on QED this trip. Severance no longer cared if he missed a few mail contracts by rushing back off-planet. He didn't care that he would be turning around to face another six weeks of empty space without more than a one night's break. All he cared about was starting the journey back to Lovelady.

The six weeks from Renaissance had been the longest and loneliest of his life, even worse than the dark season after Jeude's death. At least during that period he'd had his own bitterness and self-reproach to keep him company. But for the past six weeks the only company he'd had aside from Fred had been memories of Cidra.

The ship had seemed deserted without her. It had amazed Severance at first. He was accustomed to being alone on board with only Fred as a companion. He shouldn't have been so shocked to find himself alone again, but he was. He would wake up in the morning longing for the smell of hot coffade and someone to share it with. He would stand under the spray in the lav, and his mind would be filled with images of Cidra's charming tendency to waste water. She was so scrupulously clean and sweet-smelling.

He missed other things too. She'd had the ability to share time with him without demanding that he entertain her. Cidra was a woman with whom he could be quiet. For hours at a time she had retreated to her bunk to read or become absorbed in her programming while he worked out on the exercise machine or fiddled with a gadget. But he had always been pleasantly conscious of her presence, a satisfying sensation. She had become a companion, not just a passenger.

She had withstood his temper too. Severance knew he had been abrupt with her on more than one occasion. But she'd handled it without sulking or crying.

Most of all he missed having her in his arms. The memories of her sweet, hot warmth had plagued him every league of the way from Renaissance, and Severance knew he would be goaded by them every league of the trip back. There had been other thoughts that had eaten at him too. He'd found himself picturing her at home in Clementia, surrounded by the serenity and ritual in which she had been raised.

But a part of him had begun to insist that his Cidra could never be truly happy in Clementia. When all was said and done, she was no Harmonic. Her passion, her spirit, and her strength would forever bar her from her world just as surely as her lack of telepathy.

If Cidra wasn't fated to be happy in Clementia, then he had a right to take her with him. That knowledge had been growing steadily since he had put her on the freighter back to Lovelady. He had a right to take her, Severance decided, because she belonged to him now. She would always belong to him. If she didn't yet realize that, then he would have to make her understand.

The restless desire to be on his way back to claim his woman made Severance lengthen his stride toward the port offices. The sooner he completed his business on QED, the better. The most important thing in his life was waiting.

"You'll go with him when he comes for you, won't you, Cidra?" Talina Peacetree smiled gently at her daughter, who sat across her from on a white stone bench. The bench had been handcarved by an expert craftsman who had worked the hard substance into a light and balanced piece of sculpture. It had cost a great deal of credit, but Talina and her husband,

Garn, could afford it. The garden in which the stone bench resided was even more expensive. It was shaded with a unique variety of graceful pala trees that had been cultivated to order. Formal swirls of flowering plants added color and scent to the perfectly designed scene. All was serene.

"If he comes for me, I'll go with him." Cidra finished the last step of the highly ritualized ceremony that proceeded the serving of ether wine and handed her mother a crystal goblet full of the golden liquid. Her green eyes met those of her mother. "I will be going away even if he doesn't come for me."

Talina nodded with an air of quiet acceptance. "I know. I have always known that one day you would leave. But remember that Clementia will always be here for you when you wish to return for a while."

"I would never cut myself off from my home. Even though I am not a true Harmonic, the Way is a part of me."

"It is a part of all humans," Talina said.

Cidra's mouth curved in amusement. "That's what Severance once said."

"Your Severance sounds perceptive."

"He's also occasionally rude, arrogant, and obnoxious."

"He's a Wolf." Talina's hand moved gracefully in her lap. She was wearing one of her exquisite early afternoon gowns, a cream-colored robe embroidered with silver floss. Her silvered hair was bound in the same regal coronet that Cidra wore. She had bequeathed many of her features to her daughter, but in Talina those features were overlaid with an internal serenity that Cidra could only approximate.

"I am also a Wolf."

Talina watched her daughter as she made the quiet declaration. "It is not difficult for you to accept that now?"

"No."

"Then your adventures on Renaissance have indeed been worthwhile. You have learned much."

"I have learned to accept myself for what I am. But the most interesting part is that even if I were offered a clear choice now, I would not choose to become a Harmonic. I don't think I could bear to give up what I have found waiting inside myself."

"Then you will be content with your future. I am glad for you, my daughter. Most glad." She sipped the wine and then turned her elegant head as her husband stepped into the garden from his study. "Ah, Garn. Will you join us for a glass of wine?"

"With pleasure." Garn came forward to sit beside his wife. His clear blue eyes were full of intelligence as he regarded Cidra. Garn Oquist wore the shorter, masculine version of the early afternoon surplice, a deep brown robe belted with a knotted thong of multicolored braided floss. His handsome face with its strong nose and high forehead held the same air of inner serenity that his wife's wore.

When Garn took his seat beside his wife, Cidra sensed the brief, silent mental communion that took place between her parents. It was a quiet touching of minds that Cidra had once envied with all her heart. Once that subtle communication had made her feel left out and deprived. But today she found she was accepting it for what it was: a Harmonic way that she could not follow. She had other methods of communication open to her. They might be less certain, more vulnerable to risk, but when they worked, they worked well. She was satisfied with them now. They held their own rewards.

"What are the two of you discussing?" her father asked.

"My future," Cidra said with a smile. "But the truth is that I've got something far more immediate and important to discuss with you, Father. I need advice in one of your areas of expertise."

"Which one?" Garn sampled his wine with judicious care. He had many areas of expertise, some of which had made him rich.

"The theoretical aspects of the credit system."

"I never realized you had an interest in the financial system."

"I never had enough credit to make it worth worrying about." Cidra's smile broadened into a small grin.

"But now you do."

"Yes," she said. "Now I do. I want to invest, Father—the full five hundred thousand."

Her father had been considering his daughter's fortune ever since he learned of it. Now he spoke his mind. "Whoever negotiated the sale of your discoveries did an excellent job."

"I know. But now it's my turn. I'm in charge of investing the credit. Something high-yield and relatively short-term."

Garn reflected seriously for a long moment and then nodded. "There are some young and aggressive exploration firms that offer excellent prospects. According to my information they are presently seeking capital investment. One in particular, a firm called ExcellEx, has intrigued me lately. We can query the computer about it this afternoon if you would care to do so."

"That sounds perfect." Of course, it would be perfect, thought Cidra. Most things were perfect in Clementia. For the first time she understood one of the reasons why she had never really felt at home here. Great quantities of perfection and serenity could be a little boring.

Severance paused inside the gates of Clementia and gazed at the vista of gardens and beautifully proportioned architecture. Here there were no ugly or jarring structures that had been hastily erected or incompletely thought out prior to construction. Around him people garbed in simple, elegant robes nodded politely as they passed him on the wide stone paths that wound through the gardens. There was no shushing sound of a passing runner or sled. As far as Severance could see, there were no vehicles at all.

Behind the small, walled city rose the majestic coastal mountains. In front of the gates stretched a quiet, sheltered bay that rarely knew the turbulence of sea storms. Jeude would have been at peace here.

Severance took a deep, steadying breath and reminded himself that while this would have been the ideal environment for his brother, it was not for Cidra. He made his way toward the Archives, a structure that had been pointed out for him by the Wolf who guarded the gate.

"You can't miss it. Big domed building in the center of the campus." The Wolf had regarded Severance quizzically. "You here to attend classes?"

"No," Severance had answered. "I'm here to find someone."

"Who?"

"Cidra Rainforest. She works in the Archives." He had waited impatiently while the Wolf had contacted Cidra's home.

"I talked to her mother. Seems Otanna Rainforest is expecting you." The guard had waved him through the gates.

There were other non-Harmonics in the vicinity, probably students who attended the university, but the majority of the people wore the formal gowns and serene expressions of true Harmonics. Among them Severance felt large, awkward, and out of place. Rather like a torla in a garden. Not for the first time that day doubts rose to undermine his determination. Cidra wasn't a torla in this garden. With her grace and poise she could blend in beautifully.

But the weeks of gathering uncertainty had done their work well. He had to find her and take her with him. She might be able to mingle with Harmonics, but under the surface she was his passionate, loving woman, and if she had forgotten that in the time she had been back in Clementia, he would remind her. He needed her with him.

Severance found the Archives without further instructions. The curved structure seemed to rest almost unsupported on the ground, its diazite walls protecting the array of computers, study areas, and treasured bound volumes within. The bits and pieces of knowledge that had survived the crash of the colony ship had formed the heart of Clementia's Archives. In the intervening years a great deal of new information had been added. It was the center of learning for the Stanza Nine system.

Only when he was inside the building did Severance realize just how large it was. He would need help in locating Cidra.

"Try History. She works with First Family files a lot," an attendant at the front desk told him. "Straight ahead and to your left."

Severance followed the directions to a room that had been designated as the repository of First Family diaries and written records. He saw Cidra almost at once. She was wearing a morning robe, her neat head bent attentively toward a computer screen. She didn't notice him. For a long moment Severance simply stood staring at her, waiting for the sudden, aching surge of hunger to fade back to more manageable proportions. Sweet Harmony, but he had missed her! What in a renegade's hell was he going to do if she hadn't missed him?

She looked up at that moment and saw him.

"Severance!" Then she was on her feet, flying toward him with a lover's welcome in her eyes.

He caught her up fiercely and swung her around as she threw herself into his arms. The exhilaration washing over him was almost shattering in its intensity. He realized he was shaking. "I've come to steal you out of Paradise."

"It's about time you got here."

"I know." He captured her face between his hands and kissed her. "I know."

It was a long time later before Severance had Cidra to himself. Her parents had been gracious and hospitable, accepting him immediately. He had been grateful for that. One niggling concern he'd had to face on the long trip back to Lovelady was the issue of how he would deal with a set of Harmonic in-laws. But with Harmonic civility Talina and Garn had taken all obstacles out of his path. They were content with their daughter's decision. And with Garn, at least, Severance had found some common ground. He had spent two hours going over the investment program Cidra's father had mapped out.

After dinner, during which Severance had worried excessively about his table manners, Cidra had invited him out into the gardens. He had welcomed the escape, pulling her into his arms beneath the shelter of a flowering tree. In the moonlight her eyes were luminous. Severance knew that he could get lost in them.

"I was afraid from time to time during the past few weeks, but deep inside I think I knew you'd be waiting," he said.

"I know. I had a few anxious moments myself. But somehow I knew you'd come for me." She leaned her head on his shoulder and smiled. "We belong together. When are we leaving?"

"As soon as possible. But there are one or two things we have to take care of first."

She lifted her head and wrapped her arms around his neck. "Such as?"

"Such as getting married." He brushed a stray strand of her hair behind her ear. "I love you, Cidra. I want this done right. I want the bonds in place for life."

"I love you, Severance."

"I know." He smiled. "I saw it in your eyes today when you came running into my arms."

"It must have been in my eyes when you put me on the freighter back to Lovelady because I knew I loved you then too."

"I couldn't see things as clearly then," he admitted.

"And now you can? You're sure of your decision, Severance? I couldn't bear it if you changed your mind."

"Cidra, it was never my own mind I was unsure of. I only wanted the time so that you could be certain of what you were doing."

"We could argue about who didn't trust whom all evening, but it doesn't matter any longer. You're here now and I'm going with you."

"Yes." He stroked his hands down to her hips and smiled slightly. "Absolutely. Sometimes we Wolves sort of blunder along until we get things right, but when we finally do get them right, we stick to them. I'll never let you go, Cidra."

Her mouth curved teasingly as her eyes mirrored her love. "Wait until you hear my marriage terms before you make any rash promises."

"I'm listening," he drawled.

"I should warn you that by leaving me alone for the past few weeks you've given me plenty of time to work out these terms."

"Obviously a mistake on my part."

"Yes, well, first, I am no longer satisfied to sign on as a mere member of *Severance Pay*'s crew. I am demanding full partnership status."

"Ah."

She nodded vigorously. "Ah, indeed. Next I must insist on a full High Ritual wedding ceremony."

He groaned. "Why?"

"For luck. We can skip the two hours of telepathic meditation in the middle of the ceremony if you like."

"Given the fact that the bride and groom can't communicate telepathically and would be bored to their toes, I think that would be wise," he agreed.

"And last but not least, I want some more opportunities to learn the fine points of Free Market without having to wager every fireberyl hair comb or emerald-floss slipper I happen to own. And don't even think of suggesting I bet genuine credit. It's all invested along with yours."

"You know the game's no fun unless the stakes make it worthwhile."

"Until I get to the point where I've got half a chance of winning occasionally, we're going to have to settle for wagers that won't bankrupt me."

Severance pulled her close. "I'm sure," he said, his mouth hovering just above hers, "that we can find something for you to bet that has nothing to do with credit or fireberyl combs. Don't worry. I'll think of something."

"You're so resourceful."

"Ummm. Good with my hands too."

"Does this mean," Cidra asked as she lifted her face for his kiss, "that you're accepting my marriage terms?"

He grinned in the moonlight, all male and all Wolf. "Your terms are nothing compared to mine. Wait until you hear them. I intend to go over them in great detail with you."

"It's all right," she assured him. "Whatever they are, I accept."

"Just like that?"

"Of course. I trust you, Severance."

His silent laughter faded to reveal the intensity of the love in his eyes. "And I trust you, sweet Cidra, to the ends of the universe." He sealed the vow with a kiss.

Jayne Ann Krentz, who also writes as Stephanie James and Jayne Castle, has long been fascinated with the notion of combining romance and science fiction. She lives in the Pacific Northwest with her husband, her bird, and her word processor. She has degrees in history and librarianship, and has enjoyed the usual assortment of jobs and travel experiences that writers seem to collect before they get lucky and sell their work. She believes in a medicinal glass or two of wine before dinner.